# WALTZ ACROSS TEXAS

# WALTZ ACR

# OSS TEXAS

## MAX CRAWFORD

FARRAR · STRAUS · GIROUX / NEW YORK

Library of Congress Cataloging in Publication Data

Crawford, Max.
  Waltz across Texas.

  I. Title.
PZ4.C89924Wal3   [PS3553.R293]     813'.5'4     74-26604

# I

# 1

Son Cunningham got his nickname because that's what he called everybody else. It was a good thing he hadn't dropped the habit; when I walked into that bar in Flavannah, Texas, it was the only way I knew who he was. Granted it had been ten years since I had been home, but he had changed more than that.

It all began a couple of weeks earlier in California, when my ex-secretary called up and said I had gotten two letters from home. One was from my aunt saying my old man was dying—or so I read between the lines—the other was from Son offering me a job. My little company had just gone bankrupt and I was pretty much alone in the world at the time, so I decided to take the job. The letters themselves were a couple weeks old, so by the time I got out of L.A., let my old Chrysler blow up in Needles, and hitched the rest of the way to Texas, my old man was dead. The job was still open.

I sold the car for fifty bucks and caught a ride with a kid who I think said he had decided he was still in love with his wife. He talked about her all night long. I could have retired as a fortune-teller on what I could have told the kid about his future. He slept through New Mexico, most of the next day.

We missed the tornado by half an hour. When we got to Amarillo the night was still filled with lightning, wind, and hard rain. The streets were jammed with cars, the radio crackled with static and news of the twister. The kid let me out downtown, bidding me farewell as if I were part of the storm. The streets were littered with broken bricks, glass, limbs of trees, crowded with angry, disbelieving people. A carload of drugstore cowboys pulled across the curb and dumped out my bag and kicked through my clothes. They were merchants and worried about looting. So was I.

It was past midnight when I finally got a ride into my hometown. The place had had a motel ten years ago, but instead of looking for it, I walked down to the courthouse square and found a soft bench and stared at the stars. But the dog in the jail had smelled me and finally the night watchman dragged himself out and, pointing a little pistol and a big flashlight at me, asked if I was passing through.

"No," I said, "I'm coming back home. Flavannah. This is my hometown."

The night watchman lowered his flashlight. "I see, so yore a chicken that has come home to roost."

"I guess I am."

"And you ain't got no place to roost." He snapped off his light and I spent the rest of the night in his warm dry jail.

# 2

The next morning I woke to a locked cell door and a beady-eyed old deputy sheriff playing dominoes with his deaf cousin. But after a few minutes the old men broke out their battered grins and let me out. I had a piece of white bread and a cup of coffee and then, leaving my bag in the cell, I walked over to the John Deere place, where my old man had always come when he was in town. I wanted nothing to do with sickness, hospitals, or my aunt. Not for a while.

As if he hadn't moved since I was a kid, Gene Hausenfluke was squatting on his rocking chair among his green tractors, his gray bulldog jaws clamped on a sick-looking Roi-tan. A stiff skinny farmer sat in a straight-back chair listening to Gene cuss out the government. Gene didn't even look up when I asked him if Merce Campbell had been up and around. He chewed his cigar once and spat in a coffee can. "Naw, that old man is dead."

I must have made a noise because Gene got up and sat me in his rocker. "Sorry, son, but I caint see nothin with the light reflectin off that Farmall winder acrost the street. Have a Coke. Catracks," he muttered as he pulled up another chair for himself. "Old Merce has done died on us and yore late if you come to bury him. We did that. You knew Merce Campbell, didn't you, Ott?" he said to the farmer, who looked like life just wasn't worth living when it was too wet to plow. "Married one a them Sunshine gals."

"Shore. We went to the funeral a week ago Tuesdy."

Gene got serious, probably thinking about selling me a tractor. "You thinkin bout takin over the farm, you better jump in there and straighten things out. Yore aunt Boots is bound and determined on sendin lawyer Stigall back to Alcapulca this year. You better git in there and talk to banker Dougherty. He knows what's goin on."

The farmer nodded. "Aw yeah, Dougherty knows everything."

Gene reflected a spell. "You know, there was somebody in here just yesterday lookin for you."

"Looking for me? Nobody knows I'm coming back."

Gene ignored that. "It was Dot Cunningham's boy. You remember him, Ott. Big smart ole boy, went off to Texas University. Drives hisself a Lincoln now." Gene squinted at the Farmall dealership across the street. "He's runnin with that fancy crowd down at Toro."

Toro was a small gritty town thirty miles east of Flavannah. Down in the breaks, as the people on the high plains call the land below the cap rock—low rolling hills, scrub mesquite, ranching country. Nothing about Toro had ever struck me as fancy.

The farmer had taken to rocking in his straight-back chair. "I saw that red Lincoln settin out back a Hannah's when I come in this mornin."

"This town has gone to the dawgs. How long you been gone from home, boy?"

"I don't know—ten years. I didn't know that Merce was dead."

"Well, you know now. This town has gone to the dawgs."

"Got a speckled pup myself," said the farmer.

"Southwest precinct's been voted wet. There's a passel a *loorid* beer joints out on the Y filled with debauchery and pulchertrude." It had to be straight from the preacher's sermon: old Gene was looking drowsy.

The farmer nodded. "You wont a ride out there, son, I ain't had my wings singed in over a week."

Gene snorted. "Conners has got Merce's pickup over in the yard. Let's walk over there and we'll git it for you. I tole that gotdamn stubborn old man to write up a proper will, but he thought he was too smart to die. Pickup might be the only thing you git outta the deal. The Buick was totaled. It's over in the yard too, if you want to have a look at it." My old man's death must have finally reached my face, for Gene's attitude softened some. "That's how Merce died, son. He was goin down to that young pill-roller's in Toro and drove Boots's Buick right over the cap rock. His own sister, she didn't know if she was mad or sad." We walked out on the street, leaving the skinny farmer staring at the tractors—there was no other place on earth he could tolerate sitting. As we made our way into the automobile showroom glistening with new Chevrolets, Gene theorized: "All the Campbell boys had good heads on their shoulders but their hearts was soft. Now the sisters is hardhearted to a rock and their heads is like squarsh. I almost married one a them gals. Yore daddy was the last Campbell boy alive."

"He was."

Gene stopped and squinted at the floor. "If I sound hardened to you, boy, it's just a way I have a goin on with all my old chums dying out. I just pertend we ain't speakin." Gene pushed into Conners's office at the rear of the showroom. The auto dealer was entertaining a farmer, and though he scowled at Gene prowling through the keys hanging on the wall, he was probably just unhappy with the hick wasting his time trying to buy one of his shiny new cars. I followed Gene across the street to the used-car lot and a white pickup, four or five years old, parked on the alley. Gene patted the hood, then told me where my old man was buried. Right by my lovely mother, he said.

I let the truck warm up for a long time. The cab smelled of stale cigar smoke and dust. The glove compartment was empty. There was nothing under the seats. I backed the pickup into the alley and drove out toward the Y. Nothing much had changed in this precinct. The Baptist church had a new neon sign over the front door.

The Y was where three highways met—north to Amarillo, southwest to Lubbock, east to Toro. When I was here last, the Y had supported a grocery store, a hairdo parlor, Curly's Café, a butane trucking outfit, and a battered building that had housed a succession of Western-wear stores, radio-repair shops, and the like. Curly's and the butane outfit were still there, both faded and worn, but now there were beer joints on every corner and package liquor stores in between. The Bally Who?, The Idle Spur, Charlie's Alibi. I spotted Hannah's across the Y, on the Lubbock highway. A Lincoln was parked out back, shiny and red as a brand-new wagon.

# 3

Even in high school Son had been a big man, tall and raw-boned. The last time I had seen him, several years after graduation, he had been six two or three, a hundred and ninety pounds. True, I wasn't looking for a man two inches taller, sixty pounds heavier, but it was his face I didn't know. The voice, the laughter, the gestures, maybe I knew them too well—it was his face that had changed, as though he were wearing a mask or acting in a play. It crossed my mind that maybe he was. Son always said he wanted to live life like a drama, that his problem was he took life too seriously. Serious as a game. No, he said, he wanted to live like he was in a play, and even though he might not have a choice of role or script, still it would be better than living under the rules of a game, where if somebody wins some-body's got to lose. It turned out his philosophy of life had changed too.

Hannah's was a triangular building, the bar set across one wall, booths lining the side walls, a pool table in the center of the floor. Late-afternoon light came in from the doors on either side of the bar. The decor was slick plastic, the pool table green as a sick pond, the walls hung with dim beer ads. Of the dozen or so customers maybe I did pay special attention to the two men sitting in the booth at the back of the room. One a huge man wearing sunglasses, cowboy boots, a fancy dress shirt he had slept in, hair long enough to curl over his collar. The other man looked like a wino slipping out of the store in a two-hundred-dollar suit. The coat was too big for him but he didn't care. The men stopped talking when I walked past their booth. The little man stared at my belt buckle, the big man kept his face turned away. I wouldn't have known him anyway.

I strolled across the room, then ordered a beer at the bar. I asked the bartender if he knew Son Cunningham. The bartender said he had never heard of him.

I sipped my beer. "Well then, who does that red Lincoln out there belong to?"

The bartender didn't move his lips. "You new around here, buddy?"

"Actually I'm old around here, buddy."

I was thinking about the bartender when I felt someone standing behind me. A hand the size of a first baseman's mitt wrapped over my shoulder and pulled me around. I looked up into that strange destroyed face. A face that was still handsome—the nose, the lips had once had delicate lines—but it was too big. There was too much flesh on the skull. It had the look of a body that had been ruined— bruised and swollen. The man's eyes were hidden. Long hair streaked with gray swept back from his high forehead. His mouth was filled with gold and black, humorless laughter, laughter that I remembered as good, and now it wasn't.

"Sugar, son, you're not trying to get yourself kicked out before you barely get yourself settled in, now are you?" And still laughing, he led me to the booth in the back of the room. The small man was introduced as a business associate. He seemed pleased that two old friends had been united after so long a separation. The diamond on his finger looked as real as it was big. After a few minutes he whispered in Son's ear and left. A nod from Son seemed to have solved all the little man's problems.

After the man left, Son talked carefully about the last few years. When he mentioned my old man, it struck me I hadn't really understood he was dead. He couldn't have hit me harder.

"If you feel like taking a ride, Sugar, we can drive out to Merce's place. I got the key. There might be some mail that has piled up for you. I'm glad you came back, son, things are getting pretty interesting around here. In some precincts anyway." He smiled.

"How did you know I had decided to come back?"

"A little buzzard told me. Naw, I just figured you'd be interested. I've been keeping up with your career the last year or so. You weren't that hard to run to earth, son." His face hardened and he looked off at something that wasn't in this room. "Actually, I've been trying to track down a lot of old friends lately. Lonely maybe. And I do need somebody I can trust."

"What's this job about? The one you mentioned in your letter."

"We need cash, son. Bad."

"And I'm supposed to have it?"

Son smiled mechanically. "I thought you might be able to find it for us. That's not too much to ask of a man with your talents?"

"How much do you know about my checkered past?"

"I was sorry to hear about your little company folding, Sugar. Oil's nice work, if you can get it. I've been considering it myself."

"I felt like retiring anyway. Anyway, I wanted to get out of California for a while."

"The law's not after you, are they?"

"No. Personal problems."

"A woman?"

"And a good friend."

"Ain't falling in love a true pain in the ass." He looked at me, smiling. "Where do you think it comes from? I mean, if the mind hangs out in the head, where does love come from? The heart, maybe the gonads?" He laughed. "It's a little bit like killing somebody, you'd have to be crazy to do it. To fall in love, you'd have to be crazy, wouldn't you, Sugar?"

"Maybe."

"Maybe. But then I didn't bring you all the way back here to talk about love, did I?"

"We were talking about money."

"Cash, not money, Sugar. Out here we're still uncivilized."

"All right. You need cash. How much do you need and what do you need it for?"

"My boss needs it, son, not me. We need it to pay the premium on his insurance policy. And don't laugh. It's a big, big policy."

"What kind of insurance?"

"Life."

"How come this guy has got such a big, big policy? Is he afraid he's going to die?"

Son stared at me a second, then gave a quick laugh. "Sugar, I'm expecting a phone call. Let's take a ride and see how your crop of tumbleweeds is doing, and I'll tell you all about it."

Son spun the Lincoln out of the parking lot. We made seventy before the Wall Street red light. "A man who don't have a fast car in West Texas is giving Father Time the edge and that old bastard don't need it." His head fell back and the Lincoln's tires screamed for half a block.

We drove east on the Toro highway, then turned south on a farm road, a ribbon of asphalt that ended at the county line. My old man's land was in Wadsworth County, maybe the poorest in the state. Water from last night's storm stood in the ditches, but the roads were already dry. A buzz came from the back seat. Son reached behind me and brought out a telephone. I barely listened to the conversation, though it sounded like he was talking to a woman. After he hung up he asked me, "You ever heard of Tee Kitchens?"

"No."

"You know about El Toro, don't you?"

It was the biggest ranch between the XIT and 6666's. So that was the fancy crowd. I said I had heard of it.

Son began telling me what I didn't know. "About five years ago old man Kitchens was on his last leg and that one had been busted five times. He couldn't even sit a horse without being wired in the stirrups. So to beat creditors, taxes, and old age he formed up a corporation and yanked Tee out of college and dragged him back home and sold him most of the stock for a dollar and other considerations. What I gather transpired was that Malcolm was figuring to go on running the ranch with Tee as a messenger boy. Well, if Tee is the type, his wife Adrienne is not. When I first met them they had just kicked the old folks upstairs and had taken over the ranch themselves. The good old days."

"Where did you run across these people?"

"In Lubbock one night. At Marvin DeKalb's house. You remember him. Used to be president of the Pioneer National. Speaker of the House couple years back. Ran for governor last year."

"I remember the name."

"Marvin is still around. You'll be meeting him. Well, at the time I was land appraiser for his bank. The job didn't pay all that much, though there were some expenses that got mighty expensive. But I had Russ out running my place and I was getting bored. Plus I had to put some distance between me and Wandell. Things were getting just a little too close. I ain't the tail-chasing type, not any more, but when a lady starts crawling in the sack with you, well, to complicate matters that was back when Alma had just left."

"That didn't have anything to do with Alma leaving, did it?"

Son's eyes dimmed and in them I saw the shadow of his quick insane rages. "No, she left me for another reason. It's the truth I bedded Wandell more from being lonely than horny." He gave me a wan smile. "Though maybe when you get to our age that's more often the case than not. How does that line go about men dying but not for love. But then who knows what he'll die for till he has the chance." The car had stopped and his face turned toward me. "That's right, don't you think?"

"I wouldn't know."

Son's eyes left mine, like a gesture of contempt. He tilted his head against his chest, as if he were asleep. I grew vaguely afraid of this man who I knew but didn't know, strangely drawn toward him. "A couple of honest poor boys, we're going to be rich and famous. But we can talk about that later." He looked up. "I'll wait in the car if you want to be by yourself."

We were sitting at the side of Merce's house. In 1942, the year after my mother died, the big house had burned down and Merce had thrown up this cottage, boarding out myself and my sister in town. The concrete foundation was all that was left of the old house. Merce had always wanted to rebuild the house but had never got around to it. I walked up the crumbling brick steps and could remember only the fire. The concrete slab was just a place where Merce had stored machinery.

Pushing my way through the tangled shrubs around the porch, I let myself into the small house. It already smelled lost. Nothing left but dust and old empty ledger sheets scattered on the floor. The furniture was gone. Some bastard had even yanked the sink out. In the living room I found a large manila envelope with my name on it. It was Merce's handwriting and the envelope was empty. I had thought I had no tears left for him. As the old man had told me many times, it wasn't enough water to do anything any good.

Son was lying across the front seat, his boots sticking out the window, honky-tonk music on the radio. He had the Lincoln spinning around before I got my door closed. "You want that house, son?"

"To hell with the house, I want a drink. Then you can tell me more about your plans to make us rich and famous."

Son smiled and pulled a bottle of Scotch from under the seat.

# 4

We drove back to Hannah's and Son picked up his train of thought. His eyes were fixed on that night in Lubbock when he had first met Tee Kitchens. He watched the people as they moved around that huge flat house, but I felt that among all the others he was watching one person, maybe the woman he wasn't ready to tell me about. He talked about the others—the Speaker of the House, state senators, lobbyists, the richest men in the state. He told me about Tee, drunk, wild, he had thought he was just another crazy cowboy. Late that night they had gathered in DeKalb's library, the rich and the powerful, deciding which laws of the land were to pass this year's legislature, which weren't. "Sugar, it ain't going to be drink or women, not even money, that does me in. It's going to be that touch of power. The silky feel of it. Maybe politics is my secret vice. See, I got other irons in the fire. I could almost say that taking care of Tee is my hobby. Right now, for example, I'm working on a little bill that sets up a state deposit insurance corporation, along the lines of the FDIC. But our little state agency is going to cover deposits up to fifty thousand dollars per depositor. We hope that's going to draw a customer or two away from the feds. One or two. You know anything about banking?"

"Some."

"You ever think about being a bank president?"

"All the time. Is that going to be the currency of my wages?"

Son watched my amusement. "Might be, if you're interested. We're thinking about opening up a new bank in Toro and we're always looking for talent."

"What if I don't want to live in a burg like Toro? I mean California is big time, Son."

"You wouldn't have to live there more than a year. Then you could kick yourself upstairs and live in Dallas. And then there's always the ranch. Toro's never dull, son."

"Maybe. What happened to the bank they used to have in Toro?"

"It's still there, but it's a federal bank. This would be a state bank. You could run it with a little more imagination than the feds."

"I didn't think they had enough people in Toro for one bank."

"If you got enough money, you don't need people. Look, things are moving pretty fast around here, Sugar. If you don't want to go along, just don't get in anybody's way."

"I'm not sure what you mean by that."

Son laughed. "I'm not sure either. Look, give me a chance to shut up for a while. I bet you're hungry as hell. Let's get a little something to eat."

"More tired than anything. I got to figure out a place to stay tonight."

"That's taken care of. I've got a place here in town that I

only use for business and occasional entertainment. It's yours for the duration." He laughed. "I've also got a house at the farm, a room at the ranch, a condominium in Lubbock, and a little hideaway in Houston."

"Goddamn, did you strike oil out there at Sand Hill?"

Son massaged his neck, rotating his head. "Naw, I discovered I got a brain up here and what to do with it." His eyes were closed, his head moving around and around. "Making money is a funny thing, son. It doesn't come out of thin air, or out of the ground, and it doesn't grow on trees or little plants. You've got to take it away from somebody." He smiled and opened his eyes. "You can do it with a gun, or you can do it with your head. Now there ain't much doubt which is the best way to go, is there? I'm glad you're back home, son."

We went out to the car, but Son seemed reluctant to leave. "I'm sorry I've been talking your ear off. Sometimes I get sick of the sound of my own voice." The Lincoln's motor came to life, and as if the machine were our master, we were speeding down the highway. "Well, I'm going to ply you with a steak as thick as your skull and see if I can squeeze a little sweetness and light into your life." We drove to a new restaurant on the Toro highway. Son gave me a key to his house, told me a street number and how to get there. He touched my arm before I got out. "I'm going to have to be leaving early tonight. First, I have to have you working for me. For a couple of weeks anyway." His eyes faded, as if the words had been said before. "I need somebody I can trust. I'm into this thing over my head. There's more to it than money, Sugar, there's just some things I can't tell you tonight, but I'll be able to soon. I'm just asking you to trust me for now."

"What else is there besides money, Son?"

Son looked away. "I got some personal problems too. I can't handle them alone. It's a woman . . . and a good friend." His face seemed to freeze. "There's been too much dying going on lately, too many people dying. It's got to stop. I want you to help me stop it." He laughed abruptly. "Look, we've got plenty of time. There's no rush. I've got to go to the ranch tonight, but I'll call you tomorrow. I want you to meet these folks down at the ranch. You might even like some of them. One final thing. There's a young lady who might be in the restaurant tonight. Would you do me a favor and get her out of my fucking hair?"

I was tired and hungry and wanted no part of this girl, but I agreed. Son roared with crazed, angry laughter. To my astonishment I was laughing too.

# 5

I woke in the early-morning hours in Son's house across town. The girl had already gone. By dawn I hadn't gone back to sleep so I dressed and walked the empty streets of my hometown. Downtown I leaned against the bicycle rack and studied the movie marquee. *Too Much Too Soon.* My problem in a couple of weeks. I found my way back to Son's house and slept in a fever. I thought I had walked miles, been gone for hours, but when I woke it was only seven-thirty. I drank half a beer and went back to sleep. When I woke several hours later, for an instant I remembered the day before, my coming back home, as a dream. A bad dream.

It was one o'clock by the time I had showered and dressed. I wandered through the small house. I couldn't tell that anyone had lived here for months. The living room was bare and untouched. The kitchen, beneath a film of dust, was too clean, the bedroom disturbed only by my sleep. Whatever Son used this house for, he was awfully businesslike about it.

I found a stack of letters on the floor beneath the mail slot. I spread them out, studying them like a hand of cards. I finally opened the letter from Merce. A handwritten will that was undoubtedly worthless, deeding me his land. There were six letters from Lila, my ex-wife. Four of them were Christmas cards. By the time I had opened the last one, I had grown fond of little baby Jesus. In one of the letters, formal and vaguely worded, Lila told me she had remarried. She mentioned our daughter in passing. I left the rest of the letters unopened.

It was two-thirty by the time I got out on the highway. Since I had traveled to my mother's grave a hundred times or more, I knew the way. I stood at the foot of their graves—one flat and covered with grass, the other fresh as a plowed field—and could think of nothing but the fact that both their given names began with M. It was a large letter that stood over me, both fearful and kind, their love of me. I was suddenly physically shaken by the fear of death. No, not death, but dying—slow, quiet dying. I knew why Merce had driven that Buick over the cap rock. I didn't know what Son had in mind, but death was one way to stop people from slow, quiet dying.

# 6

Like a yellow bird my aunt Boots's laughter floated just beyond the clutches of my plodding sarcasm. She would not forgive me for having missed the funeral. The will was no good. Everyone knew that. The farm was tied up in debts and taxes. There was nothing left. Everyone knew that too.

Boots leaned back in a graceful attitude that I had seen before. At one time she had been a beautiful woman, but it meant nothing now. In her hands I was still a foolish schoolboy. "Does money mean that much to you, Rogers?" she said, the only person alive who called me by that name. "It's work that makes money bearable. I hate to see anyone get mixed up with that high-flying crowd he's mixed up with now. I believe young Cunningham had a chance when he was married to Alma. When he drove her away . . . Well, I've heard he's become an evil man."

"What does an evil man look like nowadays?"

"Looking at a good man might give you an idea."

"Why did he leave Alma?"

"Why did *she* leave *him*?" My aunt blew air through her nostrils. "What other reason is there?"

She picked up a dish towel and the conversation was over. On my way out she suggested I talk to Mr. Dougherty. I said I would.

When I got back to Son's house, I found two telegrams under the door. I lay on the bed and opened them. The first read: PRETTY PLEASE and was signed with the letter A. The second: ROPING WADSWORTH TONITE COME DOWN MEET SOME NICE FOLKS CALLED BUT YOU OUT WILL SETTLE WORLD PROBLEMS SON. I let the telegrams fall to the floor and tried to think, but it all seemed perfectly logical. A man with no money set to find money. Too many people dying. A good man going bad. I knew two things for sure. I didn't know what the hell I was getting into and I liked it.

I reached up and set the alarm for five o'clock and it rang immediately. I lay on my back, looking up at the cool blue ceiling. I had never felt less like moving. I stood under the shower, telling myself I would go right back to sleep, then unpacked my bag and spread clothes over the furniture to let the wrinkles rest. I put on a fresh pearl-button shirt and spit at the boots I had bought special for my trip back to Texas. I put a crease in my new straw hat and decided I was definitely dressed fit to kill.

I ate a steak at Curly's Café while the gas station across the street changed the points and plugs in the pickup. Then with a six-pack to go I turned the truck southeast. The sky to my back was clear red when the truck dropped over the cap rock, the sky ahead black and torn with a lightning storm so far away it had no thunder. The air was dark and heavy by the time I topped a hill and picked up the lights of Wadsworth.

Wadsworth was a small town, smaller even than Toro, but there must have been a couple hundred cars and pickups jammed into the rodeo grounds' parking lot, spilling out along the sides of the road for a quarter mile. The storm didn't look much nearer, but the air smelled rich, both dusty and wet. I parked on the road, folded three cans of beer under my arm, and walked down toward the grounds.

There were as many people in the parking lot as in the stands. Loping their huge dark horses through the parked cars, gathered around open trunks and pickup beds, drinking beer, fondling as much as repairing their equipment, they watched me carefully. I saw Son's car parked back by the stock pens, but I climbed the raw wooden bleachers, opened a beer, and watched the barrel racing, all quick mares and pretty girls. Now I could hear thunder in the distance, a faint rumble coming more from the earth than the sky. The air was tense, as if it were waiting for the wind. Shouts drifted up from behind the bleachers. People sitting at the top of the stands looked down into the parking lot. A fight going on, my beer warm, the night cool, down in front a pretty girl wearing a Stetson twirling a rope—I had finally made it home.

I saw Son walking along in front of the bleachers, in deep conversation with another man who looked as out of place at a roping as Son did. A small wiry man, he was about the same height as me, maybe fifteen pounds lighter, his face finely shaped, the bones delicate and sharp, the skin drawn tight over his skull. His forehead was high, his hairline receding, his long yellow hair pulled behind his ears, the lobe of one pierced with a short leather thong. He wore belled Levi's, endangered-species boots, a white Mexican dress shirt with six-inch cuffs. The man's hands attracted my attention—hands not so much narrow as long, moving gracefully as dancers as he argued with Son, the fingernails polished, tapered claws. The man was covered with dust and his mouth was bleeding. As they walked along he kept gently bumping into Son. It struck me as a sign of intimacy, of competition.

The two men had stopped at the end of the bleachers directly below me. I had been watching them for some time when I realized that Son's companion was looking up at me. For an instant I felt I was the subject of their conversation. The idea crawled toward me like a snake.

Son nodded a greeting, then put his arm around his companion and walked him down toward the stock pens. The barrel racing was over and cowboys were prodding calves down a long chute toward the loading pens. The two men were joined by a girl who had been riding in the barrel racing. The girl was blond and dressed all in white. She took the contestant's number from her back and pinned it to the man's shirt. A broad-shouldered cowboy handed the man a straw hat, which he put on. He and the cowboy strolled back toward the stock pens, where other ropers were galloping their horses back and forth, reining them sharply, the horses rearing and backing like wild animals. The girl stayed by the fence, watching the two men walk away. Then her eyes followed Son Cunningham as he made his way through the crowd toward me. More than ever he seemed to be playing some role, though no longer for my benefit. Three riders galloped their horses to the far end of the arena, then back. Son seemed to be laughing at them as he sat down. "That little s.o.b. is going to get us both killed someday. The cat he jumped must've been six foot four."

"Is that the woman you've got problems with?"

Deliberately Son turned his head toward the cowgirl in white. "Naw, that's a one-night stand who can't count."

"What's her name?"

"I forget."

"I got the telegrams. Both of them."

"It's four hundred a week and I didn't say month. You'll officially be working for Tee."

"That's the long-haired cowboy."

"Unofficially for me."

"What in the hell am I going to do that's worth four hundred a week, Son?"

"I haven't decided yet."

"All right. For the time being you've got yourself a hired hand."

Son shrugged, as if it was of little consequence. "There's a party going on down at the ranch tomorrow evening. Come on down and see how we live on the other side of the tracks. We'll set you up in the bunkhouse at Toro or you can stay in the Flavannah house if you want to. We're going to be on the road most of the time anyway." A rider and calf burst out of the stall. Son's boredom with the chase was so intense it verged on hatred. "Give me a ring before you come. Some of the boys down at the ranch are getting kinda jumpy. Not that I blame them. During the last month one of them's been killed and now there's another kid missing." Suddenly his face jerked away from me, back toward the stock pens. "You and Tee are going to have to meet one another. You'll like him, son, he's a good ole boy."

"Who is A.?"

"A.?"

"The pretty-please telegram was signed A."

Son stood. "She's the lady I'm much taken with. Kitchens's wife. Maybe I'll see you tomorrow. Maybe later." He went down the bleachers, toward the stock pens. He didn't speak to the cowgirl as he passed. She had turned to watch the roping.

Then the cowgirl started walking toward me. I didn't look at her till I sensed her body beside me, a perfume of woman's sweat, leather, and horse. The girl's face was perfect, her skin rich, tanned, a natural flush to her cheeks. Her eyes were cold blue, her profile strong; her father had been a handsome man. Her hair clung to her temples as she took off her hat and set it beside me. She stared down into the arena as if it were a body of water. I spoke to her and she moved those cool blue eyes over me.

"Are you the one that's going to kill him? You sorry motherfucking bastards."

I followed her gaze toward the loading chutes. The long-haired cowboy was walking a small bay horse back and forth. "Look, I don't know what you're talking about and I'm not here to kill anybody."

But the fire had died quickly in her eyes; the strength in her face crumbled, leaving nothing but her beauty. She was deathly afraid of something, maybe even me. "Then why were you with Cunningham? What were you saying?"

"It wasn't about killing anybody, good Lord."

The girl began to make a chattering noise with her teeth. "How many men have you killed?"

"What a conversation. Look, whatever your name is, I like you a lot for somebody I've just laid eyes on. I like the way you look and smell and sometimes I even like the way you talk. Let's start all over again and just sit here and try to come on like normal people. We might even get to like one another."

"You can forget it, friend. I'm so much in love with him it makes me sick."

"All right. Where are you from? You don't sound like you're from around here."

She laughed. "That's right, I'm an imposter, a college girl in the country. But so is she." And she leaned forward, her arms hugging her sides, and rocked back and forth. "I thought you looked like her type. Sick. So you're a spy for Cunningham. But you don't even know what that is. Well, you're the seediest one yet. My God, where *did* they find you? Or are you a Big House spy? Or maybe a political spy, or maybe you're just an insurance spy. But you don't even know how life insurance works, do you? Well, I'll tell you, the poor bastard dies, mysteriously dies, and then his wife and her weirdo boy friend collect millions and millions of dollars. Now do you have the picture?"

"I think I'm getting one."

The girl shook her head sadly. "But what are you willing to do to get what you want? Would you sell your soul to the devil?"

"No. And I'm not doing away with anybody either. Not even your long-haired boy friend. Now let's be some kind of friends."

She shook her head. "Have you met Adrienne? Do you have any idea what the setup is?"

"No. No, I haven't met her."

"Then you don't know what you're going to do." And she rose and ran down the steps.

I followed the girl, wondering if killing a man was the job I had really been offered—and if I had accepted it.

# 7

I lost the girl in the crowd back of the stock pens. Fifty people, maybe more, were gathered in a circle around another fight. As I made my way in, I saw only a small fat red-faced man in a silver business suit jumping around, shouting and yanking at the sides of his head, though his hair was already gone. "I'm warnin you! It's in the print!" The fat man's sentences burst from his mouth as quick as words. Off to one side, his hat cocked low on his face, a lariat coiled in his hands, stood Tee Kitchens. A smile slipped across his face—you had the impulse to step on it—he mimicked the little man, the crowd laughed, but the little man bulled on: "I'm warnin you, Tee Texas, it's no rodeos! I'm warnin you, they just lookin for a chance to cancel out on yore ass. I'm just tryin to help you out, Tee, I'm just lookin after yore best interest at heart."

Tee made a gesture and the crowd laughed. "Maury, you dig the wax out, you unnerstan . . ." His voice was mushy, with something hard boring through it—a man getting mean with something weak. "They wouldn't cancel out on me if I was to jump off a windmill tower into a Dixie cup—"

"They out to cancel, Tee, I can feel it in my bones—"

"Shut up! I'd break ever bone in your body, fat boy, then I'd set you up in your wheelchair so you could watch me fuck your wife. You ever watch me fuck Mabelline, Maury? I forget."

There was movement in the crowd. But the fat little man didn't answer. He just looked at his tormentor; he seemed to stare him down, because Tee dropped his head and mumbled on about something else. He had lost interest, like a cat finally eats a mouse just to get it out of sight. The crowd began to move off, leaving myself and half a dozen others. I then saw Son standing behind Tee, his head lowered in thought. Tee shifted nervously from one foot to the other. His voice was quiet. "Anyway, this ain't no goddamn rodeo, this is a fuckin roping contest."

"You wanna argue that in court, Tee, you wanna convince twelve city slickers this ain't no rodeo?"

"Maury, they caint cancel out on *me*." Almost as if he were mimicking the whine of a spoiled child.

Maury gazed wide-eyed at us for support. "They got people watchin you ever minute a the day."

"*Who?*"

The little man waved one arm around, like he was starting a race. "How the hell should I know. I'll tell you one thing, ever time you take a shit, Dallas knows if it was the drizzles."

Tee threw down his rope and squeezed his hands hard till he laughed. "Now wouldn't it piss the hell out of Mercury if I got the goddamn pneumonia and died. Wouldn't that gall that goddamn wop's ass." The whine had returned. "Have you told them sonofabitches there's somebody out there trying to kill me!"

"*Shuddup!*" The fat little man exploded. Tee dropped back as if he had been slapped. He reached down for his rope and lost his balance. No one made a move to help him.

"Tell Scarlett I ain't ridin tonight," he said quietly and moved back among the cars. Son caught Tee's arm as he passed, and though Tee yanked his arm away, he stopped to listen. Then he nodded and walked a few steps and threw his rope as hard as he could against the side of a new Cadillac. He walked over and kicked the car.

As Son moved toward me, the little man grabbed his arm and I was joined by the two of them. "Cunningham, believe me, if you got any power over that boy, and if you don't heaven help us cause nobody else does, you have got to git him to cut out that kinda talk. If they don't git him one way they'll git him another. They got psychiatrists studyin his goddamn handwritin, they got people listenin on the phones . . ." The man yanked a crumpled bandanna out of his pocket and smeared it around his face. Under his business suit he wore a pair of cowboy boots as small as ballet slippers. Son introduced us and Maury Mueller flashed a bright empty smile, shook my hand, and forgot I existed. Son seemed interested in hearing him out, though not now. Maury wasn't concerned with other people's problems; he rolled his eyes like a branded calf. "Is there really somebody out to kill his ass?"

"No more than there was before he got the policy. Where do you get all this talk about them canceling out on him?"

"Aw, it's common knowledge, Son. They got cold feet. You oughta know that." He became crafty, but openly so, like a man who chronically takes more than he gives. "They know what yore using that policy for. What I caint figger out is what side yore on, the insured or the insurers."

Son reached out and adjusted Maury's tie. "I'm on my side, Maury." He gave the tie a quick jerk. "There's no law against what we're doing, Maury. Is there?"

Maury wiped his face despondently and eyed a pretty cowgirl walking past. "Naw, and there ain't no law against cancelin out a policy if the covered don't fork up the premium."

"Now who told you Tee ain't going to make his premium."

"Two weeks, Cunningham," the little man said with a flatness beyond emotion. "A fortnight, as they say in Dallas." And then he slipped out a figure, so casually that I thought I had heard wrong. A hundred and seventy-five thousand dollars.

"I don't know why you're so heated up, Maury. You got yours off the top, didn't you? Or has Mabelline already run through it?" Maury nervously jabbed at Son's arm. "Naw, I got the feeling something heavy's hanging over your head, Maury. What's your game anyway? Has somebody got hold of your nuts and is squeezing, Maury?"

The little man laughed thankfully. "Nobody but that danged Mabelline. Wonder where the hell she is." And since nobody was there to stick him, he stuck himself. "Fuckin some bull rider! The bull is next!" He laughed with real pleasure. "Cunningham, look, do me a big favor." His eyes had panicked again. "Look, keep me posted, would ya? Goddamn, this operation in the dark is drivin me crazy."

"Sure thing, Maury, but I'd keep those reservations to Rio open if I were you. Who are you taking anyway? Mabelline or that funny blonde down in Wichita?"

Maury's eyes rolled. "Lord, I'd throw myself on somebody's mercy if I knew who was goin to have it."

"Now ain't that life, Maury, the thing about it is that you got to make up your mind beforehand. He who sits on the pot ends up with a lap full of shit. I got another one for you. Fence straddlers make sitting ducks. I just made that up. You like it?"

"Fuckin hilarious," said the little man and began eyeing me, edging away. I tried looking friendly, but it didn't pacify his mind. "All right," he said, "how much does he need?"

"Twenty-five thousand. From you."

Maury wheedled. He had the money, no matter what pains he took to say he didn't. I saw the cowgirl in white standing in the shadows of a barn, watching us. The next time I looked she was gone. "I don't think it's ethical,"

Maury was saying, "for the agent to loan the insured part of the first premium to pay the second. Do you?"

Son shrugged. "I don't know shit about ethics. If you got clean sheets, Maury, my advice is to ride it out. But a warning, if Mercury and those Dallas insurance boys do try to pull us down, then there's going to be a lot of other folks getting stomped besides us."

"Why don't you tell em yoreself."

"See, Maury, a lot of times being good or bad don't have a goddamned thing to do with a man's downfall. I learned that from Shakespeare, Maury. My first wife read it to me right out of the book."

"I gotta go home."

"Sure you do. Tell you what, call me up the first of next week. We'll have lunch."

The little man was already moving away, as though he were already late for that appointment. "Tell Mabelline I went home in the Pontiac. And tell that sonofabitch he can break his fuckin neck as far as I'm concerned." He was gone before he finished talking.

Son watched after him. "Let's see if we can find Tee." But he didn't move. "If anybody kills anybody around here, Maury's liable to be the one to do it. He's got himself a .45 with the sear filed off. Sawed the barrel off a three-hundred-dollar shotgun. But maybe these are the days for it. You get enough money riding on a number and people tend to get overheated." We began walking back toward a group of cars. "Why, I got my own death threat this very evening, the first all my own." He threw his head back and laughed. "That bitch."

We went back among the cars and pickups parked behind the stock barns and found Tee asleep in the back seat of a deranged old Cadillac, the front fender crushed so that the headlight pointed off into the air. Honky-tonk music blared from the radio. Son shoved Tee over, kicked a sad-

dle onto the drive-shaft hump, and got in the back seat. I
threw a couple of bridles on the floorboard and got in
front. Tee banged open his door and puked on the ground.
Son reached up and turned the radio down. Then we had a
drink. Tee stared at me, his eyes moving in quick circles
around my face. "Cunningham tells me you were a fuckin
hero in ought fifty-one. He tells me you killed forty-three
gooks with your toenail clippers. You ever killed a white
man? I killed one just the other day. White, *white!* Now
somebody's tryin to git me . . ." And he threw his head
between his knees; his shoulders heaved, he took great
deep breaths, as if he had just come up for air.

"He ain't had more than a fifth of Jack Daniel's since
noon." Son patted the man's back.

"Now why in the hell would she want to do that." He
pushed Son away and leaned back in the seat, his eyes
dusty red; he was looking at me. "Oh Lord, it's fact, that
woman will be the death of me." He smiled dreamily and
closed his eyes and laid his head back on the seat. "Where
is that little yeller sonofabitch!"

We got out of the car and wandered through the crowd,
Tee turning people around to look at their faces, then putting them back. We went up to the top of the bleachers;
Tee swayed dangerously against the railing. He yelled at a
cowboy who was dragging his saddle by the stirrup
through the dirt: "Hey *Monk*gomery! You see Coolie!"

The cowboy threw the saddle into the cluttered pickup
bed and kicked the tailgate three times before it stayed up.
He waited for it to fall back down just one more time, then
strolled toward us. "He's down by the loader cussin and
discussin with Potts." He took off his straw hat and kicked
it under the stands and walked back to his pickup.

Tee turned around. "Who's winnin this goddamn chariot
race anyway?" He passed the flask and we watched a quar-
terhorse dash after a calf, the rope snake out, the horse,

then an instant later the calf running into invisible walls. The cowboy ran down the rope, flipped the calf on its back, and began whirling an arm over the animal as if it were part of a magic trick. He suddenly straightened, jerking his hands in the air. Tee started yelling: "Check that goddamn tie! That crazy sonofabitch has got *glue* on that tie rope . . ." Tee leaned back and grinned at two women sitting in front of us; they were pretending silver hair wasn't piled on top of their heads. Tee gave them a wet smack and one of the women began cussing him out. Tee watched her, then tipped his hat over his face. "Fuck, I feel like takin the boat out tonight, Son, I'm feeling shitty and bad. One a them bad times is comin on. Let's find Coolie and get outta here." His voice was calm and sad, regretful. He rose and started down the bleacher steps but fell, tumbling all the way to the ground. The crowd gasped, rising to its feet. Son and I ran down the steps. We found Tee's head at an odd angle, one of his arms twisted behind his back. We stood above him, pushing people back. I glanced at Son's face—it had happened so fast, but his lips were drawn back in an expression of triumph. I followed his cold gaze and saw that Tee's eyes had opened; they rolled back in his head, and his mouth bubbled blood till he spewed it out in laughter, his arms and head jerking back into place as he leaped up and still spitting blood howled out his derisive laughter at those who had thought he was dead. Son's expression had not changed.

We made our way out of the crowd, then through a maze of horse trailers and pickups behind the stands, well beyond the arena lights, Tee yelling out his friend's name. Finally we heard an answer and Tee stopped us. We finished off the whiskey and Tee threw away the flask. He touched my arm. "Lemme warn you, ole Coolie has got some Jap blood in him somewheres to make him so yeller." And we went off, banging our way through the dark maze of cars.

I heard a woman's voice: "But I *do* love you, honey."

The man's voice was cool and garbled: "Naw, you don't. You fucked Shorty and Shorty wiped his cock on the curtains."

"I never had nothin to do with Shorty."

"Shorty wiped his cock on the curtains. Beat it."

A man and a woman were standing on the dark side of a pickup. The man's hand rhythmically raised and lowered, accompanied by the light metallic clash of a cigarette lighter snapped open. Tee's voice was soft and pleased: "Coolie, let's get the boat out and go water-skiing, and listen, you little gook, Shorty don't fuck nothin but sheep. Right, Potts?"

The girl shook her head. "That's right, Mr. Kitchens. I was tryin to explain—"

"Honey, would you go find June Bug and tell her we're leavin pretty quick." He patted the girl warmly.

The girl went off and Coolie lit the cigarette. His face, for that second, looked muddy, as did his eyes, the blank stare of a dog—he thought nothing of you beyond his master's command. A dent ran across Coolie's face, crushing his upper nose and part of his forehead—it looked like something that he hadn't taken good care of. I only noticed it later, but the cowboy never acknowledged that Son was in his presence. His voice was still calm: "Goddamn, boss, it's a hour to the house, then three hours down to the lodge. I gotta git up and work in the mornin."

"Who you work for anyway?"

"Some loony sonofabitch."

"To hell with him, let's put the outboard in the frog pond then. What are you doin in the mornin anyway?"

"Denton spotted buzzards out back a Soda Springs. Him and his boys is ridin out in the mornin—"

Tee turned abruptly and walked off. It sounded like he was laughing, but it made his body shudder. The cowboy shrugged and followed him at a distance, leaving Son and me standing alone in the dark. "Life gets complicated sometimes," my friend said. "If I understood what was going on, you'd be the first to know."

"We can start with the insurance policy. Why are they threatening to cancel it?"

Son watched me. "The money we need to raise is for the insurance premium. It lapses in two weeks. That's all the time we've got. But that's just peanuts. We got to keep that policy going. We're not using it for insurance, that policy is going to be collateral for a loan. It's his only hope, that one big loan in the sky so we can wipe out all his other debts so he can start over again. Without that big loan"— Son paused—"without it he's dead."

"The girl friend thinks I've been brought here to kill Tee."

"When you've really been hired to keep him alive. Now ain't that ironic?"

"Tee seems to think there's somebody out to kill him. Maybe a woman."

Son smiled. "There's no woman out to kill him, son. That's a fact."

"How about a man?"

He kept smiling. "You know, we do live like murderers, son. I'd think about taking that job if I were you." And he left without another word. I leaned against the old pickup and had a smoke and tried to think out what there was to think out. One thing stood out plain. If I wasn't being hired to kill somebody, I didn't feel like I was supposed to keep anybody alive either.

A breeze had kicked up and the air was brisk with the smell of rain. The thunder was distinct now and had moved to the north, crossing my path. I walked back through the crowd but did not see the cowgirl in white. So June was her name. That was all right: it was tomorrow's month, if May still had thirty-one days.

The streets of Flavannah were shiny and the gutters ran like small rivers. The storm had outrun me and the air was light and clear, stars hovering in the sky. A note was tacked on the front door of Son's house. I was too tired to read it, but it made little difference; the next morning I woke with Son's girl crying by my bed. I finally got her calmed down, and she smiled ruefully and ran a finger along my cheek, close to my ear. "That bitch wonts ever man in the world, but I don't care no more. I ain't no longer in love with him" was what she said just before she dropped off to sleep.

# 8

After breakfast I drove downtown to have a chat with banker Dougherty.

Enid Dougherty was a sour-looking old man, though he didn't really have the cheek muscles for it. Powdered like a cadaver, he did try to stand up to shake my hand. Boots must have warned him of my visit, because he started right in telling me how hopeless everything was. "Dry land goes for two hundred an acre and there's no buyer at that price. The mortgage—the one we have here—the figure eighteen thousand springs to mind. The taxes you'll have to speak to L. Oliver Stigall about. The machinery is old and replacing it would cost a fortune. I really believe, Mr. Campbell, that the will, if you want to call it that, was more of a gesture than anything. You see, your father labored under the impression that you would be interested in farming the land. Now, even that is next to impossible . . ."

"What are the chances of you loaning me the money to get on my feet?"

"Very slight." He exhaled as the interview neared its end. "I'll get together with Mr. Stigall and see what everyone thinks. There might have to be a cursory investigation," he said slowly, "of your business activities of the last few years."

"I think that would be all right"—I gave him a wide flat smile—"if it comes down to that."

The banker's hands made small movements around the desk: the willingness would suffice. "Before you go I would like to give you a word of warning . . ." He leaned back and looked around the bank. "I think much of what your friends at Toro are up to is unethical and probably illegal. I feel that many of their shenanigans are designed to circumvent the protective strictures of the federal banking system. I would suggest that hard sweaty money will be of more value to you, Mr. Campbell, than the sort that creates itself. So long as you maintain their acquaintance, you will have little chance of obtaining funds from this bank."

I moved closer in my chair. The banker moved back. "Look, I could be getting into something too big for me. Can you give me any advice?"

The banker was silent. "Get out. Don't get in."

"What do you mean about their getting around the federal banking system?"

The banker shook his head.

"What's going on out at Toro? What's Cunningham up to anyway?"

The banker was still shaking his head. "Ranches should be for ranching, farms for farming, insurance policies for insurance, and banks for banking. That's all you know and all you need to know." Needless to say, Dougherty didn't have the muscles for smiling either.

I walked across the street to the courthouse. It was late morning, maybe noon. The sunlight had thinned out, the sky was high, faint blue, the air cool for the first day in June. Stigall's secretary told me the lawyer would be in court all day. I left my name and strolled around the courthouse square. A small billboard on the southwest corner showed the records of the high-school football teams since World War I. Weak teams during times of war, strong teams during peace. In the Depression there had been a lot of zero-zero ties. I had a hamburger at the drugstore, then walked down to Conners Chevrolet and learned the pickup was now mine. Son Cunningham had arranged the transfer with Stigall. I dropped the papers by the courthouse, then headed the pickup, bright from the rain, east on the Toro highway. Out where the money didn't grow on trees, you had to take it away from somebody.

I didn't know much about El Toro, except that when you dropped off the cap rock you were in it. The fence flanking the highway was solid and well kept, wide firebreaks had been cleared and in some areas the mesquite poisoned and burned off. The land lay black and charred, waiting for the grass that had been knee-high before the white man had come. Somebody was spending a lot of money to turn back history. I didn't see a single head of cattle along the fifteen miles of fence that led to the outskirts of Toro, county seat of Toro County, population eighteen hundred.

I pulled into Tommy's Oil Well. Over a cup of gyp-water coffee I commented on the rattlesnakes in the pit at the side of the café. I had never seen caged snakes with so much life, or death, in them. "Yeah," Tommy said wearily, "the wind has blowed the top off it and I been too gotdamn busy to tack it back on." Tommy eyed me suspiciously. "Say, you ain't a short-order cook? No." Tommy let out a mournful sigh. "Fry cooks used to be a dime a dozen. Ever passin tramp could cook good as me. They ain't no more tramps." He gazed down the highway that led to California. "They all got where they was goin." He asked where I was headed, then shook his head. "Naw, you can save yourself the trip. They ain't hirin, they is layin off. Even if they was, you ain't the type. They ride a funny cowboy out there nowadays."

"I'm not sure I follow you."

Tommy wagged his head. "Why half a them is the meanest cocksuckers you ever laid eyes on and the other half is gangsters. Then there's that crazy bunch a kids from Toro. Anyways, they don't keep more'n a dozen honest cowboys out there to ride line. They ain't got that much to do." He looked around his empty café. "At night big double-mufflered semis come creepin around this town. All I can say is that if'n the feller gettin rustled don't say nothin about it, then who am I to gripe."

"Yeah, I heard they were rustling their own cattle."

"I din't say that."

"Why would a man steal from himself?"

"You figger it out."

"Maybe he's stealing what doesn't really belong to him."

"Some folks say he's sellin mortgaged cattle, but I don't." Tommy stirred up the dust on the counter. He looked like he had been sleeping bad. "Got to git rid a them snakes," he said with a trace of a shudder. "One Toro cowboy done died this spring. He was found bit from head to toe. They say his pony run into a den and pitched him. He was bit from head to toe. It weren't that you couldn't recognize him for who he was, you couldn't recognize him for a man but fer the shirt on his back. That was another funny thing, he musta took his pants off to git at the bites. Ain't that a funny thing to do. Take yore pants off and then put yore boots back on and walk two miles before you die. A honest cowboy. He used to come in here with them crazy Toro kids. Some folks think it wasn't no accident, but not me. Now one a them crazy kids is missin." Tommy finally let his shudder go. "Things git much worse and I'm putting rattlesnake back on the menu."

"They told me to give a ring before I go wandering around out there. You know the number?"

"Ast the operator. The phone company and Toro is quite familiar with one another."

I stopped at the door. "Say, what was the name of the cowboy who got snakebit?"

Tommy looked at me as if I had just walked in. "Palmer." The first syllable pronounced like pal.

"And the kid who's missing?"

"What about him?"

"What's his name?"

"Billy Orrance. Billy O., they call him. The O stands fer asshole." And Tommy went back to stirring up a dust storm on his counter.

I used the pay booth at the side of the café, the sound of the rattlers rising in an angry whine as I listened to the phone ring and ring. Finally the operator told me there was no one at home.

I drove ten miles south on the Wadsworth highway, crossed a wide cattleguard, and turned southeast on a blacktop road as good as any the state ever laid down. After four or five miles I caught sight of a great rock arch over the road. I stopped the truck just this side of the arch and looked across the horizon. There was nothing there. The clearance of the arch was sixteen feet or close to it, the top at least twenty, not quite symmetrical in form, the rock like rusted steel jutting out in ragged spikes, as if it had been angrily torn from the face of a cliff. At the top center of the arch was scrawled in inlaid concrete: EL

TORO. Then, beneath that, the year 1906. Lovers' initials and the dates of graduating classes were painted on the sides of the arch, but the paint had faded and no one had left a mark here for years.

As I turned back to the road, I saw three riders walking their horses toward me. One of the cowboys held a walkie-talkie to his ear, another had a rifle cradled in his arm. I started the truck and drove slowly down the blacktop. The three riders gracefully loped their horses over to the road and cut me off. I stopped the truck but left the motor running. The third cowboy had taken his .30-30 out of its scabbard and rested it in the crook of his arm, the muzzle pointed at my head.

"Where do you thank yore goin, mister?"

"I was going down to the ranch house to see some friends."

"How would you like them goddamn tares blowed out," said the cowboy with the rifle.

"I wouldn't like that a bit. I don't think Tee would either."

The cowboys glanced at each other. The talker's horse walked back and forth. He reined it up near the cab. "Could I see some ID, sir?" I gave him my driver's license. He studied the photograph on the card and my face. "California license," he said and sidled the horse to the front of the truck, "and Texas plates. You got the papers on this vehicle, Mr. Campbell?"

I told him all about just going to the county clerk and everything he had said. The talking cowboy backed his horse away from the truck and took the walkie-talkie. With nothing to do with his hands, the second cowboy took out his rifle. "Roamer One, Roamer One, this is Cowboy 69, can you read me, you goddamn queer sonofabitch?" The other two cowboys grinned and their horses stepped back and forth. The talking cowboy's face darkened as the walkie-talkie crackled. "This goddamn thang don't work. What a bunch a shit." He tossed the walkie-talkie back to the second cowboy, then rode his horse against the side of the truck, the stirrup slamming against the door. "Yore purty pitcher." He handed me my license and pulled the horse back, the animal's eyes wide and frightened. "I wouldn't wonder off the road too far. You might wonder into one a them rattlesnake dens."

"He might wonder into one keepin on the road."

"He might at that." The cowboy touched the brim of his hat, and the three of them wheeled their horses and loped off in the direction they had been going.

# 9

The truck topped a low rise overlooking a valley, a dish-shaped depression, maybe five miles across. At the far end of the valley a small community, two dozen or more buildings of various sorts, was nestled among a thick stand of trees. The pasture around the ranch headquarters was a deep green, the silver threads of irrigation pipes and their spray glistened in the sun. The pastures were empty. I was beginning to wonder if there were any cattle on this ranch at all.

As I drove down, one building definitely began to stand out from the others, a bare, four-story stucco block, one floor windowless, the floor above that entirely glass; a swimming pool and a greenhouse were on the building's roof. The roads among the buildings were laid out with military precision; the trees—oaks, poplar, cottonwood—had been planted many years ago. A huge old house was set back in the trees, but for now the Little House dominated my attention.

Son met me in front of the house. Standing on a concrete porch the size of a small house, he waved me around to the lot at the side of the building where I parked the pickup with Son's Lincoln, Tee's old Cadillac, a white XKE, an Impala, and three other late-model cars, all white and big. A pair of oversized dice hung from the Impala's rearview mirror.

Son leaned against the corner of the house, waiting for me. We walked around to the front door. Son pointed out the floodlights on the walls above the porch—they used to hold square dances here. We entered a dark hall, its beams and arches raw wood burned with cattle brands. Only working cowboys were allowed to cut their initials into the wood, I was told. As we waited for the elevator, Son laughed at the brands.

The elevator stopped at the second floor, letting us into a short hall with doors at both ends. We walked toward the Money Room, as Son called it, the Fucking Room was in the other direction. We entered a large dimly lit room that had been ransacked. Clothes, papers, pillows, blankets, books, what looked like a couple of bodies were strewn around. We made our way toward a desk in the far corner where Tee was sitting in a fan-back chair, swiveling around and around. "Eleanor, git yore hands off a me and *oil* my wheelchair!" He went around once more, returning with a pitcher of ice water in his lap. Son took a chair and I leaned against a giant pillow. "What are we doin here, where are we goin, why does it all hurt so fuckin much— what were we talking about anyway?" Tee finally opened his eyes. "Oh Lordy, it got drunk out last night. Where was you when the ship hit the sand? Have you laid out my troubles for your little friend, Son?"

"No, I haven't, Tee."

"Well, well, well—where to begin the beguine." Tee moved from side to side, the chair making a low squeak, like a trapped animal that has begun to tire. "If I was the Lord I would do the whole thing over again right from the word go. Pay close attention, friend," and Tee lifted his feet onto the desk and put his hands as a visor over his eyes. "We need lots a cash, real bad, real quick. I took over this piece a goddamn real estate from my idjit daddy up to my ass in his debts. Well, what with a little expansion out and three, four years soft beef prices, a wife who wipes her ass with twenty-dollar bills, creepin socialism, and pregnant niggers—you put it all together and the debt has piled up. Bankers are timid souls, you know that. Yassah, they're yeller-bellied little critters who want their money back." He smiled at his mimicry of someone I had not met. "It began to look dark back at the ranch. Golden Boy was about to ride off into the sunset when he happened on to this feller at a party. This feller is shy of bein a genius by a cunt hair and he has read German philosophers from whence all wisdom founts. Did you know that was where all wisdom founts? Hell, I thought they was nothin but a bunch a halitosoid goofballs that punched their sisters. But this feller said, Nosir, them whiskers had run across the secret to success. You know what that is? Why shit, it's just the ole dialectic!" He kicked his desk and laughed till it was a strangle. "What bullshit, but then all I had was a corner on bad shit—a blind idjit for a daddy, a credit-card freak for a mama, fifty thousand acres of scrub mesquite and ten thousand matchin head of scrawny Herefords, and one dick-eatin wife." His voice finally jammed. "I was fool enough to love them. Everthing but the old woman. Yessir, the kid was in bad shape, his hands was shaky, his eyes was not clear, his dreams was freakin out the help, there wasn't no lead in his pencil. He had only one pal, ole Jack Daniel's, and he was out to git him. Still is, mebbe, but he's been sent to the foot of the line. Then one night there I was chasin after some piss-aint loan like it was a soggy-drawered cheerleader, lickin that Sunday-school teacher's boots, when I happened acrost yore ole buddy here and he begun to tell me about the real world, layin on all them twenny-five-cent words: *in*flation, *de*pression, con*sol*idation, and all that other crap that I pay him to wade through. Ah fuck, you tell the rest of it, Cunningham, my tongue needs a nap." And he turned the back of the chair to us.

Son nodded like a weary teacher at the beginning of another year. "All right. Inflation reduces the principal of a debt without you ever having to pay a penny on it. If you borrow a hundred bucks and after a year there has been, say, five percent inflation, then all you pay back is ninety-five cents on the dollar. That's the idea anyway. Keep up the interest payments, skim off the profits, let old devil inflation take care of your principal. Then if someday the bottom drops out like it did back in the thirties, you ain't going to be any more bankrupt than the fool who never owed a penny."

Son turned his chair away from Tee, as if he had left the room, though in fact the man had turned around to listen. "Did I ever tell you a little lesson I learned from my granddaddy? Back in the twenties he had made him a little pile in East Texas, working his and his kids' asses off. In the end he had a couple thousand acres of bottom black land, a sawmill, a couple of cotton gins, a major share of the fat little bank in town.

"Well, he started off with nothing, like most good American heroes. After the Civil War all the menfolk in his family had been killed off, and at the tender age of twelve he took over what little cotton land wasn't fit for carpet-baggers. I remember Granny telling the story of him and his older sisters gathering in the first bale of cotton that fall and loading it onto the wagon and him driving the team into town to trade for the winter provisions. But when he got there the merchants flashed all this red ink at the kid and took away that bale of cotton and he had to ride back home with nothing in his pockets but fingers. By the time that ride was over, he had sworn never to owe another man anything and I don't guess he ever did. He built up that little fortune paying cash on the barrelhead, but then along comes the Depression and the folks who had borrowed money from his bank couldn't pay it back and the ones who had deposited their cash were lined up outside the front door wanting their nest eggs back. Well, Granddaddy was one of those rare birds who believes in the system even when it ain't working. He took the cash out of his own pocket and paid those folks back. The bank went under, and though the old man wasn't hurt that much financially, I think it broke his heart. If money can do that. He didn't understand the Depression any more than the man in the moon. He didn't understand the so-called free-enterprise system, or let's say he understood half of it. Hard work, saving, working folks as hard and as long as you can while paying them as little as you can get away with—oh, he was a master of the sunny side of capitalism, but he didn't understand the dark side. Finance, exploiting the exploiter, squeezing the man who squeezes the man who does the work. There's a lot of colorful ways to put it. The man who rides the horse don't necessarily own it." Son's eyes had grown wary; his face showed signs of strain. "On the other hand, the man who owns the horse ain't necessarily the only rider."

Son went on talking about something, but I didn't listen. I was watching Tee's face reflecting his hatred. Finally Tee cut in, his voice low, wavering with fear: "That's enough a your bullshit for today, Cunningham. Tell your little buddy what we want out of him and let's get on with it."

Son's voice was cool. "We'll go over the details later."

"Do that, friend," said Tee and leaned back in his chair and threw his feet on the desk, knocking something to the floor. "Cunningham tells me you was some kinda slick operator out in Caliphoney."

"I was for a while."

"Till they caught up with you."

"There wasn't that much illegal about it."

"Not much." Tee opened a drawer and took out a sheet of paper and studied it. "Intelligence officer in the army. A mustang."

"That's right."

"When you got out you went into the same sort of work in the oil fields around San Berdoo."

"Eventually."

"You had you a little wildcat PR firm that was supposed to get information from the majors and sell it to the independents. But you started playing both sides of the street."

"One time."

"One time too many. They busted yore ass for it." Tee put the paper back in the drawer. "That's all right, I don't trust a man less he's tasted failure. Defeat. Hoomilation, my daddy calls it." Tee swiveled the chair so that his back was to us. "I'm gettin into oil myself, I don't give a shit what they say. This place is floatin on it. Me and Gunner we're goin in together and we're makin this the biggest field north of the Permian and it's *all goin to be mine!* Fuck them cows and fuck runnin for some diddleyshit office. Fuck all your goddamn ideas, Cunningham, me and Gunner are goin to find oil just like his old man did in Plaquemines and you and my old man—both them old men, all you old men, you're just goin to eat your goddamn hearts out forkful at a time . . ." Like the night before, his voice was shrinking into a whine. "There's got to be something under there, there's got to be *something*." His back was still to us. Son said something almost in a whisper and Tee slowly turned the chair to face us. His hands shielded his eyes, but his mouth was twisted in a grin. When he spoke, his voice was smooth, heartless. "Just find me some money, Campbell, just find me some money and keep me alive and you'll be rewarded. You'll be rewarded by and by. Where is that goddamn Mabelline when I need some advice?" He reached behind his head and grabbed a book and threw it across the room. It struck someone huddled under a blanket. The person groaned. "Where is that bitch?" He threw another book at a pile of clothes. "Mabs, git your ass over here, I need some advice on some toe fucking." He looked at me. "It's easy if you got a hard toe. Even Cunningham oughta be able to do that. Mabelline, git these boots off. Pork Man, git your ass up! Guard my body!" A platinum-blond head stuck out from under a pile of pillows and newspapers. In no hurry the woman sat up and gave Tee the finger. She grabbed one of the books and threw it across the room. Tee turned and dumped a shelf of books on the floor and began throwing them around the room, laughing like a machine designed for something else. As Son was trying to move out of the way, one of the books struck the side of his head. He stood up quickly, his face a mask of pain and hatred. Tee dropped his eyes, then let the last book slide from his hands. "I'm sorry," he said and the chair slowly turned, taking him out of sight. "See what Denton's found at Soda Springs, Son. I'm sorry, I didn't want it to come out like this. Do something for me . . ." but he received no answer.

We made our way back across the wrecked room. The blonde was muttering something to the ceiling. The face of a huge fat man slid from under a blanket. If that was who Tee had called Pork Man, it fit. His red bulging eyes followed me to the door. Son's hands were trembling as we waited for the elevator; his temple pulsed where the book had struck him. But once inside the elevator, the door closed, moving upward, he smiled coldly. "Nice little speech I gave, wasn't it?"

# 1 0

The elevator let us out in a cabana on the roof of the house. Beyond I could see the swimming pool, the greenhouse, and a dark woman sitting on a lounge chair at the far end of the pool. The woman was reading a book and didn't seem to notice us. I followed Son into a small room off the cabana, where a musclebeachboy, wearing bikini shorts and a headset, was grinning into the mike of a two-way radio set. ". . . a cane? Yo eighteen year ole, boy. Aw, a cane a Lone Star, Mama . . ." The man looked up at Son, and without a word we went back out to the swimming pool.

The woman was dressed in shorts and wore large black sunglasses. She laid the book open on her lap and watched us as we skirted the swimming pool. A small umbrella table stood at her elbow; on it were an empty glass and a mute transistor radio. I paid little attention to the words of introduction. Son brought up two folding chairs and the three of us sat chatting, looking into the wavering aqua water. Adrienne didn't remove her sunglasses, so that I was acutely aware of the planned warmth of her smile, her easy sardonic attitude toward me. Each part of her I found soft, easy, yet somewhere she was cold and hard.

She and Son talked casually about people I didn't know,

an edge of sarcasm in their voices. My mind drifted off toward what I finally recognized as the distant sound of gunfire, slow and measured. Son and Adrienne were looking in that direction. "Caroline Jo," Adrienne told him.

Son's head moved slightly toward the cabana. "Whose side are they on today?"

Adrienne smiled at me. "If you haven't already discovered, Mr. Campbell, the ranch is broken up into warring factions."

"To tell the truth, Mrs. Kitchens, I haven't discovered much of anything."

She reached her hand toward my arm but moved it away just before touching. "It's because nobody talks around here. I'm not sure from day to day who's speaking to whom." Her head turned abruptly. "We're all so silent."

"Who is Caroline Jo?"

The woman's glasses scanned my face; the smile was gone. "She belongs to the body in the radio shack. I think. Caroline Jo is a gun freak, Mr. Campbell. We all are."

Son had moved to the other side of the swimming pool, too far away to be listening. "What sides are there to be on?"

She smiled. "Why not mine?"

"No other choice?"

"No better choice."

"All right then, who's the enemy?"

She turned away as though I had dropped out of sight. "Father Time for now."

"If I'm going to be working for you and Son, then I'd like to know something a little more definite than that."

Adrienne's face turned back to me. Her smile had softened. It was meant to be liked, and I liked it. "Son and me?"

"That's right."

She looked away. "You might be too fast for this job, Mr. Campbell."

"Now's the time to find out. If the gunfire belongs to the body in the radio shack, who is he?"

"Larry? I'm not sure. I think he belongs to the Big House, but I'm not sure. Maybe he works for the insurance people, maybe he works for Denton. Denton's the Toro foreman. I don't think you've met him yet." She raised her arm and pointed backward with her thumb. "That's the Big House, where the old folks live." Then she pointed down at the concrete floor. "And this is the Little House, where the young folks live. Of course, everyone officially works for Tee. Even if they hate his guts. Even me." She smiled again. "I told you, you were going too fast, Mr. Campbell. Life at Toro is too twisted for speed. Slow down and live. As the sign at the side of the road says." She was looking past me toward the cabana. I turned and saw that Larry had come out of the radio shack. He looked at us, saw Son, and went to him. They conversed briefly, then came toward us, their faces stiff and worried. Larry took the vacant chair, while Son remained standing. "Denton has finally found him," Larry said, "down in Delta Fiver."

"Soda Springs?"

Larry studied Adrienne for a moment. "Yes ma'am, they finally found Billy O. down in Soda Springs."

The woman's hands gripped the arms of the chair. "Does anybody know what sort of shape Tee's in?"

"Bad."

"Can you take care of it, Son? I'll have to go down to Tee. He's got to be sober tonight." Adrienne turned sharply to Larry, who had fallen deep into thought, feeling his pectoral muscles. "Listen, I want *two* cars out at the strip from four o'clock on. And put the radio on Tee's intercom the rest of the afternoon. Who's down there?"

"Pork Man and Mabelline are all I noticed."

Adrienne uttered a bitter, helpless curse. "Did they say what happened to him?"

Larry turned his ear to the firm, measured gunshots. "Denton claims this one was plugged smack between the middle of his eyes." He smiled. "Looks like he was dressed out just like ole Palmer. In a pair of boots and his birthday suit."

There was a silence. A cloud passed quickly and Adrienne shivered. There followed a sudden rattling burst of gunfire. "Tell that bitch of yours to stop it!"

Larry blinked, as smooth as a push-up. "That ain't Caroline Jo. Caroline Jo went into town this morning."

Adrienne had folded her book back, cracking the spine. Son stepped toward her. "It's all right, A., it's probably just one of the boys."

"No, don't. I know who it is."

"We'll take the Rover," Son said, then to Larry: "Call Sheriff Tabor and tell him to get his ass out here."

"I think they found him in Toro County, not Wadsworth."

"I don't give a damn where they found him, you call Tabor."

Larry rose and went back into the radio shack. Nobody spoke till he was gone. "My God, Son, what are we going to do?" the woman finally said. Another cloud crossed the sun, high and fast, and the pool shimmered like pale blue fire at our feet. The gunfire had stopped. To the south I could see a dirt road that led to nothing but more low rolling hills, shimmering in the heat. There seemed to be no life anywhere.

"We'll just play it by ear," Son said quietly, "and hope for the best. I'm sorry Billy O. is dead, A. It's going to stop. I'm going to stop it."

"I know you are." She shielded her eyes with one hand and waved us away with the other. "Don't stay gone too long." Son said we would be back in an hour.

The elevator took us to the basement, one section of which was a garage and equipment storage area. Trucks, a tractor, a road grader, plows, and other machinery, all arranged in stalls like animals, everything new, clean. The concrete floor was bright and damp. Son operated the rollback door at the exit ramp from within the Land Rover. Outside the sunlight seemed pale.

We drove south on the dirt road till we were out of sight of the headquarters and Son stopped the truck. He sat staring at the road. Finally he said, "Tee killed the kid." He looked at me. "That's the story that's been going around anyway. Same story has it that the kid and Tee killed Palmer. Got him all fucked up and fed him to the snakes. Palmer was just a crazy cowboy in love with A. He didn't know what he was getting into. But Billy O.," he shook his head, "he asked for what he got."

We drove through deeper hills, generally southeast. We turned off the road up a grinding pair of ruts that snaked along the side of a gulley that had deepened, by the time I caught sight of the horses below, into a narrow steep canyon. Suddenly the road pitched down into a small wooded area, widened, then stopped. Two cars had come before us, an old green Chevrolet with a splash of tar on the roof, and a late-model Ford. Son parked the Rover behind them. The horses I had seen from above were now hidden by the trees and thick undergrowth of the grove we walked toward. We climbed through a barbed-wire fence and made our way down a path cluttered with used cartridge casings. It was like entering a cave of trees, but at the end we came upon a sunny, grassy clearing where six horses were tethered, their riders standing in a loose circle, watching us approach. At the back of the clearing lay a tangle of furniture—sofas, chairs, tables, a refrigerator, a stove—left to rot in the sun and rain, everything gnawed by the teeth of thousands of bullets. A target was taped to the refrigerator door—the black silhouette of a man, his head and chest and groin blown away.

We joined the cowboys and, though no one returned

Son's greeting, after a pause one of the men said, "The body is back over yonder in the bushes. Out behind the icebox."

The cowboys spoke to each other, not to us. "The sheriff is on his way out. It coulda been a accident."

"Shore, he was out there with no clothes on. He was shot somewheres else and dragged over here."

"Mebbe, but that kid was always doped up."

The other cowboys turned toward one man, as if an agreement had been reached among them and he was their spokesman. The man said, "What this outfit needs is somebody to pull it back together, or to throw in the towel. It ain't right havin all these crazy people runnin around here. Somebody's goin to have to step in and put a stop to it. Denton is back there with the body." He turned his back to us, looking toward the thick wall of undergrowth beyond the pile of furniture. "He stanks to high heaven. He don't smell purty now."

Son watched the undergrowth but there was no movement. "Who found the body?"

One of the cowboys spat. "Who did find that sonofabitch?"

The leader shrugged angrily. "There's a trail back up that way. Then it doubles back. It ain't no more than thirty yards over."

We went up a small rise, into the trees, then a few yards on found a path that curved down and back to the right. After fifty yards we came upon a bank of grass, weeds, and tangled shrubs fed by the spring, a teeming world of insects and sweltering humidity. A few yards ahead I heard a soft hissing, like a small spray. We came upon a tall, lithe man walking through the tangled grass; he had a can of insecticide strapped to his back. He kept at his work after he saw us. "It's fer Johnson grass," he said, "but it'll kill ants too. Why it'd even kill the likes a you and me, you give it to us straight." The man turned toward us. Something had worn his face down to the bone; his eyes were red and swollen—the idea that he had been crying ran through me like a shock. "The bugs has about eat him up," he said quietly. "You tell Tee the bugs has eat him up!" Then he pointed the nozzle to a low mound a few yards away and went back to spraying. I didn't have to go nearer—there's no smell quite like the rotting flesh of an animal and no animal that I know of wears boots but man. It didn't look like this man wore anything else.

Son went forward and looked down at the body. He prodded a black leg with the toe of his boot. The leg collapsed where he touched it. He came back and for almost a minute we watched the man with the spray. Then Son said, "Are you sure it's him, Denton?"

The foreman put down the insecticide and carefully wiped his hands with a bandanna. His gestures, the grace with which he moved, were so feminine that he could have been a woman dressed as a man. He stood looking toward the body. "All that gold in his mouth," he said. "The kid was always gettin his teeth kicked out. Looks like he's been shot in the head. The hole's big enough to be a .45. It's a common gun. I used to have one myself. Bought it off a dyin nigger."

"Who found him?"

"I found him, Mr. Cunningham. You know why, cause I been lookin for him. Cause I din't believe that crap, pardon my language, about Billy runnin off to Mexico. Oh, I knowed he was dead, mister, and I know where dead men lay. He was like Palmer, all in all, good boys that got messed up with the wrong people. He shoulda stayed in town. He should never come out here."

"Was it an accident?"

There was nothing womanish about the man's laugh. "Nosir, I don't believe it was a accident."

"All right, who do you think killed him?"

"Well, mister, I believe he killed hisself. Even though he was a boy that believed that takin yore own life was damnation, I believe that's what he did. You see he saw the world around him was rotten and the people was vile and they had covered his table with filth. That's what they did to him. I can understand why a boy could see no way out. I think I can understand that. But vengeance is mine, saith the Lord, mister, and all the likes a me and you have to do is set back and watch Him take His course." The man turned toward the body. "I wouldn't have the undertaker's job. I would just sprankle a little gas around and let him go up right where he lays. But I reckon that would be destroyin evidence. There wasn't no gun that I could find, but it'll turn up." He stopped at the sound of a siren coming up the draw. "There was one perculiar thing about this. Did you notice anything peculiar, Mr. Cunningham?"

Son nodded.

The man's eyes moved over us like a cold wind. "By the way, Mr. Cunningham, I found Mr. Kitchens's lighter the other day and forgot to return it to him. I got it down in my room. Would you mind telling Mr. Kitchens that I would like to have a few words with him? You just tell him that I understand. You tell him that Denton understands."

"All right. I'd like to have a talk with you sometime myself, Denton."

"Any time."

We went back the way we had come. When we were out of earshot Son said, "Ah, it's good to be really hated every once in a while. Makes you appreciate being loved by them that do." But he stopped and leaned against a tree, as if he were suddenly exhausted. Son looked back toward the tangle of brush. "He was our foreman. He's quit now. He's gone over to the Big House." Son laughed suddenly, as if he wanted everyone to be very happy. "That should give you an idea how much they hate me. Denton and the old man teaming up. He was the guy Tee brought in to run this place after he took it away from Malcolm. Denton was the one who fired all the old man's cronies. Every last one of them. There was once the old man would've killed him if he could have walked. And now they're bed partners. That's how much they hate me."

The cowboys had been joined by a sloppy fat man wearing a gray janitor's uniform with a silver badge pinned to his chest. He was late at the scene of the crime, he was saying, because he had to stop off for a quick piece. The cowboys weren't laughing. "Baaa baaa," said the sheriff as he saw us approaching. "Hidy by God, Son, now I don't wont you to fergit to vote come Satiddy—"

"Mark, get your ass up there and look at the body, and then get on the horn and get an ambulance out here and get that stinking pile of shit off this land."

"Aw shit, Son," said the man, his voice heavy with mock hurt, "I had the amblance tailin me all the way out. He just got a flat tare, he'll be right along—"

"He stop off for a quick piece, Tabor?"

The sheriff swallowed and winked. "Aw, Abner, you know he got it shot off by that meskin—"

Son's voice was light and strained. "I'd be careful about my jokes on the day a man has died. Everybody's been kinda jumpy, Tabor, they might not see the humor in it."

The sheriff was silky with sweat. The cowboys watched with disdain, as if someone were tormenting an animal. "I wadn't talkin bout nobody in *perticuler*—"

Son started walking away. "If you're coming to the party tonight, bring a copy of the coroner's report with you." We walked back into the tunnel of trees. Looking back, we could see the sheriff telling the cowboys his side of things. Son shook his head. "I keep telling myself that someday that fool will be worth his weight in gold. Some fine day."

Son asked me to drive and I took the Rover back down the canyon. Son slouched in the seat, his head leaning against the door as he looked up at the sky. "Peculiar indeed. Oh yes. What would you call it if somebody ended up dead—shot himself and threw away the gun, dressed up in your boots and nothing else. I think I would call that peculiar."

"Whose boots did you say?"

"Tee's boots. Let me pick your brains some more. If you were a rich man and were having financial problems, real bad problems, and all you had that another man didn't have a lien on was this six-million-dollar insurance policy, but even that wasn't worth anything to you alive, let me ask you, would you consider setting up your own death to get that money?"

"You mean have another man die for me?"

Son turned his head toward me, so that it lay against the seat as if his neck were broken. "Would you kill a man for money, son?"

"No, I don't think I would. Not even for that much money."

"How much did you get paid in Korea, Sugar?"

"That was different."

"I guess it was. You know you were quite a hero back home, when you shot that chink in Korea. Nobody could talk about anything else for weeks."

"I think I've heard enough about it myself."

"But you didn't know that chink, did you? You didn't hate him, or love him, you just killed him and his friends for a couple hundred bucks a month. Didn't you?"

"No, I killed him and his friends because if I hadn't they would have killed me."

Son looked at me. "You know that's still a good excuse these days."

"Are you going to kill somebody, Son? Is somebody going to kill you?"

"No . . . I don't know what I'm going to do. I don't even know if I'm going to have a choice."

"Why did Tee kill that boy? You don't really think he did it to make it look like his own death?"

"I don't know."

"Why did you bring me back here, Son? Did you bring me back to kill him for you? My God, Son . . ."

Son moved his head, so slowly. "No. Whatever I do, I'm going to do it myself."

# 11

Son let me off in the parking lot. We talked some about the trip next week to Houston. While we were talking we heard the faint buzz of an airplane. Son turned his head. "Single prop. Gunner is flying his jet up tonight. It's a big event, the first jet since the new strip was finished. You want to come down and wait for him to come in?" He looked around the deserted headquarters. "I imagine that's where everybody is."

I said I had a little business to take care of in town before tonight. Son smiled. "It's the big leagues tonight. Sonofabitch is the thirty-second richest man in the world. Gunner and his old man." But he seemed to lose interest in what he was about to say; his voice trailed off and there was a distant look in his eyes. "He's A.'s brother. He's a ruthless bastard. Dumb as he is, he's going to chew Tee up and spit him out."

"Us rich folks do live in a small world, don't we?"

Son laughed without humor. "It's not so small there's not room in it for one more ole boy. If he plays his cards right. If you can wait just a few more days, Sugar, on the trip to Houston, I'll lay everything out. All I can say is that my future is not here with Tee, and that you'll fit right in. It'll be worth taking the chance. You still are interested in making money, aren't you, Sugar? Your little deal going belly up didn't make you gun-shy, did it?"

"I don't know. I don't guess so."

"Good." Son smiled and said he would see me tonight and pulled the Rover out of the parking lot. As I was driving out, I could see the vehicle racing north, trailing a white plume of dust.

On the way back to the main gate, I noticed a road leading away from the blacktop. I stopped and followed it with my eyes. A rutted gravel road leading over a shallow hill. Why not? I eased the pickup across the ditch and stayed in low gear up the hill.

There were at least a thousand head of Hereford steers—fat, sleek animals, startled like white-faced old men wrapped in rich fur coats—milling around a canyon maybe a mile long but only several hundred yards wide. I stood on the running board and looked down into the dark red turmoil, the animals' lowing oddly muffled. I started to go down and have a closer look, then saw that the canyon was guarded by half a dozen cowboys. One of them was already riding toward me. I backed the pickup below the crest of the hill, turned around, and had reached the blacktop by the time the rider appeared on the horizon. I floored the little truck well beyond the stone arch.

At least the ranch had cows on it.

I stopped back at Tommy's Oil Well, but Tommy was cooking and not talking, according to a waitress who had just moved up from Olney a year ago last week to get away from a pushy farmer. I paid for a cup of coffee and asked the woman what she knew about El Toro, telling her that I was an investor interested in buying the place. It had already been bought by some Houston law firm, she said, or maybe they were from Wall Street. Anyway, they had discovered oil or gas but had capped over all the holes or had already sneaked all the oil out. Something to do with taxes. She talked a while about her boy friends—the cowboys and telephone linemen around here were stuck-up shit-asses. I wasn't the only one who had been in lately asking fool questions. People were always nosing around. Just this morning somebody had been in pestering Tommy and it had upset him something terrible. I said it was a shame and asked if she had heard about the body they had found today.

"Aw yeah, pore kid. News travels fast, don't it?"

"I guess you knew him pretty well."

"Aw, he was a nice kid, well-mannered and everthang, even after he moved out to the ranch. Tommy says he was no good, but I never seen it."

"I never can remember that kid's name."

"Billy Orrance. His daddy was one a them stuck-up rich types from Brownwood. He din't belong around here. He was a rich doctor down in Brownwood and practically lived over there in Europe and just left that kid all to his-self. That's how he got hooked up with *her*."

"It's always the outsiders that cause problems."

"Some locals is purty stuck up these days themselves. *She's* never been in this place one time. Not all the years she's been out there. Tee don't come in no more. Not since he lost that last election."

"He got beat pretty bad, I guess."

"Why, he was lookin down his nose at the job. What would you expect. Thang that got him worst was losing right here in Toro County. Didn't even win down in Wadsworth and that's the biggest bunch a crooks around. They tole him to take it a couple steps at a time, but that wasn't the way that boy was raised up. Why, you know he even tried to take over the volunteer fire department. Make everbody wear uniforms and go to meetings. That ain't the way thangs are done around here. He went out and set up his own fire department out at the ranch. Bought a great big red fire engine." The waitress smiled. "Had to give it up when times got hard."

"What's your opinion on all these folks dying out there?"

The waitress gave me a quick hard look. "Tough."

"How about that cowboy—I think his name was Palmer."

"Never heard a him, buddy." And she walked away and didn't come back.

I drove back to Flavannah and called the bank from Son's house, but Mr. Dougherty wasn't in. I went to sleep and woke at five o'clock. I reached Dougherty at home and made an appointment to see him next Friday. Then I asked the banker if Marvin DeKalb was still with the Pioneer National in Lubbock. There was a pause, then Dougherty said carefully, "No, no, he's no longer there. He's in insurance now, associated with Mr. Francis Dolly . . . of the Dollywood State Bank." He paused again. "It's a suburb of Houston." Then: "I'm surprised you didn't ask Laran Cunningham. They're all business partners. As a matter of fact, I assumed you were one of them."

"No. Not yet," I said and thanked him, and he hung up.

Mr. Francis Dolly. That, I guessed, was our trip to Houston. I was beginning to wonder just how many masters Son had.

I showered and then, on my way down to Hannah's, stopped by my aunt's. She was friendlier, or maybe I was. Without uttering a word about particulars, I said I was going to be able to get hold of some money. Boots said fine, but it would probably be too late to do anything but sell by then. I agreed, but asked her to hold things up for a week. My aunt couldn't promise a thing.

I drove down to Hannah's and pretended I had known the surly bartender for years. I ordered a beer and looked around the bar. The same roughnecks were stalking each other around the pool table. My eyes rested on Son's business associate, the small man who didn't fit his clothes, which didn't fit this bar, which didn't fit this town. He was sitting at a table in the back with a woman whose face was red and whose hair was white. I took my beer and made my way through the crowd, approaching them with: "Well, they found Billy O.'s body today."

The little man looked perplexed but amiable. The woman figured I had just been let out, till I was introduced as Son's friend and she became a little friendly. She was Tillie and the little man was Fife. Deciding that the best way to learn something was to pretend you already knew it, I said, "Yeah, Son has finally talked me into it. After all these years we have finally pitched in together."

"Together?" The little man looked hurt, Tillie looked betrayed.

"Not in your field," I said.

Fife broke out a timid grin of relief, but Tillie had decided she didn't trust me at all. "Sure, sure," the little man was saying, "I know how it is."

"How have things been going, anyway?"

"Aw lissen, great. I just talked to a coupla more boys today. Playin it real cool, just like Son says. One kid's a sure thing, one's a zero. He's the frog-legged kid, too stupid to be honest, I keep tellin myself, but Son says I ain't even to approach him. Let a sleepin dog lay. Now the other kid is goin to make us a mint. You know how much cotton he walks off in a day? Guess. Why hell, thousands a acres. And the county agent don't check up on none a it. Not more than one percent anyway. You know how many acres a cotton are planted in this county alone?" He gave a six-figure number, then multiplied it several times so that it came out to several million dollars. "Now a course," Fife added modestly, "me and Son only git a percent a that, very little is direct, and a course we have to locate the farmers who are interested in purchasin our services." He sighed at the difficulties of this world, most of which sprang from some sort of honesty. "Son is handlin that part for now, though I'm afeerd he's gettin bored with it, with all that action down at Toro, so I figgered . . ." I smiled knowingly and the little man dropped into despondency. "But puffin up allotments is just peanuts. We're quittin it purty soon. We're workin on bigger game." He hunched across the small table, looking at the nearby drinkers. "I personally think we can buy up the county agents right *here.*" He pointed at the table top.

"Sounds tricky."

Fife shook his head. "That man is capable a anything. He's a genius."

"And yore a blabbermouth," said Tillie.

Fife winked good-naturedly. "Aw now, this feller and Son is best friends. How long have you two knowed each other?"

"Since we were knee-high to a grasshopper."

The little man loved country sayings. He slapped the table and the beer bottles jumped. "*See.*"

"Naw, I don't see," said Tillie, but she was fighting a losing battle. Talk for Fife was like food to a starving man: too much might kill him, but he was damned if he was going to stop now.

"But we have got to pussyfoot some," he was saying. "Some counties is different than other counties. Flavia

County here has got its pros and cons. It's a big rich county with lotsa people with the itch, but on the other hand, if you have never noticed, there is a church on just about ever corner. That tightens folks up some."

"I never noticed that churches made people any more honest."

It was like promising a kid a pony for Christmas.

"How about Toro County?"

He passed the question at just the right speed. "You know better'n that. But I shore would like to sink my teeth into Wadsworth County. Rotten to the core. The only problem is that they only grow bout fifteen thousand acres a cotton down there. They ain't got nothin to cheat for." He continued his regret: "Then there's Lubbock County, the gem a them all. There for the pluckin, but it's hands off."

"Son didn't mention that."

"He didn't?" Fife looked at me for a few seconds, then turned to watch Tillie, who had gone to the bar to get another round of beer. "It's Marvin DeKalb's home county. Son says we caint afford to mess around there. Marvin's a great man." His eyes slowly came back to me. "He's goin to be governor someday. That's what they say."

"Might be more than that by the time it's all over."

Fife whistled softly. "Boy, you hit the nail on the head. There ain't goin to be any stoppin that man. He's goin all the way. All I can say is, it's been a honor to work with one a his best friends."

Tillie came back with the beer, and I said I would drink to that. "When is Son going to move you up to Toro?"

The little man hung his head. "You oughter know. Never now."

"Now, I'm not stepping into your place, am I? I had no idea I was doing that."

Fife shook his head. "Aw, you din't know. I ain't cut out

to hobnob with them folks anyways. Son took me down there onct but . . . Well, I'm better off down here, ain't I, honey?"

"You can sleep at nights."

Fife attempted a look of commiseration. "I wouldn't be in yore shoes for nothin."

"That's all right. I've had plenty of experience." Fife and Tillie seemed to shiver in unison. "I wouldn't worry about anything if I were you. Son hasn't said anything in so many words, but I think he's going to leave the allotment business to you."

They were clutching each other like evicted tenants listening to the weather forecast. "You really thank so?"

"I really think so."

The bar clock said quarter to eight. In the last five minutes the light from the open doors had faded to pink, then light blue. A nice time to be driving east, with night moving over you. I told the couple about the party and that we would all go but I was a guest myself. Fife shook his head and said that was O.K. Son had left strict orders that things would be kept separate now. "He's movin up now," the little man said, "and he just caint take us with him. Ain't that right, Tillie?"

"That's right," said Tillie. "And I'm proud of it."

I sat in the pickup for a while, chewing a stick of gum. From farming to dealing cotton allotments to Tee Kitchens and Toro to Mr. Francis Dolly—they hung together like rungs in a ladder. It was going to be interesting to see just how far my friend had in mind to climb.

It was dark by the time I got to the ranch. I parked in the lot and walked around to the front of the house. The floodlights were on, hundreds of June bugs swirling around the beams, crackling like fat under my feet. Coolie was at the door. He nodded and said the party had started. Fiddle music drifted down from the roof; the air was thick with perfume as I stepped inside the door.

# 1 2

At the far end of the hall two doors had been thrown open to a massive room that was still too small for the fireplace at the other end. I could have walked into the hearth. In the center of the room was a circular pit where a group of teenagers were trying to interest two domestic roosters in a cockfight. About forty people were scattered around the room and most of them looked under twenty-one. Most of them looked under eighteen.

I took a stool at the bar, which occupied most of the north wall, and had a drink. A cowboy was pouring whiskey neat—if you wanted anything fancy, like ice or water, you got it yourself. A mural had been painted on the wall behind the bar. From left to right it told the history of El Toro, from the 1880's, when the first Scottish land companies had begun to consolidate the smaller ranches in this area, to when Tee had taken over from his old man. At the far right of the painting was old Malcolm Kitchens handing a bridle over to a man who looked like Tee's younger brother. The cowboy bartender caught me looking at that end of the mural. "Thangs has changed," he said, leaning his elbow on the bar and looking up at the painting. He looked back at me, to see if I was an agent of change, for he said, "Did you go to high school with Tee?"

I told him I had gone to school in Flavannah and he nodded as if that was all right. "I wasn't here in the days when this was a ranch. It must a been somethin. Onct the old man had a cattle drive; he drove em round in a big circle all around the ranch, then on down to the railhead, and that was it. Right after that the lawyers dragged Tee outta college and put him on a horse."

"Tee wasn't much of a cowboy then?"

The man's eyes flickered. "I thought you had knowed him for a while."

"No, I was invited here by a friend of his. Son Cunningham."

The man's eyes stayed dim. "Is he a friend of Tee's."

"What do you think happened to the cowboy they found today?"

"That wasn't no cowboy." His eyes moved over me slower than ever. "I thank he got what he was achin for."

"I think that's a little drastic just for a boy falling in love with your wife."

"Did I say anything about a wife?"

"Some people think he shot himself."

The cowboy laughed.

"What happens to the ranch if Tee can't raise the money he's after?"

"What happens has done happened."

"I'm not too bright. What has done happened?"

"Just take a look around you, friend."

"What happened to the cowboy who got snakebit? Did he get what he was aching for?"

"Shit." And with that the cowboy walked down to the far end of the bar, standing under the picture of Tee taking the reins from his old man.

I finished my drink and didn't want another. There were several people I wanted to talk to, but none of them was here. I was about to try the roof when I saw Maury Mueller. His soft eyes had been on me for some time, I felt. I lifted my glass and he made his way around the room.

He was happy as a puppy when he arrived. "Boy, are you in trouble!"

"The way I'm feeling tonight, the man I'm in trouble with is in trouble."

Maury pulled at his swollen eyelids. He climbed up on a barstool and yelled at the cowboy bartender, whose face was flat and empty. Maury fingered his string tie. "You ain't really a friend a Son Cunningham's, are you?"

"No, not really."

Maury looked defeated. His head swung low to the bar and I saw how drunk he was. "Let's make a deal."

"What kind of deal?"

"You tell me what yore hired to do and I'll pay you off in cash. Whatever it's worth to me."

"What if it's not worth anything to you?"

Maury's eyes were wide and frightened. "And if I don't want it done, then I'll pay you twict as much not to do it. To stop it bein done."

"What being done?"

"You been hired to kill Tee?"

My voice sounded faraway. "I haven't been hired to kill Tee. You know that."

Maury's face gathered up all the cunning he imagined existed and placed it in a smile. "Then maybe you been hired to die." He went on talking, but my mind had stopped there. Finally I asked him about the body they had found today. Maury laughed in my face. "You worried bout endin up in them boots yoreself? Well, them boots was Tee's signatoor. I bet that kid's cods was missin too."

"You think he killed the kid?"

Maury gave a well-oiled shrug. "Why not? He claims he did. He's been braggin that to everbody. Bragged how he thew Palmer to them snakes too. And maybe he did." He said in a quieter voice, "Look, I ain't the fool I may seem to be. Nothin's easy in this world. You always gotta give somethin to get somethin. Unless yore on top. Even then"—he looked around the room as though he alone saw the futility of it all—"even then, it ain't right. Nothin's ever perfeck. Look at that pore bastard now. He wants to die." His eyes were lifted toward the far end of the mural; then they dropped, his understanding of despair as smooth as silk. "I know how he feels." Now I had the chance to laugh in Maury's face. He only shrugged.

"What sort of trouble am I in, Maury?"

He waved it off. "Aw, Tee thought you was spyin this afternoon. Son has calmed him down."

"Why would anybody want to spy on Tee's cows?"

Maury stood and looked at me coldly. "You think over my offer."

"Why not? I like getting paid double not to do something I wasn't going to do in the first place."

Maury sneered and left. I studied the mural. They had painted poor old Tee into a corner. If Toro kept going, it would have to be on a different wall.

I was about to go somewhere anyway when Coolie strolled in and told me I was wanted. I did as I was told and went up to the roof.

Everything was different. This afternoon the roof had looked old, dirty. Larry had been sullen and threatening, Adrienne's beauty cold and asexual. The gunshots, the decaying body, the weakness in the windowless rooms below, they had all been displaced by another world, the idea of the rich, everything bright, seamless, glittering, the people carefree and beautiful. It was like a huge, shining photograph, except that you could walk into it and live there.

Son saw me and came around the pool—lighted from below, the water glowed in the night. He talked in a loud voice as he guided me around to the group he had left.

Tee was there—he was different too, sober, aloof—he smiled wryly as the others laughed at the idea that I had been out counting cattle this afternoon. For the rumor Maury had been banished to the ground floor for the night. The laughter was full and rich. Maury's banishment had been for his own good—the temptation to toss him off the roof might have proved too great. The man who had spoken was small, dapper, foreign-looking, though he spoke with a Texas accent. I listened carefully to the names: he was Mercury, the man Son had mentioned in connection with Tee's insurance policy. Though I remembered that Son had considered him some sort of adversary. The others' names I had not heard before. Special attention was being paid to another small dark man dressed in a subdued military uniform. He was addressed as Prince. Every time he was spoken to. Gunner was not there, though from the conversation he had landed his Lear jet and was on the grounds. The Prince had accompanied Gunner: everyone asked how the flight up had been. The Prince's English and smile were clean and clear. He looked like a man who did a great deal of boring exercise to ward off fat. He did not strike me as a shy man, not at all, but he never looked at people, his eyes always straying a few degrees off to one side of yours. The Prince was bored. Another rooftop swimming pool in the middle of another desert.

I began to distinguish the others. A flabby young European explaining to a blond matron how he had invented a hookah filter cigarette which she could market in Israel. Someone else was arguing about the Italian Communist Party. Another foreigner listened to the debate but said nothing. A woman so tan she seemed carved out of wood was being entertained by Son's scurrilous tales of country life. My attention came back to Tee. He smiled at his guests, but his eyes moved constantly, from face to face, around the pool, toward the cabana, the elevator doors, the greenhouse, scanning the luminous floor of the swimming pool. Then his eyes stopped and I followed his look to the door of the greenhouse where a couple stood.

I thought she was the most beautiful woman I had ever seen, even after I realized that I already knew her. Adrienne was standing with a man who, for that second, I took to be her husband or lover. The dark glasses she had worn this afternoon had masked her innocence. Now, walking toward us, she seemed awkward, soft, sensual, her movements those of a young animal, her limbs fresh and untried. Her smile was no longer planned or directed at anyone. Though her voice still carried intelligence, there was nothing weary or hardened in it. I suddenly had a powerful impulse to touch her, and then I realized how stupid it was—to fall in love simply by imagining how a woman felt.

Adrienne and her brother joined the group. Gunner was in his middle thirties and stood well over six feet. His body was broad, thick; his hair had already receded enough to give him a middle-aged bearing. He had the wary eyes of a man who has had to fight his father for everything he has. He was drunk but he could handle it. The only persons he took notice of, besides his sister, were the Prince and Tee. Son became subdued in his presence.

I felt the circle tightening, so I drifted away. For a time I looked down into the swimming pool; then for a while I looked out over the ranch, the sky as dark as the hills. I listened to the people moving around the roof, talking, laughing. The three-piece Western band played songs I never expected to hear again. The fiddler sang about poison and faded love. I walked back along the pool, away from the inner circle, which had grown considerably. I skirted a smaller group of people desperately ignoring their isolation, laughing hard and talking loud. By the time I came back out of the greenhouse, they had joined the circle. They no longer made much noise.

From the greenhouse's odor I had expected something rich growing there, exotic, maybe illegal, but I found nothing but cotton plants. All about three inches high, row after row, each plant in a separate container, tagged with an identification number. They had been planted about six weeks ago, after the last spring frost. At one end of the room a large purring fan circulated air. No two plants were exactly the same—the varieties differed, as did the soil, the fertilizer, and the planting date. I leafed through a large journal that recorded each plant's progress. Occasionally there were odd entries criticizing the experiment. The last entry in the journal had been made today. There was no comment, only facts and figures. I stopped reading when I thought I heard someone approaching.

There were twice as many guests on the roof now, though the party was still quiet. On the other hand, a rumbling rose from below, like maybe a polo game had started on the first floor. I was on my way to the elevator when I saw the cowgirl in white leaning against the low roof wall, looking out over the ranch headquarters. She looked posed, drunk, and young. She turned her head vaguely as I approached. Her profile was still strong, her eyes still frightened. She finally returned my look, then shrugged. "I'm sorry, I've forgotten your name. Something sticky." I told her and she apologized again. "God, what a dull-ass party," she said, watching the people.

"I think there's a little more action downstairs, if that's what you're after."

She gave a single sharp laugh. "There's where I'm supposed to be, sweetie, banned with all the other trash. But I told them to go fuck themselves. I dated Gunner in college."

"You don't look that old."

She grimaced. "We called him feral man. He used to get drunk and roll up in the floorboard and peek up your dress. I just dated him once really. I was a freshman and he had been in law school for years. He liked to fuck young girls and I like to fuck old men." She tried to laugh. "Ole Gunner, a good ole law-school alkie. He talked a great screw, his only problem was that there was this slim time somewhere between the twenty-third and the twenty-fifth beer when he could make it. And then it took quite a bit of dick-sucking and love to bring it off"—she looked at me—"and I've never been fond of either."

"Which one is his wife?"

June smiled. "The one who looks Danish, like the furniture. She's from Tulsa and could spit much farther before they capped her teeth. She farted once at a gala for Lyndon. It took her weeks to figure out what *aroma* she was wearing. No, I think she's good for Gunner really. If he got the type wife who usually latches on to sons of rich men . . . he'd probably be dead. He'd wish he was anyway."

"What type is that, June?"

"Who else do you want me to tell you about?"

"How about the Prince?"

"You really have been away a long time." She looked away. "Have you ever seen a cartoon—I think it was French, or I saw it when I was in France—it shows a tiny fish about to be eaten by a little fish about to be eaten by a medium-sized fish about to be eaten by . . . well, the Prince is the big big huge fish. He's so big big and huge that he's not even in the picture. He eats the picture."

"What has he got to do with Tee?"

"Nothing. Though Tee doesn't know it. He's got to do with Gunner. No, not with Gunner, with his old man. Dolph, old Dolph. They're going to sign an oil lease on the Prince's whole entire sandbox." She paused. "The whole country, whichever one it is. It's never been done before. It's going to make them a billion dollars. They're going to be the most rich men in the entire world. Big Big Fish. And Tee only wants to be a Little Fish and they won't let him. But you don't give a shit, do you, Sugar-booger? Who are you anyway? You're like a eunuch, you don't react. Are you a money eunuch, sweetie?" She slapped her forehead. "Of course, that's exactly what you are. The man who cares nothing for money is hired to guard it. Or get it? Or take it away? Or what?"

"I like money well enough, June."

"Do you? Your friend hates it, I think. That's why he pursues it so single-mindedly . . ." I followed her look across the pool. Son now seemed to be the center of the circle. June pointed out the three men standing with him. "The Three Wise Men," she called them: they looked different, but they looked the same, wavy shiny hair, smiles curling their thin lips, eyes narrow and wary. "Why, they're our leaders," she said. "Why, they've just crawled out from under that big rock down in Austin . . ." She stopped as her voice began to rise. She touched my arm. "I'm sorry. You see, I used to be a liberal. I used to believe in democracy et cetera. I used to love the good guys. I thought they were going to save us. But there's nobody going to save us, is there? I'm sorry again. There's nothing more heartbreaking than a sniveling ex-liberal, is there? So you see, the one standing there, the oilier-looking one with the patent-leather hair, well, that's Marvin DeKalb. He was Speaker of the House a few years back and he wants so desperately to be governor. That's why he's running for attorney general. He and Cunningham are thick as thieves. They're letting Tee play at eminence grise. Do you see the big one with sand in his mouth? Well, he wants to be Speaker, but he's going to have to wait. Too long. And the other one, with the ten-pound bifocals, well, he wants to be— But you have the idea, verdad?"

"What about the man called Mercury?"

"You are curious, my dear. Why, he's the wop genius who wrote Tee's policy. Six point five big ones. Third largest life ever written west of the Mississippi. And once again Cunningham enters the picture."

"How?"

The girl twisted her body as she laughed. "Have you ever heard of Dolly? Dollywood State Bank?" Another laugh twisted her back toward me. "Yes, oh yes, Sugar dear, Francis Dolly, he owns the policy that Mercury wrote that Maury sold that Kitchens bought that Adrienne stole that Cunningham . . . Cunningham, Cunningham, I know his ambition well. It goes far beyond Tee, or Dolly, or even A.'s papa. He's going all the way."

"So he's working for somebody else besides Tee."

"What is that light I see in your eye, Sugar? Is it stupidity or ignorance or . . . What are you doing here, Sugar?"

"I'm trying to find that out myself. I still haven't come here to kill anybody, June."

I didn't move but she held my arm. Her touch trickled through my groin. "Would you like to shoot, Sugar, would you like to practice? We could walk out to the range. It's all right," she said. "You see, I need your help and you need mine. I can tell you something that you want very badly to know." Her hand still grasped my arm. "You aren't going to kill anybody, Sugar," she said, and her hand dropped away. "You've been brought here to die."

# 1 3

Nobody noticed us leave. June's hand trembled while we waited for the elevator. I couldn't help wondering if the dead cowboy had left the party too early with the wrong woman. The idea that he had died for something that small had suddenly become very real and frightening.

The elevator door opened onto a witch. She was a short witch with wide hips that jiggled as she rushed toward us. A foot from June's face she hissed, rolled her eyes, and bared her fangs; then hurried on past us straight toward the swimming pool. Going away, she was a cape of wild, frizzled hair. In the elevator June laughed. "That's my buddy, C.J. She's crazy like me. I like her."

"June, let's go some place where we can talk."

"Talk?"

"I want to know who killed those men. I've got to find out what's going on around here."

"I wish Adrienne had killed them." Her eyes moved rapidly over my face. "You think I'm joking." She drew away. "I do wish she had." She laughed again; it was a sad, frail sound, even if it was meant to be. "But she didn't do it. She loved them, she loves them all. For a while."

The elevator opened onto the hallway where six horses were tethered. We excused ourselves through the horses, into the Little Room, which had been invaded by six drunk cowboys—the same number as the horses, if you felt like counting them. June looked around the room. "Wait for me, Sugar, I'll be back, I promise, and then we can talk and talk and talk." And she disappeared into a cluster of cowboys.

I saw that Larry was behind the bar now, but before I could get near him, Mabelline had attached herself to my sleeve. Like an abject supplicant a very drunk cowboy was following the insurance agent's wife around, tinkering with her bra catch through her blouse. As she talked, Mabelline kept looking over her shoulder. "What's the first *guid* joke you ever heard? Lotsa people like the Silver Saddle. Myself I thank that's a pisspore joke. All them travelin-salesmen jokes is sorry. They're too much like real life. What's yore philosophy a life? If you caint put it in words, that means you ain't got one." She turned around and gave the cowboy a swat, and he wandered over and began trying to unbutton somebody else's blouse. Mabelline looked back at me, no longer playing drunk. "You know, Maury is a rich man now, but they're out to git him for it. They caint stand it. Pore lil Fuckerfaster, I tole him it wasn't worth it. For all the riches. Nothin but riches. Don't do it, Maury, don't you git messed up with them. But now it's too late. That's my advice to you, Fuckerfaster, don't git messed up with them till it's too late!" And she wandered off, playing drunk again.

I went over and sat at the bar. Larry was busy chewing his gum. Probably some sort of exercise. It looked like I was going to have to resort to violence to get a word out of him. I toasted him. "Were you a good friend of Billy O.'s?"

Larry grinned, then cracked his jaw. His teeth were big. "Shit yes."

"What I don't understand is why they're letting Tee get away with it. Does the old man have that much pull with the law?"

Larry kept grinning. "Get away with what?"

"Get away with killing all those people."

"You believe everthing Cunningham tells you?" Larry folded up his grin and leaned across the bar. "Some advice to *you*, buddy boy. Tee ain't killed nobody. Yet."

"Then who did kill those boys, Muscles?"

"Keep it up, keep nosin around here, you pear-shaped bastard, and the little brains you got is goin to be decorating the chanderliers." And Larry walked down to the far end of the bar, flexing his fingers as if he were going to throttle the next person who asked for a drink.

Since it was the third time tonight somebody had taken a dim view of my life expectancy, I jumped, just a little, when June ran her hand down my spine. "Are you ready to go?"

"Any time."

She looked at me quizzically. "Don't you have a gun?" I didn't say anything. "Don't worry," the girl said. "I always carry two."

The front door had been lashed open. The strains of the "Tennessee Waltz" drifted down from the roof—somebody like me was introducing his girl to his best friend. Coolie and his girl were leaning against a car, still arguing. June and I walked past them. Coolie's eyes left the toes of his boots and trailed along behind us.

We walked up a grade that gradually steepened till, after a mile, we were making our way up stairs that had been hacked out of a caliche wall. We came out on a wide, flat expanse. It had once been some sort of quarry, June said, but that had been long ago. The floor of the quarry was white and hard so that we had no trouble walking, though I couldn't really see where we were going. The dark walls of the quarry rose above us. When we stopped I saw that June held a small automatic in her hand. She was staring at a row of dark figures lined up against the white cliff. They were the size and shape of men. I felt I was in a tunnel, trapped; then a strange idea seized me—those men standing against the wall were blindfolded, their hands tied behind their backs. Then my mind shifted and I saw the silhouettes as a firing squad and I so realized that things could be the opposite of what I had thought.

The girl was watching me, the gun held casually, pointing neither at me nor at the targets. "It's too dark to shoot," she said. "Let's talk instead."

"All right, let's talk."

June turned her body; the gun now pointed at me. "Who are you?"

"I thought you were going to tell me."

"Tee killed them for her. It wasn't his idea. He had to do it. He did it for her. The past was closing in on her. She had to get away from them." The girl looked away and I thought about taking the gun from her, but my arms weighed a hundred pounds. "She's insane. Do you know how many years she's spent in a mental hospital? She used to be fat . . ." She raised the gun toward the target and fired. The report was sharp and I flinched. "They had been lovers. She fucked every man on this ranch, every kid in Toro . . ."

"You were going to tell me why they brought me here, June."

"She and Cunningham moved the body. I saw them." She lowered the gun and handed it to me. "Tee had been gone for a week. I was going crazy. They told me he was off in Mexico drunk. But I was sure he was dead. That they had killed him, like they had been threatening to do, to get the insurance money. Don't you see, the two of them are in this together. It was her idea. And then Cunningham came along. So much stronger. Even the insurance company knows they're going to kill him. Why do you think they want to pull out? Pork Man's their spy. He's the only one who wants him to live. That man's his only friend. God, how horrible . . ." She hid her face in her hands.

I said, "You said you saw Son and Adrienne moving the body."

"Billy O. had been missing a week, and she only laughed about it. She told me they had killed him, but they had to wait and make it look like an accident. You see," she said, her voice flat, "if she has anything to do with death, then the policy is void. One night I came out here, but it was too dark to shoot. As I was going back— I couldn't sleep; there is a little draw over there, and I was walking and walking, and I heard the sound of a truck and then I looked down through the trees and I saw them unloading the body from a truck. It was a white truck like yours. A man who looked like you and Cunningham were unloading Tee's body into a grave. And she was standing by, watching . . ." She tried to kiss me and take away the gun, but I pushed her back. She cried for a short while. I held her as if she were going to fall. Then she drew back. "But you weren't even here and Tee's not dead. Is he? See how crazy I am. These dreams, they get all mixed up with what I imagine happens. There's no longer any truth in the world. You can't see the dancer for the dance and I can't see the world for me."

"Let's go back now, June."

"Will you let me have my gun back?"

"When we get back to the house."

"Will you help me?"

"I'm going to help you, June—"

"*Their plan is to make it look like you killed Tee!* Don't you understand . . ."

By the time we got down to the headquarters, June had stopped crying. Her eyes were dark, exhausted, but her tears seemed gone forever. "Look, I know I'm going to pieces, at least I know it. But Tee doesn't know, he doesn't understand what's happening to him. He has a beautiful soul, like a little boy. They've turned him into something ugly." She looked at me. "His body is something ugly. Even his face. All his boys had beautiful faces . . . Palmer, Billy O. . . . He didn't kill them, Sugar, he couldn't . . ."

I finally gave her her gun back and she put it away. We walked back through the trees, past dark sheds and buildings, till we came upon the glaring façade of the Little House. I could hear the faint, scraping fiddle from the roof; otherwise the house was quiet. Coolie was still leaning against the car, watching us. His girl friend was gone. As we were crossing the porch he called out, "The party's moved down to the bunkhouse, folks, but they wont to see you upstairs. Up in the Money Room, the both a you."

The front doors were closed, the horses gone. The Little Room was empty. Everybody was gone, except for the band, whose plaintive song echoed over the intercom.

# 1 4

A cowboy opened the door to the Money Room. The large room was empty, but a small study off the entrance was packed with people, many of whom I had seen earlier that evening. No special notice was taken of us. Almost everyone sat on the floor, leaning against pillows or the walls. The man June had pointed out as Marvin DeKalb, the ex-Speaker of the House, was holding forth on Texas politics. Son had one of the few chairs; he was listening with flawless intensity. Tee sprawled on the floor behind a desk. Gunner had a chair in the corner. The Prince had been placed in the leather rocker behind the desk and now was peering at book titles through his fingers, which he had arched tip to tip over his face. Mercury sat cross-legged on the floor, and behind him Pork Man's red, bulging eyes studied me without interest or expression. My attention kept coming back to Son's face, deteriorating, stained with confidence and ambition. I had begun to hate it as you would hate someone who has destroyed a friend and now was trying to take his place.

There was laughter at something the ex-Speaker said, and as I followed his roving eyes, I saw Adrienne sitting across the room. Our eyes met and she looked away, the movement slow.

The laughter died out, except for Tee, who continued to make a strange, painful noise. He finally stopped and made an apology that came out as an insult. The ex-

Speaker smiled and went on with another story, which Tee interrupted. There was a silence. Everyone seemed to be watching Gunner, whose sullen, drunken eyes hovered over the Prince. The Prince was still studying book titles through his fingers—they had simple ways of handling hecklers in his country. June had fallen asleep by my side. Only the impression of a smile remained on Son's face.

"Do you know what you are talking about, Kitchens?" Gunner's voice moved heavy and slow, as if each word were a burden.

"You understand English, don't you, Gunner? What Marvin says is bullshit."

The ex-Speaker laughed lightly. "It *was* a joke, Tee Texas."

"A *joke?*"

"You know what a joke is, don't you, Kitchens?"

"Yeah, Gunner, it's something funny. Did you say something funny, Marvin?"

The ex-Speaker smiled. "You've got a good point there. My daddy always did tell me to hold up one finger when I was joking." The ex-Speaker held up a third finger and everyone laughed, finally even Gunner and Tee, though again Tee's forced laughter went on long after everyone else's had stopped.

"What—" said Gunner's wife, breaking in, "why don't you tell us about the night you and Hank Gomez took Price down to Scholtz's?"

Marvin DeKalb went on with a story about a drunk who had been governor. Tee continually interrupted the tale, laughing at the wrong places, shouting. The ex-Speaker ignored him, but many of the others were growing angry and embarrassed. Finally the ex-Speaker stopped. Nobody said anything. Tee's voice trembled with anger. "Marvin, let me ask you a question. Who do you think is the greatest governor in the history of this state?"

"Past, present, or future?" The ex-Speaker smiled.

"I think Shakey was the greatest governor this state has ever had."

"He could have been. If he'd handled the insurance scandals with a little more aplomb. And if he hadn't sold his party out."

"And what do you mean by that, *Marvin?* What's wrong with bein a Republican? You're insultin Mercury. Apologize."

The ex-Speaker shrugged and smiled at Mercury. "Other than being slightly stupid, it's perfectly legal. But Shakey tried to be both, that's where he fucked up, Tee Texas. But now I guess he's gone straight Republican. He's opted for money over people, as my daddy used to put it. That's the difference between the two. Right, Mercury?"

"What about you, Gunner? You vote Republican."

Gunner was sitting on the edge of his chair. "I only vote Republican when the Democrats get some eggshellhead to run for President. I always vote Republican on the state level and always will."

"You mean Democrat, Gunner"—the ex-Speaker laughed—"tell me you mean Democrat."

Gunner looked at him blankly. His wife said, "You said Republican, dear."

"Freudian slip," said Tee.

"Fuck Freud!" said Gunner, and led by his wife, everyone laughed.

"I'm still goin to be governor," said Tee. "What do you think about that, *Marvin?*"

"Ah."

"Naw, I wanna be President."

"Now I think you would make a great *President*, Tee Texas."

The Prince had begun to listen to the conversation.

Presidents kept him awake. He started to speak but Tee interrupted him. Gunner savagely broke in on Tee. "God-damn you, *you let him talk!*"

The room erupted. Tee and Gunner stood facing each other, breathing hard, fists clenched, their wives telling them to sit down, people's reactions ranging from fear to the Prince's amusement. One of Tee's cowboys stuck his head in the door. "Boss, they are shootin up the bunk-house agin. C.J. has done winged Lone Star."

Tee waited a moment, then stepped back from Gunner, stuffed his shirt in his Levi's and, as if nothing had happened, apologized. As he came around the desk, I had to jerk my foot back to keep him from tromping on it. At the door he turned back and looked at June lying at my side, his eyes crawling with anger. He left with the cowboy.

With a burst of relief people were on their feet talking. Gunner ignored his wife, who was trying to calm him down. He and the Prince talked about flying on to Las Vegas tonight. I moved toward Son in time to hear him apologize to Marvin DeKalb, whose face was tense and drawn. Adrienne came up to Son and touched his arm. I turned away. June was still asleep, curled on the floor. I lifted her face. Her eyes opened. I told her I had to go, but I would be back. But her reddened, dull eyes didn't un-derstand. I caught Son's attention and in a few minutes we walked down the stairs to the Little Room and out to the parking lot. We talked about the trip to Houston, which Son was excited about. I finally asked him about the money, ten thousand bucks, telling him I was thinking about paying off the mortgage on Merce's land. The an-swer came slow. "I don't think there would be any prob-lem. We sometimes prepay our money broker's fees. Ten grand is no problem."

"Good. Then everything is on."

Son smiled. "Sugar, sometimes you have the patience of

Job. And like that old story, the wait is going to be worth it."

"What was that little get-together about tonight? Anything I should know about?"

"Just a few friends rubbing elbows, son. Though sometimes a lot of business does get done in that room." Son thought a moment. "That goddamn Marvin is doing his best to blow his chance of ever becoming governor of this state."

"Is it that easy? Cross Tee Kitchens and you're out?"

Son smiled. "Cross me and you're out."

I turned as if I were going to walk away. "By the way, I'm looking forward to meeting Francis Dolly."

"Sounds like you've been doing your homework, Sugar."

"No, people just keep telling me things. Very interesting things."

We walked over to the pickup. Son leaned against the door. "Like what?"

"Like what I'm doing here. Like who really killed that kid."

Son pushed himself away from the truck and opened the door. "But you already know that, son. Don't you remember, I told you." He started walking away. "Be sure to get a good night's sleep, Sugar. We're starting out for Houston first thing Monday morning." He stopped. "And, Sugar, I'm glad to see you taking an active interest in things."

Tonight there was no note tacked on my door, no crying girl in my bed. It took me hours to go to sleep. They all kept stepping forward, bowing, introducing themselves, telling me who they were and what they were doing on this stage. June was crazy, Maury beaten, Pork Man watchful, Gunner rich, the Prince bored, Tommy afraid, Denton vengeful, Adrienne beautiful, Son powerful, Palmer and

Billy O. dead, and Tee—in a few hours or days or weeks, Tee told me he would be dead too. The only question I hadn't answered was who would kill him. But by then I was dreaming.

# II

# 1

It was more night than morning when the phone rang. A quarter hour later Son was banging around the house like a brother sent to see if I was living right. In another three minutes the Lincoln was easing onto the highway that would take us six hundred miles to Houston. It was still dark, four-thirty Monday morning.

About ten miles out on the highway we turned off on a dirt road, toward Son's old home place at Sand Hill. Ten minutes later I caught sight of a lonely grove of trees on the horizon. The house looked smaller and newer than I remembered. The cottonwoods seemed thicker, and a large quonset barn had been built behind the house, the first slice of sunlight rippling like electricity off its curved sides. Most of the old barns and sheds had been torn down. The corral was gone, the horse tank a rusted, empty shell. The machinery looked new and well kept; there were no animals around to get in its way.

We parked back of the house. A breeze rustled the paper leaves above us. The east side of the house was warm and bright as bread, the north side cool blue. Hundreds of sparrows fled the trees when we got out of the car. We walked toward the quonset barn. I waited in the cold shade of the barn, the sliding doors open at both ends, so the fields of new cotton beyond were framed like a picture. The barn was dark and cavernous; inside I could make out a combine, several tractors, a single-prop airplane. The low sounds of conversation and a wrench repeatedly grasping metal came from within. I went back to the car. A woman came out to the car with a sack lunch. Dressed in slacks, her hair pulled back, her dark eyes neither solemn nor playful, she told me not to let him drive too fast.

A few minutes later the Lincoln was headed back toward the highway. Son was silent for a while; then he said, "I always go back there to lick my wounds. No matter what happens, whether my luck is going up or down, I'm always going to keep that place. It'd be the last thing I'd ever get rid of. It hasn't changed a bit, has it?"

"Not much."

"No, not much."

We made Abilene by nine-thirty and Austin by noon. We stopped for lunch at a place where stuffed animals watched us eat. Son was relaxed, he laughed and joked; it almost was as if we were two old friends who hadn't seen each other in ten years. Back on the freeway Son pointed out the capitol building and the tower at the university. "You never did spend much time around here, did you?"

"No, not much at all."

"Well, after we graduated I did my time here, two years, but I finally had to drop out. No dinero. I tried to make it waiting on tables in one of the girls' dorms, but I didn't have what it takes. Too scared to make good grades, too lonely to get a rich girl friend, too horny to fuck. Oh yeah, I was a real loner, waiting around for some millionaire in his yacht to happen along and take me away from my misery. What bullshit." His voice was relaxed and easy. "I used to write poetry in those days. Most of it junk, but there were some good lines if I remember right. One night I burned it all. Now I wish I hadn't. Not that I yearn for

the days of my youth, no thanks. I'm so goddamn glad
they're over, I actually look forward to being old. It's
funny, Sugar, how we grew up pretty much the same and
then split up and have led such different lives. But now,"
he said, looking out the window, "we're back together."
We turned onto a freeway which took us past an air-force
base, lines of bombers, fat-bellied, their wings drooping
like engorged insects. He was silent till we had passed the
base. "I turned into an anti-rich type for a while. A bitter,
twisted little anarchist. I used to hate the haves so much, I
hated the have-nots even more. The frat boys had a place
on the mall where they hung out between classes. I used
to walk out of my way to avoid that place. Then I would
torture myself and turn around and go back. They were
always laughing at me. Or so I thought." He looked at me
coldly. "The person I hate the most in this world was me
when I was young. After I dropped out of school I got a
night job beating up crazies out at the insane asylum and I
started living in this rooming house that made the nuthouse look good. There was this guy across the hall who
saw Jews under the bed. They were putting chlorine in
the water to wear us down. Like those bombers back
there, he used to tell me, 'See, see that triangle on the tail?
That's half the star of David. They're halfway to taking us
over.' One night I was typing and he came in and started
walking around the room, picking up things and putting
them down. 'Haven't I seen you some place before? How
bout Forty-second Street. Yeah yeah. You're an FBI agent.
What are you writing there? You writing something bout
me there?' And he yanks the paper out of the typewriter
and runs across the hall and locks himself in. Well, I forget
what I was writing, but after that I imagined this nut
laughing at me all the time . . ." He laughed to himself.
"There were a couple other guys living on the same floor.
One of them was this young kid, he had a lot of money to
be living in that dump, queer as a three-bit piece, some

kind of opera singer. He was keeping this older guy, who was some kind of minor-league baseball jock. What a couple. The baseballer was a first-class mean sonofabitch. The kid was beautiful; he looked like a girl, wide soft hips, fluttery eyelashes, big cowy eyes. They had some kind of sado-masochist thing going, though at the time I didn't know that some folks like it like that. The baseballer used to beat the shit out of the baritone, with me and the Nazi laying there on our sacks listening to the kid shriek. Well, after a month or so, something in me snapped. I got to imagining that this shortstop was after me. I couldn't look him in the eye. I couldn't walk past him in the hall, because I knew if he brushed my arm, just touched me that much, I'd kill him. I really did want to kill him. I wanted him dead. All that kept me going was the idea of him dead. I used to lie there and kill him, over and over again. Then one day I had my radio on, with the door open, the wind blowing through, I remember it was a nice day. Then all of a sudden the door slammed to. It was the wind I kept telling myself, but I hadn't seen it. It was a disease overpowering me, the idea that he had kicked my door closed. I got out my hunting knife and I went down the hall and I kicked their door in and I murdered that room. I tore the holy hell out of it. They weren't there. I would have killed either of them. Both of them." His voice stopped and he could do nothing but stare straight ahead. "After that I left Texas and bummed around for six months. All over the place. Then I came back and worked in a warehouse in Lubbock for two years. After that I knew what I wanted. I went back to school at Lubbock Tech and I pledged a fraternity and I sat out on the mall and I laughed at all those poor fucked-up poets walking by." We drove in silence for a while. "You know, Marvin DeKalb and I met waiting on tables at that girls' dorm at Texas." Then he said in a different voice, "I guess you did have an interesting talk with June the other night."

"It was interesting, yeah."

Son made a weary expression. "It's not A. who's done time on the funny farm, son, it's June. Check out her wrists sometime. It seems like she would get tired of slicing herself up just for a little sympathy. Still, she does liven up a dull life, doesn't she, with all her cloak-and-dagger stories. Now, why would I want to kill Tee, son, why would anybody?"

"I can think of a couple of reasons. Maybe for money, maybe somebody hates him enough. Maybe there's another reason. Maybe somebody would kill him for her."

"Maybe."

"And if June is crazy, Son, she's not the only one. Maury told me almost the same thing the other night. As a matter of fact, he even tried to buy me off, to keep me from killing Tee."

Son's eyes had grown dark, his face rigid. "Look, let's get one thing straight. I'm out to keep that little bastard alive, no matter how much he might deserve otherwise. As far as money goes, if you're talking about insurance, there's no way that insurance company is going to pay off unless Tee dies in bed with Mercury holding his hand. And even then they'll wriggle out of it. That policy is good for one thing and that's to secure a loan big enough to get Tee out from under all these little loans that are choking us to death. As far as Adrienne is concerned, she is not going to benefit from Tee being dead, one way or another. And she's free to walk away from him any time she wants to." Son let the Lincoln slow, then drift off the highway onto the shoulder. He stared down the highway, the heat shimmering and close now that we had stopped. "All right, maybe I haven't been playing it straight with you about why I brought you back here. Maybe I have been thinking about killing the bastard, but not now, that's over with now. Up till the last couple of days, I haven't been sure what was going on myself. She hasn't been sure what she's going to do. But now she knows. I've been staying on at the ranch the last month only because of her. To see that no harm comes to her and that she's treated right. You'd do the same if you knew some of the shit he used to pull. He's scared to death of me and he goddamn better be. Right now it's the only thing keeping him together. If I thought A. really would get the insurance, I'd do him the favor myself. But the only way out for her is if he stays alive and she can get a divorce before the whole house of cards collapses. Our job is to keep him alive and healthy for the time being, and to see that if he does want to go on that long trip, he doesn't try to take her along with him. She's the only woman I've ever loved, Sugar." Son paused. "I do hate him enough to kill him. But I don't have any plans along that line. Not any longer. All right, old friend?"

Son pulled the car back onto the highway. My body felt empty; the world looked like a shell, nothing moved. I watched the trees and houses, the towns and fields, as we passed they weren't really there. Nothing existed outside my mind, and into it kept slipping the idea that Son was lying and I could think of no reason for his lie except that June had been telling the truth. That I was being lured into a trap where I would kill a man, be blamed for his death, or be killed myself. And that falling in love with Adrienne was exactly what they wanted me to do.

# 2

I woke on the outskirts of Houston. I had lived in the city a long time ago. Son was telling me how much it had changed in the last three years. We passed mile after mile of industrial suburbs mixed with crumbling tract houses and cheap apartment buildings that always looked unfinished. Son talked about the plants—he always seemed to know the men who owned them.

We were soon on a freeway which grew wider and more congested, then began to rise toward what looked like a bridge into the sky. We took the top sweeping curve of the cloverleaf and from there we could see downtown Houston, ten miles away. A storm was building out over the Gulf, and the afternoon sun struck the skyscrapers so that they looked like dwellings of light carved out of a massive black cliff.

The freeway took us down and to the east, and we lost sight of the city. Soon we left the freeway and the Lincoln eased its way among other Lincolns, Jags, El Dorados; large, deep houses set back in small forests; walls of trees, hedges, bamboo, glass, iron, brick, everything was a wall. The air was heavy with the smell of rain, but here its perfume came from the sea.

Son turned the Lincoln through a hedge arch and parked beneath a slender high-rise apartment. The first floor was without walls, and as we waited for the elevator, we watched the rain begin. We went up to the seventh floor, where Son let me into a small frigid apartment. He drew back the curtains and slid open the plate-glass doors to the balcony, where we stood watching the rain sweep over the city. Son went back inside. I stayed there for a while, watching the curtain of rain grow dense, seeing this plain as it must have looked five hundred years ago.

Son was on the phone when I went back inside. He pointed me toward the kitchen, where I made a drink. Son hung up, went into the kitchen, and came out with a glass. "That man is a genius," he told me and smiled. "Bob Zeeburg. He's Dolph Gunther's top assistant."

"Gunther is Adrienne's old man?"

"That's right." He picked up the phone again, dialed a number, and began taking notes from the answering service. He wrote down several names and numbers, then hung up and dialed the first. It was Adrienne. We had been invited to a party tonight. The next call was to Mercury. They agreed that everything was fine at the ranch: Tee healthy, no money in sight. Son and Mr. Dolly were going to talk to Lon that night. Son foresaw no problems. Lon was the current Speaker of the House and just a good ole country boy. "Mercury's a big-city kid," Son told me afterward, "and he just can't quite get over the shock of seeing crackers with money. He's president of ABL in Dallas. That's Mr. Dolly's company. They're the ones who underwrote Tee's policy. Actually they got only about five percent of it." He dialed another number, his eyes roaming the list of names. "They farmed out the rest. Of course," he said slowly, "ABL and Mercury and that goddamn Maury got about ninety percent of the first year's premium. It's a little high, but that's the way it goes sometimes." He slammed down the telephone. "That bastard thinks he's so good at fucking he won't answer his goddamn telephone." He quickly folded the paper and slipped it into his pocket, as if he had memorized the numbers and wanted to recite them before they slipped his mind. "Sugar, I'm getting out. Don't mention that to anybody here in Houston. Hell, Dolly knows something is up, but I just don't want to get into a knock-down drag-out with him right now. Up until a couple weeks ago it was all unfolding pretty easy, but then Mercury or Dolly or somebody at the insurance company decided they wanted out from under Tee's policy. And now you've got your basic contradiction. One of your masters needs money bad and the other master needs just as bad for him not to get it. That's called being caught between a rock and a hard place, ain't it?" Son smiled. "Sugar, we've got a little time to kill here. Let's take a ride. There's a couple things I want to show you before dark."

As we drove into the rain, Son talked. "You know that ranch would sink anyway, no matter who was running it. Grazing cattle is all over with, son. Tee should've seen the handwriting on the wall a long time ago. The cowboy days are dead and gone, buried under feedlots. And there ain't a drop of oil under that sun-baked piece of shit, I don't care what Gunner's geologists say. If there was, Dolph would be in on it instead of Junior. Naw, that ranch is nothing but a way for Tee to make a profession out of feeling sorry for himself." We were silent for a while. "You haven't met old man Kitchens, have you?"

"No, I haven't."

"He's a mean s.o.b., blind, crippled, and crazy now. But I'll tell you one thing, back when he was young, if it'd made money, he would've divided Toro up into eighty-by-eighty lots and sold stucco and swimming pools. Now people would think you were crazy if you started crying over a steak, wouldn't they? No, feedlots close to production and transportation, son, and that's all being pre-empted by the meat-packing boys. The only future in ranching is figuring out how to eat a cow that can live like a coolie."

"What would you do with the ranch if you owned it?"

"If I didn't sell it? Why, I'd help get a President elected, find some water, get me a couple of thousand acres of cotton allotments, and grow old gracefully."

"Is that your little cotton patch up in the greenhouse?"

"No, that's Adrienne's. She's got quite a way with plants. Some people say she's a biological genius. Nature did do some fine selecting there, I think." Son broke off and pointed out a group of towers and buildings just off the freeway. Through the rain they were the blurred shapes of a fortress. "Dollywood. Can you believe it?" He laughed. "Well, six months ago I thought it was a monument to a genius. Six months ago, maybe it was." As we left the freeway and drove aimlessly through the streets that curved among the towers, he explained: "During World War II Dolly saw that there was going to be a lot of boys coming home with back pay, GI Bills, new jobs, and all of them looking for peace, quiet, and ranch-style homes. He started out by buying a cheap tract of swamp over in Deer Park, near the refineries, and threw up forty crackerboxes in twelve weeks. But the working class in this country didn't want to live under the shadow of the smokestack, so he traded the Deer Park development for an undeveloped piece of land out by the airport. Now, to the untrained eye, living under an airport doesn't seem any more attractive than a factory, but Dolly knows how the minds of us lower classes work. He also knew that the new Gulf Freeway was going to run a mile to the east of his little subdivision and what was now forty-five minutes downtown would pretty soon be ten. In a couple of years he made a pile in middle-income housing out by the airport. He cashed his chips in and took down a map of Houston and had a look at it. Dolly knows what every poor boy who's ever grown up in a small town knows by heart. New money lives west." We had pulled into a large covered parking lot and were now inside a shopping center whose mall was enclosed and air-conditioned. The rain beat down on the vinyl sky as we strolled along with the crowd of window-shoppers. We went into a private club and Son ordered us Scotch. "Well, Dolly started speculating in real estate out around Bellaire and biding his time, and he was doing all right, but he wasn't making money fast enough. So he started looking over demographic figures, birth rates, population shifts, and so forth and he began to visualize Houston as a city of a million souls by 1960. This was back in the early fifties. So he went out seven miles on the other side of Bellaire, which itself was about half rice paddy at the time, and bought up two thousand acres of farmland for top money. Nice folks downtown thought he was crazy. But like he told me himself, he got back about half of that in free advertising the day of the sale. 'Realtor Buys Cotton Patch. Predicts City of Future in Ten Years.' And Dolly had other things going for him. He could smell where freeways were going to be built like some folks can divine water, though some fuzzyballs claim that Dolly makes the future more than he predicts it.

"The other part of the genius of Dollywood was that he knew that Houston wouldn't want to be forever dependent on Dallas as its financial center. There is a distressing habit—to some Houstonians—of Houston industry having its executive suites in Dallas. Dolly began making not a few enemies among the old-line families, the Downtown Gang. The same bunch that are trying to keep Dolph Gunther down where they think he belongs. But Dolly also made some friends. I mean, a Texas Who's Who reads like Rednecks Who Have Made Good. Anyway, Dolly set out to make Dollywood a financial center, trying to draw banks, insurance companies, savings-and-loans, brokers, what have you, to set up shop out here. He wasn't having much luck, and being an impatient man, he decided to get into the financial swing himself. And that ain't easy. With no branch banking in the state, the big downtown banks had begun to make it tough on suburban banks, especially suburbs that claimed one day they were going to be the financial center of the state.

"The old man put in an application for a state charter and the first time it was voted down, two to one. But some sort of mistake was made in the paper work"—Son laughed—"and the whole application had to be processed again, and lo and behold, one of those nay votes switched and Dolly had himself a state charter. There were some big bankers in a state of high dudgeon that night. I wish I had been around to see the looks on their fat red faces. But things were still a little rocky. Contractors, developers, just

plain folks like you and me were flocking out to Dollywood to live and shop, but they were keeping their money
downtown. Still are to some extent. That's what Dolly's
working on now, pushing this bill to beef up state banks.
Might end up that his own insurance companies can sell
his own banks the deposit insurance. Ole Mercury's so
hungry he's about to drown in his own spit. But I don't
know, Sugar, I'm getting real nervous about all this paper
flying around. There's nothing real there, nothing you can
lay your hands on and say, *this is mine*, like Dolph
Gunther can do. I know that's old-fashioned, but I can't
help it. And Dolly is fucking it up too. For one thing, he's
pushing this banking bill outside the banking lobby and,
son, that's just not done. I tried to reason with him, but he
just won't listen. That's just one of the reasons I'm getting
out." Son looked at his watch. "Sugar, how would you like
to drop in on some old, old friends?"

"That depends on who they are."

"Why, Mr. and Mrs. F.H.S. Who else?" He pushed away
from the table. "Let me make a couple of phone calls and
we'll be on our way. They live out on the other side of
town. Whenever I really get to thinking it all ain't worth it,
I just drop out and visit old Kenny and Idalou and I cheer
right up." He snapped his fingers and the bartender
brought me another drink. In fifteen minutes we were
walking back through the air-conditioned shopping center.
You could tell it was dark outside and it had stopped rain-
ing, for the time being.


# 3


It took thirty-five minutes of hard driving to get across
town to Pasadena, a flat, dirty, oil-refinery town south of

the ship channel. Son cackled fiendishly (no other way to describe it) most of the trip: Mr. and Mrs. F.H.S., Sweethearts of Flavannah High—there was some justice in life.

This part of Pasadena looked like the country with city streets. Small farms, a place to keep a horse, where you could work in a Houston warehouse and kid yourself with a half-acre garden. If there were street signs they had been torn down, and we got lost, though we agreed the day you didn't get lost in Pasadena was when you had better start worrying.

I remembered Idalou as a saucy little basketball-playing cheerleader who believed that everybody but a few of her mother's friends was going to hell. Kenny was a typical high-school quarterback in that he could think ten yards ahead and that was it. They had been a handsome couple, the last to fuck in their class, married right after graduation day, with the kid born nine months later to the day. They had gone off to one of those religious colleges in Abilene and I hadn't seen them since.

The living room could have served as a midget's roller rink, the hardwood floor glowing, empty, six or seven straight-back chairs on the sidelines. We were hustled past a small room off the living room where people actually enjoyed themselves—I could hear a TV, the sound of children, and the comments of Idalou's mother rising from a reclining chair. I never did figure out who the old woman was yelling at—the kids, the TV announcer, or us. Son, Idalou, and I sat on the straight-back chairs. I began talking wildly about the good old high-school days, mainly because Idalou was scowling at me as though I were an imposter. Kenny hadn't gotten home from work yet. He was a bookkeeper at Comet Rice. Idalou's body had grown sloppy, her tongue sharp, and her mind narrow. Narrower. She warned us: "And he won't have much time to chew the fat when he gets here. He has to be to work at eight o'clock."

"But I thought you said he was just getting off work."

"His job floorwalkin out at Gulf Gate," Idalou sneered. "What's goin to pay for the camper and the pony and this land we're settin on? And Mama's goin to need that operation any time now, I can feel it in my bones."

"What's eating the old girl?"

The old woman howled and Idalou said, "See?" We heard a car pull into the driveway and the three German shepherds in the back yard began to slather. Fenced in, chained down, muzzled, they still believed they had a fifty-fifty chance of getting you. "What's Kenny driving these days?" Son asked.

"Still that old station wagon," said Idalou, her eye on the door so that she could start harping the second it opened. "Kenny wanted to buy me one of them little Jap idgit cars, but I put my foot down." So much for that little car.

Kenny was no fool. He opened the door and called out his apologies for being late before he came in. Idalou yelled out that guests were visiting. "Sugar Campbell, well, I'll be darned." I could hear him whistling on the front porch.

"Draft!" yelled the old woman and the front door closed. Kenny was still outside.

"What's he doing out there?"

Idalou was dismayed. "Cleanin off his shoes, I should hope. Just look at this floor." Idalou was watching my muddy boots. I hooked the heels on the rung of the chair, but I had a feeling that was worse. I stretched my legs out and crossed my feet. It only gave Idalou a better look at the grimy soles. She finally could take it no longer and went out and got us each a piece of the sports section. Son read the baseball scores as he ground his heels into the floor.

Kenny came in in his stocking feet and grinned at seeing

me again. We shook hands and he sat across the room and devoured one of those nineteen-cent hamburgers which he had pulled out of a large brown sack. When he was finished he folded the sack and put it in his jacket pocket. Kenny was bald and looked as out of shape as I was now, and his spirit looked like it had taken licks that quarterbacks never dream of. Still, there was some life left in his eyes, though most of the sparkle was directed toward one of those do-it-yourself tax books. Kenny cradled the book in his lap and, when the conversation drifted away from him, would flip through the pages and read at random.

"Well, Sugar," Kenny said over the last bite of hamburger, "I never thought I'd see you again."

"I did," said Idalou.

"I *thought* I heard voices," said the old woman and had the kids turn her chair so that it faced the doorway. I could still only see her puffy feet and orthopedic shoes laid out on the footrest, but she was in on the conversation. Idalou and Kenny ignored her.

"What have you been doin with yourself, Sugar—"

"The last ten years."

"Well, after graduation I went into the army—"

"Some tax relief there—"

"Fightin old men's wars," yelled the old woman. "Who is that in there?"

"I got out and came back—"

"One a Merce Campbell's boys, Mama."

"That old man is dead."

"He can still have boys!"

"What are you doin with yourself these days, Sugar?"

"Do you still go by that nickname? I'll swan."

"Well, I'm kind of taking it easy, a little vacation—"

"Have you got any beer?" Son said. "I'm parched."

"I don't think we got any beer—"

"Has some old man brung beer in this house!"

"Shut up, Mama! We have never had beer in this house in our lives, Laran Charles."

"Aw naw, I remember that time me and Shug and Kenny got drunk."

"Got drunk?"

"Sock-puking drunk."

"I don't remember ever—"

"Good night, nurse!"

"We stole that eight cans of warm Coors right out of Mr. Garner's garage and rode around town sipping it through straws. Then we picked up those girls from Longton and started courting up a storm. Remember all those dips? Dip dip whoops dip. Who was it had the dry heaves—"

"We wadn't goin steady at that time—"

"That pore woman, she did the best she could."

"Remember the next day? The coach had caught Teen Hartsell and that South Plains bunch down in niggertown drinking Cokes with carbonated water."

"Yeah, I remember." Kenny grinned sheepishly. "Twelve laps, forty-five minutes of calisthentics, and then rollin down that football field six times. It's a funny thing but if somebody ever asked me what was the hardest task of labor I've ever done, I'd say rollin six hundred yards like I was a log. They'd think I was crazy."

Idalou's eyes had grown distant. "It seems so long ago."

"Yes, the good times are over," said Son and shook his head. "Well, we better be going, Sugar. I know you folks have got to get to work. And me and Shug here got to go down to the Rice Hotel for a meeting with the Speaker of the House of Representatives . . ." And everyone was up bustling around as we walked outside. Even the old woman got out of her chair, if only to shout, "Turn the rascals out!" Amid the confusion of Idalou shouting back at the old woman, the kids screaming as some guy's guts splattered across the precinct-station floor, the shepherds

chewing through their muzzles, Kenny apologizing for
having a Republican in the house, Son and I were escorted
out to the car. The old woman, the kids, then Idalou went
back inside the house. Kenny hung on to the car door,
telling Son about the franchise chicken stand he was
thinking about leasing. Son asked him how his income-tax
business was doing and Kenny said fine, though it didn't
leave him much time to study for the C.P.A. exams. Kenny
asked us out for Sunday dinner, but we said we wouldn't
be in town. Idalou called out from the doorway that Kenny
was going to be late for work. Her voice came as close to
sounding girlish as it ever would. Son put the Lincoln in
reverse but Kenny still held on to the door.

"If you ever need any help, Kenny," Son told him, "be
sure I'm the first man you talk to."

Kenny smiled faintly and shook his head. "Thanks, but
I'm doin all right on my own right now."

As we pulled away I saw that Kenny had let out the
shepherds and they were bounding around him like pup-
pies. A block away Son stopped the car, he was laughing
so hard. "Don't it feel good to be outta there? I'd trade that
ole woman in on a sack of day-old horseshit." We found
our way back to the freeway. "Now, Sugar, if anybody in
this country could make it rich, the textbook would make
you think it'd be a guy like Kenny, right? I mean, four
fucking jobs. He works his ass off, loves the flag, honors
the system; he'd slit the gullet of a godless Communist
without batting an eye. But you know, the chances are that
old Kenny will end up, well, maybe never broke or hungry, maybe, but wishing he was. Now, take all that good
Calvinist labor he's suffering through. The theory on that
is that all that hard work is to accumulate capital, to get a
little bit ahead, so that he can turn around and start buying
up other men's labor and start living off that. Those are the
good old days indeed. Kenny is busting his balls, not to get

ahead, but just to keep from going under. You know how much he gets for keeping books for Comic Rice? Maybe a little over four hundred a month. He's been there six years and he's a senior bookkeeper and the stevedores down at the docks make more money than he does. And he loves it. That's because he's management. He wears a white shirt, one of the vice-presidents simpers good morning to him once a week, and they can pay him that miserable salary, work him overtime with no pay, lay him off any time they want to, and they don't even have to worry about him joining a union. He thinks he's in the same class as the man whose mama owns Comet Rice and lives up on Turtle Creek and drops down twice a year to see how his peons are doing. Kenny's worked there six years, he's seen the man twelve times, and he believes he has more in common with him than he does with the niggers down stuffing boxcars. I'm telling you, if Kenny and the rest of those deluded bookkeepers ever stood up on their hind legs, this country would come to a stop. But they won't. You know why? It's their fucking dreams that keep them down. That's something I know quite a bit about.

"Like I was telling you earlier, I went back to school, got a crew cut, and enrolled in business school and joined a fraternity and started chasing sorority girls. Except I didn't have enough sense to know the rich girls from the ones who acted rich. There was this one blind date and I thought she had the money and she thought I had it and goddamn, son, it wasn't till the honeymoon that we found out different. We laughed our asses off. Well, I took my B.B.A. and got a grimy little job selling oil-well parts down in Midland. I used to take down that *Fortune* magazine with the top five hundred corporations in it and I'd run my finger down to Mid-American Tool, four hundred and sixty-three, and then in my daydreams I'd work myself all the way up that ladder to chairman of the board of GM. I'd still be there if I hadn't of inherited that land. Alma almost shit a brick. She was from Odessa, and even though her daddy wasn't any more than a glorified drugstore clerk, they had a membership in the country club and she could go out and play rich with all her little high-school chums. It was the beginning of the end, though I never had any intention of Alma slopping hogs or having my little brain shook loose on a popping johnny. I already knew what I was looking for when I met Mr. Dolly. That was over at Marvin DeKalb's house in Lubbock. In a lot of ways that man was like a father to me. My economic father." Son smiled. "Do you think this is an American tragedy, Sugar? Is it time for me to do the old man in?".

# 4

Cabs were lined up for half a block in front of the Rice Hotel—people struggling in and out, luggage piled in a maze on the sidewalk, cabbies, porters, doormen hustling passengers back and forth like sides of beef. The conservative Democrats were caucusing this week, Son told me as we pushed through the crowd; they were figuring out who was going to win what.

The new Speaker had taken over the Presidential suite and several adjoining rooms on the twelfth floor. On the way up Son explained that Lon wasn't really new to the speakership: this was merely the first time he had gathered pledge cards on his own. Lon had taken over the job when Marvin DeKalb resigned; he already had a commanding lead over his liberal opponent.

The elevator let us, along with a drunk, into a hall that led toward two young men with faces as soft as sirloin and eyes as hard as gristle. They didn't move a muscle as we walked between them into a mirrored anteroom. The last I saw of the drunk he was staggering down the hall, casually squinting at door numbers.

We entered a large room cluttered with antiques and velvet and heavy, well-dressed men standing in small groups, moving from one to the other, laughing mechanically and talking loud, as if this was a rehearsal for an important drama. We stood by the door for a moment, then stepped into the swirling play.

A tall weary young man came toward us. He was blond, tanned, and wore a crumpled seersucker suit. He paused to ask if Son was coming down for the weekend. Both Son and the young man seemed to be looking for someone else. "I would like to," Son said. "Have you seen Francis Dolly?"

The young man waved an arm. "Have you heard about the SEC investigation in Dallas?"

The two men's eyes slowly met. "What's up?"

"Nobody knows. There's an odd rumor going around that it has to do with the state banking system. I thought you might know."

Son's eyes hardened and he looked away from the man. "I would like to know. This is the first I've heard of it."

"Really?"

"Really."

The young man waved the same arm and fled through the door. A state senator from Galveston, I was told: old money, a wife who could double back her long legs behind her head. Son refused a drink offered by a Negro waiter and we went back through a labyrinthine hall. A small grinning man stopped us. He seemed so happy and young that it had to have something to do with sex. "You've backed a winner, Cunningham. Lon has just passed a hundred."

"We all knew he would. He'll make a great Speaker."

Without answering, the young man went on. Son was about to say something when we came upon a breakfast nook. Two men sat on the same side of the table; the older man looked up at us with puzzled innocence, the young man with apprehension. Once again I had the impression their reaction was sexual. The older man raised a hand as if to warn us to be quiet. "Laran," he said, "could you come back in a few minutes? But no, Harry and I have had our say." He looked toward the young man, who was trying hard to relax. "Sit down. Lon is such a busy man these days, we all have to wait our turn." He spoke while studying me. I was introduced. "Good, are you with Gunther Oil, Mr. Campbell?"

"No," Son said slowly, "we're old friends. Very close friends."

"That's nice. Harry and I have been having a discussion. Do you spend much time with philosophical matters, Mr. Campbell?"

"Not as much as I should."

"Mr. Dolly is a great philosopher. You should publish some of your thoughts, sir."

Mr. Dolly ignored the young man. "I have developed Five Points to save the world. One, end poverty. Two, end war. Three, end disease. Four, ban all monopolies, including labor unions. And five, outlaw Communism."

"Like the Pope said, sir, you can just picture it as a better world." Harry had shoved his hands under his thighs.

"The Catholic Church was founded for the betterment of mankind."

"Mr. Dolly had an audience with the Pope last year," I was told.

"Laran, do you think Marvin was miffed because I didn't take him on our trip to Rome?"

"I think he understood."

"It wouldn't have been right leaving Mercury at home."

"Mercury is Catholic, and Marvin—what religion is Marvin?"

"I believe Marvin is Episcopalian," said Mr. Dolly.

"Mr. Dolly is Methodist," said Harry.

Mr. Dolly looked peeved. "I believe there is a deep religion of good men. The Pope and I talked about that. He was deeply thankful for the help we have offered the Fathers."

"Mr. Dolly has really helped out the Fathers out there in Dollywood—"

But Mr. Dolly raised his hand and Harry fell into a fretful silence. Once you start putting your foot in your mouth, it stretches your smile till your own mother wouldn't recognize you. "Friendship, good friendship," Mr. Dolly said, "is an act of faith. It embodies neither blood, nor money, nor sex, not even love. It can be a pure thing, but it can also be ephemeral, a thing that the wind will sweep away. A good friend is worth his weight in gold. They also make delightful enemies." Mr. Dolly smiled at Son—his lips told his face they were smiling. Harry was panting as though truth were heat. The banker looked tall sitting next to Harry, whose thick shoulders didn't quite fit into his black and yellow checkered sport coat. Not to be a dandy, Harry wore a dirty white tie over his clean white shirt; his neck was sweaty and red and raw where he had shaved. His eyes had grown sinister and cloudy, and I realized he was drunk and that some kind of fear had only temporarily sobered him. His hair had been cut this afternoon—you could still smell the Lucky Tiger and the sides of his head softly gleamed.

Mr. Dolly's expression was so bland and unchanging that if you closed your eyes or looked away it was difficult to remember what he looked like. His head was shaped like a blunt bullet and fit solidly and without much neck into shoulders as heavy and powerful-looking as the younger man's. But his body looked pampered—milk-fed, exercised, steamed—he had no reason to be strong. He was telling Harry goodbye. "Tomorrow," he said, "tomorrow meet me at the club for lunch. And bring along your friend."

Harry thanked us all, thought about shaking hands, then left. Mr. Dolly leaned over and watched him go down the hall. "Harry is a good boy. Is Mr. Campbell aware of the discretion with which our business must be conducted?"

"He's never met Harry before."

"Well, you see," said Mr. Dolly, frowning, "we have a demand for bright young junior executives, but business schools, except for the finest graduate schools, hardly meet our standards. We need young men with experience in the rough-and-tumble. Bank examiners are far and away our best bet. They are thrown into a thousand situations which the young man in the smaller bank would rarely come up against. They are bright, honest young men. The discretion comes in the recruiting, you see, for other banks are equally interested in young men like Harry. And these young men are, in a manner of speaking, on the other side. An effort to woo him away from a competitor might be taken as an attempt to deflect his honesty. I wish you would forget you saw him in my presence. How is Tee doing? Will he pull through?"

"Things are looking up."

"You know, Laran, we can't afford to carry that policy another year. I hope it's settled soon. I'm anxious to have your full attention. I am so looking forward to having your attention, Laran." The banker turned to me. "The dream of every American boy in this country, sir, is to make absolutely as much money as possible. You've been doing a magnificent job up there, Laran, or so Mercury seems to think. With little remuneration. There will be our reward this side of paradise. How is our lovely Adrienne?"

"As lovely as ever."

"I heard young Gunner and Marvin had a misunderstanding the other night."

"It was Marvin and Tee, then Gunner and Tee."

"Gunner and Tee?" The banker thought a moment. "Still, Marvin should be careful. History is what people *think* happened. Has Mr. Campbell seen a copy of our bill?"

"No sir, but I've told him about it. He's been active."

"Then he should appreciate the delicacy of the negotiations." He held up his hand. "It shouldn't take long. You can't come over to the Shamrock later on?"

"I don't think so. We've accepted an invite to the Dowdens'."

Mr. Dolly arched his eyebrows. "The Seniors?"

Son laughed politely. "Juniors."

"Some of his wife's friends are beginning to sound strange. Strange people to hobnob with, Laran. That young architect's wife on the school board is a lovely young woman."

The young happy man appeared at the table. "I'm afraid you'll have to move into the other room, Mr. Dolly. There are other people waiting to see the Speaker."

For an instant the banker seemed genuinely flustered. "But we haven't talked to Lon yet!"

"Oh. Sorry," said the young man without marring his beatific expression. "It should be three minutes, Mr. Dolly." His eyes swept over Son and he disappeared.

Mr. Dolly regained what little composure he had lost. "A really good man would never make a mistake like that. Marvin tells me you turned down his offer this year."

"There were no hard feelings. I just didn't have the time."

"I know, I understand. Politics is a public vice. Marvin is just depressed about losing. He keeps telling me he hasn't lost an election since high school. He feels it's going to be bad luck. It could be, actually."

"Do you really think so? Everyone else seems to think that running now is the only thing he can do."

Mr. Dolly smiled wanly. "Oh, I'm not worried about Marvin. Even if he loses, he's set for the next few years. I'm worried about you, my boy."

"I'm doing fine, Mr. Dolly."

Mr. Dolly's tongue protruded ever so slightly between his lips, then darted back in his mouth. "Wherever your future lies, Laran, I hope you'll be careful. I hope you won't get hurt . . . in any form or fashion." Again his hand rose. "No. There are some things a wise man doesn't know. I *would* like to know what young Gunner is up to."

"I'll see what I can do. You're probably aware of as much as I am."

"Probably."

"I don't think Tee and Gunner will go much beyond the talking stage."

"Probably not. Prince Whatshisface is a cunning rascal, but I guess he knows that. I've heard that Dolph is getting cozy with the Foundation people. Fath in particular. I've heard he's going to buy this very hotel." The banker studied Son. "I've heard he's going to buy the publishing establishment across the street." The banker smiled. "See what you can find out . . . from your new friends."

Another man appeared before us, popping onto our stage like a bumbling stand-up comedian, but nobody laughed. Mr. Dolly stood and shook the man's hand, a vigorous act. The man greeted Son by name and nodded at me, then sat by Mr. Dolly. He looked like another bank examiner—squat, sweating, wearing a green silk suit with an electric-yellow sheen, thick plastic-rimmed glasses that kept inching down his nose; he occasionally would silently snarl to push them back—but both Son and Mr. Dolly began touching the man and congratulating him on his victory. The man didn't seem surprised. He apologized for not having read the bill.

"Oh Lon, that's not all we wanted to see you about," said Mr. Dolly, "though I would have appreciated more than three minutes with you, sir." Lon stared blankly at the banker. Mr. Dolly was hurt. "That's what Leon said, Lon. Three minutes, then clear out of the suite—" The Speaker started to protest, but Mr. Dolly had built the slight into a monument. "Laran will vouch for me, Lon, we were asked to leave."

"Francis, you have as much of my time as you want. And you always will."

"I'm glad to hear that it was Leon's mistake, Lon. Now I want to make you some money, Lon, by giving you an old-fashioned tip on the market. Is there anything in the world wrong with that?" he asked everyone.

"Yessir," said Lon. His eyes had drawn down to a bead; he took a cigar tube out of his pocket, removed the cap, and pressed the tape on the table.

"Fathoming the public's wishes is your business, Lon, knowing the ins and outs of the money jungle is mine. We are both explorers and serve mankind by mapping out these regions. Yours is often a thankless trek. Rewarded by fame during your journey, often forgotten at your destination. On the other hand, I am relatively unknown but receive some remuneration from my work. The people are capricious, money is not. Their love can be transferred without token or ticket. Needless to say, cash esteem abides. If it's handled properly."

"Yeah, but on our last stock deal, Francis, I got my ass burned."

"It was the market, it was the market. We all lost, Lon, expert and amateur alike. There are no *true* winners in a recession, my boy." The banker's face turned with distaste.

"All right, what's the deal?" Lon said, with caution so heavy he seemed exhausted.

"I'm prepared to offer you $y$ amount of ABL common, which traded over the counter this afternoon for eleven dollars and twelve and a half cents. At some future date, if you're so inclined, you can sell the stock and repay my loan. From my knowledge, I should imagine in three months' time you will have made a handsome profit. Of course, Lon, I could hardly advise you on that. By the way, the governor and Dr. Lebarron have already invested in ABL, with a loan provided by Dollywood. I imagine the same avenue would be open to you."

Lon's eyes were almost closed. "Is that a fact?"

Mr. Dolly lifted his shoulders. "Of course. I can have Dr. Lebarron call you any time. By the way, ABL has gone up two whole points since they came in."

"What about Rabine?"

"He's more interested in highway construction these days."

Lon took off his glasses, cleaned them, lit his fifty-cent cigar, and put his glasses back on, tight. "What sort of collateral would I need for twenty-five thousand?"

The banker leaned back and spread his hands as though he were parting waters. "Your good word, Lon, your honesty, your integrity, your good name." He leaned forward confidentially. "I don't think anyone would blame you if you bought in for fifty thousand. You don't have to lift a finger, Lon, we'll take care of everything at the bank. I personally will mail you the papers in the morning. We'll be able to come in below twelve. And we'll top twenty by September, mark my words. If the creek doesn't rise"—the banker smiled—"as Lyndon says."

"Sell at twenty. What's in the bill?"

"Nothing, nothing of great importance. A small matter," said Mr. Dolly, elation swelling his chest and neck and head. "When you get back to Austin, I'll come up myself."

"You know that Watson's going to have to O.K. the introduction and Rabine will have to get it through the Senate."

Mr. Dolly smiled broadly. "Oh yes, of course. Of course."

A smile spread across the Speaker's face. "I can only promise a fair hearing, Francis." Now everyone was smiling, rising to shake hands. Lon took a minute to tell Son how much luck he wished Marvin. Everyone was predicting a cliff-hanger, Marvin was an in-fighter, and so on.

After the Speaker left, we sat down. Mr. Dolly seemed spent, Son wiped his forehead with a handkerchief, and I needed a drink. "Let's get out of here," said the banker, rising and flexing his arms. "I need to go somewhere and talk to my muscles. And I don't want to run into Leon again." He peered into the hallway. "He's a frightening person, don't you think? So cold." We went down the hall and through the large room without being noticed. Someone had brought in a carload of girls. We stood on the sidewalk with Mr. Dolly as he studied the line of waiting cabs. "What do you young men think of the Speaker? Do you think he'll be a great man someday?"

"I don't think he's in the same class as Marvin."

"Ah, but he is ambitious though, isn't he? But ambition itself is cheap. Yes, common as bright ideas. What makes the difference, Laran?"

"A sense of reality."

The banker raised his eyebrows. "Do you think Marvin

has a sense of reality, Laran?" Son, with a troubled look, didn't answer. I was beginning to appreciate my friend's talent—deeply troubled by the shortcomings of those he loved and worked for, steadfast and loyal up to the point of their failure, it was they who failed him.

With a fatherly expression Mr. Dolly touched his arm. "I think you're right about Lon. I wonder how he got someone like Leon to work for him." The driver of the first cab in line began motioning at Mr. Dolly, who stared at the man without expression. "He's too young to have a stomach. I can't abide young people who are fat. Great men do things, Laran, without expecting praise or reward. And in turn they expect that sacrifice from those who work for them." Then he went down the line and got in a cab that pleased him.

"Bet you didn't know they still stacked bullshit that high," said my friend as he waved at the fleeing cab.

# 5

Sometimes the nights in Houston are hotter than the days and we were glad to get back to the air-conditioned apartment. Son broiled two steaks and after we had eaten talked about the scene we had left. "I'm afraid I do have a contempt for politics that I have to be watchful of. I make the mistake of mistaking politicians for politics. Hell, not too long ago I thought all governors were equally powerful men. God, I'm tired, Sugar." He laid his head back on the couch, his eyes moving around the ceiling. "Everything down here is in a turmoil, worse than that fucking ranch. There's a stampede coming on, and though God knows I want to stay in the game as long as I can, I got a feeling the

gittin time is gittin near. It's a little bit like the market—
you got to be able to tell the difference between real and
apparent motion." He had walked over to the window,
looking out across the lush western section of the city.
After a moment of silence he said, "Things are working
out pretty much like I had planned . . ." But his voice
sounded old. "I'm going to be happy soon." He laughed,
then turned and looked at me. "Sometimes I find myself in
the middle of a roomful of the richest people in the world
and I have no idea what I'm doing there. Strong men
aren't afraid of going back to the way they used to be. I
think I'd rather die than go back to being poor. I can't go
back."

"There doesn't seem to be much danger of that."

He laughed faintly. "Maybe not. But it makes me too
cautious. Part of the time I hide my timidity, part of the
time I'm too reckless. A man like Dolph Gunther never
looks back. A man like me, I'm in love with the present.
But I don't believe it's really going to last. I'm always pic-
turing the future as over with. My life is like a dream. In a
lot of ways it's all like a dream." He went into the kitchen
and came back with two drinks. "When I was a kid I used
to have these waves of timelessness come over me. It
seemed like it usually happened when I was standing out
in the open some place, like in the fields back of the
house. All of a sudden everything would seem foolish—no,
that's not really the word for it. It was much stronger than
that. It was an overwhelming physical sensation, like
something had drawn my mind outside my body. I could
see the whole world and all of time, just like that. Like
they were nothing. I would be moving along like everybody else, but it meant nothing. Nothing mattered. It was
like the people around me were speaking a foreign language, or I was from another planet. I no longer existed. I
used to dread those spells worse than nightmares, worse

than anything. You ever have anything like that happen to you?"

"No, I never have."

Son slumped in his chair. The weariness in his voice had spread throughout his body. "It's good to have you back, Sugar. It's not often I get to let my hair down these days. Though I guess that's part of my problem, always trying to figure out how I tick. I had a good buddy in college like that. He wanted to be a writer and he used to take his portable typewriter and hitchhike out to a motel on the outskirts of town and hole up for the weekend and write a story about a guy taking his typewriter and hitchhiking out to a motel . . . We called him S.S." He smiled. "Silver Screen, your life is but a dream." He finished his drink and stood. "Son, tell you what let's do, let's go to that party tonight and mingle amongst the rich and the powerful. They'll never know the difference, not until it's too late. Let's fool them, for a while anyway. What do you say?"

I let myself be driven through the city without noticing where we were going.

We parked in a dark woods, except that now I noticed huge houses back among the trees. Other cars were parked ahead of us. Son switched off the headlights. "Bill doesn't like people smoking in his house," he said and drew on his cigarette and tossed it out the window. "His fucking cats are allergic to the smoke. Dowden's a good liberal. He can afford to be. His old man owns about a tenth of Harris County. He's the editor of the *Press*. I don't know if you remember, but that's the other big paper in town. Fairly liberal. Democratic." Son shook his head. "I don't believe that Dolph is really buying the *Examiner*. What I don't understand is why Dolly dropped the news in my lap." He smiled. "I guess you could say he's begun to have doubts about my loyalty. Of course, we should never rule out any possibility. Dolph is going to need a newspaper if he wants to make little Gunner governor. That's what the spat the other night was about. Three men in that room want to be governor and not one of them is going to make dog-catcher. By the way, Toi, Bill's wife, is a gossip columnist, so you better watch your $p$'s and $q$'s." We got out of the car and walked up the circular drive. "I hope you get to liking A., Sugar. I had the feeling you didn't."

"I haven't really talked to her."

"Good, good," and we walked up the steps of a huge colonial house. A man and a woman were standing behind one of the columns. They and Son exchanged cool greetings.

# 6

All the rooms of the mansion were lined with books and draped with people. The main room, where we now stood, was two stories high: a catwalk ran around three sides of the room, the fourth side was a balcony with an entrance to other rooms on the second floor. People strolled along the catwalk looking at books. Son called my attention to a small man standing beneath the spiral library staircase which led up to the catwalk. "One of A.'s little buddies. There's no one hornier than a bibliophile"—he turned away from the small man—"and no one more drastically mistakes it for love. Have you seen A.? I want to introduce you to Bill or Toi and then turn you loose. There's a man I got to see a dog about. Hey," he said to a man who was hurrying by with three martinis, "where is everybody?"

"Hiya. Upstairs watching TV."

"Oh yeah, I forgot. There's an election special on tonight." He looked at his watch. "Let's go up and take a look."

We went up a broad carpeted stairway, then down a hall toward the sound of a TV and people laughing. The room was dark but for the TV set and we stood in the doorway till someone called out Son's name and he went across the room, toward the back. I sat on the floor near the door, with a bed as a backrest. To my right was a wall plastered with children's drawings, mainly monsters, and to my left a woman with teeth that glowed green in the TV light. The rouge on her cheeks glowed purple. She was wrinkled all over; even her tongue looked wrinkled. She wore some kind of moth-eaten cap, or it could have been her hair. She immediately began impugning my sexuality. There seemed to be beautifully polished women sitting everywhere else. The wrinkled woman moved across the room and began, I guessed, impugning my sexuality to one of the beautifully polished women. I tried to follow the TV commentator, but everybody was laughing at things I thought were sad. The program was coming to a close. The conservatives were going to win by a landslide. The people in the room had grown despondent; by twos and threes they began to leave. I don't know how I missed Son leaving, but when I looked back, with only a few people remaining, he was not there. But then I saw no one but Adrienne, her face pensive, her mouth tensed slightly as she watched the TV program. I had known she was going to be there, but still I was struck by that small knife of fear and desire especially honed for unrequited love. I turned back and watched the gray, distorted picture. What the man said was so far beneath meaning, yet his words, the sound of them, were indelibly fixed in my mind—percentages, voters, parties, the hopes of victory and the chances of defeat. The man disappeared, and music and a cascading stream appeared, and then there was a young couple strolling along the rocky bank, leaping from stone to stone; their fingertips touched, the man pulled his beloved to safety, they embraced and split a beer. Adrienne came and sat by me on the floor, aimed a small box at the TV set, and the picture sank into a small dot of light which grew very bright before it disappeared. Light from the doorway fell across us; it seemed rich and yellow, like sunlight on a summer morning.

"I said, you look sad tonight. You look as though you miss someone."

"No, I don't miss anyone."

Adrienne nodded brusquely. "I think I'm the world's worst at sensing how other people feel. How do you feel?"

"Oh, I think I'm mainly confused. Confused about what you're doing here with me."

She blushed, not with pleasure, and looked at the floor across the room. "I've been terribly confused at times in my life, but now that's over." She looked at me, her face drawn. She believed what she was saying, that she had never been happier in her life.

"You didn't seem so happy three days ago. But then I guess I came into your life at just the right time." She laughed. "What has happened for the better?" I asked her.

"Oh, everything has taken a turn . . . for the better." She paused and said sharply, "Tee's going to be all right. Son says he's going to be able to raise the money and then everything will be for the better."

"Then you'll be able to leave him with a clear conscience?"

She flushed. "Did Son say that?"

"No, I did."

She was still angry. "What did he say?"

"He said that he loved you."

She ignored me. "We're not going to live together for a

while. I'm so uncertain of him. What was he like when he was young?"

"He was smart."

"I can imagine that. What else?"

"I don't know, he was different. Different than he is now. People didn't know what to make of him. I guess you either loved him or hated him."

"And you loved him?"

"I didn't hate him."

"And now?"

"I don't know about now."

She lowered her head. "I know. If I didn't love him I would hate him."

"Do you love him, Adrienne?"

There should have been a stillness, but she shrugged. "I don't know. When I love anyone I love him. If I could only trust him. Oh, I do, there's never been any cause . . . It's not that." She looked into the dark TV screen. "It's just at times I feel that he doesn't need me. That he doesn't need anyone."

"He might not."

She looked at me, in her eyes a fear that drew me toward her. She said, "No, he doesn't love anyone." She looked at me steadily. "Not even himself." Then she stood and asked if I would like to see the books and offered me a hand to my feet.

We went along the hall, then into a large room which was half kitchen: a chopping block stood like a statue in the center of the room. We stepped out onto the balcony overlooking the main room. Another couple was on the catwalk along the far wall. The room had filled with people. Many of them had gone to the ballet tonight, Adrienne explained, but now the troupe was here. Adrienne picked up a book and pretended to read it, but when the people across the way went down the stairs, she climbed over the balcony railing and I followed her. Her eyes sparkled with mischief, her face was bright. We walked halfway down the catwalk and Adrienne took down another book. "If I have a secret vice," she said, "it's watching people." She laughed and blushed and was incredibly beautiful. "My open vice must be talking about them. I'm terrible. Do you see Toi anywhere? But then you don't know her." I pointed out the wrinkled woman and Adrienne laughed. "*That's* not Toi. Did she say she was? Well, whatever you do," she mocked, "don't ever let it get back to Anna that you thought she was Toi. She's impossible to live with as it is. Do you see the four young men languishing on the sofa? And the attractive woman there. She's Elizabeth Browning, she's on the school board, and is she ever raising hell. She might be our first woman mayor. Those are the ballet boys she's flirting with. Poor boys, they don't stand a chance, not that they probably care. Oh, there's my friend Ty." She blew a kiss toward the bibliophile standing beside the spiral staircase. He raised his glass and gave us a mystified smile. It was difficult to tell how old he was; his glasses were so thick they looked frosted, but his devotion to Adrienne was apparent. "He's one of the sweetest men I know. He's a private eye, of all things. He's also very liberal and knows everybody. He's a book collector too. He's bought half the books in this room. Poor Bill, his father is so brilliant, and he is so nice. Bill has read four books in his lifetime, if you count *Giant* twice. I told you I was nasty. He and Gunner are so much alike, it's a shame they have to fight. And over politics of all things. Gunner is so incredibly stupid about parties and politics. Christ, what difference does it make? By the way, Gunner and Tee have made up. What happened the other night is nothing new. They're always rearing up at each other. Gunner at least has the sense to know he would kill Tee . . . if they ever did fight. Gunner is an incredibly strong man—physically." Her voice had lost most of its energy. She stared down into the room without seeing the people. "He knows he's not a strong person. Not like—" She laughed strangely. "I was going to say, Not like my father. But I had a picture of Son. That's strange, isn't it? No, what's strange is my thinking it is. Gunner used to be such a nice man. A nice boy. Once he told me about a movie he had seen. A man is wounded in some kind of robbery, I think, and he gets this crazy idea that he has to go back to his father's farm. God knows, I guess the place doesn't exist. But he is driving along and he sees a thoroughbred ranch and he thinks it's his father's place, and he stops the car and starts running toward the horses. He never catches them, but he dreams he does, he dreams that he is riding . . . He was only sixteen when he told me that. He once told me something, the dreams of the poor, and now I've forgotten—haunting him, perhaps. At any rate, it didn't last long. He wasn't enough of a man to shoulder his simplicity. Most of the time now he's a small person, wallowing in his shrewdness. But then again I'm talking about somebody else, aren't I? A man who takes kindness for weakness isn't strong, is he? He's just weak in a different way. I've always pictured Son as a sensitive boy. Was he?"

"He didn't cry at movies."

"I think I know him as well as you do."

"And I don't think you do."

"And I think you're probably right." She looked away and brought back her brilliant smile. "But then I didn't cry at movies either. Did I?"

"No," I said, heartbroken or something close, "I don't think you did."

"Let's go upstairs," she said with a sudden tension. "This place smells like a gym. Do you see Son anywhere? But I guess he can take care of himself." Her casual toughness was frail, almost tender.

We went back through the kitchen, up a narrow spiral staircase to a deck which extended the length of the house. An empty swimming pool lay flat and dull beneath us. Three stories up and still the cypress and willows reached higher, their branches draped with the ghostly cobwebs of Spanish moss. We walked the length of the deck. Adrienne said that Bill, who was crazy about games, had once held a track meet here, finishing the race in the swimming pool three stories below. No one had really wanted to win. She was laughing when we kissed. We were so surprised it was almost as though it hadn't happened. Adrienne sat in a lounge and I leaned against the rail, the moonlight so bright I could barely see her face. She began to talk again, but with only a mask of enthusiasm.

"You're not an easy person to understand."

"Oh yes, I am. I'm really very simple and trusting. Isn't that what you're counting on?"

"Do you try to sleep with most women you meet? That's just a question."

"I'm not trying to sleep with you, Adrienne."

"Did you sleep with June? She said you did."

I became slowly angry. "Is having me fall in love with you part of his plan?"

"Whose plan? There's no plan."

"It's not going to be that hard, Adrienne, if you really want that. If you think it's really worth it."

"You don't know what you're talking about."

"Has he told you why he brought me here? I'd like to know myself. Is it that I once killed a man in cold blood? Has Son told you about it? I was quite a hometown hero for a while. It was in Korea and I was interrogating a Chinese officer and I didn't like the way he parted his hair so I blew his head off. No one's told you that? Now, it was a long time ago and I told them he attacked me, so I even got a medal for it and a hometown parade and my picture in the paper. But you know how that sort of thing goes, it twists a man. Once you get started, once you taste blood—maybe he'll do it again. Is that what you want, Adrienne? Is it your idea or his?" I had never imagined the look on her face. At that moment, if she had asked me, I would have killed him. "Now maybe I'm wrong, but when June first met me, she thought the same thing. She thought I had been hired to kill Tee. But that's crazy, isn't it? That's what Son says. That's not really why I'm here, or is it?"

"June is crazy, you know that. She got that idea from Tee anyway. He's as crazy as she is. They all are. Nobody wants to kill him."

"Are you sure? He's got a pack of enemies. There's a lot of people who would like to see him dead, there's a lot of people who would benefit by it."

"But they don't want to kill him—"

"But they do want him dead."

She moved her head and had no energy left. "I don't know any who do."

"Are you sure you don't want him dead, Adrienne?" Her face was white, like a skull, as she raised it to the moonlight. She collapsed back in the chair and began to cry. I didn't move. "Another crazy idea that June came up with was that I was being lured into a trap." She finally brought her eyes into mine. "She said that someone is planning to make it look like I killed Tee, and then that someone and you would collect the insurance money. Is that right?"

"That can't be true," she whispered. "I came down here to get away from that."

"Was that what happened to Billy O.? Was he supposed to kill Tee, but he couldn't?"

"He killed himself. She knows that—"

"Was he your lover?"

"He was just a boy."

"What about the man who was snakebit? Did he fall in love with you, too? Was he supposed to kill Tee too?"

"I don't know what you're talking about." As she started to get up, I pulled her toward me. Her body grew soft with trembling. But she drew away and I let her go. She could barely talk. "I've got to get away from there. I can't go back to him. I can't ever go through it again! *Ever!*"

She moved farther away. I turned and saw Son standing in the shadows halfway down the deck. He moved toward us. I was elated, for his face was distorted with defeat. He came up silently, touched Adrienne's back, and she turned gently into his arms. "It looks like the bottom has finally dropped out, baby," he said softly. "Tee has disappeared again." She began to cry as though she were in pain. Son watched me indifferently. "Tee has run off, Denton has quit, Toro County has drummed up a grand jury to look after what's left of Billy O., and poor little June has had her another nervous breakdown. Poor little June Bug, when it rains it pours." His cold eyes left mine and I knew that this was no game, no drama, there were no rules, no words to follow. We were killing a man—it was as simple as that.

# 7

The three of us flew back to Lubbock that night and rented a car at the airport. We didn't talk at all. Son had been able to sleep on the plane, while Adrienne and I had not. It was four o'clock and still dark when we headed east from Lubbock. Son drove, looking bitterly tired. Adrienne curled in the back seat and slept. I fought exhaustion for a while, as though staying awake were a test of strength, but eventually I closed my eyes and my aching mind collapsed.

It was just light when I woke. We were headed north on the highway between Wadsworth and Toro. The grass was thick and heavy; the dew-covered blacktop looked as rich as chocolate cake. The sun had yet to appear on the horizon; it was that brief time before dawn when the world always seems to be at peace. Our peace didn't last long. Pork Man met us at the door of the Little House, a six gun strapped to his waist, two cartridge belts crossing his chest, a carbine held at port arms. He came across the porch and leaned down into the car window. "Where you turds been? Mornin, Miz Kitchens, we bout got things under control. We been keepin guard throughout the night."

Son only sounded angry. "What in the hell for?"

Pork Man blinked, then squinted. "You don't know the half of it, buddy boy." The fat man's eyes were red and looked rimmed with salt; his clothes were wrinkled and filthy. He stood back, letting us out of the car. He and Adrienne walked back toward the house, Adrienne leaning slightly to one side, limping; Pork Man talking excitedly, slinging the carbine over his fat shoulder. They disappeared into the house.

Son gave me two keys. "You know where the bunkhouse is. This is the key to my room. Far end, my name is on the door. This key is to a small safe under the bed. It should have two guns in it. Bring the .45 back to me. Keep the other gun for yourself. O.K., now, in the safe there are some papers, letters mainly. I want you to burn them all, right there in that goddamn room." He thought for a second. "I don't know what the hell is going on, but be careful till you get the gun. We'll be up in the Money Room." He went inside and I drove the car around to the side of the house, where the sun was already hot.

I walked down through the cottonwoods, alive with sparrows and rustling leaves. Throughout the ranch there was no human movement. The bunkhouse—a long concrete-block building—was quiet, the windows and doors thrown open. A light breeze flapped a blind. I hesitated on the porch, then stepped into the building, closing the screen door behind me. The place was a wreck. Bunks overturned, mattresses ripped apart, cotton stuffing strewn over everything, windows and bottles smashed, the floor gritty with broken glass. I found a small pool of blood beneath one of the bunks; pieces of cotton fluttered on its surface. I pushed open the door to Son's room and went in.

The small room had been demolished. The raw smell of smoke lay in the air, the window glass had been broken, the ceiling was blackened with soot. In the center of the floor sat the safe, broken open, the interior charred, the bottom thick with a layer of black scum. The guns were gone, the letters had been dealt with. I stood and a chill crept over me. A man on horseback stood just outside the window, a .30-30 propped against his leg. The horse moved forward a few feet and the man turned his head and I saw that it was Coolie. My attention narrowed to the fine point of his face, calm, turned up at the trees. I did not move. The horse walked several feet more, Coolie reined it in, then fired the rifle into the trees. The sparrows took flight like leaves being ripped away by a silent storm. The horse moved on, out of my line of vision. A few seconds later came another rifle shot, but too distant to be Coolie. It had come from the direction of the main houses.

I waited five minutes, till my legs stopped trembling, then walked back to the Little House. I neither saw nor heard anything. The front door was open. I tried the elevator but it was broken. I climbed the spiral staircase behind the fireplace. Everyone was in the Money Room. A meeting was in progress; Son sat behind Tee's desk. Talking on the phone when I came in, he periodically interrupted that conversation to question those in the room. I sat at the back of the group of a dozen people. Adrienne wasn't there. Half the people were armed—Pork Man, Larry, a couple of cowboys; Maury fingered an engraved shotgun. Caroline Jo was missing too. Mabelline was asleep on the floor. Mexican servants slipped in and out of the room. I could not take my eyes from Son's face as he talked into the receiver. "Look, Mark, you get your ass up to Toro courthouse with some kind of affidavit swearing when, where, and how you found that body. I'll see if I can cool down that goddamn grand jury from the other end. Well, who the hell is running that county, Maxwell or the D.A.? Then goddamnit, Tabor, get a surveyor out there and survey it." Son put the receiver to his chest. "Does anybody know what county that fucking spring is in?" One of the cowboys said it was a couple miles inside Wadsworth County. Son asked the man if he would be willing to go down to Wadsworth and get Tabor straightened out. "You might have to swear out an affidavit yourself."

The cowboy shrugged. "I'm goin to have to borrer somebody's wheels. Coolie done blowed out all the tares on mine."

Son had hung up the phone, without another word to Tabor that I had noticed. "What in the hell has gone wrong with Coolie?"

The cowboy shrugged again, glancing at his partner. "Loco."

"Is he working for the old man?"

"Naw, I thank he'd just as soon shoot the old man, myself." He looked toward the second cowboy, who dipped his head an inch.

"Somebody shoulda put that old man away a long time ago."

"Maybe Adrienne could sign some papers against him,"

said Larry, his voice languid. "Well hell, he's been tryin to put Tee away for three months now."

Son hesitated. "We'll wait till Tee gets back and get him then. There's going to be beaucoup lawsuits as it is." Son looked at something he had written on a pad and was about to speak when there was another rifle shot, not too close, followed by what sounded like a shotgun blast from the roof. Son turned casually to Larry. "If you don't get C.J. down from there, I'm going to have her thrown off."

Pork Man answered, "What the hell, the Big House was the ones who started it. She's just lettin them know we ain't goin to take their shit layin down!"

Maury spoke for the first time. He seemed exhausted. "I'm tellin you, Son, it was rough out there last night. Somebody over at the Big House potshotted out ever piece a winderglass in the greenhouse."

"You know who's doing the shooting?"

Someone laughed. "It ain't the old lady."

"Who's over at the Big House now?"

"The old folks. Stanley. That's about it. None a the boys have nothin to do with them."

"How about Denton?"

"Naw, he packed up his saddlebags and took off for them fuckin caves."

Son wrote something down. "Roxie, ride out this morning and have a talk with him. If he stays out there it's going to look bad."

The cowboy chewed his teeth. "I reckon he rode out there just so's he don't have to talk to the likes a me."

"He might know where Tee is."

"If he knows where Tee is at and he wants us to know it, then he'll come and tell us."

"You think June might know where he's holed up?"

There was a silence, then Maury coughed. "Hell, Son, her flippin out is what drove him off."

"One a the thangs."

"She won't know nothin and wouldn't tell us anyhow. She thanks there's a goddamn conspiracy afoot."

"How'd it start, Maury?"

"You don't have to tell everthang, Maury," said Mabelline, who still looked asleep. "As a matter a fact, please don't."

Suddenly Maury began to talk fast. "Hell, I don't know what happened first. Did she try to plug him or herself? Actually, it started with the grand jury thang, actually it started with that cocksuckin Montreal bank crawfishin out. Me and June was out walkin around, and Tee rides up and he tries to shoot me, for God's sake, his best buddy for a long time. Then he rides off laughin his ass off. An me and June Bug was just out diggin up old Injun graves. I wasn't tryin to git into *no*body's pants. Well, Junie says, Let's go git our guns. When we got back to the Little House, Tee was downstairs blazin away into the fireplace with two guns, ricochets everwhere. We hurried on upstairs and armed ourselves. Somebody told us that he had tried to burn down the bunkhouse and had tried to rape Potts and that him and Coolie had got into a fistfight. This was about four o'clock in the evenin.

"Me and Junie was up on the roof, lookin off at everthang, but it was deadly still. She said she was goin to go down and try to cool him down. She said I had better hook up with Mabs for my own good. She had this screwy look in her eyes when she left. The day before, Tee had took the clip to her Brownie away, so's she didn't have no bullets. I had the idea she was goin to look for the clip first. Then I got to worryin. I got to thinkin about some a the poetry she'd been readin me that afternoon—the coolin warters of Zanatoplis, the city a death it was—so's I got on the horn down to White Hope to have him come up here and guard the roof so's nobody wouldn't do nothin foolish.

They tole me over at the Big House that White Hope had gone off with all them other cowboys who had gone on strike down in Wadsworth, gettin all liquored up and threatenin to come back here and stretch Tee's neck if'n he didn't pay them their arrears. The old woman started in tellin me that Cunningham here was behind it all. He was at work for the banks with secret plans to foreclose the ranch and divide it all up amongst himself and his Houston buddies. Son, I tried to convince her, but they don't listen to nobody now. She said that A. had a bunch a jewelry in the wall safe and that Tee had a hundred thousand bucks sewed into one a his saddles, crazy stories like that. She said for safety sake I had better bring all the jewels over to the Big House. She was expecting the cowboys to raid the place later on that night. I said I would cooperate, which just goes to show you. Well, I drained the fuckin pool just to be on the safe side and you know how it lets out behind the house, well, somebody was down in that culvert hidin out, just waitin to ambush Tee Texas when he come by. I thank it was one a them damned crazy kids from Toro. Anyway, that's when the shootin started. He got all pissed off and took a coupla shots at me, then knocked out a coupla winderglass in the greenhouse just for the meanness of it. It didn't make that much difference anyways, somebody had done yanked out all the potted plants earlier in the day and stomped all over them.

"Well, the shootin stopped pretty soon. The kid got off a coupla shots and got skeered and left. But everbody was edgy. Shootin gits started and it's hard to stop. Towards dark somebody over in the Big House got pissed off and started it all over again." As if to punctuate his point, another shotgun blast came from the roof.

"I've had enough of this shit," Son said to the cowboys. "Get that gun away from that crazy broad any way you have to." The cowboys hitched up their Levi's and left.

Larry watched Son without expression. Son explained, "Look, if we don't stop this shooting, somebody from the outside's going to find out about it and we'll all end up in the loony bin. Maury, is there any part of your life story that's going to shed any light on where we might find Tee? Larry, where were you during all this shooting?"

"I don't have to answer your goddamn questions, Cunningham. Who appointed you boss of this outfit anyway?"

"Adrienne—"

"Fuck that goddamn whoor," Larry said, but Mabelline was on her feet.

"Say one more word about that woman, you butterfat bastard, and I'll slice you up like white bread." But she sat back down, as if slightly bored by the idea. Pork Man yawned. Larry smirked and slid down in his chair. Maury seemed to have lost interest in his story. With a few sentences it was over.

After the shooting on the roof, Maury had come down to the Money Room and found Tee arguing violently with a telephone operator. June was nowhere in sight and Tee ignored his questions. Maury didn't find her downstairs either. He went outside and walked around the house. He was about to go back in when Pork Man came along and said he had seen June headed toward the bunkhouse. "I got down there just quick enough and found her lyin on a cot. She had cut her wrists, not too deep, the doc said, but she did almost die from the pills. They didn't find out about them till it was almost too late. Fastest trip anybody's ever made to town. She woke up there once and said the funniest thing . . ." But Mabelline had begun to cry and he didn't say anything else.

"She's a lost little girl, Son," said Mabelline. "It wadn't no fake this time. She really wanted to go. She was going down there to die, goddamn sonofabitch, caint you all leave her outta this?" Son asked Mabelline if she would drive over to the hospital, but the woman shook her head. "I caint do it, Son, I'm just too worn out."

From where I was sitting it seemed like an awfully long way to say anything, but I told them I would make the trip. Everyone looked at me, then looked away. The meeting went on. Son and Pork Man got into an argument over a loan that Pork Man had promised to deliver—a hundred thousand dollars. Near the end, Pork Man took out a checkbook and wrote a check and waved it in the air. Son studied the check, folded it, and put it in his shirt pocket. The discussion turned to making peace with the Big House. They had to decide who would make the best ambassador. Eventually the meeting broke up. It looked like a sad party, people milling around, touching one another. Son came over to me. "She's in the Methodist hospital in Lubbock. I don't imagine she's in any shape to talk, but find out what you can."

"You don't have any idea where he might have gone?"

"Naw, but I'll be able to find out." He grimaced from weariness. "He always tells somebody. I might send you after him. If you're willing."

I shrugged as nonchalantly as possible. "The guns were gone. The letters or whatever had already been burned."

"They had?" Son looked around the room. "We'll check around here for the guns. Maybe we'll find something by the time you get back." He looked at me. "I wouldn't send you into anything I wouldn't go into myself."

"Fair enough."

He seemed to be disagreeing with himself. "Ahh, he's just down on the border getting drunk. He's pulled it before. Look, I've got to see how A.'s doing. This is harder on her than these bastards will ever realize. After you finish at the hospital, take the rent car back to the airport and take a cab to Flavannah and get some sleep. I should know something by dark. If we can get him back in one piece, I got an idea how to settle all this. This ought to take care of it." He gave me three hundred dollars and a gas credit card.

# 8

From the parking lot I could see hawks wheeling and circling far to the east. In the corner of the lot I had found in a pile a saddle and bridle, a rifle, hat, shirt, boots, a billfold, some change. I put everything in the trunk of the car and then drove past the Big House. Everything was quiet now. I let the car wind out on the road out to the highway.

I turned south toward Lubbock. Farmers were combining wheat and trucks were backed up at all the elevators. In some fields six combines worked at once. I could see the rain in the clouds to the southeast, the smell of hot dust and wheat straw heavy in the wind.

The bleak structure looked unhealthy for a hospital. The trees surrounding the building were barely taller than my reach. The outside walls were dirty pink; inside, everything was green. A receptionist told me where I could find June. I rode the elevator to the sixth floor, then walked up to the seventh, no more than a small tower. At the top of the stairs I was met by a short, distracted woman who looked like she was wandering around unattended. But behind her stood a windowless steel-plated door.

I told the woman June's name and she asked me to wait and disappeared through the door. I could see nothing beyond but another door. I walked to the window at the end of the corridor and looked out on southwest Lubbock. The way I was looking at things, each car in the parking lot was someone sick or dying.

The steel door opened and the nurse came out, followed by a man who seemed given to hiding the fact that he was very bright. Lithe, dressed in a lightweight summer suit, his hair so short and thin his skull looked shaved, the man identified himself as a sergeant in the Lubbock Police Department and asked if I would mind telling him a few things about June—it would be impossible to see her till tomorrow. On the ride down to the basement coffee shop, I told him I would try and be as helpful as possible, but I didn't know much about June at all.

He apologized to me. "But you must have some idea why she tried to kill herself."

"She's been trying to do that for a long time, Sergeant."

"Then there's no reason for it, other than *Weltschmerz*?"

"No, there's a reason for it. I just don't think it would interest you. As a police officer."

"Well, it's a true fact that Toro and Wadsworth Counties are far beyond my jurisdiction. Let's just say I'm curious. Not as a police officer."

"I'm not sure I would know where to start."

"Sometimes getting people started is my job."

"All right. She's in love with a man who's being driven mad."

"Do you really think it was a suicide attempt?"

"If it wasn't, she'd be dead. They would've killed her."

"They?"

"Whoever you're theorizing about."

"There's been two unsolved murders out there already."

"They say one was an accident and one was a suicide."

The cop smiled. It hurt his face. It hurt mine. "Do you know who you're playing around with out there, Campbell? Do you know that P. M. Estep, Larry McGaha, and that girl friend of theirs have between them run up twenty years in various state and federal pens?"

"They seem to be totally rehabilitated."

"What's your angle, Campbell?"

"I'm a business associate of Son Cunningham's."

"Ah, Ronnie Rice's buddy. Have you met Ronnie yet?"

"No. Should I have?"

The cop stood and laughed with precision. "He's a colleague of mine. You know, no matter how much money he's got or how many senators his daddy knows or how many cows he can call his own, you're still going to have to shoot a mad dog down. I've enjoyed the talk. El Toro is becoming downright famous in law-enforcement circles."

After he left I drank another cup of scalding, watery coffee and didn't feel so cute. For the life of me I couldn't figure out why I hadn't told the cop everything I knew. About June eighty feet above us, wrists slashed, stomach and mind pumped empty; about Coolie riding naked through the hills; about Denton gone to earth like an animal; about old Malcolm Kitchens so bent on revenge he was willing to send his son to a prison for the insane. And then there were the others, the two dead men, the Toro teenagers, the striking cowboys; then the insurance, the politics, the finance, the machinery that was driving these people mad. And then there was Tee in a helpless, drunken rage in some bordertown cantina; and Adrienne, was she frightened, confused, or did she know exactly what was happening? And Son Cunningham set on his elaborate plan of destruction, and then there was myself— what was I doing? I could no longer tell us apart: If I wanted what Son wanted, then I had to become like him, didn't I? I held my head in my hands, as if that would stop my mind from slipping. I wanted to sleep more than I had ever wanted anything, but I couldn't close my eyes. I had to stay awake, I had to get back to Toro. I found myself driving along, laughing crazily. I didn't want to miss a thing.

A single-prop Mooney was parked on the road south of

the Little House. Several cars were now parked around the Big House, which no longer seemed so ominously still. The doors of the Little House were lashed open, the elevator had been fixed. I found Son, Pork Man, Larry, and a young man I didn't know sitting at the far end of the pool. The greenhouse had been cleaned up; the shattered glass, the ruined plants were gone. Things had been patched up, Son said: he had convinced the old man that everyone was working for the ranch's best interest. They had decided to sell some of the ranch's land. Their only problem now was to find Tee and convince him to go along with them. Only a few minutes earlier they had received a call from a private investigator in Houston: Tee had been seen at his house in River Oaks. Pork Man and I were to fly to Houston this afternoon, dry him out, and bring him back tomorrow. Through Gunner, Son had lined up a powwow with some financial people from Houston for tomorrow afternoon. Son drew me to one side and told me Tee had gone on one of his jealous rages and had been on his way down to Houston when we heard he was missing. "I guess we passed him in the night." Son leaned his head back and inhaled deeply. "Well, these Foundation boys aren't coming up here for their health, Sugar. Fath himself might make it. That means that day after tomorrow all our troubles are going to be little ones. No more expansion, no more grubbing after capital. We'll start cutting back and digging in and enjoying our short little lives some."

"Where's Adrienne? I want to talk to her."

"I don't think she wants to talk to anyone right now."

"Look, I'm going to talk to her if I have to tear this place apart."

He stared at me a second. "You'll never get her. You want her too much, and then you don't want her enough." And he walked over to the elevator and went downstairs ahead of me.

I got a jacket out of the pickup and locked it and walked down the south road. Pork Man had turned the plane into the wind, which had risen cool and thick with rain. As I came up, Son crawled out of the cockpit. We stood directly behind the tail. He gave me a thick manila envelope and, yelling above the roar of the engine, told me the instructions were inside, he wanted me to deliver the envelope in Houston. He then took a step back, looked at me oddly, and turned and walked back up the road. When I climbed into the cockpit, P.M. was draining beer out of one bottle and pissing into another. When we were airborne and the sound of the motor fell off some, the first thing he said was, "So you wanna pound Adern's peehole, huh? Well, yore gonna have to wait in line, needledick the bugfucker!"

# 9

We landed at sundown at a small private field west of Houston. We taxied back toward the hangars—pools of water stood on the asphalt strip, reflecting the dying light like molten silver. After tying down, P.M. went on to the airport office and I opened the manila envelope. Son's instructions were brief. I was to deliver the papers in the envelope to Mr. Dolly and in anything concerning Tee was to take orders from Ty Foose, a private detective and a close friend of Adrienne.

Though I hadn't recognized the name, there was no mistaking the bibliophile's solitary figure standing outside the airport office. His head thrown back, his coat draped like a cape over his shoulders, he wore sunglasses now and held his cigarette as you would a flower, occasionally lifting it to the sky as if he were comparing its glow to the evening star. I introduced myself, and he replied that if I was in charge I had fucked up. "You should have chartered a jet or something," he said, staring at me inscrutably. "Tee has given me the slip."

After Pork Man had finished in the office, the three of us trudged out to Foose's '56 Studebaker. Foose told Pork Man the bad news, but the small man's bravado cracked and P.M. announced that he was taking charge. First we would get something to eat, then go straight to Tee's place in River Oaks. The fat man hummed a cha-cha for the rest of the trip.

SIX BILLION HAMBURGERS, a large sign told us as we pulled into the drive-in and parked. "It's a known fact," Foose said as we took our place in line, "that out of that number eighty-five people have been known to come back and eat here a second time." Throughout the meal P.M.'s steerlike gaze moved back and forth between the sign and Foose. Pork Man ate his six little hamburgers two at a time—while one was being swallowed, another was bitten and chewed. Foose took one sip of his milk shake and then in disgust blew smoke rings above our heads. Finally P.M. leaned across the table and opened his mouth wide so that Foose could have a good look at the mess inside. After that nobody spoke for a while.

We were sitting at a picnic table in front of the drive-in, the heavy Houston bugs cracking against the concrete, the overhead lights beating down on us like a pale sun. Foose and I tried to talk about what we should do, but P.M. ignored our petty conversation. Instead he poked my arm and nodded toward a girl standing in line. "Bet that one's a dick-eatin sonofabitch." Foose closed his eyes. "Aw, yore lookin at the wrong spick, Michelangelo. The one up front, not her fat-ass girl friend. I'm a nose man myself." He winked at me, then grinned at Foose, who was drumming his fingers on the table and staring almost straight up. "I was reared on a farm, boy, milked so damned many a them old cows I caint stand the ones with the big titties. Ain't that the way it is with you, Typhoid?"

Foose tightened his shoulders and doubled up one of the smallest fists I had ever seen. "I'm a mind man, my-self—"

"A mind man! I never heard a that. Where do you fuck em, in the ear! Haw haw haw."

Foose grimly went on. "For me sex is an outgrowth of love—"

"I got yer outgrowth hangin, Typhoid."

"Redneck!" Foose hissed.

Pork Man looked over at me to see how that had regis-tered on the insult scale. He decided to change the sub-ject. "Man, this is my time a day. Night! Boy, when the sun goes down, that's when I howl. If I ain't castin a neon shadder by dark-thirty, I start getting nervous. I was reared in the country and you can kick that place in the ass. Nightfall in the big city, that's me. That's how I got my name. That's what P.M. really stans for." He turned to Foose, as an expert. "Say, turd, what does P.M. stan for anyway? I mean the actual words."

Foose studied the fat man carefully. "P.M.," he said, "P.M. stands for pussle mouth."

Pork Man blinked at me: that wasn't Latin.

I went and sat in the back seat of the Studebaker. There were so many beer and oil cans stomped down into the floorboard that I had to stretch my legs out on the seat. I pulled my hat down over my eyes when I saw Foose com-ing. The front door opened and slammed. I snored a little, but Foose said, "You're a regular Albert Schweitzer com-pared to that guy."

I grunted.

"I think he'll be a fascist someday."

"O.K.," I said, tipping my hat back. "Where's Tee?"

"I think I know," he said, grimly watching Pork Man

back in line for another hamburger. "I have a man working on it." He turned around to study me. "Who's in charge, him or you?" I gave him Son's letter. His face showed strain as he read it. He handed the paper back. "So I'm in charge. I wish I believed she knew what she was doing. She's a fine person. Delicate and sensitive . . . Are you a friend of his?"

"I don't know whose friend I am yet. Hers, I guess."

"You too." He looked away, his voice heavy with self-pity. "I guess you want to know some details."

"Might as well."

"Well, to begin, I guess you know he was coming down here to shoot Cunningham."

"How much does he know about them?"

"Everything. He's known about them from the word go. Cunningham has made sure of that. He's a vicious bastard. I hope you don't mind my insulting your friend."

"Well, if Tee has known about them from the beginning, why did he wait till now to shoot Cunningham?"

"Maybe he's just now got up the courage." He shook his head. "No, I don't know. You know, I feel very strongly about her too. I hope you won't say anything about that. Of course I don't think he was serious about shooting anyone. I don't think he *has* shot anyone." He shuddered. "If anything, I think it's . . . it's more likely he'll shoot himself someday . . ."

"Sounds like he ought to go into a rest home or something for a while—"

Foose lashed out, "Where the hell have you been, mister? Don't you know that if he's committed to any kind of psychiatric care the whole house of cards collapses? That sort of talk is playing right into their hands."

"Whose hands is having Tee kill himself or kill somebody else going to play into?" He gave me a look of such guilt that I pushed my hat back over my face.

"I'm not a very religious man. I'm a Unitarian . . ." He

looked to see if I knew what that meant. "Unless of course he's positive that's what he wants to do." He removed his glasses and cleaned them. His eyes were old, bleared with myopia. "But I don't think Tee does."

"Neither do I."

Foose squinted. "But I am afraid he might go down to the border and wise off to some Mexicano and get himself killed that way." He slid his glasses on and looked around. "See, I don't trust you and your fat friend. I think in a way that you or him or both of you have been sent down here by some demented party named Cunningham to see that Tee never gets back across that border alive!"

We studied Pork Man, who was sitting at a table of girls. "How can I get you to trust me, Foose?" He looked back into my face, which had never felt less innocent. "Would you trust me on Adrienne's word?"

His face seemed to grow older; his body shrank. "If she's a fool over one man, she can be a fool over another."

He shook his head sorrowfully.

With P.M. heading back to the car, I said quickly, "Look, I've got an hour's business here before we can take off after him. Call Adrienne, whatever you want to do, but you've got to make up your mind. We've got to try and figure out what the hell is going on and what we're going to do." I paused. "Look, it's going to be me or him. An hour, all right?"

He eyed me balefully. "That's all right. I trust you now. We have more in common than you might think."

# 1 0

Foose let me off at a rent-a-car stand before P.M. had time to protest. Foose said he had a call in to his man in Nuevo

Laredo, so we would know something soon. We agreed to meet at Tee's place in an hour. Foose wrote out the address. River Oaks: Dolly lived in Tanglewood, which was nearby. I rented the biggest car the place had and drove downtown. I parked down by the bayou and started making my way up the skid-row pawnshops. At the third place I found what I wanted. A Spanish Llama .380, nickel-plated, hand-carved grips, a slide action that worked like a rocking chair—but for a hundred bucks it was mine, no questions asked, and a clip filled with ammo. It was the first gun I had touched in fifteen years.

I took the freeway southwest to Tanglewood. I had no trouble finding the new suburb, the streets wide, well marked, and straight. The houses were all one story, dark, sharing lawns as long as the streets. Mr. Dolly's house looked like all the rest.

I rang the bell and after a minute a dim porch light came on and an electronic voice from the peephole asked me to identify myself. After another wait a woman in a cold quilted robe let me in and pointed through a darkened room. The woman disappeared down a hall to a room where a TV talked.

I waited for the banker in a large, dim room. At one end of the room was a fireplace that had never seen fire, shelves of books that had never been read, a large cabinet that probably hid another TV set. Faded etchings hung around the fireplace—scenes from the Old West; a buffalo hunt; a lone coyote howling to the moon; an Indian astride his pony, their heads hung low with exhaustion.

Mr. Dolly appeared quietly. He wore his bathrobe like a business suit. He took the envelope and sat on the couch and studied the contents. I had forgotten to remove Son's instructions, which he read several times, sighing with weariness. He talked as if I were not there—as if I were an animal trained to repeat the sounds of his words. "The primary is set for Saturday. After that the governor will call a special session of the legislature to consider the tax bill. That's when the banking bill will get in. Quick passage is a must. Before our enemies marshal their forces. Now, Laran is to join me in Austin *as soon as possible.*" He again picked up Son's sheet of instructions. "There are to be no more phone calls to me at the bank. None." He tossed the paper and it whirled to the floor. "Did you say you worked for Gunner?"

"No. You asked me that before. I used to be in the oil business, but that was in California."

"Son says you need a loan of some money."

"I might. If I decide to settle down."

"Would you like to work for me?"

"I don't think so, but you never can tell."

"It's worth a retainer of two thousand dollars. The job is simple." Dolly raised his feathery white hands. "I know Laran's plans. I'm amazed that he might think I don't." Then the banker's face twisted, as if he tasted the venom in his voice. "Everybody knows he's buying another man's wife! Buying his way in!" And then his calm returned, as if it had never disappeared. "I know that Laran will leave me for another, I know it well. I simply want to know when—in advance. *We must stick together during the coming trials!* Have him call me. And not at the office." The banker rose and with no gesture of dismissal left me to find my way out of the house.

I drove to Son's apartment. I was beginning to feel crazy from the lack of sleep. I tried to call the ranch but the operator said the line was down. An hour had already passed, but for some reason I sat reading a newspaper. A small item caught my eye. Some politician had committed suicide. I glanced at the front page and saw that I had read the same stories in California over a month ago. The phone rang. It was Foose. Adrienne had called: Caroline

Jo had told her that someone had a contract on Tee. Foose knew it was Pork Man—almost as soon as they had got to Tee's house, the fat man had disappeared. Foose's voice was garbled and piteous: "He said he was going out to get something to eat."

"It's all right, Foose. Did she say anything else?"

"She said—she said they were going to kill us too."

"O.K. Have you got a gun?"

"A gun?"

"Lock the doors and windows, Foose, and don't let anybody in till I get there."

"Lock the doors and windows, that would take hours—"

"O.K., leave them open." And I hung up.

Down the hall a door slammed and I flinched. I took out the Llama and unloaded and cleaned the gun with a dish towel, then loaded it again. Then I drove to River Oaks.

I parked across the street from the address Foose had given me. His old Studebaker sat in the drive, cowering like a beggar before the house that was too big, too opulent, too white. Every light in the house was on, everything perfectly still. I left the pistol in my pocket and walked along the grass border of the drive. The front door was open. I could hear nothing. I pushed the door back as far as it would go, then stepped inside. The front room was empty and dark; it smelled stale. In the center of the room stood a pool table; beyond was a dining room so long it looked like a hall. A table ran its length. The dining room was dark too, but at the far end was a lighted doorway. I could hear someone moving around, the sound of bottles clinking. I started to call out, then waited. I heard another person walking around on the second floor. I found a chair just inside the door to the dining room. I took out the gun, sat down, and called out softly, "Hey."

The movement in the kitchen stopped. Then Pork Man's voice: "Who is that out there?"

I steadied the gun with my left hand and didn't answer. P.M. came through the door, faster than I had expected, but he stopped, silhouetted against the lighted doorway. He held something in his hands. "Drop it, you goddamn sonofabitch," I told the fat man.

Pork Man didn't move. His voice broke the calm: "Whaddaya mean, drop it?"

"Drop it, P.M., or I'm going to blow you half in two."

"Aw lissen, what're you talkin about it's just a plate a food all right all right!" And he dropped the plate to the floor. It made a very loud crash. Then footsteps came along the hall upstairs, then silence, then at the top of the stairs Foose's querulous voice:

"What's going on down there?"

I tried to speak to the fat man reasonably: "P.M., if you move I'm going to kill you." Then I yelled at Foose: "Get your ass down here!"

I could hear the little man angrily banging down the stairs, muttering when he came into the room.

"Watch it, he's got a gun!" yelled Pork Man and leaped back through the kitchen door. I just couldn't shoot him, not with Foose standing there sucking his cheeks. P.M. switched on the dining-room chandelier and for a second we were all blinking. "That idjit made me drop a plate a food with a sandwich on it."

Foose turned white as he stared at the gun. "I've been trying to get this place cleaned up."

"Are you goin outta your head?"

"Come in and have a seat, P.M. You too, Foose. Now *you* tell me what's going on around here."

Pork Man and Foose glanced at each other, then sat down at the long table, Pork Man at the end, Foose near me. I think Foose gave me a meaningful look behind his frosted glasses. "All right, Foose," I said, "what's this about P.M. going to kill Tee?" Pork Man looked surprised too late. It was enough. I handed the gun to Foose, who wouldn't look at it. "I'm not sure I'm giving this to the right man, but you keep an eye on our fat friend here while I call Son. If he makes a funny move, just jerk back on that little thing right there." Showing good judgment, Pork Man was more afraid of Foose with a gun than me. "Where's the telephone?"

"Under the pool table. Here's the number you can reach him at." Foose handed me a scrap of paper.

"He's not at the ranch?"

"No, no," said Foose, holding the gun with both hands. "He's in Lubbock. Everything's all right. He called back and said Adrienne got everything confused."

"Maybe. Just keep that gun pointed at our friend." I watched the two men till the phone began to ring, then I closed the doors. Son answered the phone laughing. He kept laughing when I told him what had happened. "It's all my fault, Sugar, with all this shit going on, Adrienne panicked and I let myself get a little carried away. See, Caroline Jo and Larry had this row over P.M. and whether they ought to move over to the Big House, and C.J. had one of her fits and comes out with this story about over-hearing P.M. talking on the phone yesterday, and well, A. has been under sedation, and when the two of them got together everything got all fucked up. A. just wasn't in shape to handle C.J. and vice versa. But she's all right now, we got her sleeping it off."

"Sleeping it off. What did she say, Cunningham?" I heard a woman's voice interrupt: "Is that her?"

Son didn't muffle the receiver. "Keep your mouth shut, honey." Then to me: "I'd still keep my eye on P.M. if I were you. He's erratic."

"I'm beginning to think I'm the one who's erratic. I don't know what the hell is going on, Son."

"No, you boys are doing a good job. Ty said you'd narrowed it down to Nuevo Laredo. Why don't you pick up my car at the airport and drive on down tonight and poke around and see if you can find him. P.M. can bring the plane back when the weather clears up. Treat it as a little vacation, son."

"Are you sure P.M. isn't out to kill anybody?"

"No, no, you can trust him, son, he's harmless. Take Foose along with you if you want to. He's a friend of the family, you can trust him."

"For what it's worth." But Son was laughing again, so I hung up the phone. There were at least a hundred questions I hadn't asked him.

When I got back to the other room, Pork Man had the gun. Foose lowered his head and grinned. P.M. pointed the gun at me a second, then slid it down the table. "I was just tellin yore little buddy you oughter file off that front sight, Campbell, cause someday somebody's goin to jam that sonofabitch up yore ass."

# 1 1

Foose didn't want to go with us. He apologized for the mix-up. Son had called back after Foose had talked to me, changing the story about P.M. Foose had assumed that Son would call me. He said he hadn't trusted Cunningham till P.M. had returned and convinced him of the truth. By the time they had called me back, I had left Son's apartment.

Tee's car had been traced to Laredo. Foose gave us the number of a man there who was already out combing boystown. Probably he would have found Tee by the time we got to the border. We would call in every two hours to be sure everything was all right. To save time Foose would drive us to the airport where Son's car was, then return the rent car. When Pork Man went upstairs, Foose took me aside. His voice trembling, he warned me about P.M. "See, I still don't trust him. I still think he's been hired to kill Tee."

"I'll keep an eye on him. You got anything to keep me awake?"

"Pills." We went into the kitchen, where I stuck my head under the faucet, and, hoping I could trust Foose, swallowed some of his pills with my whiskey. I leaned against something and watched Foose. He was crying or his eyes were watering an awful lot.

"I can't seem to think," I said. "Who do you think has hired P.M.?"

Foose sneered. "You know who."

"No, I don't know who. Why not Adrienne herself? She has as good a reason to see Tee dead as Cunningham. Maybe that call was just to throw us off."

"She'd never—"

"And how about the old man? He sounds like the sort of bastard who would kill a man for his own good."

"I don't think so—"

"And what about Denton, or maybe one of those crazy kids from Toro, or any number of other folks, Foose? Why is everybody always picking on poor old Son Cunningham?"

"Picking? If you think . . . why, you're mad!"

"Maybe so. Maybe we all are. But just because everything points to Cunningham, that doesn't mean that somebody else might not be setting it up to look that way. That ever cross your mind?"

Foose looked away. "It could be. The world *is* standing on its head."

"I'm glad we agree about one thing. Now tell me what you know about P.M."

"I don't know much. He's not from around here. I think

he used to operate out in California." He looked at me. "That's why I thought you might know him."

"Somebody said he's served some time. You got any idea what for?"

Foose shook his head. "Something violent, I bet."

"June told me that Pork Man was actually working for the insurance companies, that he really wants to keep Tee alive."

"Could be, still . . . I just feel it in my bones, that he's working for Cunningham."

"So what do you think we're going to find down in Mexico?"

"Tee. Drunk, helpless, an easy target."

"If Cunningham has hired the fat man to see that Tee never gets back across the border, then why am I being dragged along?"

When he spoke his voice was listless: "I don't know, I don't know."

We found Pork Man waiting for us on the front steps. Foose drove us to the airport, where we picked up Son's car. I let Pork Man drive and fell asleep on the outskirts of Houston. I woke in San Antonio. I touched the gun in my pocket and P.M. laughed. "You fuckin amatoor."

I hurt everywhere, but that was real. What my mind would not accept was that I was holding this fat bastard's hand while he went to Mexico to kill a man. I sat up and let my head fall back against the seat. My neck cracked like a board. "What are we doing off the freeway?"

P.M. shrugged his mouth. "Seein a man about a dog." We drove on in silence. The more Pork Man thought about it, the more pissed off he got. Finally he said, "I'm gettin me a .44 magnum, by God, then I'll teach you to fuck with me!"

To see if it would help, I apologized for making P.M. drop his sandwich.

We had stopped at a blinking signal and P.M. looked at

me closely. "You wanna know my advice, buddyboy. With the friends you got, you don't need no enemies." We drove on through the dark ghetto of west San Antonio. Pork Man told me he had once had a church in this part of town. He laughed and laughed. "Bet you din't figger me for a preacher, huh? What a racket that was. Made *The Noo Yark Times* when they caught up with us. Only problem we hared a crooked crook to keep books. Still figger there's somethin fishy bout that law they got me on. Boy, was life sweet back in them days. Anyway, I did my time in the joint. I paid for it." He eyed me carefully. "You ever been inside? It's terrible. You know how much it costs to get you a broad in there? Bet you din't know you could fuck a whoor while you was in the joint."

"No, I thought everybody was queer."

"Huh?"

Why not get tough for a while, like they do in the movies? "That's what I read in the bus station one time. Cornholing going on all the time."

Pork Man's face had risen like a blister. "Naw, that's just some bushit wrote by one a them—"

"Aw, come on, P.M., I bet you got fucked in the ass so much your turds are going thirty miles an hour by the time they hit ground. I bet they bounce like golf balls."

"Golf balls," Pork Man muttered, wildly searching the empty street for a woman.

"This where your friend with a dog lives?"

We had stopped on a dark street. Pork Man looked around. "Yeah. See that telephone booth right down there, chubby cheeks? Well, you just trot down there and call up the shrimp while I talk turkey to this feller."

I held out my left hand. "Give me the car keys."

"Huh? Nothin doin, shit breath—"

With my right hand I pulled the gun out of my pocket and punched it where everybody else has ribs. "Give me those keys, you tub of guts." He gave me the keys.

"All right," he said, doing a miserable job of faking hurt feelings, "if you ain't goin to trust me, I ain't goin to trust you. We'll go inside together. We'll stick together like the fuckin gold-dust twins. And lissen," he said as we stumbled across the pitch-dark street, "this here used to be my brother-in-law, so watch it." Pork Man pounded on a door that looked like the lid to a pine box. We waited, for hours, it seemed, in that narrow tunnel of black. Then a Mexican woman stuck her head out the door and began speaking a low, hurried Spanish. Pork Man started cussing her out, mainly in English. Leaving the door open, the woman went across the room, opened another door, and spoke to someone within. She came back and in stilted English asked us to come in. P.M. had called her a few really terrible names, but she nodded and climbed back onto a foldaway bed in the corner of the room, joining two children. She blew out the candle, leaving us standing in the dark room. "You don't know how much I do for these people," Pork Man said bitterly.

In a moment a Mexican man holding a candle came out of the bedroom. Short, brawny, dressed in khaki pants and an undershirt, he yawned at us quizzically. Pork Man pushed him back into the bedroom and closed the door behind them. There in the dark room, listening to the children's steady breathing as they dropped off to sleep, everything began to make too much sense. If Foose was right and Pork Man had plans for Tee, then he would have to have the same plans for me. Or maybe the plans were just for me. I yanked open the front door. The Lincoln was still parked across the street. A drunk was stumbling along the sidewalk. He started toward me, mumbling Spanish. I shut the door and he pounded on it. The woman yelled something out, and he cursed her and went away. I had had enough of this. I went over to the bedroom door and shoved it open. On the bed sat a dresser drawer, one end of it stacked with twenty-dollar bills, the rest of the space piled with handguns. The Mexican and P.M. watched me with cool surprise. Pork Man's hand moved and I saw dull-gray metal slide into his pocket, as smooth as the grin he wiped across his face. He spoke to the Mexican in fluent Spanish. The Mexican nodded, picked up the drawer, and slid it back into the dresser. P.M. hitched up his pants and smirked. "See you later, coonyow." The Mexican blew out the candle.

We went back to the car. I said I would drive, and that was a mistake. Pork Man was snoring outside Cotulla and didn't wake up till we got to Laredo. I thought about trying to take the gun away from him, but he was using it for a pillow. When I pulled the Lincoln into a gas station on the edge of Laredo, I was numb with exhaustion, Pork Man red-eyed and arrogant. I called the number Foose had given me and a woman's voice, lightly accented, told me Abel was across the border. She thought one of his men had located Tee, but she wasn't sure. She gave me a Nuevo Laredo number to call. I was to call back in an hour if I couldn't reach anyone there. When I got back to the car, P.M. had slid under the wheel. We parked on the American side and walked across the International Bridge. It was just after midnight and the streets were still crowded.

We took a cab out to boystown and were dropped in front of the Club Chi Chi Mango. We climbed high broad steps to a pastel patio lightly scattered with Mexican whores. We found a table and were joined by two plump whores, one who had been around and one who hadn't. P.M. bought mom and the kid a couple of tequila glasses of water and told them to go play with the jukebox. After they had gone he said, "Well, whadda you think we ought to do first?" His face twitched as if someone had kicked him under the table. "Actually I gotta make a phone call first."

"What phone call have you got to make? Another man with a dog?" But I was hurting his feelings again. "All right, all right. Why don't you call up this number and see if Foose's friend has found Tee. Then we'll decide what to do."

Pork Man studied the scrap of paper. "All right, you stay here."

"All right, P.M." And the fat man left, his face strained and uncertain. The older whore came back and I gave her five bucks and asked her if she had seen a crazy gringo cowboy, one with long blond hair. She hadn't, she didn't even understand what I was talking about. I had finished my tequila when I realized Pork Man wasn't coming back. Why should he? He had the keys to the car, the airplane, the phone number in Nuevo Laredo, the number in Laredo; I didn't even know the number at Tee's house in River Oaks. Instead of considering any number of sane actions, like walking back to West Texas, I went out looking for the fat man.

It was easy. I went back inside the Chi Chi Mango—a cold tile cavern inhabited by three drunk flyboys—and found the phone sitting at the end of the bar. I was standing there looking at it when the bartender came down and asked if I was looking for my friend. My head had begun to ache, something inside it was frozen solid. The bartender had overheard the conversation and had written down the address. I looked at the piece of paper: Hotel La Amazona 19. It was near the plaza near the bridge. Maybe there was a cab waiting out behind the club, he said, if I wanted to join my friend. I asked how many calls my friend had made. The bartender's English broke down. The cab driver turned up stone deaf. He could have driven to the hotel without being told.

The hotel fronted on a small dark plaza. I had the driver let me out on the far side of the plaza. I sat on a cold stone bench and considered the hotel. The nicest thing would be to find P.M. trying to sober Tee up. But why couldn't we do that together? Maybe P.M. was working for old man Kitchens and was supposed to take Tee back to the Big House, away from Adrienne, Son, myself, the other bad influences. The thing is, sitting there in that dark and lonely plaza, it didn't seem like a bad idea. Maybe life with Mom and Dad visiting every other Sunday wouldn't be all that bad. Maybe Foose was right. Maybe P.M. would find Tee unconscious, maybe he would kill him. Maybe he would kill me—dress me up in a pair of cowboy boots and feed me to the snakes. I rose and began walking along the gravel path. I could see Tee huddled naked in a cell. I could see him dead. I could see him lying in wait for me in that room. I could see anything. I could even see why I was about to go prowling through this cheap hotel on the Mexican border—that in a matter of a few minutes I could be killing a man.

Hotel La Amazona was dark and grim. Built American-style, with a false front, and behind that a patio and swimming pool flanked by two stories of rooms which opened onto facing balconies that served as open hallways. The night desk was empty, dark, though beyond a bead curtain I could hear low music, voices, the sounds of a cocktail lounge. When my eyes grew accustomed to the dark, I saw the burned-out neon sign: CLUB AMAZONA. There was no register at the desk, no sign of a clerk, and I didn't look around for either.

The patio was lighted only by the two or three night lights still burning. The pool was half-filled, the lawn furniture ragged, the stone floor grimy. Everything looked worn and dirty. Twenty rooms looked out on the patio, ten to a side, five a story. The patio abutted a ten-foot brick wall. Number 11 was the first room to my left, 16 directly above that. My eyes went down the wall to the next-to-last room, 19, the door in shadows, as if it were slightly ajar. No lights came from any of the rooms, they were all silent. I wanted to go back into the lounge, to have a drink, to ask the barman about Tee, about P.M.; maybe they were there, waiting for me, we would have a nice talk—but I began climbing the stairs. I stopped in the shadows by the first door and took out the little gun and looked at it. My hands were trembling. I took the gun off safety and cocked the hammer. There was a noise below, toward the front of the hotel. A man came out of the club and walked alongside the pool. He seemed to be looking for something in the water. He laughed and threw a small object into the pool, then, muttering curses, went back into the lounge. Then everything was quiet. I could not hear the music from here.

I tried the door to 16. It was open but I didn't go in. I waited another minute, then walked quickly down to 19. The door was cracked open. I stepped into the room and closed the door after me. I knew the smell—rich, choking—but it was too late. There was a blinding flash inside my eyes, then an explosion which jarred my arm, and the side of my head danced with pain. I was on my hands and knees and was kicked or I fell against something sharp. I thought quite clearly that I had fucked up once too often and that I was going to die. A gray light spread out beneath me, and then even in the dark room blackness began to push my sight into a small shrinking gray circle. I lay down and waited for the circle to come to me. But my head began to ache, and the wall and a window and part of the ceiling appeared and slowly brightened and sharpened till I could study their most minute details. For a moment I experienced a fantastic elation. I tried to get up and the side of my head and face burned. I touched the pain and my head was wet and sticky. My fingers left dark streaks on the carpet. I saw the gun in my other hand, miles away.

The door had swung open but I heard nothing. I leaned against the wall and tried to operate the gun's safety; I finally forced it into my pocket. I heard voices somewhere in the distance, but they didn't seem concerned. I was looking toward the window, walking toward it, when I saw someone lying on the floor, his legs hidden by a door to another room. My fear became dull, so heavy I could barely move. I leaned over the man. He lay twisted on his side. I pulled him onto his back. I couldn't see him. I felt his chest and it was mushy. Then with both hands I turned his head. The man's hair was short and dark, his face was covered with blood. I pulled him up into the light. I had never seen him before, so I let him drop.

# 1 2

From the window it was ten feet down to a dead-end alley. I walked back out to the balcony. Two men stood frozen part way up the stairs. Two more stood below them, near the pool, turning around as if they were lost. The men on the stairs were watching me. I waved my arm. "El otro lado," and began walking very carefully toward the stairs. The men on the stairs retreated. They didn't speak or try to stop me, and I walked out the front door and across the plaza toward a cab. It was the bartender's friend. He had been waiting for me. "Una problema," I told him as I got in the front seat. "Una accidento. Necisito un médico, necisito un médico amigo. Sabe?" And I gave him a hundred-dollar bill and he said he understood. He even became friendly. The doctor's apartment was green. I thought it was a hospital—through a darkened courtyard, up four flights of stairs greased with broken glass, the grumpy nurse in slippers and housecoat, the children sleeping in the waiting room, the doctor working on me in the kitchen, the driver closely supervising, drinking mescal from a green bottle with a worm curled stiff and dead at the bottom. I gave the doctor another hundred-dollar bill. In Spanish he told me about the wound. I said I wanted a hat and they laughed. The bandage bulged from my temple like a slippery turban. I began to laugh too and the doctor gave me a shot of mescal.

The driver got me back across the border with no problem. I almost fell asleep in the cab. It was two-thirty when he let me off in front of the bus station, which looked like the bottom of a boot. I bought a ticket only as far as Lubbock. That would throw them off. I sat by four old women who kept arguing about everything. They changed into college kids but they still didn't like each other. I fought sleep, for I knew if I couldn't stay awake they would catch me. I kept whispering my departure time to the clock on the wall. My mouth was dry but the idea of water made me sick. To stay awake I began to imagine that I hadn't killed the man in the room. Then piece by piece I remembered that someone else had been there with us. He had shot at me, not the dead man. He had killed the dead man, not me. He had kicked me and run out. He had left the door open. Now I remembered the sound of his exertion. The strain. The dead man was a stranger, but the fat killer I knew.

I wanted to see if I had fired my gun. But my pocket was empty. I checked again. The little gun was gone. Two cops in heavy boots strolled around the waiting room, but they checked only Mexicans. Someone woke me at three-thirty and said our bus was about to leave. When I woke again it was light, early morning, the bus had stopped. Out the window I could see people lined up, the driver taking their tickets. A woman sat by me. I told her to wake me up before we got to Lubbock. She moved to another seat. In Lubbock I bought a ticket for Flavannah. The air was hot, dry. Something was wrong with my body, but there was no locus for my pain. I had the driver let me out on the highway and I walked to Son's house. I puked in a ditch alongside some lady's flowers. I was sick again at the house. My sphincter collapsed. I threw the mess in the bathtub and feebly tried to clean myself. Naked I curled around the toilet; the floor there was soft and I was warm.

I dreamed they came and got me. My name was being called out. I repeated it and smiled. Then I remembered Son picking me up and carrying me out to a car. He carried me as if I were a child. Adrienne was in the back seat and I buried my face in her lap, where everything was soft and warm. I then dreamed that Tee had cut off his hair and dyed it black and I had killed him and I reached down and found a soft hole in his chest. I put my hand through and was sucked into a whirlpool of eyes which became mouths that told me I was never coming back, never coming back. I drifted up and there was a small rusted man sitting beside my bed. I told him the oxygen tanks had kept me from sinking and he grinned. His teeth were black but I didn't care. Adrienne was standing at the foot of the bed. I told her she loved me and I dreamed she smiled and turned away.

When I woke, a knife was thrashing inside my head. They had been waiting for days for my eyes to open and they dragged me up and began trying to make me drink something. It was delicious. I thanked them and dropped the glass, but I never heard it hit the floor. I drifted back into a painless sleep. They were all standing around the room, but something was wrong. Pork Man was there and I didn't want to kill him. And Tee, Tee had cut his hair and dyed it black.

"What day is it?" I finally said.

"It's Thursday or Friday," somebody said and we both laughed. I tried to sit up but my head was swollen and sore. The old man helped me, stuffing a pillow behind my back. I asked who he was and he said a horse doctor and we laughed again.

"Where am I?"

"Yore here at the ranch. What's left of it."

"What's happened to it? Has it burned down?"

"You don't worry about that. There's enough chiefs around here to take care of everything."

"But I want to help her. Get her out of here."

"We're all gettin out a here, old boy, so you don't worry about that neither."

"Where the hell am I?" But I didn't hear the answer. This time I dreamed about what happened and I saw clearly why Tee wanted to kill me, why they both wanted to kill me. I was unstoppable. I dreamed about Adrienne. She was dressed in a white shirt and I reached out and touched her face. She dropped her head and I raised her face. I held her face in my hands. I thought how friendly her look was. Son was sitting at a desk, pretending to study a curving line of figures, but he was watching us. He looked bored, but his expression changed—to dread and fear, till finally he was dead. Adrienne touched his shoulder, so that he toppled onto the floor.

Someone helped me sit up in bed and my head throbbed like an explosion; it lasted fifteen seconds. I asked somebody to draw the curtains and in the dark I could see. Son stood by the window, Tee sat in a chair at the foot of the bed. Pork Man sat to my right. Everyone looked serious. Someone was standing behind me, but my neck was solid pain when I tried to turn my head. They asked how my head was and I asked what had happened. Tee opened a notebook and began looking it over. "That's what we've come here to find out from you." He flipped through the notebook, then smiled at me across the foot of the bed like a doctor who's glad you're never going to get well. "What did happen, ole buddy?"

"Why don't you ask that fat sonofabitch over there?"

Pork Man made a motion like under normal circumstances he would have rushed me. "Whaddaya mean, ast me? Why don't you start in splainin where you run out on me—"

"Shut up, P.M. Why did you leave P.M. and go off on your own?"

"What are you talking about? He ran off and left me and then took a shot at me in that goddamned hotel room, whatever the name of that hotel was."

"See, still delirous. He ought be over there with June Bug—"

"What hotel?"

Like a chill the faintest idea of what was happening came over me. The dead man in Mexico needed a killer. "No, I can't remember the name of the place. But P.M. ought to remember. He took the phone call telling us you were there."

Pork Man did the number of laughing so hard he almost fell off his chair. Tee cut him off. "All right, Campbell, let's hear your side of it."

"The side with the nuts on it."

"I'm warning you, fat boy—"

"You and what other twenny flab-bellied—"

Tee threw down his notebook and yelled. Then he smoothed back his hair and picked up the notebook, his hands unsteady. His nails were pared and I noticed now that he wore a business suit and tie. His face was ghostly, stained white except for the dark circles under his eyes. He tried to smile. "You said somebody tried to shoot you. That place on your head wasn't made by a bullet. Is that what you meant?" It was a nurse standing behind me. Her white arm reached out and adjusted the covers. "What do you—why do you think P.M. tried to shoot you?"

"Because he thought it was you, Kitchens." Nobody moved or spoke. "Because he left this message telling me to meet him there. And when I walked in the door, he tried to kill me. He thought he was killing you."

P.M. made a noise with his lips. Tee considered it as carefully as words. "What were you doing in Mexico?" But he waved off an answer. "You were only chasing my car. I loaned it to a friend. I was shacked up in Galveston. Who told you I was in Mexico?"

"I can't remember his name."

"Foose."

"What the hell was he doing in on this?"

There was a pause. Son said, "It was Adrienne who—"

"Shut up!" Tee suddenly clutched his temples, then released his hands into fists. "These goddamn headaches are driving me crazy! Why are we talkin about this shit?"

P.M. said in a hushed tone, "Better ast him what he said when he was delirous."

Tee let his hands fall over the arms of the chair. His head dropped against his chest, though his eyes were still open. "I can't remember anything."

It was Son who spoke. "You said there was a dead man in your hotel room."

"He shot that mother—"

"Shut up, P.M.," Son said pleasantly.

With effort Tee raised his head. His eyes looked weak. "How about it? Did you think it was me?"

I looked very confused. "I don't know what you're talking about."

Pork Man looked like he had been lied to, betrayed, and shortchanged. "Why, you said layin right there talkin in yore sleep—"

"There was no dead man in that hotel room, not unless

you count me as close. How in the hell would I shoot any-body anyway? I don't even have a gun."

"Why you lyin sack a shit. He was threatenin me and Foose all night long."

"The only person who had a gun was fat boy there. We made a special stop in San Antone so he could pick one up."

There was another silence, which Son broke. "I think Jamie better leave the room for a few minutes." Tee nodded, and the nurse tugged at the covers, gave my shoulder a pat, and left.

Tee turned to Pork Man. "Who did you see in San An-tone?"

Pork Man glared at me. "Raphael."

"Are you workin for me or not?"

"For you—"

"Then goddamnit I don't want you seein that bunch any more!"

The fat man's hatred swung around. "Yessir."

Tee watched me. "Better tell us if you did shoot that ole boy. Maybe we can get you out of it."

"I'm telling you, there's nobody dead in Mexico. Not to my knowledge. P.M. and I drove down there together, he disappeared, planted a phony message with the bartender, one of his Mexican buddies took me to the place where they said you were, P.M. or some sloppy pig just like him took a shot at me. I hit my head falling down. On the way back home I got sick. Maybe he doctored my drink. That's it."

Everyone looked at Pork Man. Thinking for him was like running, he was almost swinging his arms. Then it came to him: "I didn't want to tell you before, boss, I wanted to perteck the punk, but I guess I better tell now to perteck him from hisself." He nodded: that was pretty good. "See, when we got to 'co, I went off to git me a little pussy. I was tellin the wino here you wadn't down there, it was just bushit concocted up by that little niggerlover in Houston. I tole him a little pussy would relax him, but he said it was just another dirty hole to him. Anyways, when I got back the turd had gone. Now you know the stories C.J. was handin out durin her epilepsy about a hared gun out to gun you down like a dawg. Well, that got me nervous bout this lizard. I mean, what's he doin here anyways. Well, I got to astin round and the bartender said he had overheard the phone talk and had wrote down this here address. Right here"—he put his hand in his pocket and wiggled his fingers around—"19 Hotel Amazona, it said. Well," said P.M., rolling his tongue as if lies were marbles, "I went there right away and there was a dead man strung out on the floor. It scared me to death, Tee Texas, I thought it was you."

"How come you didn't think it was me?" I said.

Pork Man chortled. "Wishful thinkin."

"*You* say there was a dead body there and *you* say there wasn't a dead body there. It wasn't the right one." Tee had slumped in his chair, a hand shielding his eyes. His shoulders began jumping, a chattering noise distorted his face. The noise became laughter. He waved his hand. "Was it? *Was it?* So you boys killed some spick while you was layin for me. Fuck it all, Son, you shoulda known it wouldn't work. I coulda told you so." He listlessly made his way to the door, which he opened by letting his body sag against it but slammed with a sudden violence. Son walked over and stood in front of Pork Man. He reached down but didn't touch him. "Fat man, don't ever fuck up like that again." Somehow Pork Man got out of the chair and left the room without touching Son and without Son having moved. Son came over and sat on the edge of the bed. "Well, I don't know what happened, but if you got anything to worry about, don't. I got a federale down in

Monterrey covering everybody's tracks whether they need it or not." He watched me and I didn't say anything. He nodded. "Did you see Dolly?"

"Yeah. I got the papers to him."

"Did he say anything interesting?"

"He misses you. He wants you in Austin right after the election."

"I'm going to be in Austin, but it ain't going to be for him. I've got to find somebody to take over my place here toot sweet."

"Hell, Son, that might take light-years."

"Don't be bitter, Sugar." He smiled. "Next week we'll be down in Austin drinking out of doors. A couple of rats leaving the ship. What do you think?"

"You're the expert. What do you think?"

He looked around the room. "Yeah," he said slowly, looking back at me, "she is sinking fast. Tee wants to give it one more try. We're going to take one more little trip. I'll call you tomorrow night. Be sure your bags are packed."

"Wait, I want to go . . ." I said, but found myself falling asleep. Like really falling, I knew it was happening but couldn't do anything about it. Several people came in later that afternoon and night, bringing food or medicine, but I never really woke. At one time during the night Adrienne sat on my bed. She leaned down and kissed me, but it was just another dream.


# 1 3


The next morning I woke early and found some clothes left for me and slipped out of the house. It felt like escaping from a jail abandoned by its keepers. I walked around the ranch headquarters; everything was at peace. But I quickly grew tired and went back to my room and lay on the bed and watched the ceiling. If I was going to do anything, I was going to have to get up. I was woken by someone setting a breakfast tray on the table. I seemed to be able to do nothing but sleep. The old doctor woke me the next time. He told me about Coolie, that he had been fired. These were his clothes I was wearing. The ones he had left behind.

About noon I ate a few bites from the tray, then went up to the roof, where I met Anna, Adrienne's friend with the green teeth. Her teeth weren't quite as green in the daylight. I sat on the lounge beside her. We impugned each other's sexuality for a while; then I began laughing and found that I couldn't stop. "What are you doing up here anyway? At the ranch, I mean."

"Drying out my sinuses."

"Let's talk about something else. What's going to happen now? Is she going to leave him?"

"You said it. But you're boy friend's boy friend, aren't you? Well, boy friend is going to be left behind too. But that doesn't bother you, does it? Your penis is hanging out, mister." Her bitterness dissolved itself. "It's a sad mistake."

"What is she going to do?"

"Leave him. I don't know what she's going to do." She took a breath. "Go to Houston and set up the gallery she's always wanted. And be among her friends, where she's always belonged."

Anna started to go on but stopped. I turned and saw Adrienne and a small dark woman standing at the shallow end of the pool. It was as though they hadn't seen us; they stood looking into the water. Adrienne was talking so quietly that we both watched the gentle movement of her lips. The two women moved around to the far side of the pool. Adrienne smiled at us, but the other woman did not look up, as if there were something caught at the bottom of the pool. Anna raised her glass. "Five o'clock somewhere," she called out in a harsh, nervous voice. They joined us, Adrienne sitting on the deck, her knees drawn up under her chin. The dark woman—they told me her name was Michelle—kept staring into the water. Adrienne shifted her smile to me. "I'm sorry, but you were very funny last night."

"I felt hilarious."

She looked away, lightly tapping the knuckle of her thumb against her lips.

"Nothing seems funny any more," said Anna. "The world is dark and ugly and gray."

Michelle and Anna talked about a picnic. I was invited. "We're going to ride out to Sour Tongue Creek," Adrienne said. "It might be good for you."

"It might at that."

"I'll phone down and have another horse saddled. You're well enough to ride?"

"A nice old horse."

Adrienne smiled. "I think the Rover might be better."

I agreed to meet them downstairs in fifteen minutes. The three women left. I lay back on the lounge. The sunlight felt gritty, like hot yellow dust. I was falling asleep again. I forced myself to my feet and went over and looked out across the ranch. Toward the south burning silver clouds hung in the sky; they looked like monuments to great dead heroes.

We took the Land Rover out the south road, but before long Adrienne turned off and headed overland. Michelle pointed out a field of wildflowers, and at the top of a ridge we stopped. Anna and Michelle walked on down toward a larger field of flowers, their colors mixed, blue, orange, white. Adrienne and I sat on a ledge, its rocks soft and crumbling, and watched the two women kneeling, gently resting the flowers' blossoms in their hands. "For a long time I wanted to write the history of this ranch," Adrienne said, "but now I don't guess I ever will. I've finally realized it's only people I'm interested in, not things, or people who I know only as things. The person who should write it is Tee, but of course he'll never do it, not now, and when he dies it will be lost. I have some stories on tape, the stories Tee got from his grandfather. He was a fascinating man." She looked down toward the women who had moved beyond the field of flowers and were watching a hawk soar up and up and up. "Tee's grandfather drove all over this ranch before there were roads. He bought a car back in ought thirteen and they had to go up to Trinidad to pick it up. I don't think Mr. Kitchens had ever seen a car before but he had such an uncanny mechanical sense that he seemed to know all about them. He drove back through Raton Pass when it was nothing but a wagon trail. There was a good road down from Amarillo but it stopped at the cap rock. Mr. Kitchens simply headed across the plains, with hard rubber tires and carbon lights and a way of doing things with baling wire. How he had a son like Malcolm, God only knows."

"You don't sound fond of your father-in-law."

"He's not worth hating, amigo." She paused. "He has cancer, I guess you know."

"No, I didn't know."

"It's a terrible disease, but he's a terrible man. I know that sounds terrible itself, but it's true."

"How bad is he?"

She looked at me strangely, then shuddered. "Not this bad." She looked away. "Tee used to be good. If I hadn't come along, it never would have happened. Tee would've given up, he would've let Malcolm have him. Without me he would have never known the difference. He would have been better off, wouldn't he?"

"I don't know. Maybe."

"I wonder if we're not all much weaker than we think we are. Life is a terrible game, isn't it? Did you kill that man in Mexico?"

"No."

"They say you did. Will you tell me what happened?"

"Not today."

"How did you really get that wound?"

"Someone tried to shoot me."

"Are you sure?"

"No. They could have been shooting at somebody else. Why did you call and warn me, Adrienne?"

She shook her head. "Somebody thought you might have tried to kill yourself."

"I'm not the type."

"He is, I'm afraid." She looked up quickly. "Tee is. Did you know that?"

"No, I don't know. Adrienne, we've got to talk."

"About us?"

"No, about the two men who died, about what was supposed to happen in Mexico, about what I almost did in Mexico." She didn't speak. "What's happening to Tee, Adrienne? What's happening to all of us?"

"Not now. Later," she said, as if she hadn't understood what I had said. She looked down the hill. "Did you know that Anna and I were roommates at Smith? I flatter myself to think she was in love with me at one time. There's hardly ever been anything sexual between us. Hardly ever." Her anger disappeared before I realized it had been directed at someone else. "You know, I do long for the days when we were"—she smiled—"not so rich. It's as if he has no control over it. There's something driving him.

My first friend used to say that money has a will of its own, one that man can't govern. Oh, you can push around a dollar or a million of them, but the whole thing is out of control. In its rational way money goes berserk. And the seductive thing about it is that it drags you up, not down. No, there's the illusion you're going up, something like a diver who has gone so deep that he's drawn down and down, thinking that at any moment he will break through to the surface. Daddy hated my friend so much. I once thought he had hired a man to kill him. My friend just laughed. He was always laughing at me, such kind laughter. I haven't told you about him, have I? That's what he called himself. My first friend. You remind me of him. So calm and resigned. I don't mean to say that. I don't know if you are resigned or calm. My friend's placidity was like an illness. He knew that. He was the first man I loved. I sometimes think the only one. It's odd that I've never told Son about him." She moved her shoulders. "When Tee found out he went crazy with jealousy. He thought someone else was the father of the baby. But there never was a baby. She didn't even die. Our lovemaking turned so cold after that, as if he were trying to reach down inside me and kill what was already dead. Kill whatever he might be making." She was silent for a moment. "For a while after the miscarriage I stopped eating. He thought I was losing weight for someone else. I know it sounds funny now—sometimes I can even laugh about it. One night three or four years ago, he held a gun at my head and made me fuck him and we haven't touched since." She tried to smile. "When I was a girl Daddy told me that only the passage of time cured a hangover and healed a broken heart. I'm sure his hangover that morning lasted longer than my broken heart. But memories, some memories, I think time makes worse. Don't you think that's so?"

"I think time makes most things easier."

"I hope so, I really hope so. I'm so tired of remembering."

"You make it sound like everything is in the past."

"Do I?"

"When are they supposed to be back?"

We looked across the field of wildflowers and the pale-green prairie beyond. The two women were not in sight. Adrienne's face was set, as if an old argument were about to break out. "The men? Who gives a damn. No, not really. Son said he would call tonight. They're in California. Their schemes get wilder and wilder as he nears the end of his rope." She tried to laugh. "Did you know that the other day P.M. was waving around his incredible check for hundreds of thousands of dollars. I mean, it was his check, he had signed it. God, what a farce." She was silent for a moment. "Would you like to see the caves?" We rose and made our way down through the wildflowers. "Do you know a funny thing? Flowers are the sexual organs of plants. You'd think they'd be their faces. Bright, cheerful little faces, wouldn't you?"

# 1 4

I left the women picnicking on the banks of a tree-lined creek which was hidden from the ridge. They would go on to the caves, Adrienne said, and then hike back in. I drove back to the ranch.

There had been a phone call for me. A phone with a portable jack sat on the night stand by the bed and under that a sheet of paper with a Los Angeles number written on it. I called the number, but a woman's voice said my party wasn't in. I gave her my number, hung up, and went to sleep in the chair. The ringing woke me. I felt as clear-headed as if I had been sitting watching the phone. Son sounded tired. He asked me something I didn't understand and he laughed. "Don't tell me you haven't voted."

"I don't know what you're talking about."

"Hell, son, this is election day. Get out and give old Marvin a hand."

"I've got a feeling my poll tax isn't up to date."

"Nobody's perfect. Last year couple hundred dead men voted. What've you been up to while the cat's been away?"

"Sleeping."

"When can you come out here?"

"You're going to have to run that by again."

Son laughed. "I want you out here. Tee's already almost got us killed twice and that ain't counting freeways. Actually, things are looking pretty good. We might actually rustle up some cash, son, might have to go a little bit outside normal anking circles to do it, but c'est la enterprise. How are you feeling?"

"Sleepy."

"I hope you're not getting too much, with ole Anna around."

"No, that's not my problem."

"That's no good either. By the way, son, have I ever told you the world's half full of women and you can have any one of them but her? Have I ever told you that?" I didn't say anything. "That's good. When can you come out?"

"I'm not coming out."

There was a silence. "All right. There are a couple of items you can check out for me there."

"I'm not checking any more items out for you, Son. You're on your own."

Another silence. "That's what it's going to be, Sugar. You're the only man I can trust."

"Then you're hard up, Cunningham."

"This does change things. Would I be boring you if I told you that if you go off by yourself, you might be getting into things you don't know a goddamn thing about."

"I might know more about what's going on than you think."

"Too bad. This does change things. I mean, you might be the difference in making it go one way or the other."

"You're breaking my heart, Son."

"I guess there's always that faint possibility. I'll be seeing you before long." He hung up.

For a moment I thought about dialing him back and telling him that I knew exactly what was going on and his trips to California and his phony promises of money and happiness forever after didn't fool me one goddamn bit. But I think he already knew that. I put down the phone and rolled up in a blanket and decided to wait a little while longer. The phone rang but I didn't answer it. I curled around my burning stomach and waited. Someone came into the room and asked if I was going to the rodeo, and I closed my eyes and went to sleep. When I woke I felt moist and weak, and when I moved my arm, there was no pain to yank it back. The lamp by the bed had been turned off, but light and the sound of voices cut upward through the blinds. The window looked out over the parking lot, where a half dozen cars and four times that number of people had gathered. I closed the blinds and waited till the last car had driven off and everything was quiet. Then I went up to the roof.

About an hour's light was left, the sky a deep blue. The vapor trail of a jet stretched west as far as I could see; above me the smoke crumbled like bone. Nighthawks dived below me, their movement more like falling than flying. I mixed a drink and lay back on one of the lounges and watched the sky turn black. I was no longer sleepy. It was the best I had felt in days. I would be the hero and save them all. I had another drink.

When I got back down to my room, there was another message on the night stand. Adrienne wanted to be sure that I came to the rodeo.

# 1 5

The rodeo was in Estacado, a larger town fifteen miles south of Wadsworth. The road was straight and flat, through a valley that was being irrigated and farmed. Tall, stately trees lined portions of the highway. The town was set into the side of a hill so that I saw the lights from the rodeo grounds from a great distance.

I parked the car on the highway and walked back. The parking lot was almost dark; the arena glared like a small loud day. I leaned against a car and let the cool night breeze drift over me like peace of mind.

I bought a half pint of something from a small worn-out drunk and went up into the stands and watched the great big men on great big horses chase after little bitty calves. I was already attracting some attention by cheering the calves, so talking to myself fit right in. When I saw Pork Man—outfitted in fly-eye sunglasses, a plantation owner's straw hat, ice-creamy sport jacket, and black and white wing-tipped shoes—I yelled at him. He stopped in his tracks and glared at me. He looked just like a big bug. He went down through the crowd, circled the concession stand, climbed the stairs at the far end of the bleachers to the top row, then came down toward me. I patted the empty seat next to me. I think he tried to sit on my hand. "I thought you were in California, big shot. What are you doing lurking around here?" Out of the corner of his mouth, P.M. asked me to shut up. "Fuck you," I said. "Was that you that took a shot at me?"

The people around us were listening carefully—they wanted to know too. Pork Man grabbed my arm. "Let's take a little walk. If you can walk, shit-fer-brains."

"I can walk. I ain't taking a goddamn walk. We're going to sit right here and you're going to tell me what the hell is going on." We were walking down into the crowd. "But I won't let myself be led into any dark alleys with you. You want some Seven-Up?"

P.M. took the Dixie cup and looked into it suspiciously. "What you got in it?" He took a sip and almost choked. "Got me some new threads out in Hollywood," he finally said. "That way they wouldn't recognize me. Whadda you think?"

"Did you come back here to spy on me?"

"Aw, you think yore the center a the fuckin universe, don't you? Nobody gives a good goddamn what you do."

"I thought you were in California bringing home the bacon, fat boy. How come you came back early?"

P.M. hesitated, then doggedly spread his lips. "Aw, don't tell me you hadn't heard. Cunningham beat pore ole Tee up. Hoomiliated. You ain't really in cahoots with that sorry sonofabitch, are you?"

I no longer felt very drunk. "When did it happen?"

"Shit, sometime last night. What difference does it make?"

"But I talked to Cunningham this afternoon. He didn't say anything about it."

Pork Man looked at me suspiciously. "What did he say?"

"He wanted me to come out and help raise money."

The fat man shook his head. "He called you this afternoon and wanted you to come out to California?" He kept shaking his head. "That man is tryin to set somebody up."

"Me? Like Palmer and Billy O.? Is that what was going on in Mexico?"

He shrugged. "I don't know nothin bout them two queers. All I know is that man ain't out fer nobody but hisself and I'd watch it if I was you."

"What happened between him and Tee?"

Pork Man wearily set the cup on the hood of a car. "Ever goddamn deal we had lined up has fell through. Ever goddamn one. It's like it was planned. Naw, nothin this bad coulda been planned." He watched me carefully. "But I can tell you one thing, buddy, if Cunningham is tryin to do Tee in like some people been blabbin, then he's takin his time goin about it. He had plenty a opportunity out there in L.A."

"Maybe it's not time yet. Are they still in L.A.?"

"Not by now. Fact, Cunningham might not a been there when he called you. Everbody's windin their way back home. There's goin to be a big powwow when everbody gits back. I got some real good ideas to save the ranch. If they let me in. Tee has threatened to fare me."

"What for?"

"That goddamn Cunningham's been poisinin Tee's mind against me, that's what for. Tellin him I'm some kinda insurance investigator. When I really care fer that boy, too."

"Bullshit."

"Naw, it's true, I have really growed fond a that man. He's just a crazy squirt, you know that. Gittin fucked-up drunk, runnin stoplights, yellin at niggers, runnin out on fifty-buck whoors, drinkin enough gin to pickle yore wienie." Pork Man morosely hitched up his orange-sherbet trousers. "Lissen, it was touch and go there fer a while. I'm so well-knowed out in the L.A. area that I had to stay in separate motels and everything. I had a run-in with the mob out there in '58. There's a coupla them wouldn't mind seein me worm shit."

"You tried to kill me, you goddamn sonofabitch."

The fat man just laughed. His face was shining way too bright. I carefully set my cup of white lightning on the fender and then hit him in the belly as hard as I could. It felt like he was wearing a steel T-shirt. I thought I would try again with my other hand, but I was so enthusiastic about it, the punch turned the corner like a Greyhound bus. P.M. hit me twice real fast with the same hand and then helped me up. I was starting to like the fat man again—if I had been healthy enough to stand up very long, he probably would have killed me. I went out behind the parking lot and bled into a ditch, while P.M. stood around trying to find the Big Dipper. He finally came over and patted me on the back. "You know, I didn't really try to kill you, boy. It was a accident. I thought it was them comin to git me. I didn't know it was you till I thought you was dead. By that time, I had to think a myself."

"Get your goddamned hands off me. How come you killed that man in the hotel room?"

Pork Man looked me over for a second. If I ever hit him again, it was going to be with something heavy from behind. "It was self-defense, pardner. He tried to kill me first. Anyways, he wasn't dead when I left him."

"Was he part of the mob, P.M.?"

He answered in a low voice. "He thought I was Tee. You know who he was, don'tcha?"

"No, I don't."

"I think it was somebody that snivelin little pinko in Houston hared to rub Tee out."

"Come on, P.M., you can do better than that."

"Why don't you grow up, Campbell. He's in cahoots with that goddamn A."

"That doesn't mean he's going to kill anybody. He just happens to be in love with her too."

"Oh yeah. Well, I wouldn't fuck that bull dyke with yore dick. Aw lissen, buddy, don't you know about her? She ain't no good fer you. I'm just givin out friendly advice now, no matter whether she was married to Tee Texas or not. She'll just throw you over. She's a hardhearted woman. If you ast me, she's the one that wants to git shed a Tee, not Cunningham."

"You don't know what you're talking about."

Pork Man fanned himself with his hat. "Yeah, I do too. Lissen, there's two separate worlds in this country and the railroad tracks runs smack right down the middle a them. Give up them pipe dreams, boy. I had the sweetass on the daughter a one a the J. C. Penney's onct, one a the store managers. It never worked out." I offered him the bottle to deaden the terrible pain, but he shook his head. "Naw, I don't feel like gettin drunk. You feel like pickin up some teenagers?"

"No, I've got some things I want to look into."

"I'm so goddamn low I think I'll go back to the ranch and fuck a cow."

"Maybe you ought to think about settling down. Buy you a dairy farm."

P.M. shook his head and grinned. "Naw, the worst woman is better than the best cow. You wanta drink a coupla beers and tool over to niggertown in Lubbock?"

"No, I'm supposed to meet somebody later on."

"Is that a fact." His face darkened. "Who?"

"Well, I'm thinking about talking to some people over at the Big House. You know, I think I'm going to start nosing around and see if I can find out what the hell is going on around here. I might even try to find out who you are, fat boy."

"Is that a fact. Well, I'd watch my step if I was you,

sweetheart. I'd knock fore I stuck my head through any more whoorhouse doors. I'd let a sleepin dawg lay if I was you." He ambled off through the parking lot, checking out back seats.


# 1 6


Adrienne found me sitting in the stands. She wanted me to take her home. She pressed her face into her hands as if she were crying. "Those fools have let June out," she said, her voice dry. "She's going to kill herself, I know she is. They've practically accused me of putting her there because she was screwing Tee. God, people are vicious. And stupid."

My mind barely moved. "June is out?"

"She's gone off down to Houston. Foose knows where she is, if you want to help her. The old man was here earlier. With Son gone he thinks he can get away with anything. I wish he would go ahead and die. Then things might work out for all of us, instead of . . . I just can't stand their accusations tonight, Sugar."

"What accusations?"

She laid her hand on my arm. "What happened to your face? Did Denton do that?"

"No, P.M."

She looked away. "That bastard. Did he tell you what they've been doing out in California?"

"Some. What about Denton?"

"Denton? He's crawled out of his cave." She spoke in a different voice. "I'll leave my car with Anna, if that's all right."

I drove slowly on the highway. Adrienne laid her head

back on the seat, a strand of her hair trailing out the window. When we got back to the ranch, she packed a basket of cold chicken and with a bottle of wine we went up to her room to wait for the early election returns to begin.

Adrienne began to talk, speaking as if someone else was in the room with us. "Don't think I'm ridiculous, but I envy Son his life. You too, Sugar. I've never had to struggle against anything. I also know what a selfish monster I am." On the TV news were refugees, streams of people fleeing from one demolished city to another. She turned the TV off. The blank tube sat before us like cold gray flesh. "I've got to change my life," she said in a low voice, "or I'll go crazy."

"Anna said you were moving to Houston."

"What does she know. I moved to Houston long ago. No, she's right. I've got to do it officially, finally. I sometimes think the cruelest people are those who can't make up their minds. They gather strong people around them but only to see them as weak as they are. Are you a strong person? I think you must be," she said, not looking at me, "or I wouldn't be attracted to you." She laughed suddenly. "Have you ever wondered what it would be like to have everyone in the world in love with you? It would be like having no one at all." Her eyes didn't move. "I sometimes think I'm looking for someone who doesn't love me. And I sometimes think I've found him. But that's not true. He loves me, only at times . . . I don't know what it is that I feel for him. Only that I've never felt this way about anybody before."

"Not even Tee?"

"Tee might as well be dead." Her head jerked away. She drew her knees up to her body. "I'm sorry, I'm truly sorry."

"Did you ever love Billy?"

"Billy?"

"Did you love him?"

"No. I slept with him of course—but I didn't love him. He was such a strange boy, twenty, twenty-one when he died. It sounds so long ago. He'd been an alcoholic since he was sixteen. He was never the leader of the bunch; the house made him the center. His father built a big house on the outskirts of Toro and then they left him there alone. They went off to Europe and sent him all the money in the world, and all those crazy kids started living there. I met him at a rodeo, some place south of here. Back in my silent period, before things got bad. I was already bad. Tee was good to me then. I remember him as good. It was my birthday and I hadn't been out of my room for something like eighty days—I counted the days by tearing cards in two, and then I put them back together again, except that they never matched, there would be the head of a black queen and the head of a red jack . . . I would sit and watch all the things I had bought. I could see all my previous selves in their faces. I could will people's actions. Everyone at the ranch loved me then. I was the city girl with the crazy saddle and the funny way of riding in my stirrups. They decided to take me to this rodeo, some place. The cowboys, the cooks, Tee, they all came in laughing and joking and dragged me out and threw me in a car and we went off, about thirty or forty cars. I fought them, but then I got drunk. I got so drunk. I was wandering around in the parking lot puking when I ran into this boy wandering around the parking lot puking. It was afternoon and we started driving around, and I mean around all of West Texas. Billy's Impala, my credit card, we drove all over West Texas. For six or seven days we didn't stop. Finally they caught us and brought us back. But instead of beating Billy up, Tee took him in. We had done nothing but talk anyway. Billy's ideas were so strange, but I can't remember them—there was one thing, a strange story about an evil girl who threw a loaf of bread into the mud so that she could step across, but she sank down into the depths of hell, and the insects, the flies she had tortured, she had pulled off their wings, they walked over her face because they could not fly, and finally they walked over her eyes because she could not close them. He told me that was me, that I would never be able to close my eyes. He hated me so much. Sex is so dull, he said, it has no dark side like love. All I ever wanted to do was touch his face and it has come to this."

"Is that why Tee killed him, Adrienne?"

"No." There was no anger in her voice. "Did June tell you that? You know, liars often tell the truth about themselves in their little lies."

"No, I got that idea some place else." Something in her eyes moved. "What about the other man who died? Who was in love with him? Who killed him?"

"My God, how should I know? What are you after anyway?"

"What I'm after is what's happening at this ranch. What's happening underneath all the games you're playing, Adrienne?"

"Why in the world do you want to know, Sugar? Surely you're not driven by a sense of justice."

"Curiosity maybe. It killed the cat, I know."

She laughed. "No, no. It's the engine of science. It's all right." She looked at me coldly. "You want to know about the other man. I loved him too, if you're curious. I fucked him too, if you're curious. I think I'm beginning to dislike you. I think what Son said about you is true."

"You once told me there were many sides here. How many sides are there, Adrienne?"

"What an old-fashioned idea of the world you have, Sugar. There aren't sides any more, just confusion and hatred and despair. Revolutions can never be successful because they don't account for despair." She laughed suddenly. "My friend told me that too, before I even knew what revolutions were. I have it written down in a notebook and I know exactly where it is."

"All right. It's Tee against Son. But they're not fighting over you. They're not fighting over anything. One man hates and the other man is hated. And they love it. They need it that way. *He* needs it, do you know that? And when Tee is dead, he's going to have to find someone else to hate. Do you know that?"

"No—"

"What he's doing to Tee, he'll do to you."

"No. Yes, maybe he will, I don't care. I don't even want to understand what they're doing." She buried her face in her arms. "Do you love me, Sugar? Do you love anyone?"

I knelt by her and lifted her face. She wasn't crying.

"I don't know. I would have killed him in Mexico. If he'd been there, I would have killed him."

"Who would you have killed, Sugar? Do you know who you're talking about?"

"I'm going to do what you want me to do. What you both want me to do."

"A person always does what he wants to do, Sugar. That's what my friend said, and he knew." Her eyes didn't leave mine; her mouth was cold.


# 1 7


I walked outside. The ranch headquarters was quiet. I could see a light through the trees and hear the sound of a motor idling. I walked down toward the Big House.

A black late-model Cadillac was parked in the circle

drive, lights off, the doors locked. I climbed the steps of the house, a huge Victorian structure which had developed a colonial façade, massive pillars coated with stucco as thick as cake. The ceiling of the porch was dark and high, the door half again as tall as I was, wide enough that it had to be dragged open. The windows were set three feet into the walls, barred on the outside, curtained from within. It was like walking in a forest and suddenly coming up against a solid cliff face: I knocked on the door like a man trying to part the stones.

A Mexican wearing whites and tire-tread sandals opened the door. Without a question he led me into the cavernous house. The dark glowed with rich wood and low, hidden lights. The Mexican opened a door into a long room and told me in Spanish to go in. The room was dark, lighted only by a fireplace at its far end and, to one side, a TV set. Four old men sat in front of the TV set, pushed down into enormous hide-covered chairs, staring without expression at the TV screen. The announcer was reading off a long list of numbers; it sounded like everyone was losing.

A small dark man slid out of a chair and escorted me back toward the door. He was in his fifties, but his face was smooth and young; he talked with the quickness of an intelligent child. My pickup, if I was looking for it, had been moved down to the motor pool. The keys were in his office, which we moved toward without effort, as though caught up on a mechanical track. With a slight smile the secretary told me where I could find Denton and wished me luck.

I followed the secretary's directions to the billiard room on the second floor. His mouth too large for his head, his head too large for his body, Denton smiled at me when I came in. At first I thought he was alone, but his movements around the pool table were too stylized, a performance, and then in the shadows I saw Larry leaning on a pool cue studying Denton make shot after shot. Larry didn't seem to notice me. I sat on the leather couch and waited for the game to end. Larry moved around the table, avoiding Denton's backstroke. Larry's face had changed—it seemed softer, lips red and swollen. He stood near me. He almost whispered, "What do you want?"

"I want to talk."

He almost whispered again, "What do you want to talk about?"

I was almost whispering myself. "I'm not sure. They're going to kill Tee. They want me to kill him."

Denton had stopped moving, but he kept looking at the table. "Is that a fact? Well, good luck."

Larry was laughing. "Where's he come from, huh, Denton? Where's he come from?"

"I mean it. Son is going to murder him. Just like Tee murdered Billy Orrance."

Larry had stopped laughing. Denton was smiling at him. "So Tee Texas murdered that boy. Well now, everbody knows that. I thought you was in on it yoreself."

Larry was quite serious now. "I don't think he was around here at the time, Denton."

The foreman laughed. "Well, well."

"Billy was working for the old man. That's why he did it. That's why Cunningham drove him to it."

"I don't understand any of this."

Denton laid the cue on the table, then rolled it against the balls. "You don't? Well now I'll be darned. Well, let me put it plain for you, Campbell. It was little Tee that pulled the trigger on Billy O., but it was Cunningham who was the cause of it. And her. I got that much figgered out now. You still don't git it? O.K., the old man has been going to cut Tee out for quite a whiles now, he's just been too softhearted about it. Cunningham's the only one who was inside enough to figger out the financial arrangements set up between Tee and the old man and had the sense to see that Tee is nothin but a foul-up and that the old man, when he was pushed up against the wall, he would cut him out. You know Tee's been milking this place for all it's worth. He was doing it through A. She was in charge of the books till a couple months back. One night we loaded up and went over there and took the books and brung them over here. Me and Billy. We bought Billy, Campbell, me and the old man. We bought him like a piece of meat. Just like they bought you.

"Well, the old man was right, them books was fouled up enough to send the lot of them to Huntsville for a long, long spell, but the old man wouldn't see it. Tee was his only hope in life and he has turned out bad. Now nothin makes a darn to him. You have to be careful around a man who don't care about nothin."

"They killed Billy because he went over to you?"

"He was the one who helped Tee kill pore ole Palmer. He set that up. It was a bad way for a man to die, Campbell."

"Why did they want Palmer dead?"

Denton smiled. "Why, he was just part of that line that keeps goin all the way back to Cain. Man is a murderous creature and his sin can never stop. It's carried with us like a disease. The man who killed Palmer died and the man who killed Billy O. is going to die and the man who kills that man will die too." He walked over to the pool table. "It ain't ever goin to stop. It's best not to even try. Myself, Campbell, I'd let Tee wear his own life out. I wouldn't kill him if I was you." He picked up the cue and made a shot, the ball striking the pocket like a fist. "I think you'd best be leavin now, Campbell."

Larry made a quick movement. "I'll show him to the door, Denton. So he won't be snooping around."

We left Denton staring at the pool table—there was no

shot he couldn't make. Out in the hall Larry raised a finger to his lips and smiled, like a bad boy whose mother's back was turned. We didn't speak till we were outside, on the road between the two houses. Music and laughter drifted down from the roof of the Little House. The party had returned from the rodeo. "That was something, man, when you asked him about that Orrance kid—" He laughed. "Man, you know he had the sweetass on that kid."

"I think I heard something about it."

"And you just forgot. I got to give you credit, Campbell, you're cold. But I like em like that." He gave me a look I didn't feel like returning. "You sure were hitting some good shots there."

"Like what?"

"Like the way you set Cunningham up. That was fine fine superfine. Let Cunningham take care of Tee and Denton will take care of him. Beautiful."

"So that's the way you think it will all work out?"

"Why not? Hey, how do you like my job of infiltrating? Pretty fucking good. Sure, we got everbody fooled now, buddy. We just play them one against the other." He gave me a feely sort of slap on the back and a chuckle with little dimples. "Say, did you hear they got it all settled out there in California?"

"Not exactly."

Larry shrugged. "Well, I got the last word that Cunningham and Tee have come to an understanding. Cunningham will give up the snatch and Tee will sell out." I didn't say anything. "Caught you by surprise, huh? Then he lowers the boom when Tee's guard is down."

"Did Son tell you that?"

"I got eyes, ain't I? You just let them think everthing's goin hunky-dory over here and I'll keep workin Denton up to a froth. Sometime you get a chance, you oughta come in and meet the old man. He's gonna like you."

"I wouldn't mind meeting him myself."

"Well, he's sleeping now." And he placed a finger to his swollen lips and moved back toward the Big House. It looked like he was tiptoeing.

I stood in the road between the two houses, listening to the music and laughter coming from the Little House roof. I wasn't going to kill Tee, I knew that. Now all I had to do was figure out if I was going to keep him alive.

I walked down to the parking shed and found my truck and drove back to Flavannah. The truck ran cold and the house was stale. I couldn't remember ever having felt more at home. I lay on the couch and watched TV. I fell asleep thinking how I was going to buy this house from Son and settle down. I woke up to the burning white TV screen, turned off the set, and lay on the bed. I could still see the figure in that Mexican hotel room moving toward me through the darkness. Only now, when I closed my eyes, it was no longer P.M. I saw coming for me but Son. I woke again, during the early-morning hours, to what I thought was still part of my dream, it was so strange. Son sat in a chair by my bed, a gun lying in his hand. The gun, I kept thinking, wasn't pointed at anything. We had been talking for some time when he handed the gun across the bed and said it was for me. I held the gun so that it aimed at his head. He laughed. "It's not to shoot me with."

"That might not be a bad idea."

He pushed the barrel to one side. "We can talk about that later. How have things been back at the ranch?"

"Cozy."

"You sure got a pretty nose."

"I busted one of P.M.'s hands with it."

"What's wrong with you two lovebirds? You're always fighting and feuding."

"I think we've just about come to an understanding. We had a long talk about our little misunderstanding in Mexico. We had a long talk about you. As a matter of fact, I've been having a lot of long talks about you with a lot of people."

"Who have you been talking to, Sugar?" He leaned back so that his face was lost in shadows.

"I've been talking to Adrienne quite a bit. And I just had an interesting little chat with Denton."

"What did the fag have to say?"

"He said that Tee killed the Orrance kid."

"No shit. What else?"

"That you're going to kill Tee."

Son was silent for a while. He didn't move. I realized I still had the gun pointed in his direction and I lowered it. "What else?"

"I talked to Larry. He says you and Tee have made a deal. You give up Adrienne, he sells the ranch."

Son spoke slowly. "Tee killed the kid all right. I was with him at the time."

I leaned back against the wall. "Why did he want to kill him? It must've been your goddamn idea!"

"No, it wasn't my idea. It was his. I just watched."

"I don't understand, I just don't understand. The man is crazy, Son, why in the hell would you let him kill somebody? My God, why!"

"I don't know. Maybe I was crazy myself. Maybe I wanted the little bastard dead myself. I don't know why I'm letting him go on like this. He is crazy and he is a murderer."

"Did he kill the other man?"

"He did."

"I don't know if you're telling the truth. You could be protecting somebody. Maybe you killed those men, maybe she did."

"No, Sugar, that's not the way it is."

"What's the gun for?"

"Tee went wild out in L.A. after P.M. left. He tried to kill me; maybe he was really trying to kill himself—maybe he's been trying to kill himself all along. He found out that A. is leaving him. He'll probably be all right when he sobers up, but you never can be sure. He's made it back to the ranch in one piece anyway. We're going to have to watch our step the next couple of days. He could be about to give up the ghost, and if he does, all hell is going to break loose. And I don't think there's any doubt he's going to try to get me again. That's why I need you to stick around for a while, Sugar. It ain't just some little whim, it's for real." I didn't answer and Son shrugged. "There is going to be a meeting with the Foundation people some-time tomorrow or the next day. I don't know if Tee is going to sell out or not. We'll just have to wait and see. And, son, I'd never bargain A. away, not for anything." He was silent for a while. "I guess it does look like we're slic-ing up the meat while it's still alive, but something's got to be done and I'm going to need a hand doing it. I want to get it over with quick, Sugar, I got a beachhouse down in Galveston all staked out, a little hideaway. Come the mid-dle of next week, we'll be down there drinking Pearl and watching the clouds pass by just like they were our trou-bles. Then after a little vacation maybe we can open up a little office down in Houston and start consulting. You ever consulted, son? Well, I hear it's a wonderful way of life. What do you say?"

"All right, Son. For a couple of days."

"Ah, that's good news, Sugar. And, Sugar, we're all going to live through it. All of us." And he left.

I lay back and waited for the dawn. For the first time since I had come back, I felt I was ahead of him.

# 1 8

I slept much too long. When I woke it was almost noon. I
was dry, my mouth felt like it hadn't been swept out,
clothes scraped my skin. I walked through the house a
hundred times. Nothing on the radio but gospel. The TV
didn't work this morning. I kept picking up the phone. I
walked outside: up and down the street nothing moved.
It was hot, the clouds thin and high, the light searing,
gray. I went back inside and sat by the phone. I placed a
call to a woman in California, then hung up. I decided
to walk downtown to get a newspaper but only got to the
end of the block. I began searching the house for
signs of Adrienne. I realized they had made love here. I
lay on the bed and tried to feel them. I searched the house
for a picture of her. I found some papers in a hidden file
box. They had nothing to do with us, they were from
Son's past. A file of letters was at the bottom. At the back
were four letters from Son's wife. No date, no address,
they were cool and logical. The last letter was an answer
to her. It had never been mailed. My eyes moved down
the page—a man was going crazy with grief, loneliness,
remorse. And he got nothing but understanding, nothing
but these simple dry words explaining something that
couldn't be explained. I put the file back and went into
the bathroom and stood over the washbasin, looking down
into it as if it were a mirror. After a long time I was able
to move and went in and hid the gun and lay spent on
the bed. A hot stiff breeze blew across me. After a while
I got up and dressed and drove down to the Y, then
headed the truck east on the Toro highway.

I stopped the truck on the ridge overlooking the ranch. I stood on the running board. The ranch looked the same as the first time I had seen it, except there were dozens of cars parked around the Big House. I drove down into the ranch headquarters with the crazy understanding that I didn't want anybody's troubles to be over.

I parked behind the Little House. A crew of Mexicans was cleaning the Little Room. They told me the señora had left. A silver-haired woman sitting at the desk in Adrienne's study said that Adrienne had flown to Houston this morning with friends. I asked where Son was. There was a meeting going on at the Big House, the cool woman imagined he was there.

Today a uniformed guard stood at the door of the Big House. He told me to wait in the shade of one of the columns. In a few minutes Maury came out, followed by the guard. Maury was hustling and grinning. He said they were working miracles and handed me a slip of paper. "Now you drive out to Toro and call ole George, he's the caretaker down there at Lake Snyder, you call him and tell him to git the lodge ready for tonight. Hell, the way that Cunningham is wheelin and dealin, better make that this afternoon."

"Why did Adrienne leave?"

"Who? Aw, one last fling at Neiman's before the old man cuts her credit cards in two. Take Mabelline along with you. She's bored. You can find her up on the roof broilin. Make that call, boy, ski daddy is gone to hit them waves agin!"

"I want to talk to Tee."

"Talk to Tee? Lord, man, he caint talk to nobody now. You know who's in that room right now? Why Mercy Fath a the Fath Foundation himself—"

"I've got to talk to Tee. It's a matter of life and death."

"Shit, Campbell, yore a card. You can talk to him later

on down at the lake. Everbody's comin down. You tell George to thaw out enough grub fer hunderds!"

"Maury, do you know what's been happening around here? Do you know what's going to happen to Tee?"

"Why, he's goin to come outta this smellin like a rose. What else! Good Lord, boy, that buddy a yores is a genius." And Maury slipped back behind the huge door.

I went back to the Little House and tried to phone out but the line was dead. On the roof I found Mabelline, Caroline Jo, and Pork Man. Larry was in the radio room, working on the transmitter, but he didn't look up. The others stared at me as I pulled up a chair and joined them. They were drunk. Pork Man kept looking at me with what I took to be astonishment, though through his new sunglasses I couldn't be certain.

I patted the fat man's shoulder. "Cat got your tongue, P.M.?"

"I oughta throw yore ass off this roof."

"What for this time?"

P.M. cussed for a while. Caroline Jo had been inching her chair closer to mine. Larry came out of the radio shack, got a beer, and disappeared again. Finally Pork Man sneered, "What happened, bird brain, the meetin let out early?"

"I think you've been sitting out in the sun too long, P.M. I haven't been to any meeting."

"Better stop tryin to bushit the boys."

Mabelline nodded, but it was more like falling asleep.

"Benedict Arnold," Caroline Jo said.

"Aw, he's as stupid as he looks," the fat man said gloomily. "Yore shitass buddy has cut up the pie and divided us out. What have you got to say to that?"

"Nothing. I'm driving down to Houston tonight. Maybe this afternoon."

"Houston. Good place for you. Chase that cunt all over the country far as I'm concerned."

Caroline Jo moved her chair so that she could reach out and touch my arm. "Tee is givin up the ghost. Even though P.M. don't think it's the right thing to do. Right, P.M.?"

"Right, baby. I think we coulda pulled that sucker outta the fire. Still think so, if there hadn't been somebody monkeyin around behind the scenes." I looked at him questioningly. "That's right. All along that fuckin Cunningham's been workin loggerheads to Tee. Him and his little pals down in Houston been plannin to sink this ship all along."

"I could've told you that a long time ago, P.M."

Pork Man scowled. "And you makin a asshole outta yourself over that million-dollar piece a tail. When you goin to learn you throw a sack on their head, it's all the same."

"Except when you're in love, P.M.," said Caroline Jo.

The fat man frowned. "So you ain't in on the inner circlejerk. I wonder what's goin on over there." He went over to the edge of the roof, then came back. "Probly laughin their asses off."

"I talked to Maury. He seemed to think they were doing the right thing."

"That bastard's a traitor too. He's sellin Tee right down the drain. Right, Mabelline?"

Mabelline nodded slowly. "Naw, I have decided he knows what he's doin. He knows how to handle things. He ain't goin to give up the ghost on Tee Texas."

"He shore is a shitass," said Caroline Jo.

"I love that man, but I think he needs a rest."

Pork Man split open a wet grin for me. "The love a yore life shore took off like a scalded dawg when she found out

the old man was takin over the reins agin." He nodded
toward C.J., who hadn't taken her eyes off me. "Purty little
Larry shore has been grouchy today. One good thing was
them kickin his cheatin ass out."

"He caint git the radio set to work."

"What do you mean, kicked his ass out?"

C.J. shook her head. "That boy was always tryin to play
two ends against the middle. Right, P.M.?"

"Yeah, sure."

There was a pause, then I said, "Has anybody seen June
since she got out of the hospital?"

Everyone looked at me; even Mabelline turned her
glazed eyes in my direction. "Man, you been outta touch,"
P.M. said. "Little June Bug has done tried to kill herself
agin. They had to put her back in the loony bin down in
Houston."

"How come you think we're gittin so stinkin shit-
faced?" said Mabelline, her voice thick and aggressive.

There was nothing to say but that I had to leave.

Pork Man watched me. "Where the hell you think yore
goin?"

"Don't get worked up, P.M., I'm just calling a man about
a party they're throwing after the meeting."

"I'm goin with you."

"You can go in my place if you're so goddamned enthusiastic about it."

"Nothin doin. I'm stickin close to you as a blood tick on
a battlefield." Pork Man shook his head at Caroline Jo.
"You stay here, C.J., and carry out the emergency plan.
Just in case the emergency comes up."

"What emergency is that, P.M.?"

"If you ever do somethin smart."

"I'm tired," said Caroline Jo and closed her eyes and let
her head fall over on her shoulder.

We turned at the sound of a car being started up; a horn

sounded, then another engine roared. We went to the wall and saw people streaming down the front steps of the Big House, cars driving across the grass, the men shouting, waving, and laughing. Pork Man's face was dark. "Let's git outta here. I don't wanta be seen by any a them bastards."

On our way past the radio room we found Larry in a crying rage, ripping wires and tubes out of the set, throwing them around the room. "Sob sister," Pork Man told me.

P.M. wanted to stop by a friend's house in Toro. She lived in an odd-shaped shack—it looked like it had been sliced in two—that sat between a truck stop and the railroad tracks. The door was painted a chalky blue, wildflowers grew in the yard, the soft porch sagged under P.M.'s weight. A puffy Mexican woman came to the door. P.M. told me to wait a couple of minutes and disappeared into the house. I drove to Flavannah.

I called the number Maury had given me, but there was no answer. I called Tee's house in River Oaks and there was no answer there. No one answered the phone at Ty Foose's house either. I went over to the bed and slipped the .38 Son had left from under the mattress.

When I got back to Toro, Pork Man was waiting on the porch. He took a long time walking out to the truck. "That was one helluva block you rode around, buddy." He got in the cab and handed me a quart of vodka. "Tastes like warter alongside that stuff you had the other night." I pointed the truck back toward the highway and P.M. grew morose. "I can't figger out women. They either fuck too much or they don't fuck enough. Makes em meaner than hell." He was studying me. "What you got in that pocket, Dick Tracy? Another popgun?"

"That's right, P.M."

"It's against the law," he said and we drove along in silence. Suddenly he slammed both feet against the floorboard and banged his fist on the roof of the cab. I slammed on the brakes. "Jumpy huh? You better be." Again we rode in silence, for maybe a mile. "I know why you got that gun," he said, as if the subject had just occurred to him. I concentrated a lot on driving. "Friday," was all he would say, and he said that several times.

Finally I said, "What the hell are you babbling about?"

"What am I babblin about, my ass. You gotta do it by next Friday, don'tcha?"

"Do what by next Friday?"

Pork Man began growling like a dog. "Don't git smart with me. That policy runs out next Friday and you goddamn well know it."

"No, I don't know it, and you know that's not the reason I'm carrying this gun."

"It ain't, is it." He was silent for a while; then he spoke in a different tone. "Just remember, I got my eye on you. You ain't goin to git away with it. You and him."

"And I've got my eye on you too, P.M., and you don't fool me one goddamn bit. Either one of you. You tell him that."

After that we rode to the ranch without saying anything else.

The place was deserted again. The big cars, the important people were gone. A harsh, gritty wind blew up the south canyon, and though the afternoon was hot and dry, everything looked cold. A few cars were still parked behind the Little House, but Adrienne's car was gone. The Mexicans had finished cleaning the Little Room. We went up to the roof. The radio shack was a shambles. Caroline Jo hadn't moved, she sat staring into the pool. She smiled wanly at P.M. as he sat by her and patted her arm. "How you doin, honeybunch?"

"Everbody has gone off and left. I thought I'd wait for you."

"You shoulda gone on with somebody else. It ain't good for you to be sittin here by yoreself."

"I don't think I can git up."

P.M. glanced at me. "Shore you can. It's goin to be a party, right? You gotta cheer up."

"Larry went off with Mabelline."

"Aw, that turd is just a overgrowed kid. Where's Maury?"

"He went off with Tee and Son. They're all going down to the lodge."

"Did Adrienne come back? Her car is gone."

Caroline Jo turned her wispy face in my direction. "I hope she don't never come back."

Pork Man made a movement to stand. "We better git on down to the lake, honey. Just to see what the hell is goin on. Maybe we can do some warter-skiin. How's that sound? Might cheer you up."

"Warter was the grave a mankind onct."

The fat man gestured abruptly. "Well, you can stay here, C.J., if you don't feel like goin. You can take a little nap."

"I'd never wake up agin. This place is like a wound. It oozes blood. Love has turned to hate, the sun burns like I don't know what."

"Goddamn, C.J., how many beers you had?"

"Fourteen."

P.M. took off his sunglasses and held his head in one hand. "You puked yet?"

"Once yesterdy." She giggled.

"Well, why don't you run on down to the ladies' room, honey, and git it over with, and then we'll take off. Go on, you'll feel a lot better."

Caroline Jo became tearful. "I caint do it. I'd *die*."

"Aw, baby, take a look at Campbell; a wino like him has puked a coupla thousand times and he ain't ever choked onct."

The girl smiled faintly. "I onct knew a gal who puked more than she ate. She was feelin awful bad." And she rose and weaved toward the elevator.

After she disappeared P.M. shook his head. "That kid is a froot cake. It wouldn't be so bad cept she used to be a fortune-teller. What I mean is, she's been predictin another killin around here for some time."

"Who does she think's going to get killed, P.M.?"

"It ain't you, sorry to say," said the fat man and put his sunglasses back on.


# 1 9


Pork Man hated the idea of driving down to the lake in my pickup, but someone had taken the keys out of all the ranch vehicles. He gave me wrong directions; he figured a man who didn't have a radio in his pickup was the lowest creature on earth; he told C.J. he wished I was married so he could fuck my wife; he wished I had several things so he could burn them down, rip them up, and piss on them. He finally settled on rolling the window down about an inch farther than it had ever gone before and singing.

The lake had once been a wide, barren canyon down near Snyder, 175 miles to the southwest, but about five years ago they had piled an earth dam across the Snyder River and now it had gathered behind it a respectable body of water. We had bought beer at Wadsworth but what we hadn't drunk had grown hot, so we stopped at the inn above the dam. While Pork Man and Caroline Jo were inside the bar, I stood on the patio overlooking the lake. The shore was rocky; small beaches more gravel than sand had begun to form in the coves; saplings had been planted along the shore but they only added to the sense of desolation. It was four o'clock, the sun small and high over the lake; a bitter southwesterly wind whipped up choppy waves the color of steel. In the bar Pork Man was standing over the jukebox as if it were work. I sat by Caroline Jo. Her eyes had followed me in. I ordered a beer so cold I couldn't taste it. "Did you see Tee after the meeting?" I asked her after P.M. had gotten more change from the bar and returned to stand over the jukebox.

Caroline Jo laid her head on the bar. "Yeah, I saw him. He looked pretty happy."

"Did he say anything about the meeting?"

"I don't know. I was looking at him through the binoculars. Somebody said Cunningham was responsible for it all."

"What kind of emergency is P.M. planning for?"

"I don't know and I don't care."

Pork Man came up on the other side of Caroline Jo. "Let's git outta here."

"Christ, P.M., you just put two bucks in the jukebox."

"I'm restless. Let's go."

"Whatever P.M. says is law around here," Caroline Jo told me as we walked out to the pickup.

"Would you two shut up. I'm thinkin."

"What're you thinking about, P.M.?"

"Nothin. None a yore goddamn business. I don't like the looks a this place. I never have. Too goddamn much warter."

We drove in silence around the south side of the lake, at times losing sight of it, the road rising and winding through the barren, rocky hills. The earth was dry and yellowish white. P.M. pointed out a caliche road which took us down to an inlet thick with live oak and elm. It looked as if there had been a spring here long before the lake had existed: the trunks of the trees on the shore line were under water. P.M. said the lodge parking lot was probably packed, so we parked on the road behind two other cars and walked down through the scrub oak, a haze of fine white dust rising after us. We came upon a bungalow set back in the trees. The narrow road circled around the house to a parking area I could see through the trees, but we angled off on a path which took us directly to the rear of the house, a large shaded patio. I waited here while Pork Man and Caroline Jo went into the house. I could hear the voices calling out, but no one answered. There was a silence, then a screen door on the lake side of the house slammed. A few moments later Caroline Jo appeared at the door to the patio and said that everyone was down at the lake. I followed her through the house—low-ceilinged, dark, and cool—down a flagstone stairway set into the side of the hill. The party had moved to the screened boathouse at the end of the dock. Twenty or so people stood around the berths, which held only one boat, a large outboard. There were no rich bankers here, no oil men, no one from Houston or any foundations, no one from the Big House, aside from Maury no one who had been at the meeting. Only Mabelline, a man who could have been Coolie's seedy older brother, a group of cackling, paunchy men, one of whom I recognized as Sheriff Tabor. Adrienne was not here, nor was Denton, nor were what seemed like hundreds of others. Larry, Tee, and Son were not here. Pork Man was not here. I looked back up toward the house but saw no one there.

Caroline Jo and I were set down in chairs near the water, handed beer, and asked where the dickens everyone was. I moved away from their hospitality and introduced myself to Sheriff Tabor. He remembered me from a town I had never set foot in. We talked a little about football; then I asked him what had come of the case of the boy who had been shot at Soda Springs.

The sheriff winked. "That case is closed. That boy killed hisself."

"You know, I'm not so sure about that."

The sheriff was still grinning. He opened me another can of beer. "How's that?"

"Well, somebody told me that he knows for a fact that that boy was killed. That he was murdered."

Half the people had moved out on the dock and the others were out of earshot, but the sheriff drew me to the far end of the boathouse. In the inlet the water was smooth, the wind had dropped, the sun was disappearing behind the hills. "Now, who told you that story, son?"

"It seems like to me you'd be more interested in who the murderer is."

"You let me hannle the investigatin." His voice wanted to be hard and cold. "You tell me who tole you that story and we'll forgit all about it."

"Well, if we're going to forget about it, let's just forget about it." I stood and the sheriff's hand went to his belt, though nothing was there. I sat down anyway. "All right, but you're not going to like it."

"I ain't in this business to like thangs. Spit it out."

"Tee Kitchens killed Billy Orrance."

The sheriff stared off into the water. His voice was frail. "Who tole you a thang like that?"

"Son Cunningham told me that. He said he was with Tee when he did it. He saw him do it."

The sheriff groaned. "Yore gettin yoreself into deep trouble."

"All I'm doing is telling you what Son told me himself. That's just good citizenship."

"They used to berry people that brung bad news. If I had my gun I'd be tempted to shoot you myself. Them are both fine young men. Why yore doin it only heaven knows."

"Look, Sheriff, I never put any stock in the story anyway. Why, Son and Tee are my closest friends. I just thought I had an obligation to mention it to a peace officer. I've done my duty and I'm going to forget the whole thing. The kid was just looking for trouble anyway, right? The way I look at it, a man who messes around with another

man's wife deserves to get shot. Down here in Texas."
The sheriff nodded involuntarily. "Let's forget I ever
brought it up, Mark. Let me buy you a drink."

"Mebbe," said the sheriff. "I gotta git me a cold beer
right now."

"Now don't you move a muscle, I'll get it for you,
Sheriff. But listen, before you go, Mark, I guess what I'm
really worried about is Tee Texas himself. I don't know
exactly how to put it, but I think Tee might be in some
kind of danger over the next couple of days. You know,
before the insurance policy runs out."

"What kinda danger is that?"

"Why, I think somebody might kill him for the money,
Sheriff."

Tabor was staring down into the water again. "Did Cunningham tell you that too?"

"No, it's just a feeling I've got. There's probably nothing
to it. Still, maybe we ought to stick with ole Tee tonight,
just to be on the safe side. What do you think?"

"Mebbe. I gotta git that beer now. I need the exercise."
And though I wasn't blocking his way, he pushed me to
one side and went out and joined the others on the dock.

Mabelline and an old woman who kept pushing up a watery smile for my benefit were the only others left in the
boathouse. The people on the dock were throwing rocks
down into the water. Tabor was standing off to one side. I
saw him look once in my direction, but generally his head
was turned toward the house. Mabelline jabbed me with
her finger. The old woman cackled, "Hit him agin!"

"Did you hear what happened at the meeting, Campbell?"

"I heard that everything went off all right."

"Maury fixed his little red wagon."

"Is that right?"

"Tee's goin to fix his little red wagon, buddy."

"Whoooeee!" said the old woman.

There was a noise—laughter—and I looked up the hill and saw Tee and Pork Man coming down the stairs. Both men carefully watched where they put their feet. The crowd on the dock shouted as though they were conquering heroes. Tabor went up the steps to meet them, but Tee wouldn't listen to what he said. Followed closely by P.M., Tee pushed his way down the stairs, trotting the last few feet out onto the dock. Tabor and Pork Man stayed behind, talking. Tee was embraced by several people. He seemed to be looking for someone. P.M. and the sheriff came strolling down the steps, so satisfied with one another. Tee's face had been reamed out, his eyes were glassy, his smile dead. He was talking so rapidly that his lips seemed to be trembling. Pork Man drew away from Tabor and grasped Tee's arm, and the crowd followed them into the boathouse. Tee and P.M. drew up in front of me. The crowd formed behind them. I could see the sheriff standing alone on the dock, sipping at a forgotten can of beer.

"Here he is, Tee Texas," said P.M. "You want me to kick the shit outta him?"

Tee put a hand on the fat man's arm. "I just took good care of his buddy. I figger I can handle him." His free hand moved across his chest like an animal. "I figger I can handle this one whenever it pleasures me. I just sent yore buddy runnin for good. I think it's about time you headed right down that same trail."

The crowd tightened around me and I laughed in their faces. Twenty overweight winos and their friends, they were going to throw me in the lake. Pork Man warned them I had a gun and they stopped. Tee held out his hand, smiling as if he was waiting to be paid for it. "You don't have a gun, do you?"

"No." I smiled back. "I don't have a gun. I'm no enemy of yours, Tee. I'm on your side."

"On my side. You're right. Let's have a drink. That would help me. Somebody run up and get the case of Scotch in my car." He dangled a key chain in front of me. "Would you mind doin that for me, Campbell? That would help me out. It's in the trunk. The white Pontiac. Come on back down and let's have a drink. You need any help helpin me?"

"I don't need any help."

"Good." He smiled. "Run on up there now."

Tee patted me on the back and the crowd parted. I went up the steps, around the side of the house to the parking lot. I walked on up to the road. All four tires on the pickup were flat. The valve stems had been cut. I went back down to the Pontiac. The car was blocked in; there was no ignition key on the chain Tee had given me. I unlocked the trunk and set the case of Scotch on the ground. I searched through the trunk but found nothing. I slid into the front seat and unlocked the glove compartment. A .45 lay under a couple of road maps. I took the clip out, ejected the shell in the chamber, and put the clip back in. The missing bullet would give me or Tee's killer a few seconds, but I had no choice. I put the gun back and locked the compartment. I took the coil wire off the Pontiac and dropped it into my pocket. I tucked the .38 in the back of my belt and looked around, up at the empty house. I hoisted the case of Scotch on my shoulder. As I was going down the stairs, I heard the sound of someone trying to start the outboard.


# 2 0


It was almost dark and nobody but Tee wanted to go out on the lake. Mabelline had passed out; what was left of

Coolie was lying on the floor, his eyes and mouth hanging open. Almost everybody was going up to the house to watch Tabor cook frozen steaks. That left myself, Maury, P.M., and Tee in the boat. Maury had stripped down to a pair of swimming trunks. He cast off the bow line and climbed onto the boat's hood. Tee held the boat wide open in reverse, turning sharply, almost throwing Maury overboard. Tee pushed the throttle forward and the prow of the boat stood out of the water. We headed toward the middle of the lake.

The sun was heavy and red, hanging only a few feet above the horizon. The wind had died, the lake was motionless, the surrounding hills had turned a soft violet. Lights sparkled from the inn; the sound of the jukebox carried clearly across the water. Tee cut the power and the boat drifted. While Maury was strapping on an orange life jacket, Tee tossed two water skis overboard. Maury tossed the tow rope off and jumped into the lake, yelling as he hit the water. Tee eased the boat forward till Maury caught hold of the tow bar. He signaled with the other hand; the bow of the boat shot up, and Maury and water skis splattered everywhere. Tee cackled and wheeled the boat around. P.M. gave a wheedling laugh. "Lord intended only one man to ever walk on warter." Going back to religion till he got back on dry land.

Tee pulled the boat up beside Maury, who was coughing and spitting water. "Come on, ski daddy, gotta do better than that."

"Slipped," said Maury and grabbed on to the tow bar. Tee eased the boat out till there was about a yard of slack in the rope, then slammed the throttle full ahead. It took a long time for Maury to come up. Tee sat on the side of the boat giggling. The third time Maury got up, but Tee opened up the motor and headed straight in to shore and Maury dropped the line. Tee took the boat about a quarter mile out and cut the power and we sat watching Maury's head bob on the surface of the water. P.M. was staring at his own feet. After a minute one of Maury's arms raised and fell against the water, then the other, and he began laboriously swimming toward us, pushing the skis ahead of him. Tee started the motor and let him get no closer than the outstretched tow rope. I could barely hear Maury's voice: "Too tared, Tee—caint raise one a my arms—"

Tee's face was alive with fury, his body wouldn't stay still. "Next time you drop off like that, I'll leave your goddamn ass out here!"

"Don't go so fuckin fast, Tee . . ." He splashed the skis around and once more caught hold of the tow bar. Tee pulled him up gently but then took the boat around in ever-tightening circles, slinging Maury around faster and faster till he could no longer hold on. It looked like he disintegrated, skis flying everywhere. Tee didn't seem to notice; his face was expressionless. He turned the boat in a wide arc toward the north shore. P.M. hadn't looked up. Maury could dog-paddle to China as far as I was concerned, but I climbed over the seat and took Tee's hand off the throttle. He offered no resistance. The boat drifted. The sun had set: I could only imagine I saw Maury's head. Tee looked at me blankly. "You want to water-ski?"

"No, let's go back and pick up Maury and go back in. It's getting dark, Tee."

"P.M., you want to help me toss this guy in. We'll teach him how to water-ski with a rope tied around his neck."

Pork Man shook his head. "Naw, I'm sick a warter. Let's git outta here."

Tee began to laugh. "O.K., let's go back and pick him up." And he took the throttle and turned back toward where Maury had fallen. Tee stopped the boat and we called out, but there was no answer. It had grown dark and we could have been a quarter mile off. Tee let the boat idle forward and took an oar and began probing the water, talking to himself in a high, choked voice. The boat started going in small aimless circles, so I took the wheel and steered toward the lights above the dam. If Maury had swum in that direction, he did not answer us. Finally Tee pulled the oar back and I let him have the wheel. We headed full speed north across the lake. Eventually Tee cut the motor and we glided into the berth under the boat-house. I tied the line and gave P.M. a hand out of the boat. He went up to the house ahead of us. Tee took my arm. "You don't think he really drowned, do you?"

"No, I imagine he paddled in to shore."

Tee's voice caught. "I hope so. He's a good man."

"Tee, listen, we've got to talk."

"It's tonight—but you know that, don't you? You got to come with me. I caint talk now. But later, we can do it later." He went up to the house ahead of me.

Upstairs, the roll of the unconscious had grown. The warm Scotch and Tabor's steaks, half burned, half frozen, had laid out just about everybody but Tabor. The sheriff was sitting before the TV set, drinking something hor-rible—he had chopped up the frozen center of his steak as ice cubes for his Scotch and soda and couldn't understand why everybody had got so upset. He called it a Bloody Kilt. Caroline Jo was wide awake; she served Pork Man a plate and whispered to him while he ate. P.M. looked at me and listened. Tabor gave me a smile of sexual satisfaction when he saw me watching Caroline Jo. I ate the fringe of one of the steaks. Tee slammed around the kitchen looking for ice cubes. He talked to Tabor a while and told me the sheriff could take care of everything. "If anybody drowns in this state, it's their own goddamn fault." We went in and sat in front of the TV. The sheriff had dozed off. "In Texas," Tee said in a drunk blare, "if you catch a man beddin your wife, you can shoot him. You know that. He was suppose to drive over to Lubbock and meet her plane. I don't give a shit. I didn't want to drive all the fuckin way to Lubbock to meet a shit-eatin airplane. Maybe we oughta leave. Maury's goin to be pissed off as hell. He's goin to need a coupla days to cool off. He's gotta awful temper. Me and Maury's like the buffalo and the bear. You can push us and push us and push us, but then . . . then we don't push no more. You want to go over to Post and drink a beer?"

"You sure you don't want to stay here?"

"Naw, naw, she's comin back tonight and I got to talk to her. She's still my girl. I'm sure she is." His voice was slow and heavy. "She's comin home tonight. The three of us are going to hash things out. Let's go, whadda you say, ole buddy, you're the only friend I got left." He fell back on the couch, laughing. "Shit, even ole C.J. is beginnin to look good." We looked into the next room, where Caroline Jo and Pork Man were peering back at us. "I once put all my hopes in that man. I'm really gettin worried about Maury not comin back. I think I better take off or I'll get caught."

"I'll go with you."

"Why do you want to go with me?"

"You know why. I want to go back to the ranch and I need a ride."

"But I'm goin to Post and drink beer with a ole buddy of mine. We don't want you taggin along."

"Thanks. But I don't think we ought to let P.M. and C.J. go along with us. See, I don't trust either of them." The brightly lit room they were sitting in looked like a stage. Caroline Jo's head was cocked; P.M. was chewing the center of his steak, cutting it with a butcher knife. "I wouldn't trust anybody if I were you. Except me."

Tee barely nodded, fear had almost frozen him. "We'll tell them we're goin to the Cotton Club in Lubbock."

I nodded toward Tabor. "Let's take pusslegut with us."

"Okeydokey," Tee said. "I'll drive." While I woke Tabor, Tee went in and sat at the table with Pork Man. I coaxed and dragged the sheriff out to the parking lot and pushed him into the back seat of the Pontiac. I put the coil wire back and quietly closed the hood. I leaned against the fender and thought about the .45 and decided to leave it like it was. I listened to the silence till Tabor began to snore, then went back to the house. Tee was standing at one end of the kitchen, his back to the couple at the other end of the room. The door was situated so that I came between them. Pork Man and Caroline Jo seemed to be waiting for Tee to make up his mind. I let the screen door slam and Tee turned around. His face had gone wild, nothing fit together; his eyes swept the room in a desperate search for something that wasn't there. He never looked at any of us. Without a word he went past me, down to the car. I took my key chain out of my pocket. "Why don't you all follow us in my pickup," and I threw the keys to Pork Man; they fell to the floor. We stared at one another, then the fat man's eyes moved away and I went down to the parking lot.

# 2 1

Tee hadn't moved the car. The motor was running; he leaned against the wheel, his head pitched forward, his eyes sightless. Finally he pushed himself away from the wheel, holding on to it. "Do you really think I killed him, do you really think I killed him . . ." He backed the car out of the parking area and up the narrow road. In the Pontiac's headlights my pickup looked short and tired. "Do you really think I'm going to kill him?"

"Kill who?"

He smiled at me almost coquettishly. "Don't give me that shit, friend."

He settled the gear in low and then, with his left foot on the brake, slowly pressed down the gas pedal. His foot snapped off the brake and the Pontiac slithered across the road, bouncing off one of the parked cars, spinning back across the road, in and out of the ditch and up the winding road, the white dust as thick as mud. We turned south on the blacktop. Banging the brake and the gas with both feet, Tee pushed the Pontiac down through the winding road around the south side of the lake. He hit eighty on one short straightaway, spun out on the next turn but gunned out of the ditch, the car bucking like a horse. Tabor groaned as his head slammed against the door. Tee deliberately sideswiped a mailbox, then after a hundred yards let the car slow. His eyes were dull and frightened. He stopped the car and got out. He looked back in at me. "What was that I hit?" He started running back down the road. I took the keys out of the ignition and followed him. I found him on his hands and knees searching through the tall grass in the ditch. "My God, I hit something."

"You hit a goddamn mailbox. Now get up."

"No, it was alive."

"Look, I've got the keys to the car and I'm driving back to the ranch. You want to crawl around here all night, that's fine with me."

He stood. "You can't leave me out here. He's out here looking for me. Hurt."

"All right, get back in the car. I'm driving."

We walked back to the car. Tabor was sitting up in the back seat, wild-eyed. When he saw us he lay back down. I started driving, hoping this road led back to the dam. At one point Tee began mumbling to himself, then quit. Once he reached toward the glove compartment but drew his hand back. We stopped at the inn and Tee went inside. I let him go. Tabor sat up and asked where we were. He lay down saying, "Good, good." I checked the glove compartment; the .45 was still there. I took the .38 out of my belt and slid it into my pocket and went up the steps toward the inn.

I thought I had lost him. He wasn't in the bar—only the bartender and a woman, their heads together over a drink. They looked up when I came in. I started toward the patio but saw Tee in the phone booth across the dance floor. I went back to the bar and waited. The bartender strolled down and I asked if he had seen a little fat man wearing a bathing suit wandering around. The bartender gave me a grin somebody had punched a couple of holes in. "Naw, but we got a fruitcake over in the tellyphone if you want a bite a something." I ordered a beer and watched Tee in the phone booth. The bartender went down and leaned toward his girl friend. They laughed. Tee kicked himself out of the phone booth. He weaved over toward the woman, then changed directions and came over and sat by me. "Line was busy," he said and started slapping the bar. "Get your ass down here! Get your goddamn ass down here!"

The bartender drew himself up. He had a belly as lumpy as a sack of potatoes. On the way down he drew two beers out of a cooler and set them and his hands on the bar in front of us. His arms went on a yard before they made an elbow. I paid for the beer and he went back to where he belonged. Tee grinned at him all the way. To change the subject, I asked who he had called.

"Nobody." He smiled. "I was just takin a piss."

I looked around at the puddle on the floor of the booth and slowly looked toward the bartender. Tee was pounding the bar. "Get your ass down here!"

"Tee, look, let's get out of here."

He stopped laughing abruptly and stood. "I'm the god-damn boss around here and don't you ever forget it. *Don't you ever forget it!*" He slammed out the door.

The bartender came down and wiped the bar. "Yore buddy must be lookin for trouble."

"I think he's already found it."

"Well," said the bartender, delicately moving the two beers across the bar, "you tell yore friend that if he ever comes back in here agin, it's goin to hurt for years."

"I'm afraid nothing's going to hurt very much longer."

I went out to the car. Tee was sitting behind the wheel, the beginning of a snarl on his face. The glove-compartment door lay open. I got in and snapped it shut. We got back on the highway and headed north. Tee drove eighty, but the road ran straight and we met no cars. At the intersection with Highway 84 we turned left and northwest away from Toro. I watched Tee as he drove; he seemed smaller, older. He hunched over the wheel, drawn forward by the deadly center stripe. I didn't look at him again till we got to Post. Then his look had changed.

Post was a small oil town set down between an ocean of sand dunes and the Lubbock highway. Strung out along the highway, backed up to the railroad tracks, were half a dozen beer joints. Liquor had come to Post years earlier than any of the surrounding towns and the beer joints showed signs of wear, battle, and decay. We stopped at the first place in line. I looked at the broken, flashing names on up the road—Hut Two, Kelly Green's, the Wagon Wheel, Mr. & Mrs. Shorty's, the Christmas Tree, with an oil derrick strung with lights on top of the building. The plump waitress wore a black dress with a little white apron and the bartender bounced on the balls of his feet when he walked. The jukebox was loud and the songs were old and there was no dancing and little talk among the dozen or so drinkers. No one seemed to notice us, except for a scrawny roughneck at the pool table who watched Tee for a while before he went back to his game. The waitress came over and we ordered beer and she brought it and went away and things were going pretty well till Tee started yelling about bottled skunk piss. The bartender no longer bounced on the balls of his feet and the waitress didn't wait on us.

There must have been a hundred beams holding up the next place's Sheetrock ceiling. The dance floor looked like a forest. The dancing was lively, just two couples weaving themselves and their partners through the poles in a design that betrayed years of practice. During the slow numbers the couples would sit together at a table near the jukebox and drink beer and gaze happily at one another. The men were tall and thin, with neat wavy hair. The women, short and plump, did all the talking between dances. The song changed to a bunny hop and they were up again.

Tee pointed his beer bottle toward the bar. "You ever seen that guy before?"

It was the scrawny roughneck from next door. He sipped a beer and openly studied Tee. "I've never seen him before."

"He's been following me. I think I saw him out there in L.A. He's the one they hired to git me."

I looked at the man again. He wore a battered hard hat, a cowboy shirt black with weeks of grime; his face was dark and hungry for trouble.

"I seen him before that too. He's the one. Let's git outta here."

We left our beer and stepped outside. The man watched us all the way. Tee was shivering.

"Look, you go back to the car and get Tabor. I'm goin to wait in the doorway and jump that s.o.b. when he comes out." He felt his jacket pocket. "I'll wait for you in there. It ain't goin to hurt havin a lawman around in case we have to kill him." And Tee slipped into the next bar.

I looked back in the bar we had left. The roughneck was hitching up his pants and looking right at me. I stepped inside and put my finger on his chest. "I got a nervous friend. How come you're staring at him? How come you're following us?"

The roughneck stepped back in surprise; then he put a finger on my chest. "I thank I seen him somewheres before. I'm gonna git it straightened out right now."

I started toward the door. "Yeah, and I'm going to go get the sheriff. So you better forget any ideas you got right now."

"Oh yeah," the roughneck said. "Fuck that Porto Rican."

I went back to the Pontiac and began pushing and pulling Tabor. I finally got him sitting up and told him Tee needed help. He bulled his way out of the car. I was able to keep him upright and moving. The next bar looked like the others, except there were a lot of old women sitting around sipping mugs of beer. A couple of them were doing the schottish as if somebody had a stopwatch on them. Tee and the roughneck were sitting at a table in the back, staring at each other with malice. The old women studied me pushing the sheriff along. I sat Tabor on one side of the table and myself across from him. "Hey, you're crazy, man," Tee was saying, "you don't know nothin. You got the year all wrong. I don't know you."

"Yeah, you was the quarback and you fubbled five times. I remember hittin you and yore belly was squishy. You oiked."

Tee shuddered with anger. "You can't talk to me like that, you fuckin redneck."

"Aw, yer mama sucks down at Gruddy's," said the roughneck, beaming at the insult. "She fucks a Porto Rican in a jeller pickupa." His laughter showed the inside of his mouth—no teeth and a stubby tongue. Tabor was trying to keep his head up but his eyelids kept dragging it down. "Yer pappy shovels shit with a fork; he ain't that dumb, it keeps his plate clean." Tee was dumbfounded by the flow of the little man's insults. "Everbody round here is quarter queer, quarter dog doctor." I went to the bar and bought a beer for a weapon. When I got back, the sheriff's head was lying on the table. The roughneck was examining Tabor's face with his fingers. "Is this fatso really a sheriff? Are you his deppity?" I set my beer on the table. "Shut up, deppity." He turned lazily to Tee. "All right, let's tie it on, buddy. I'm gonna kick the livin shit outta you."

Tee was looking down at his hands as if he couldn't move them. "I think we ought to go back home," he said. "This guy is crazy. He ain't the one."

The roughneck reached across the table and slapped Tee. It was a harder blow than it appeared, throwing Tee's face open. He was held helpless between his fear and his rage. He started to move but the roughneck hit him again, with his fist— Tee's nose seemed to explode, his chair jumped straight back. He sat looking at the floor as if something had fallen off his face. The roughneck was thinking about diving across the table when I hit him as hard as I could on the ear, slamming his hard hat against the wall. He leaped more than fell onto the floor, his hands clutching the side of his face, his legs drawn up in spasms of pain. I kicked him in the back and tried to kick him in the head but missed. He rolled under the table. Tabor had been thrown back from the table and was blinking and rubbing his eyes. The bartender had taken out a shotgun but was staying behind the bar. I raised both hands and showed them to him. "This is the sheriff of Wadsworth County and we're just leaving." I kept my hands in the air and kicked Tabor's chair, and he stumbled to his feet.

Tee's eyes were still open, still he sat hunched over his face. I yelled at him and started toward the door, hoping he was behind me. One of the old women said, "I thank they ought to stay fer questionin." I pushed Tabor out the door and looked back. Tee was standing so that the bar blocked my view of his legs, but he was stomping on some part of the roughneck. The bartender was yelling, waving the shotgun at him. The old women were turning around and running away. I shut the door. Tabor was already in the car. Tee came out right behind me, cursing and gasping. He pounded the car door till his fists had to be broken. He threw himself into the car and screamed— I couldn't describe it if I wanted to. Then he shuddered and his body relaxed and his breathing gradually became shallower till I could make out what he was saying.

That now he was going to do what he had to do.


# 2 2


By the time we got to Wadsworth the sheriff had passed out again. Tee turned toward the ranch, driving no more than fifty. His nose was swollen, broken, jammed back into his face; occasionally he would wince. He talked under his breath, laughing to himself. His mind seemed strangely at peace; then abruptly he collapsed at the wheel, the car veered, his foot fell against the gas pedal. As I was fighting to get his arm untangled from the wheel, he jerked back, put on the brakes, and pulled the car to a stop on the shoulder. I sat there a moment, staring ahead at the empty highway. When I turned, Tee held the .45 in his hand. He smiled and laid the barrel against his temple and clicked his tongue. "You fooled me with that trick," he said, "but never again. Get out of the car."

"Tee, what are you doing?"

"I want you to drive. Get out of the car."

"It won't be worth killing him."

"I'm goin to kill him and I'm goin to kill her. You're like the rest, you don't believe me, you don't think I got the guts, you think he did it. He said I couldn't do it, but I did. He saw me. I waited till they got right up close and then I blew his head off. See, he's never killed a man—*it was easy!* Get out of the fuckin car!" I got out and stood on the shoulder. In neutral he revved the engine as high as it would go; then he told me to get in and drive.

After less than a mile he told me to stop. We sat motionless for a moment, then he slumped against the door, but his eyes were open and he laughed when I looked at him. He got out and stumbled into the ditch behind the car. I could hear him retching. He came back to the driver's side and motioned me over. He pushed the car past a hundred; we were outrunning the headlights, hurtling into the darkness. I caught a glimpse of the ranch turnoff; Tee's shoulders flinched. He hit the brakes and the Pontiac skidded down the highway like a wounded animal. He backed the car at full speed, the yawing finally throwing us off the road. He hit the brakes again and the car spun around, coming to rest in the middle of the highway, the turnoff a few yards away. Tee was breathing hard; he had dropped his hands from the wheel and was looking around as if he didn't know which way to go. With his head turned so that I couldn't see his face, he asked me if I wanted to go hunting with him.

From the crest of the ridge the roof of the Little House was a small square of light. I thought, or maybe I just imagined, I saw two figures standing by the pool watching us approach. Tee drove down to the ranch compound, winding through the roads behind the Big House. A light shone on the third floor. Through the trees I saw a car pull out of the parking lot and disappear behind the Little House. A moment later it appeared on the west road headed toward the highway. I hadn't been able to tell whose car it was. Tee stopped the Pontiac in the grove of cottonwoods near the bunkhouse. He shut off the motor and we watched the entrance to the Little House. Then behind us, in the direction of the Big House, a door slammed. Then a motor started up, but no car appeared and the sound of the motor idling, if it was still on, was too low to hear. Tee started the Pontiac and we drove once around the Little House. He honked the horn but didn't stop. He jumped the Pontiac off the parking lot, across the wide gravel ditch, churning up the bank to the south road. He turned off the headlights. There was no need for them: the road was white in the darkness and easy to follow.

I knew where we were going without recognizing the way. It was as though I weren't in the car. The .38 lay heavy and unnecessary in my pocket. I looked at Tabor asleep in the back seat—he wasn't here either—there was just Tee, sinking deeper and deeper into his brutal, destructive dream. I wasn't going to wake him, I wasn't even going to try.

Tee turned the car east into the hills and we followed the winding road up the ravine toward the springs where Billy Orrance had been killed. Tee parked the car at the fence and told me to get out. I caught his arm before he stepped through the fence. He yanked free of the barbed wire and began backing away. I followed him along the fence. "Why are you coming back here, Tee? There's no one here."

He stopped, his face in shadows. "I told you I wanted you to go hunting with me. You've got to believe me."

"I've already seen the place where you killed him, Tee. They're back at the Little House, if you want to go hunting."

"No! That's not what I meant!" And he started walking down into the black tunnel of trees. His head was the last thing to disappear. I gripped the barbed wire with both hands and listened, but there was no sound. I let go of the wire and still did not move. The path through the trees was a black hole. I was about to go back to the car when I heard the shot. I crawled through the fence. On the other side I stopped and listened: still, there was no sound. I took out the pistol, but I felt no danger. He was hunting himself, not me. I began walking slowly forward, calling out Tee's name.

I didn't find him. I had walked down through the trees to the clearing when I heard the car start up. I stood motionless, in that absolute stillness, and listened as the Pontiac turned around and went back down the road. I could see it for a distance; then it disappeared and I was alone. For the briefest time I was fantastically happy. *Someone else would kill him now!* I put the gun away and started walking back to the ranch.

When I caught sight of the ranch compound, nothing had changed. The Little House was as brightly lit, as still as before. I left the road and cut across the gravel ditch, up the embankment to the parking lot. I found the Pontiac parked in front of the Little House. Tabor was still asleep in the back seat. I leaned against the car and tried to get my breath, but it seemed impossible. I kept looking down through the window at the man's flaccid head. I kept seeing him dead. I finally went inside.

Tee was lying in the pit of the Little Room. I thought he was lying facedown, the back of his head blown away. Then I saw it was his face that was missing. It had been beaten back into his head. His hair was still golden, it looked new. His body seemed alive, only his face was gone. I heard a noise on the second floor and lifted the gun and went up the stairway. The noise was coming from a small bathroom off the main corridor—the sound of running water; something else, a voice, crying, laughing, talking, I couldn't tell. With the gun I pushed back the door and went in. Son was standing over the basin, looking down at the running water. He didn't look at me, he watched the gun. His face was swollen, bruised, distorted; he didn't look human, there was so much pain. He held a towel red with blood.

"Tee is dead. Do you know that?"

I looked into his eyes. They didn't seem to be there. His head barely moved. "Yeah, I know it. I killed him," he said and walked past me.

A few moments later I followed him downstairs.

# III

# 1

The body had been covered with an Indian blanket. Son stood off to one side, as though he were studying a colorful creation. A sweet odor hung in the air; Son's face was stiffened by it. He said something—he asked if I had seen them—but I couldn't understand what he meant. He repeated the question and I shook my head. The room felt stale despite the blood's perfume. The ancestral figures on the wall had never looked more lifeless. Son's voice said, "There were two of them. One of them shot me." I saw a towel around Son's arm, which he held clamped to his side. The towel was stained by his wound; I was surprised at how red his blood was. "You had better put that gun away," he said and staggered one step to keep from falling. "You had better drive into Wadsworth and get Tabor. Be sure to get Tabor. Don't get that fucking Maxwell from Toro."

"Tabor's out in the car. He's blind drunk."

"Drag him out and let's get some coffee down him. We finally need him."

Tabor was sitting up in the back seat, his eyes wide and frightened. His shirt was soaked with sweat; he was shaking and couldn't talk. I opened the door and pushed the seat forward, but he refused to get out. "My God, what's happened?"

I grabbed his shirt and yanked him forward. "Did you see anybody come by here? Goddamnit!" I slapped him but he didn't seem to notice. "Did you see two men come by here? Did you see anybody come by here? Did you hear any shots?"

"What's happened?"

"Tee is dead. Now get out of this goddamn car—"

The man groaned and closed his eyes and pitched forward. By throwing myself under his arm I was able to wedge him out of the car. He stood facing me, panting and wary. "Son's inside. He says he needs you now." And the sheriff followed me in.

We found Son collapsed in the corner of one of the couches, his eyes closed, his body folded over his wounded arm. Tabor came no farther than the door. He stared at the body, the boots and one hand protruding from beneath the blanket. As I moved toward Son, he opened his eyes and turned his head toward Tabor. "Somebody has killed Tee, Mark. Come sit over here by me." He patted the couch and the sheriff, circling away from the body, walked to the other end of the couch. "Somebody has killed Tee, Mark. What do you think we ought to do?"

The sheriff's voice was high-pitched and faint. "What're we goin to do?"

"I think it might be a good idea to get Al Fondren out here."

"Yeah, git Al Fondren out here. He'll know what to do."

"He can certify the cause of death, Mark, and we can move the body into the funeral parlor in Wadsworth. We don't want it lying around here any longer than necessary, do we? We don't want Maxwell's people in Toro to get a hold of it, do we?"

The sheriff shuddered. "Naw, we don't want that. Oh my Lord, all hell is goin to break loose now."

"You can start by taking mine and Sugar's statements, Mark. Maybe you even saw the killers. Maybe you heard the car leave. You were parked right out front, right?"

Tabor was staring at Son with dumb fear. "I didn't hear no car leave."

"It might be a good idea to get Roxie out here too, Mark."

"Roxie—"

"Get your secretary out here, Mark, she can take down our statements. There's been a senseless murder here, Mark, and you're going to have to do things right."

The sheriff seemed to try to pull himself together: he squared his shoulders. "Yeah, where's the phone? I'll call her."

"The phones are dead. We're going to have to send somebody into town. I think you and me had better stick around here till the coroner shows up. Just in case somebody else comes along, we can explain what happened. We can send Sugar into town, if you want to, Mark. You can trust him. He wasn't the one who killed Tee." The sheriff flinched and Son's face twisted under a smile. "There were two of them. I'd never seen them before. Mexicans, nationals probably. I was upstairs and I heard a commotion and I started down and there was a shot, and by the time I got downstairs one of them was standing over Tee beating his face with a gun. I didn't see the second man. He hit me as I came down the stairs and then the other man shot me. He got me in the arm and I rolled down behind the couch and the second man started kicking me in the head. But something scared them off. I didn't even know it was Tee till I was practically on top of him. I didn't even know Tee was anywhere around here. I thought he had left."

"Oh my Lord, somebody has killed Tee Texas. Tee Texas is dead."

"You better get control of yourself, Mark. You were one

of Tee's best friends, I think everybody will understand that, but you're also sheriff of Wadsworth County till next January, and if you want a future outside a goddamn ditch, you're going to have to get control of yourself."

The sheriff barely noticed. It looked like he was sweating butter. "All right, all right. What do we gotta do? We gotta git Al Fondren out here and git Roxie out here—"

"You better get a doctor lined up to meet Al back at the funeral parlor."

"Yeah, we gotta git that autopsy. Keep them grand juries off our necks."

"Maybe you ought to get Sugar here on his way. You can take his statement when he gets back."

"Oh sure. He didn't have nothin to do with it anyway. You git Al Fondren out here with his amblance and tell him to set up for a autopsy and have him call Doc Collins and git everthang ready when he gits back. We're goin to do this thang right the first time."

"Collins is a good man, isn't he? He'll do a good fast job?"

"Roxie lives out on the Jacksboro highway. You caint miss it. Little pink house bout a mile outta town on the right-hand side a the road."

Son held out a key chain. "You can take my car if you want to. It's parked down at the Big House. We better leave the Pontiac where it is for the time being."

"Yeah, we better do that. Tee was drivin it." The sheriff's face tightened. "Say, you was with him, wadn't you?"

"I was for a while. But then I got let off."

Son had stood. "Mark, he's all right. Tee was by himself when he came in. He said he let Sugar off down at the bunkhouse. You can have a talk with him later."

Tabor patted his chest for his badge. "All right, but don't talk to nobody else. Unnerstand?"

As I left the room, the two men had moved over to the

body. Son had pulled the blanket away from the head; the sheriff stood looking down into the ruined face, his legs spread wide. He gave a low whistle and touched the corpse with the toe of his boot.

The Wadsworth funeral parlor occupied a large, low house with an ambulance parked in the driveway and a proprietary sign nailed to a stake in the front yard. I rang the night bell, which I could barely hear, and in a short time a wispy man in a bathrobe and slippers let me into the front room. He showed no surprise when I told him who was dead. He stepped through a curtained doorway. The only furniture in the room where I waited was three humpbacked coffins weighted with ornate trim that in the pale darkness glowed like gold braid. The man returned in a few minutes, dressed in a business suit and carrying a satchel. I mentioned the doctor and the undertaker smiled that everything was being taken care of.

I found the secretary's house where the sheriff said I would. But there was no life about it, the blinds pulled, the garage locked; nothing moved or protested as I banged on the front door, then walked through the stiff, dry grass to the back. I knocked on the screen door till my knuckles ached. I was about to leave when I heard a voice, small and crouched, like an animal. I leaned against the door and listened. "Roxie—"

"Go away or I'll call the sheriff."

"That's who sent me."

"Go away or I'll call the sheriff."

"Look—"

"Go away or I'll call the sheriff! I know who you are!"

I drove around the square three times before I stopped at the pay phone behind the Wadsworth courthouse and called the Toro sheriff's night number. I told the sleepy man on the line that there had been a murder at the ranch, that Tee Kitchens was dead. He didn't believe me.

# 2

When I got back the body was gone. The blood on the floor had dried; it looked like crusted oil. Everything else was perfectly clean. The Little Room was filled with people. Pork Man, Caroline Jo, Maury, dressed in tight Levi's and a bathrobe, were hunched around Tabor at one end of the room. Denton, Larry, the Big House secretary gathered in another corner. Son lay on the couch, his eyes closed. His arm had been bandaged and bound to his side. The undertaker came down the stairs, went over to the sheriff, they spoke, then the undertaker went out. Everyone watched me with suspicion. Tabor got up and came toward me, smiling. He carried a small notebook and a pencil. He led me over to a leather chair near the bar. "Look, boy, ready to make your statement now? Let's go."

"I don't have a statement to make right now."

"Come on, we're just tryin to git a description a the killers. Mebbe you seen em."

"I don't think I saw them."

The sheriff was affable, easygoing. "Aw come on, nothin ain't goin to be held against you. Son's already vouched fer you. We just need to know what size and shape them spicks was and we can put it out on the radio. Git the Highway Patrol out after em. Mebbe you seen their car."

"No, I want to talk to a lawyer first."

Tabor threw down his pencil. He seemed pleasantly surprised by how high it bounced. "A *law*yer? What in the world for?"

"Maybe I did see a car."

"That's more like it." He picked up the pencil and

flipped through his notebook till he found his place. He licked the pencil lead and propped a boot on the arm of the chair. He knew he had talent. "What kinda car was it? Probly all niggered up."

"What did the others say it looked like?"

The sheriff got serious. "Whaddaya mean by that?"

"I mean, we've got to all stick together, right? We're just one big happy family. Right?"

The sheriff took his foot down and brushed off the arm of the chair. He put his notebook away. "You must a got hit over the top a the head too. You ain't talkin sense."

"You're right, I'm not. I'll make a statement in a little while. I want to talk to Son first."

The sheriff spread his legs and started walking away. "Make it quick. He ain't feelin too good." Tabor began to strut around the room. There was a siren in the distance, and in a minute or less the room was in turmoil. A man I later learned was the Wadsworth sheriff-elect and several of his cronies came strolling in. Tabor began yelling at them about using the siren before swearing-in day. It was illegal. Leaving one of the cronies stationed by the door, the argument swaggered outside. Maury rose and hobbled up the stairs. P.M. and Caroline Jo remained motionless; it took such effort to look so innocent. Denton and the secretary had gone; I hadn't seen them leave. Larry stood by himself, looking innocent too. I went over and sat by Son. He didn't open his eyes, but he raised his free arm and let it drop. "What a mess. Did Mark take your statement?"

"Not yet. I decided to wait a little while."

"Might not be a bad idea. I don't guess you saw the Mexicans or the car."

"I haven't decided yet."

Son smiled, his eyes still closed. "Might not be a bad idea to see them. Their car anyway."

"What kind of car was it?"

"I don't know. I didn't see it. Mark might be able to refresh your memory. I believe he saw it."

"I did see a car. But I don't know if it was the right one."

"It would be nice if it was. I think Mark saw an Olds. Pink and white, of all fucking things."

"Is Adrienne upstairs?"

For the moment before he spoke Son was absolutely still. "She's not here. She doesn't know anything about it."

"She's still in Houston?"

Son sat up. His eyes were dark red, as if they had been burned. "No, she came here. Tee found us here. She was leaving him for good. We got into a fight. He messed up my face, though it would be best to let the spicks take credit for it. He was crazy. He was going to kill her. He went off to find a gun—"

"He didn't have one with him?"

"There wasn't one around the body."

"One of the Mexicans must've taken it. Tee had a gun when I last saw him."

Son smiled slowly. "Maybe he did. At any rate, I wanted to get her out of here before he came back. She drove over to my place in Lubbock. She doesn't even know he's dead."

"Somebody had better tell her." I waited, but he didn't speak. "I'll go if you want me to."

Son leaned forward and wearily covered his face with his hands. "All right. Go on."

I stood. "I still have the keys to your car. I'll be back as soon as I can."

Son leaned back, his hands lying worthless by his side. I couldn't look at him. "Don't stay gone too long. I'm going to need some help when the Big House blows up."

"I'll be back as soon as I know she's all right."

"There's one thing I want you to keep in mind, son.

There were two men here. They did kill Tee. I want you to know that's true. I don't know what I said upstairs, but I was out of my head. I didn't kill him. All right?"

"All right."

Son's Lubbock house sat on a bluff overlooking a country-club golf course. The area looked underdeveloped, only three or four houses on each block, weeds thick on the vacant lots. Across from Son's house lay an orchard: the trees were dead. Below, the golf course lay silent, the sand bunkers glowing like phosphorus. I parked the car and looked at my watch. Two a.m. The house was one story, low, the windows set high in the walls. I could hear nothing from within. I unlocked the door and let myself into the house. I went down a short hall to the living room, the air was heavy with cigarette smoke. I called out Adrienne's name but there was no answer. I called her name again and heard the sound of crying. I moved through the house slowly. Adrienne lay facedown on the bed. Her crying grew quieter. I sat in a chair across the room and watched her huddled beneath a sheet. I felt calm and wise, but why was she crying now? I asked her what was wrong—why was she crying now?—but she didn't answer. She kept asking what had happened. Why was I here? I moved to the bed and grasped her arms and shook her and told her it was all right, Tee was finally dead. I thought she was going to embrace me, but her head smashed into my face. She yanked her arm free and I lost balance. She ran from the room. I followed her but grew dizzy and fell against a sliding wall. I found her in the kitchen. She had dumped the contents of a drawer on the floor and was on her hands and knees tearing through the strewn objects. I saw the flash of a knife and I pinned her arms to her sides and lifted her away from it. She feebly swung her arms at my head. I carried her back to the bedroom and held her down on the bed. She lashed her head from side to side, crying, calling out for Tee. I held her till she stopped struggling, then ceased to call out, then stopped crying. For what seemed like hours I watched her lying exhausted on the bed. She did not move or speak, her face turned away from me. Finally she asked me to leave and a few minutes later went to sleep.

I drove out to the highway and checked into the first motel I saw.

# 3

I woke about ten. The motel room was hot and white. I had slept in my clothes, so I walked out the door and drove to Son's house. The house was empty, the front door wide open. I drove downtown, where I bought a newspaper. There was no story about the death. I drove back to the ranch.

During the night, I was told, things had grown complex. I was wanted for questioning by the Toro sheriff, a man named Maxwell. Tabor was out of the case. He was all but under arrest. Someone said he was under sedation, sleeping it off in a room on the second floor. The murder had occurred ten miles outside his jurisdiction. The Toro sheriff had set up a temporary office on the same floor. It seemed to take me a quarter hour to climb the stairs.

Sheriff Maxwell was a young man who fit loosely into his expensive-looking cavalry twill uniform. His face was untanned, open, and intelligent. He looked more like a lawyer than a sheriff, and later when I met the district attorney, a swarthy, wind-beaten man, I had the impression the men had switched jobs. The sheriff greeted me civilly and asked me to sit down. Maxwell had a deputy named Phelan who made Tabor look svelte.

We were in a guest bedroom in the southwest corner of the house. The canopied bed had been pushed against one wall and a long folding table placed near the windows. The drapes were drawn and two lamps stood beside the table. Maxwell worked at a desk near the door. Phelan paced back and forth, from the bed, where dozens of photographs were spread out, to the door. He would pick up a photograph and walking back and forth peer over it at me. A telephone line had been brought into the room, and for fifteen minutes Maxwell did nothing but assure people that everything was all right. He didn't seem much interested in solving the murder. By the time he drew a chair next to me he had given me too much time to think about what I wasn't going to say. Maxwell told the deputy to ask Mrs. Jones in, and to bring another chair. Mrs. Jones, he explained, was the Toro court stenographer. She seemed very kind and sympathetic. She crossed her legs and propped a steno pad on her knee. The sheriff had pulled his chair in close too. There was a narrow path between them, but it led directly to Phelan, whose eyes were rapidly sinking into his fat-filled face. The sheriff spoke to me in a direct fashion, his voice slightly louder than I had expected.

"Would you like to make your statement now, Mr. Campbell?"

"No, not exactly. As a matter of fact, I've already given one. You see," I said, after not very much of an absolutely perfect silence, "I gave a statement to Sheriff Tabor last night."

"Have you signed it?"

"No, I haven't signed anything."

"Has it been transcribed?"

"I don't think so. I haven't seen it."

Maxwell glanced at Phelan. "Was it written down?"

"Not that I had anything to do with."

"Tabor just memorized it."

"I believe he had a little notebook."

Phelan snorted. Mrs. Jones looked toward him sympathetically. Maxwell seemed to take a greater interest in my future. He lightly touched my knee. "Would you tell us what happened?"

"I don't think so. I think I would like to talk to a lawyer."

"Did you kill Tee Kitchens, Campbell?" Each of the interrogators seemed to draw nearer.

"No, I didn't," I said, and something within me broke and I began to relax; they would never catch me now.

Maxwell's voice was lower, his words measured; he even seemed to sneer slightly. "We know you didn't kill Tee Kitchens." He took a breath, as carefully thought out as a speech. "On the other hand, we think you know who did kill Tee Kitchens." The sheriff was my friend. So was Mrs. Jones. They would protect me from Phelan, who had walked back over to the bed to look at photographs. "Do you know who killed Tee Kitchens?"

"No, I don't. I would like to see a lawyer now."

"We'll get to that in a minute. Why did you report the murder to us last night?"

"I don't know what you're talking about, Sheriff."

Maxwell grimaced wearily. "Yes, you do, Campbell. That was a long-distance call you made last night. It went through the switchboard in Estacado."

"I still don't know what you're talking about."

Maxwell sighed. Phelan had his back to us, listening. Mrs. Jones finally cracked and yawned.

"Where did you go last night? Where'd you spend the night?"

"Sheriff, I'm not answering any more questions right now."

Phelan moved around to stand directly in front of me.

"That's your right," said Maxwell, pushing his chair away from me, looking at Phelan. He took a cigarette from his pocket, offered me one, and lit his. "What happened to you? You look like you've been in a wreck."

"It happened a couple of days ago."

"You look tired, Campbell. Maybe you'd like to get some sleep."

"I think I would."

"Would you help us out with a little polygraph exam this afternoon, Campbell? After you've cleared it with your lawyer."

"I'll see what he thinks about it."

"Good. There's really no need for it." We both rose. Maxwell took my arm as we moved toward the door. "As far as I'm concerned, with two eyewitnesses having seen the killers, I figure we'll pick them up sometime today. It's just that old man Kitchens has raised all sorts of fuss with the papers and the district attorney and so forth. We just have to be on our toes and follow every lead to the end. Do you know what the book says, Campbell? It says that no investigation at all is better than a half-assed one like Tabor pulled last night." Maxwell was smiling coldly, blocking the doorway. I could feel Phelan and Mrs. Jones behind me. Maxwell laughed. "Do you know that the body had been moved, autopsied, embalmed, and the wounds closed before I was ever really aware that a crime had been committed? Do you realize that after the death certificate had been signed, the means of death listed as bludgeoning, the cause of death hemorrhaging within the dura, that a man from Lubbock came over and that, though the body was already powdered and puckered, that he poked around the back of the dead body's head and found a bullet exit hole about the size of a goddamn quarter of a dollar? Do you know what else happened? We sent a man back over to Fondren's and found a .45 slug lying in the bottom of this poor sonofabitch's bucket of blood. And there's another little thing, by goddamn, all you witnesses traipsing around the country like school was out!"

"Easy, Slapsy, take it easy," said Phelan.

Mrs. Jones looked over the deputy's shoulder. "It's Mr. Renquist on the phone again, Sheriff Maxwell."

"Goddamn sonofabitch," said Maxwell and went back into the bedroom.

Phelan nodded at me. "Just stay put for a minute."

I leaned against the wall just outside the door. I could hear voices in the kitchen down the hall. Two booted highway patrolmen came out, blowing into their coffee cups. Whoever Maxwell was talking to was doing the talking. The sheriff had a way of drawing out his yeses and nos that reminded me of cooing. Phelan leaned against the other side of the door, watching me. I said cheerfully, "I wonder if I could get a cup of coffee."

Phelan clicked his teeth together, like banging a box of dominoes out on a marble table. "In a minute." Then Phelan got quizzical. "You from around here?"

"I used to be. But I've been gone."

"Where?"

"California."

"How long?"

"Ten years, I guess."

"Ten years is a long time to be gone and come back real sudden."

"I think maybe you're right."

Maxwell came to the door, his face tense with anger. He smiled, making it worse. "That was the district attorney. It looks like we're going to have us a little inquest. But then there's no worry about that, is there? Whatever it's going to be, Judge Thomas will preside." Phelan nodded. Maxwell spoke to me, "You know Judge Thomas?"

"I never heard of him."

"That's funny," Maxwell said slowly, "I thought you two would be asshole buddies."

"I don't know why you would think that."

"He doesn't know why I would think that." Then to me: "So you don't have a thing to worry about now, Campbell. You probably won't even need that lawyer."

"I'd like to get some sleep anyway."

Maxwell nodded. "You can sack out here if you're welcome. If you're not, we can get you a motel in Toro. We would appreciate it if you stayed close till after tomorrow. When you testify."

"I was thinking about going to Flavannah, if that's all right with you. It's my hometown and I sleep better there."

"It's all right." Maxwell took out a notebook. "Just give me the address." I told him; he wrote the address down and then, as if Phelan were deaf, showed him what he had written. "You're staying with Cunningham."

"I'm staying at one of Cunningham's rent houses."

"Oh? He gave me this as his home address."

"I don't know much about it, except that I thought he lived in Lubbock. Something Tophill Lane."

The sheriff looked down at the piece of paper. "It's not that important. Are you a close friend of Cunningham's?"

"Fairly close."

"You've been staying at his house for a couple of weeks."

"That's right."

"You've known each other for a long time—but you hadn't seen each other in a long time."

"No. It had been a long time."

"Do you work for Cunningham?"

"No, we're just good friends."

"He says you work for him."

"That's wrong."

"He says you're his bodyguard."

I waited for a second, but I was pretty far behind. "No. No, we were thinking about forming a partnership. It never came off."

"But other people have said the same thing. That you were Cunningham's bodyguard."

"It's not true. Do I look like a bodyguard?"

"One person has said you were hired to kill Tee Kitchens."

"That's bullshit."

"I know it is." He shuffled through papers on the desk. "The whole thing is bullshit. But what are you doing here then, Campbell? What are you doing here at the ranch?"

"I'm on vacation. I was a guest here."

"A guest of Mr. Kitchens."

"Yes," I said. "I was."

"What kind of car"—the sheriff smiled to himself—"did you see leaving the ranch?"

"It was an old car. Oldsmobile, I think."

"What color?"

"Pink and white, orange and white. Something faded."

"And there were two men in it?"

"I don't want to answer any more questions right now."

"Of course you don't. Did you know the men?" Phelan and Mrs. Jones moved around a lot. Maxwell didn't seem to care if I answered. "I thought you were a friend of *Mrs.* Kitchens."

"I am. But I got to know her through her husband."

"How long have you known her?"

"Not long."

"How long had you known Tee Kitchens?"

I pushed away from the wall. "Look, I'm not answering any more questions."

"Longer than you had known his wife. So you saw the killers' car. But then anyone could have been in it. You didn't see who was in it." I didn't answer and Maxwell nodded. "Do you know where Mrs. Kitchens is?"

"No."

"You haven't seen her?"

"Not lately."

"Not in a couple of days."

"That's right. She was in Houston the last I heard."

"She wasn't here last night?"

"Not to my knowledge. I didn't see her."

"And no one told you she was here?"

"No."

"We know she was here last night." He smiled. "We would like to talk to her before the inquest, if you see her. As far as I'm concerned, Mrs. Kitchens is as much a suspect in this case as you and Cunningham. Did you see anybody else while you were wandering around last night?"

"Tabor."

"But he was passed out."

"Maybe."

"You think he might've been awake at the time of the murder?"

"It makes as much sense as having me or Mrs. Kitchens as suspects. Hell, we weren't even there."

"Were you together? Then how the hell do you know she wasn't there?"

"I'm taking Son Cunningham's word for it."

Maxwell smiled. "Did you see anybody in the Big House?"

"No."

"When was the last time you saw P. M. Estep?"

"Before the murder? At Tee's lodge on Lake Snyder. About ten-thirty."

"Do you know what time he came back to the ranch?"

"The first I saw of them was after I got back from Wadsworth."

"Maury Mueller was with Estep?"

"As far as I know."

"And a woman named Caroline Jo Magaha."

"As far as I know."

"Why did you go into Wadsworth?"

"Cunningham sent me."

"Why?"

"The phones were dead. Somebody had to go."

"No, why didn't you go into Toro? The murder occurred in Toro County."

"I didn't know that."

"Then why did you call me when you got into Wadsworth?"

"Look, Sheriff, I need some sleep. I'll answer all your questions after I talk to a lawyer."

"The phones in the Big House weren't dead."

"Look, Maxwell—"

The phone rang and the sheriff smiled. "It seems to me the Big House would have been the logical place to go. When the son is dead, the father should be the first to know."

"Maybe so, but that's just not the way things happen around here."

"No, it's not, is it, Campbell? Things aren't right around here, are they? Things stink around here, don't they?"

Mrs. Jones came to the door. "Senator Alberts on the phone, Sheriff Maxwell."

Maxwell stared at me, but his face had become still, as if I had made the winning move. "Senator Alberts," he said. "I bet he saw that car too, a pink and white Olds, two Mexicans in it. I bet he was out watering his roses last night and they drove right by and waved. Howdy, Senator. Howdy, boys." He turned and went back into the room.

# 4

I drove straight to Flavannah and found Son asleep in the bedroom. I went into the living room and turned on the TV and lay on the couch and waited. I woke to the sound of a typewriter. It was dusk and the house was filled with a soft blue light. I got up and turned the TV off and went into the kitchen, where Son sat shirtless before a type-writer. He didn't look up. The typewriter was too small for him; there didn't seem to be room for his hands.

"Be through in a minute. I got a little masterpiece here I want you to read. How did everything go?"

"All right."

He finished the page and started another. But after a few lines he pulled the paper from the roller. He shuffled the papers he had typed. "Did you see A. last night?"

"I saw her."

Son stopped, looking down at the papers in his hand. "How was she?"

"Not too good."

"What happened?"

"She went a little crazy for a while, but she's all right now."

"Did you stay with her last night?"

"No."

"Why the hell not?"

"She was all right. She didn't want me to stay. I got a motel room."

Son went back to the papers. "You haven't seen her since last night?"

"No. I went back this morning but she was gone."

"I've been trying to get hold of her all day. I couldn't go over myself. I imagine she's gone down to Houston. We'll find her. Here, read this while I take a shower." I took the papers and Son stood. "Have you talked to anybody today?"

"Just Maxwell."

"What do you think of him?"

"He's smart."

Son nodded. "I just hope he's smart enough. What did you tell him?"

"Nothing."

"Nothing at all?"

"I told him I saw the car. That's all."

Son studied me a few seconds, then nodded brusquely and went into the bathroom and turned on the shower. I read his statement.

Previous to the day of June 13, 19__, I was in the employ of The Kitchens as the manager of his farm lands in Toro, Wadsworth, Flavia and White Deer Counties. I had been in this position since September of 19__. On the day of June 13, 19__, there was a meeting at the El Toro headquarters. It concerned the financial position of the ranch. Myself, Mr. Kitchens, and others were in attendance. Among the decisions reached was that to sell the farm land mentioned, approx. 2500 acres, and to terminate my employ at the ranch. I was in agreement with this action, feeling that the farm land was among the best available sources of capital for the ranch. I had for some time been anxious to turn my attention to my own affairs which had been neglected since I had gone to work for Mr. Kitchens.

The meeting at the ranch broke up at approx. 1:00 PM. Everyone was in optimistic spirits since with consolidation of ranching operations more capital would be available for operations. Mr. Kitchens, as was everyone, left the meeting in high spirits.

Myself, Mr. Kitchens and Maury Mueller drove down to Mr. Kitchens' lodge on Lake Snyder. Several of Mr. Kitchens' closest friends joined us there. We arrived at approx. 3:00 PM. Some guests had arrived before us, but most came afterward. At approx. 4:00 PM. Mr. Kitchens informed me that his wife was flying in from Houston early that evening and asked if I would mind meeting her plane. Mr. Kitchens gave the excuse that he did not want to leave his guests for the several hours it would take to drive to Lubbock and back. He asked me to drive her back to the lodge or to the ranch if she was too tired. I agreed and Mr. Kitchens asked me to phone him in case his wife would be at the ranch, since he wanted to tell her about the meeting earlier that day.

At approx. 5:00 PM. I left the lodge, driving Mr. Mueller's car. I was leaving somewhat early to meet the nine o'clock plane, but I wanted to stop by Marvin DeKalb's office in Lubbock for an appointment I had made earlier in the week. Mr. DeKalb was in his office and we talked for over an hour and then went out to dinner.

I arrived at the airport at 9:10 PM. to find that the plane had come in thirty minutes before. Mrs. Kitchens had expected her husband to meet her and was upset at that and the fact she had not been told of the meeting earlier that day. We ate in a restaurant in Lubbock and then drove to the ranch, arriving at approx. 11:00 PM. I had forgotten to call Mr. Kitchens and the ranch phones were out of order. I was going to drive to Wadsworth to the nearest phone, but Mrs. Kitchens asked me not to. Instead we sat in the Little Room and Mrs. Kitchens questioned me about the meeting which had occurred earlier that day. She mentioned her plans to divorce Mr. Kitchens and felt somehow betrayed by the plans to consolidate the ranch. We were having this discussion when Mr. Kitchens came in. This was approx. midnight.

Kitchens' mood was totally changed. He was drinking and had been in a fight. He seemed irrational, swearing at both of us, accusing Mrs. Kitchens and myself of plotting against him. He kept tormenting Mrs. Kitchens, physically abusing her. I became angry at his bullying and pushed him away and he struck me and I struck him in return. Then Mr. Kitchens got control of himself and became subdued and apologetic. I left the room and went to the bathroom on the second floor. I was there a few minutes and I heard Mrs. Kitchens leave. I went down to the kitchen and approx. 5 minutes later I heard something which sounded like a door slamming, so I went back downstairs. It must have taken me two minutes to get downstairs. I was in no particular hurry.

I found a man, a Mexican male, kneeling over Mr. Kitchens' body, repeatedly striking his face with the butt of a gun. I yelled at him as I came downstairs and another man who I hadn't seen shot me, wounding me in the arm. The first man struck me in the face with his gun and they ran out. I went over and saw that Tee Kitchens was dead. His face was mutilated almost beyond recognition. Since my arm was bleeding a great deal I went upstairs to fashion a tourniquet out of a towel.

At this time Rogers Campbell came into the bathroom. He told me he had seen an old car driven by two Mexicans leaving the ranch grounds just prior to his discovery of the body. Campbell gave chase to the car but with no success. Meanwhile Sheriff Tabor, who was a guest at the ranch at the time, had begun a preliminary investigation.

Son had finished his shower and stood watching me stare at the last page. He sat down at the table, leaning against the wall. He was naked, dripping water like sweat. "What do you think of it?"

"It's all right. A couple of things need to be changed."

"Like what?"

"Like you make it look like Adrienne killed Tee, you goddamn sonofabitch."

"Look, we can't all come out smelling like Sunday-school teachers. Maybe she had a reason and the opportunity to kill Tee. Maybe I did. Maybe you did. We'd be fools to try to hide it. We've got to admit what's true."

"Sure, Son."

"Anything else wrong?"

"Yeah, one little point. There weren't any Mexicans there. You killed Tee and everybody knows it."

Son didn't move. "What would you do if I told you I did?"

"You already have."

"And you believed me?"

"It seemed pretty logical at the time."

"I told you, I was half out of my head, Sugar. I didn't know what to do. I had to think up something. I was going to try self-defense, but then it finally got through my thick skull that that wouldn't look too good with the body messed up like it was."

"You shot yourself?"

"Oh yes. Never thought I'd be able to, but it wasn't that bad. Al patched me up before anybody had a good look at the wound. It's not going to make that much difference anyway."

"You want me to believe you did all this because you think Adrienne killed him?"

"Tell you the truth, son, I don't know. She might have, yeah. If it looked to you like I killed him, then it looked even more to me like she did. O.K., I left the two of them downstairs, like I said. About ten minutes later I heard a shot, I ran downstairs, and Tee was dead. Adrienne was gone. Like I said, it was about ten minutes between the time I left them and the time I heard the shot, and well, a lot of things can happen in ten minutes and the fact that she had worked up the nerve to shoot him did seem like one possibility."

"There weren't any two Mexicans?"

"There were two Mexicans all right and they actually might have killed Tee, but I doubt it. Adrienne and I ran into them on the ranch road when we were coming back from the airport. They said they had gotten lost and their car had broken down and maybe they were acting a little suspicious, but I threw them in the story without really thinking that much about it. Now it's too late to change."

"His face . . . she couldn't have done that."

Son took a deep breath. "No, I did that. I don't know what happened, Sugar, I must have blacked out there for a while. I guess I was killing him again . . . I had wanted to kill him, but somebody had beat me there." He stopped. "Look, we can go over all this later, maybe we can come up with something better, but right now we've got to concentrate on helping A. . . . just in case she did kill him, Sugar. We've got to find her, be sure she's all right, get her with a lawyer so she can get everything straight. And, son, if I sound callous or calculating, it's only because I'm scared to death. I don't want to lose that girl. Or myself, if I can help it."

I finally moved my head. "I don't want to lose her either."

"Good." Son stood, looking down at his body as if he had just discovered his nakedness. "You might have to go down to Houston tonight. If Adrienne's there, somebody's going to have to bring her back for the inquest. You better see if you can get some sleep."

"Son, what are we doing?"

"We're doing what's right. See if you can get some more sleep."

"Sleep? All I've been doing is sleeping." I sat in the kitchen a long time after Son had dressed and gone.

# 5

When I woke I found ten one-hundred-dollar bills on the kitchen table, along with a business card and a note from Son telling me I could find Adrienne at this address. In the center of the card sat the word FOOSE, in the lower left corner INVESTIGATIONS, RARE BOOKS, ETC. . . . and in the lower right corner a Houston address and phone number. I went through the bills again. They were ten of the cleanest things I had ever seen. The keys to the red Lincoln were clipped to the business card. It was nine o'clock; seven hours later I was driving around Houston, trying to find West Gray Street.

I parked in front of a dance hall atop which stretched a billboard with a neon facsimile of a girl's twitching ass. Rock music ground out the front door. The street was narrow, dark, and jammed with parked cars. The number of the business card fit the vacant lot across from the dance hall. At the rear of the vacant lot I found a rambling, labyrinthine structure. A hall ran like a maze through the building; at intervals stairways led up into the darkness. Most of the offices were vacant, littered with debris, empty so long they looked like caves. Senseless, gapped lettering still clung to the frosted-glass doors. Dim lights were strung down the ceiling of the hall, which led to the back of the building, where I found a wall of mailboxes. One of the few with a name and number was Foose's.

Foose unlocked the door and I followed him through a bare waiting room into another room not much larger than the first but choked with books. There was no furniture, no walls, nothing but books. Foose disappeared behind a desk of books and asked me to sit in a chair stacked with books. The window behind Foose looked out on the dance-hall billboard.

"Well, what can I do for you?" said Foose, and we stared at each other.

"Have you heard what's happened?"

Foose threw himself forward, peering down at something on his desk. "Of course I've heard what's happened. How uninformed do you think I am?" He leaned back, clasped his hands behind his head, and smiled. "Fairly uninformed, I guess."

"Look, I'm not feeling that bright myself. I drove down here to find Adrienne and get her back to Toro in time for the inquest tomorrow. Are you ready to go?"

Foose stared at me, then looked away. "Maybe. Life is never simple."

"Well, something is simple. If Adrienne doesn't get back in time for that inquest tomorrow—today—she's going to be in worse trouble than she is now."

"Trouble—"

"They suspect her of murder, Foose."

Foose looked over his desk, his eyes darting around his trembling hands. "I hadn't decided whether I was going to take this case, but I guess I probably will. Now, there are a few facts I want to get straight first."

"Foose, let's find Adrienne and get started back to West Texas, and then we can start getting facts straight."

The small man flushed and his hands disappeared under his desk. "You let me be in charge of things here. We've got plenty of time. What time is it?"

"Two o'clock."

"We've got plenty of time." He watched me alertly. "We've got to be some place at three." He laughed. "You see, *I* know where Adrienne is and *I* know what has to be done." He clasped the back of his head. "I also know who killed her husband and by God I'm going to prove it." I didn't say anything. "She's no murder suspect and you know it. I'm going to run that bastard down with or without your help. Why don't you start by telling me what happened."

"Which story do you want? Mine, Son's, or the one we're going to tell the judge?"

"The truth will do. Actually, I would like to hear your version. I already know Cunningham's." He looked at me quickly. "He called me earlier this evening. He read me his statement and told me your part in it."

"Did he tell you it was a lie?"

He made a weary noise. "He told me why he was lying."

"Do you really think she could have killed him, Foose?"

"No—*what?* Is that why he is lying? Did he say he was protecting her?"

"What story did he tell you, Foose?"

He was talking to himself. "I suppose she's capable, I have no illusions, *still* . . ." Then to me: "That might mean he really *is* trying to protect her."

"Maybe."

His eyebrows shot up. "Ah, but then it might be a smoke screen. He might be trying to cover his own guilt . . . by appearing guilty!"

"It's faintly possible."

Foose was thinking about something else. "And you would like to see him brought to justice."

"I guess you could call it justice."

"Yes. Why don't you tell me what Cunningham told you."

"That the two Mexicans didn't kill Tee. That he went upstairs, leaving Adrienne in the Little Room with Tee, that he heard Adrienne's car leave; then about ten minutes later he heard a shot, ran down, and found Tee dead. There was nobody in the room. He shot himself, with the idea of making it look like he had killed Tee in self-defense, then he got scared and changed it to the two Mexicans story."

"He didn't tell you anything else?"

"No."

"Nothing about what had happened before?"

"He picked Adrienne up from the airport, they went back to the ranch, Tee came back, they had an argument. That's all. They did run into two Mexicans on the road, but I don't think they had anything to do with it."

"He didn't mention anyone else? He didn't mention going over to the Big House, or that that fat thug was with Tee when he came in and found him and Adrienne together? And Maury Mueller was there too, and some crazy woman?"

My mind was working in slow motion again. "No, he didn't tell me any of that. He probably hadn't made it up by then."

"Maybe. He told me much the same story he told you, except for all those other potential suspects traipsing around. Still, it smacks of truth . . . but he did say that someone shot him. He didn't see the man, or he could barely see him, standing back in the shadows; he lifted the gun and fired. I couldn't tell if he didn't know the man or didn't see him or just didn't want to tell me . . ." Foose watched me. "He said he didn't shoot himself. Do you have any idea . . ."

"It wasn't me, Foose."

"All right, another lie. Or he could be just developing a better cover story, bit by bit, and I got the later version."

"It's possible."

"I don't like Pork Man being there"—he glanced up from a note he had found amid a stack of books—"at the time of the murder." He looked at me for a long time, like a man searching for something he hadn't really lost. Then he stood. "Sometime I want to go over what happened between you two in Mexico. But not now."

"No, not now."

"Good. Right now there are more links missing than found, but for now your attitude is enough." He reached his hand across the desk. "Let's be partners against this crime." Our clasped hands felt cold and small. "First, let's go see what the papers have to say. Then we'll talk to a friend of mine who might have some answers. Perhaps this was not an act of passion. Not an act of passion at all."

We drove downtown in the Lincoln. Foose directed me to stop across from the Rice Hotel, where Son and I had met Mr. Dolly. I waited in the car while Foose went across the street and bought the final edition of the morning paper. The news story was brief: a young West Texas rancher had been allegedly murdered by two itinerant laborers. The suspects had not been apprehended. There were no photographs and no mention of any of us. We sat for a while saying nothing. "I think there's a massive cover-up going on, Campbell. It's going to be up to us to learn who is protecting whom. Let's go see what Moser can tell us. This is no mere murder." He gave me directions and we drove across town.

Moser, a reporter for the *Examiner*, lived in a neighborhood of crumbling boardinghouses, radiator shops, used-paperback stores, and dank, closed bars. We climbed to the second floor of a yellowing apartment house. The door was ajar and Foose went in without knocking. The apartment was one large, dim room, with a half dozen windows looking out on what Foose said were the grounds of an abandoned madhouse. A number of what looked like ex-inmates were wandering around the room, but they paid no attention to us. Foose went across the room and sat by a man with a tumbleweed hairdo and an open book slammed up against his face. The hair moved in small jerks behind the book, which he finally put down. It was a little like opening a coffin. The reporter's face was pitted, jaundiced, and flaccid in the dim light. He wore black rimless sunglasses, and now that the book had been drawn aside, his jittery head moved from side to side as if he weren't quite sure where we were. He sipped wine from a jelly glass and was so drunk he looked spastic. He made a growling sound and moved his hands around what I took to be an imaginary steering wheel. Foose started telling about the news story, but was stopped short. The reporter knew about the story, he had written the headline. He tore through the paper. "Cowboy killed in West Texas, no, lemme show you some real news." He tore through the paper again, pressing each sheet against his face. "No head, no story, just one little name change and it's more news than any cowboy killed in Texas." He handed a sheet of the paper to Foose, who scanned it, then handed it to me. "The masthead. The real news is in the masthead!" Moser's black glasses were aimed at me. "That's the way they work in this fucking town. When the *Examiner* is sold, you read about it in the *Press*."

"You don't think there's any connection, do you?"

"*What?*"

"Between Dolph Gunther's buying the *Examiner* and Kitchens's death."

Moser turned away and called out, "Payne! *Payne!*" A thin blond woman came out of the kitchen and sat at the reporter's feet. She stared at Foose and myself with distrust. Moser looked down at the top of her head. His voice was heavy with self-pity. "Whatever happened to Marianne?" The girl got up and slammed out the front door. For a minute Moser stared at the floor she had walked across, and when his eyes reached the door, he rose and followed her out.

"Let's wait," Foose said. "He'll be back." We were alone now. Whoever had been wandering around the room had wandered out. "Moser is willing to help us," Foose said, "but he's really after bigger game. While we bring Cunningham to justice, Moser is going to expose the financial bones of this mammon. You see, the part about the masthead—Dolph Gunther has just bought the *Examiner* from the Fath Foundation and Fath Foundation, they are the ones who were negotiating to buy out El Toro. Don't you see the possible connection? Maybe Dolph Gunther has been trying to buy El Toro and he hasn't been able to do it!"

"And now he won't have to buy something he already owns?"

"Yes. Now the Fath deal won't go through. Adrienne will inherit the ranch. He won't have to buy something his daughter already owns. That's Moser's point. Tee was killed for his ranch, not by Adrienne, but by her father. *Her father's agent.*"

"It sounds a little farfetched to me, Foose."

"I know." There was a crash on the stairs. Foose held up a hand you could see light through. "You might laugh, but all along I think June was right. There was a conspiracy, a conspiracy among the most powerful men in this state to murder Tee Kitchens. Let's wait and see."

The reporter slammed through the door. He moved toward me, grinning wildly, as if I were his favorite creation. "Ah, so you are Foose's evil, clever friend! You know why I drink? So I can foretell the future." He laughed. "It's

just that sometimes I can't remember it in the morning." Moser poured wine so that his glass stayed exactly
full. "Do you want me to predict your future, friend?"

"Not particularly. Are you ready to go, Foose?"

"No, wait . . ."

The reporter shrugged. "Your future is murky, friend,
because it's so closely linked to your past. That's your future, friend, your past. See, I'm the perfect fortune-teller, I
can tell your future without knowing it. I transmit mes-
sages by memorizing the shapes of the letters. I'm safe,
honey, there's no need to bury me along with the truth.
What is the truth? You can tell me. I'll only know the
shape of it. You can tell me that you killed Kitchens. Nothing will happen to you at all. Absolutely nothing. You're
safe as a hangman. There are some murders that are *sanc-
tified*. I love truth as the Epicurean loves pleasure. I
*writhe* in it."

Foose was looking worried. "Moser, this is not the guy
who killed Kitchens. This is my friend."

"Eighty percent of them are killed by their friends and
family. Husbands kill wives, wives kill husbands; they kill
their children and their children kill them. Do you really
want to know who killed that strange man, Foose? You
don't. He doesn't. The cops don't want to know. *The New
York Times* doesn't want to know. I am the only one in the
world who wants to know." Moser poured wine in his
glass. "Do you still love that bitch, Foose?"

"Moser, we're busy men!"

"What are the facts, Foose? Adrienne Kitchens, née
Gunther, killed her husband. That's the simple truth. Now
the law is a clumsy tool at best, friend, and it might call it
justifiable homicide, temporary insanity, self-defense, old-
fashioned down-home murder . . . But what role does
your friend here play in this tragic farce? He's either the
best of men or the worst. Totally good or absolutely

evil . . ." Foose was trying to interrupt, but Moser kept talking, his hands moving out as if he were caressing his words as they floated in the air. "At times I believe Cunningham here must possess her soul. She acted as a murderous agent of his will. Then other times I see him as the victim. Sacrificing himself with a terrible deliberation. But I don't know why he is acting out this role. But I do know one thing . . . good or evil, he is only a small showing part of a giant machine—a mad, rational machine that devours people's lives like flesh. That's how I can predict the future, buddy, by our relationships to this machine. Adrienne Kitchens will come out of all this unscathed. Who knows where Cunningham here will end up—"

"This is not Cunningham, Moser, this is *Campbell.*"

"The machine takes ambivalent attitudes toward ambitious men, but you, Foose, had better watch your ass."

"Moser, we have got a lot to do tonight—"

"—and miles to go before we sleep. Gotcha!"

"I want you to tell Campbell here what you told me earlier this evening."

"Are you very fond of June McChesney? Then you had better watch her very carefully. She knows too much. She's told *me* everything I know."

"I'm afraid we're going to have to leave."

Moser replied matter-of-factly, "Don't leave me alone. Don't leave me alone now."

"Then tell Campbell what you told me, about Dolph Gunther."

"He'll laugh."

"No, he won't laugh."

"The President of the United States killed Tee Kitchens." Moser giggled. Then he screamed out the girl's strange name: "Payne, oh my Payne!" And he went downstairs again. We could hear him staggering around the asylum grounds, giggling. Foose went over and stood by the window. "I'm sorry, Campbell, I thought Moser might be some help." He came back to the center of the room. "Everybody I know is going nuts. Let's go back to my place before we pick up Adrienne. There's somebody there I want you to talk to."

We drove to Foose's house. It was dawn and several open-air beer joints on Alabama were serving breakfast, the leather-faced drinkers eyeing one another. Foose lived only a half block from the freeway, which here was sunken and quiet as a canal. Two hours from now the morning traffic would be rising like a swollen river. We parked in front of a small frame house with faded blue shingles, a scruffy yard, and a couple of stunted trees whose limbs batted us at the front door. The house held as many books as the office. Foose put his finger to his lips and motioned me to follow him down a dark, book-lined hallway. Midway down the hall Foose stopped before facing doors. He laid a hand on my shoulder and then with a stiff, manly gesture turned me toward the door on the right. He disappeared into the other room. I pushed open the door. June was lying on a narrow bed, her eyes open, staring across the room. I don't know why I was so surprised that her hair was still golden; it curled around her face like a soft crown. She was more beautiful now than she had ever been. I sat in a chair near the head of the bed, so that had I wanted to, I could have reached out and touched her. She moved back but only so that she could watch me.

"Are you all right?"

"I'm all right," I said. "How about you?"

"I'm fine," she said and yawned. She watched me closely. "I was worried about you. For a while I didn't think you were going to live."

"I had doubts myself for a while."

She looked away and we were silent. Finally she said, "I know what happened." I could find nothing to say.

"They only killed his body. Didn't they? He knew that. What did he look like when he was dead? Like he was sleeping?"

"Like he was sleeping."

"Have they buried him yet?"

"Not yet."

"I'm glad I don't have to go. I don't want to have anything to do with that body. Did he have any last words? But no, he would only have spoken to his killer. What would he have said, Sugar? *Goddamn you!* Something like that. What is there in her that can cause so much love?" She lowered her face against the pillow. I turned and saw Foose standing at the door. I went out into the hall. He was crying and had taken off his glasses; without them his eyes were weak and deformed. June followed me to the doorway. She was unsteady on her feet and smiling vacantly. She leaned against us for support. Her back, as we helped her to the bed, was frail and warm. "It's all right, Sugar, he's always liked me and, see, to make it I'm going to have to have someone to love." She yawned and turned her face toward the wall.

I left Foose sitting on the bed, awkwardly rubbing June's hands, and went back to the front room and lay on the couch. The sun had risen and a shaft of light cut across my face. I picked up a book but it made no sense. I couldn't even understand the title. I put the book down and adjusted the blinds so that the light spread softly across the ceiling. In a few minutes Foose came out and sat on a box of books. He hung his head, then raised it to speak. "I had to get her out. If she had learned he was dead while she was in there . . . I don't know, I don't think she would have made it. I don't think she would have wanted to make it." He hung his head. "Did I do the right thing?"

"I think you did."

"I just don't know. She might have been happy there. They watched her so sympathetically. They were so understanding, but they didn't understand. What's so frightening is that I'm finally responsible for her. Is that love? She was asleep and I looked at her and realized that for the first time in my life someone's life depends on me. I realize that doesn't seem like much to a man like you, but . . . but the sad fact is that I've never been much of this world. I've never really understood what was going on." He looked around the room. "That's why I've always surrounded myself with the understanding of other men. It hasn't helped much."

"When did you get her out?"

"Yesterday afternoon. I guess it was yesterday. Days and nights don't seem to fit together any more. Things don't happen when they should." He stopped. "When we got back here, the sun was shining . . . I carried her into the house. She didn't wake till I had her safely in bed. You know, I didn't have to tell her a thing. She asked if he was dead, but she knew. It was like he had been suffering from a long illness and had finally passed on. She cried with relief. All my theories are crackpot, aren't they, Campbell? There was no conspiracy. He drove Cunningham to kill him. He *made* him kill him. I don't see how we can pursue any so-called justice. It would only be retribution. Then Cunningham would be the victim. But that's what we've got to find out. The truth. It exists. A lucid mind can touch it. I hope you don't think my interest in detection is merely mechanical." He tried to smile. "You see, I am a metaphysical detective."

"Let's get going, Foose."

Foose didn't move from his throne of books. "Do you know, he liked me. June told me that. In a lot of ways we were very much alike. He was frightened under that tough skin, Campbell. Like you are." Foose raised his hand. "I know, I know. Time to hit the road. You cowboys are all alike." He looked at his watch. "I guess we had better wake Adrienne up and you two can be on your way. Like you say, it wouldn't look good for her if she didn't show up for the investigation of her husband's death. If you left right now, what time could you have her there?"

"One o'clock."

"Wouldn't it be quicker to fly?"

"Not in the mood I'm in."

"O.K., let's get rolling."

In a few minutes we were driving into River Oaks. We parked across from a narrow three-story house that went on developing in odd shapes as far back as I could see. Foose pressed a buzzer at the gate and a Negro maid let us into a courtyard which ran along the side and back of the house where we climbed a flight of stairs to an apartment on the third floor. We followed the maid into a large octagonal room with nothing but glass for walls. Adrienne was sitting at one of the windows, looking out over the trees and rooftops of River Oaks. Foose took my arm and pushed me ahead. Adrienne turned and smiled and asked me to sit by her. "I'm sorry about last night, night before last," she said. "About what happened. You see, I had just dreamed that it had happened, that he was dead, and then you came in and told me it was so." And she put her head against my shoulder and, as June must have done, cried quietly with relief.

# 6

It was like a farce, people dashing on and off stage, their lips fluttering, their eyes glassy as they stood around memorizing their lines. Son, P.M., Maury, the people from the Big House had testified that morning. Tabor had been on the stand when we pulled up in front of the Toro courthouse, at about one-thirty. Adrienne had slept the entire trip and was so exhausted and frightened she refused to get out of the car. I found Son in the courthouse, we talked briefly, then he went down to the courtroom at the far end of the hall. In a few minutes Son and a man who looked like a retired rancher went out to the Lincoln. They sat in the car for fifteen minutes; then the two men helped Adrienne up the long shiny steps to the courthouse and into the courtroom. Almost immediately Tabor came bursting through the courtroom's double doors. He came straight toward me, either grimacing or grinning, either winking or squeezing one last tear out of the corner of his eye. We moved away from the sheriff's door, toward the other end of the hall, where a frightened little woman sat in a roomful of books. "That Miz Kitchens has been sufferin. You can read it in her face," said Tabor as he punched and hammered at the levers on the Coke machine. "Gotta dime? I was in the middle a my testimony, but they figgered it might be best let her go on in and git it over with. Then they can git some rest pills down her and let her sleep it off."

"How were you doing?"

Tabor sucked on his Coke and watched me. "I always found out tellin the truth is the easiest thang to do." He tossed the bottle at the case of empties. Phelan stuck his head out of the sheriff's door and stared at us. Tabor hitched up his belt and turned his back to the deputy. The little librarian looked trapped by all this criminality. "How bout you?"

"I'm doing all right. I think I'll probably take a little vacation on my money."

Tabor nodded. "Thad probly be a good idea. You been

workin too hard, Son says. On the verge a one a them nervous breakdowns." He grinned.

"Yeah." I grinned back. "I got paid a thousand bucks. How much are you getting for lying your ass off?"

Tabor leaned down and scrambled the Coke bottles. Then he turned and headed down the long hall toward the courtroom. It looked like he was trotting by the time he got to the double doors. I walked down and stood in the doorway and stared at Phelan. He glanced at me once but that was all. The room beyond, Maxwell's office, was empty. I walked in the direction of the courtroom. In a few minutes Son came out of the courtroom and smiled at me. He thought it was funny. "You looked wiped out, Sugar. Like the ole girl said, all you got to do is relax. But that's not your problem, is it? What is your problem, Sugar, are you just tired? You want to check into a motel and get a good night's sleep and come back and testify in the morning?"

"No, I want to get it over with."

"We think that's probably a good idea, but we want you to go in there with a clear head."

"Don't worry about it, Cunningham, my head's clear enough for what I'm going to say."

Son started to speak, then hesitated. "I guess we'll just have to wait and see."

"I guess you will."

Son clapped me on the shoulder. "I'll tell you what, Sugar, there's a razor out in the Lincoln; why don't you take it and run over to the washroom in the jail and get cleaned up. You've got fifteen, twenty minutes. You'll feel a hell of a lot better. And listen, there's no sweat in there. Everything's real relaxed. The coroner's out of town on a little fishing trip, so Judge Thomas is presiding and the D.A. is handling the questions. Maxwell is still a little hot under the collar, but he's a young man, he'll get over it."

He started to go back through the double doors but stopped. "Just keep one thing in the front of your mind, Sugar, all we want you to do is tell the truth. That's all I've ever asked of you."

"Why didn't you tell me that P.M. and Maury were back at the ranch before Tee's death?"

Son stared at me. I could have been the wall. "I did tell you, Sugar, you must have forgot. Your fan belt must be slipping, Sugar. Sure, like I told you, me and Tee and P.M. and Maury, we all went over to the Big House and hashed a few things out. We had to get all that bad blood out of our system. I mean, just because the ranch's money problems got solved, that doesn't mean there weren't some bad personal problems we still had to deal with."

"Where was Adrienne? Where was she when Tee died?"

Son smiled coldly. "Sugar, if I knew that, we wouldn't have to be going to all this fuss, would we? You wouldn't have to be lying your ass off, would you? Now, I don't know what ideas that little bastard down in Houston has been putting in your head, but if you don't go along with us, Sugar, then you're going to be pulling everything down on all our heads. You ain't just going to be getting me, you're going to get her, and you're going to get yourself into a bad crack." He paused. "Sugar, if you're really out after me, do it some other way. O.K.? I got to get back inside. Good luck on your testimony." And he disappeared through the doors. From where I was standing I could see only the jury box, with a half dozen people sitting in it, listening to someone's testimony.

The sky was overcast, the grass on the courtyard looked gray and cold as metal. I went to the café across the street. Fifteen minutes later Phelan came over and said the jury was ready. I left my coffee untouched.

P.M., Mabelline, Maury sat in the back row. Adrienne's

secretary and two men I assumed were lawyers sat at one of the counsel tables. Sitting alone at the other table was the district attorney, the man who looked like a rancher. Neither Son nor Adrienne was in the courtroom.

The district attorney patted the chair next to him when Phelan brought me in. Phelan took the bench directly behind us. Aside from the six men in the jury box, most of the people present looked like cops and lawyers. The district attorney's eyes sparkled with mischief. He nodded toward the judge—an indifferent-looking man seated high on his bench, reading a newspaper as if the rest of us were illiterate—and I was told again that the Toro County coroner was on a fishing trip. "I'm afeared he'll be back mad as a hornet"—the district attorney winked—"for his wife went along to bait the hook. Them six sad gents there are ranchers and merchants who'd rather be out somewheres else. They're nominally the grand jury here in Toro County, the ones I could drag up." The judge went on reading the paper, the jurors looking subordinate, distrustful, as the district attorney whispered instructions in my ear. "I know this is an odd kettle, neither fish nor fowl, not a grand jury, not a prelim, and not much of a coroner's inquest, but we tend to do things like this out here in the sticks. I suppose it galls some of these big-city boys"—he turned in his chair and grinned at one of the well-dressed lawyers—"but we get some good deeds done this way and keep some bad ones from happenin." He had turned his easy grin back at the judge, who had propped his alligator boots on the corner of his bench. "Now, there's no need to be frettin over a thing, if in fact you are. Sheriff Maxwell said you were concerned to have a lawyer settin at your side, but there's no need for him. You are not protected by the Constitution here, there's no swearing, no Bibles, no perjury. This is all just hearsay evidence and can only be used to impeach you as a witness at some future date. But there's no call to fret. Everbody that has run through here this morning has been singin the same song." He winked. "You feelin in good tune this afternoon, Campbell?"

"I'm going to tell the truth, if that's what you mean."

The district attorney's laugh was like his whisper, no one could hear it but me. "Well now, I wouldn't go that far, now ain't that right." He had clasped his hands behind his head and was gazing at the ceiling. Two highway patrolmen came into the courtroom and took a bench near the door. The bailiff watched them like criminals. Toward the rear of the courtroom someone coughed and the judge glanced out over our heads. "Don't you think, Campbell," the district attorney was saying, "that it was a tragic time for this boy to die? Yes, he seemed to be settin on the top of the world, didn't he? What problems that pore boy had was bein cleared up. He had tightened up his business and financial activities so that what losses he had this year was goin to turn up gains the next. Him and his daddy, on the outs for years now, had buried the hatchet. Why, even him and his lovely wife had come upon an equitable and charitable manner of splitting the blanket, so that the division would not rend them asunder, as it sometimes does to folks. Why, I had even heard that little Tee had settled on him a new career. Yessir, he was thinkin about runnin for office agin." He smiled. "Nothin so umble as district attorney, thank your stars. Most people don't know it, but little Tee—that's what he was called in school, you know, because up till he was fifteen, sixteen he was such a runt—most folks don't know it, but little Tee was always very civic-minded. My wife taught him over there in the high school, and she said civics and govermint was always his favorite course of study. He'd been student president but he slapped this teacher down one day—she'd slapped him first, but they had to move him out. Toro, Estacado, Flavannah, for the next couple years he was poppin teachers all over the South Plains." The district attorney chuckled. "Well, it got purty nasty for a while; then one day he laid out this woman in the supermarket. Laid her out cold. After that there was a lot of people hard after him." He looked at me. "Nobody around here was surprised at the way he died, Campbell, some even figgered he deserved it. Do you figger we'll ever ketch them two murderin Meskin boys? Maybe not. If I wasn't an officer of this court, I'd be tempted to say just as well."

He looked away as Maxwell and Son entered the courtroom from a door beyond the jury box. The two men moved stiffly, as if they had been together for a long time. The district attorney turned back to me, shielding his mouth with his hand. "The sheriff might be askin you a couple things now and then. He's upset with the complexity of life. I always tell my wife he was a good boy before he went off to Texas University and they turned his mind to shit." He called out to the sheriff, who was standing directly across the table, "Did you boys git Miz Kitchens restin nice?" Son had moved around behind us, sitting by an open window, staring out at nothing. Maxwell came around the table to a chair on the other side of the district attorney, who was saying, ". . . tellin Mr. Campbell here that it's a cryin shame to put a fine lady through this trial of fire, but in the long run it'll be worth it. You have met Mr. Campbell, haven't you, Slapsy?"

"We've met."

"We might as well put Campbell on the stand now. You got any more witnesses lined up for this afternoon?"

"He's the last one for now."

"Then have a seat right up there, Mr. Campbell, and we'll git this over with and *all* go fishin."

I took the witness stand and the judge folded his newspaper in his lap and studied his fingernails. Maxwell, Phelan, and the district attorney conferred for a few moments;

then the district attorney approached the witness stand. He laid his old leathery hand on the railing in front of me. "Campbell, let's dive into this business headfirst. Bout midnight on the night in question, did you see a certain two-toned Oldsmobile or some such with two occupants unknown to you leave the whereabouts of little Tee Kitchens's death?"

Son, P.M., Maxwell, the jurors, even the sleepy judge, they watched me closely as I told them about the Oldsmobile. Pink and white, orange and white—I couldn't remember which.


# 7


Tee Kitchens had two funerals. The previous day had been a running battle between two camps of lawyers, with Adrienne's side finally winning. The body was quasi-property and the wife had rights to burial superseding other parties. But to keep things peaceful it was decided to allow the old folks to bury a coffin filled with rocks and to keep the real service a secret.

The Toro undertaker didn't like the idea of burning bodies. When the urn came from Lubbock, in its huge black hearse, he had two of his men set it on the grass in front of the funeral home. He said it was the law and laid a hand on the urn and then went inside the funeral home and closed the door.

Adrienne had rented a limousine and she rode alone with the urn down to the lake. The rest of us followed behind her. It was pretty much the same bunch that had celebrated Tee's victory less than a week before. Outside Toro the headlights were switched off and the limousine led the caravan south at eighty miles an hour.

The car I was in was near the end of the line, so after we parked on the road, I stayed back as the others followed the limousine on down to the lodge. I walked over to what was left of my old pickup. The tires had been slashed, every window broken, the headlights, taillights smashed, the fenders beaten to a crumpled shine. The wiring under the hood had been ripped out, the battery overturned on the motor, its acid gnawing into the tangle of steel. The seats had been slashed with a knife and the gear lever and the door to the glove compartment broken off. They had even tried to twist off the steering wheel. I wouldn't have minded cremating the truck too.

I walked down through the trees, their leaves ashen from the dust, and found the lodge empty. It had not been cleaned since the party; bottles, broken glass, rotted food strewn around the kitchen. The mourners were on the dock. Someone had started up the big outboard, but its motor had been shut down and they were easing it back into its berth, lashing lines to its bow. Someone else was dragging a rowboat out of the boathouse and pushing its belly into the water. Adrienne stood off to one side, looking out across the water. Dressed in black she looked strangely ordinary. A group of her Houston friends had gathered possessively around the urn. I didn't notice Son till Adrienne moved toward the boat and I saw he was there, in the boat, reaching out toward her. So many people helped with the urn they stumbled against one another. Son rowed quickly, and soon he and Adrienne were far enough away that you couldn't see their faces.

Adrienne's friends gathered in the boathouse and the rest of us went back up to the lodge. I stood alone for a while, watching the boat, but then Pork Man came over and threw a heavy, sad arm around my shoulder and drew me away. "Come on out to the parkin lot, Campbell, I got a little surprise for you." As soon as we were out of sight of the others, he drew his arm away and came up with the evil version of his grin. "Too bad what happened to yore pickup. Somebody shore fucked it up. Bunch a teenage hoods, I bet."

"That's all right, P.M. I've got plenty of insurance. I might even end up making money on the deal."

"So you got some insurance too. Well well. Well, I tell you one thing, there's some people around here ain't goin to be makin quite as much money on insurance as they got figgered out." P.M. shrugged angrily. "Mebbe losin six million bucks ain't goin to git under yore buddy's skin, but I bet watchin his girl friend fry for murder will."

"What have you got on your mind, P.M.?"

"I mean, the only way them insurance turds is goin to be able to wiggle outta payin A. six million bucks is make it look like she murdered Tee Texas. There's a specific law against the beneficiary murderin the insuree. I think it's just terrible that a gal that purty will be hangin for a ugly bastard like Cunningham."

"Pork Man, what's really on your mind?"

The fat man started walking up toward the road, but when I didn't follow, he came back. "See, I already know that you think Cunningham killed that pore boy and that yore out to prove it. All I want to do is pitch in and give you a helpin hand."

"Now who in the world told you a story like that, P.M.?"

"None a yore business. I got a piece a information you might be interested in."

"Like what?"

"Like I know Cunningham killed that crazy cowboy, I know it for a fact."

"How do you know it for a fact? How do you know anything for a fact, you pussle-gut sonofabitch?"

"You better git hot under the collar, you perjurin little bastard." He looked around to see if the trees were listening. "See, I know you was lyin yore goddamn ass off yes-tidy. There wadn't any two Meskins in no pink and white Oldsmobile."

"Did I say anything about any Mexicans?"

"There wasn't no pink and white Oldsmobile."

"Now how the hell do you know that? That's like saying there's not a spider in the room. If you weren't there, P.M., it's just going to be awful hard to say, one way or the other."

"Aw, there's plenty a spiders in the room, ole buddy, but them two Meskins ain't one of them." He looked me straight between the eyes. "See, I *was* there."

I waited and then I waited some more. It seemed like I stood there looking at the dust on P.M.'s boots for hours. He was going to stand there grinning forever. When I spoke, my voice sounded thin. "If that's true, then you ought to tell them."

"Tell who what?"

"Tell them you saw the murder. Tell them you saw Son kill him."

"Now hold yore horses, Campbell. I didn't say nothin bout *seein* a goddamn thing. I just happened to be watchin the Little House at the time a the murder; I just so happened to be standin where I could see the front door and I din't see no goddamn spicks and no goddamn Olds. Now maybe them spicks coulda sprouted angel wings and flew over to the highway, but me and you know they din't sprout no goddamn wings, me an you know them spicks exist in one place and one place only. And that's right in the middle a yore buddy's twisted little mind."

"How do you know you were watching the Little House at the time of the murder, P.M.?"

"I'll tell you how, motor mouth. And I'll tell you another thing. I got a witness with me. She din't see nothin neither."

"Sounds like you got the case all wrapped up. Why don't

you just trot over to the sheriff's and tell him you didn't see a thing."

"Aw, I do wish life was as simpleminded as you, Campbell. If I walked in right now and laid out my theory, our lives wouldn't be worth a plug nickel." He paused to give me time to catch my breath. "That's right. I lied my ass off just like you an that sow-bellied sheriff. Though I got a better reason than stupidness. But I'll tell you agin, if iny a us lets out a peep, our lives ain't goin to be worth a plug nickel. Might not be anyway." The fat man didn't look quite unhappy enough about it. "This whole thing, Tee's murder and everthing, there's one big pumpkin settin behind it all."

"Let me take a guess. Dolph Gunther?"

Pork Man grabbed my arm and hustled me up the hill toward the road, now coming out with a series of low sharp yips, like an angry little dog on a big man's leash. When we reached the road, he got control of his emotions and let go of my arm. It was like putting me down. "I gotta give you credit, Campbell." He unlocked the passenger door to a new orange Mustang. "You ain't right, but you ain't wrong neither. That oughter be a lesson. Don't never figger you got this life figgered out, cause one a them spiders that ain't in the room is liable to leap up and bite you on the muffet." His paw made pitty-pats on his chest. "Dearie me, I almost had me a spasm." He sat in the Mustang and slipped a key in the lock of the glove compartment. The car moved under his weight. "You know somethin, Campbell, of all the weirdos around here, I'm beginnin to think yore the chief. Nawsir, it ain't Cunningham I ain't got figgered out." He turned the key in the lock. "Well, here's a little surprise for you. A little Christmas early. Just be shore you git the right man with it." And he reached in the pocket and brought out the Llama .380 I hadn't seen since

Mexico. I held the small gun in my hand like a bright new toy. "Never thought you'd see her agin, did you, killer?"

"Where did you get it?"

Pork Man leered. "Now where did you lose it? Aw, there ain't no mystery to it, you left the little popper in my buddy's cab. Coulda framed yore ass tighter'n hell," the fat man sighed, "but at the time there wasn't no need for it. Now look, I'm goin to do some straight shootin with you, Campbell, and I want some straight shootin back. O.K.?"

"Maybe."

"All right, asshole, now Cunningham killed that boy. Now lissen, Tabor saw him doin it, saw him committin the foul murder. Pore ole man, he was passed out out in the car and he heard this shot. This shot woke him up. He goes inside and finds Cunningham beatin on pore Tee's head like it was a drum. Screamin and yellin like a lunatic. It must a been terrible," P.M. said with great sadness. "So bad ole Tabor blocked it right out a his memry box. He just went right back out to the car and lay down and din't remember a thing till later on."

"When was that?"

"Pore ole boy tole me the whole story last night. See, I was over in Lubbock seein a man bout a speckled pup when I run into Tabor, and me and him run out to the Cotton Club and had a few. We got to talking bout that night and his memry started comin back in. It was almost like he was in a trance. He tole me ever detail. He was the one who helped Cunningham smuggle the gun outta the house."

"Are you still working for Cunningham, P.M.?"

"You don't trust nobody, do you, Campbell? You must be the loneliest man on the face a this earth."

I cocked the gun. "You know, P.M., I sure am tired of all this lying and deceit. It's just worn me out. You know, I was thinking about killing you, but now I think maybe I'm too tired. But then you never can tell when I might get a second wind."

P.M. smiled and his ears ran two inches up the side of his head. "What would you want to kill me for anyway?"

"Because I don't like you. Because you're planning to kill me."

"You flipped yore fuckin lid, boy."

"But I'm not goin to do it, P.M. You know why? Because he's playing us one against the other. Don't you see? He's hired you to kill me and then he's going to kill you."

There was nothing left of Pork Man's eyes but some glint. "I don't know what yore talkin about. I ain't been hired to kill nobody, let alone you. Mebbe they thought they was hirin me to git you onct, but I wasn't really ever goin to do it."

"No, you were hired to kill Kitchens, just like me. It was the same deal. It didn't work out. Son went crazy and killed Tee himself. I know that's what happened. Isn't that what happened?"

The fat man's mouth slid back over his face like they were skinning him. "You wasn't hired to kill Kitchens, Campbell. That was just to keep you interested. You was hired to die for the little sonofabitch. You was donatin yore body to science, Campbell, the science a makin money."

"That's what the little trip to Mexico was all about, right?"

"That's right. See, I was supposed to lay out there on the bed in that hotel room with some red goop smeared all over my face and with this here piller layin over my belly with my little .45 right under there. You was supposed to come rushin in and lean over me, and I was goin to reach up and bop the shit outta you. Cept I wasn't goin to do that, of course, I was goin to tell you the whole plan and then sneak you back acrost the border. I wasn't goin to git tied up in iny a their murderin schemes and that's the Lord's truth, Campbell. O.K., but there was this greaser already hidin in the room there and he took a swing at me and I tried to grab a holt a him and he squirted away and I guess I hit him just a little bit too hard. Too bad. See, I wasn't really tryin to kill you when you stuck yore head in that door. I thought you was the rest a them comin to git me. I popped you one before I saw who you was. By then I had to think bout gittin the hell outta there and I had to leave you behind to face the music. Now, a course, they coulda pinned that dead spick on you, if they'd a caught you, but that's the way it goes down in ole Mexico."

"So Tee was planning on fitting me out in his clothes so that he could collect his own insurance money?"

"Well, that's what the smoke screen was anyway. That's what Son and Tee was tellin each other they was doin, working on this crazy scheme to git Tee's insurance money, while in fact they was trackin each other down. The whole thing sprung up from that crazy Billy O.'s idea; he read it in *The Reader's ·Digest* somewheres, how this feller dresses this wino up in his own clothes and kills him and collects the insurance money. Somethin like that. Anyhow, that's how Billy O. and Tee killed that cowboy, the one that got snake bit."

"P.M., I've got a feeling that it ought to be a hell of a lot simpler than this."

"Oh yeah?"

"So Tee killed the first man?"

"Him an Billy O. It was this crazy idea how to git the ranch outta hock. Nobody took them nuts serious, not till Palmer shows up dead. Then I guess Tee got nervous or mebbe he figgered the kid was settin him up, with him holed up down there in Rio and with the kid up here nibblin on A.; anyway, Tee kills the kid. Some people says it was a fight and some says it was in cold blood, but everbody has purty much agreed that Tee did it. Everbody cept C.J., pore ole gal, she has gone an put herself in a sanitarium down in Shrevesport and now she caint git herself out. We'll have to go down and visit her some Satiddy."

"Did Adrienne have anything to do with any of this?"

"I wisht that cunt did, but it's too harebrained for her. Naw, she was in some kinda love with that boy. It almost drove her crazy when he disappeared. I figger her and Cunningham might a been in on helpin Tee move the body out to Soda Springs, helpin him cover things up, but I don't think neither one a them had nothin to do with the killin. Cunningham coulda been eggin Tee on to kill Billy O., but there ain't any more witnesses to that. Naw, Cunningham's too smart to git his own hands dirty. See, he egged Tee on, hopin Tee would go up for murder, but then after Tee killed the kid, he saw he couldn't pin it on him without pullin himself down too. Tee wasn't nobody's fool. Cunningham had just as much reason to knock off the kid as Tee did. And he din't figger how much pull ole Malcolm had with the local law. I don't guess anybody did— nobody figgered a man could commit a ball-face murder and git scot-free away with it—but Tee did. Naw, see, that's why Cunningham brought you down here. He figgered if Tee killed one more time, they'd put him away. Sweet buddy you got there, buddy." Pork Man laughed. "Well, I don't know that he was that hardhearted. That's just pure speculation on my part. See, I think by the time you showed up, Cunningham's plans had changed. By that time I think he had realized he was goin to have to kill Tee hisself. I think that Tee killin them other boys was just kinda practice, so he'd git up the guts to knock off Cunningham. It sounds crazy as hell, but that's my way a thinkin."

"Probably just crazy enough to be right."

Pork Man blinked so slowly I thought he was going to sleep. "You know, Campbell, it's a true fact I was hired to keep Tee Texas alive, not to kill him. That's no shit."

"Who hired you?"

P.M. looked at the gun and shook his head. "Naw, Campbell, you ain't ever goin to kill nobody. That's why Cunningham dragged you in. He knowed you wasn't the type. With me it's different." He grinned, his mouth level. "Yeah, I was supposed to conk you in the Meskin hotel, then Tee an some pilot buddy a Cunningham's was goin to fly out over the Gulf with you all dressed up like Tee and strap a bad chute on yore ass and drop you out at ten thousand feet. You woulda splattered like warm snot, Campbell. But it never came off. Tee figgered out Cunningham had the double cross on him with the pilot, and anyways his plan was to drop Cunningham out right after you, and when Cunningham didn't show up in Houston, the whole thing got called off. Ain't that a lick? Both a them boys plannin on doin away with one another down in ole Mexico and neither one a them shows up."

"And now you think Cunningham has finally killed Tee?"

P.M. shrugged. "I caint prove nothin. All I know is that Cunningham was lyin his ass off bout them spicks and there had to be some reason for it. Yeah, me and C.J. was just headed over to the Big House at the time it happened. Tee had been alive no more'n five minutes before, and there wasn't nobody in the Little House but Cunningham and her. She coulda done it, but I kinda doubt it."

"You heard the shots?"

"I think C.J. did. Either that or that extrasense stuff a hers, cause we was climbin up the Big House steps bout the time that Tee got it, and she turned to me and says real calm and collected, You know that Tee Texas is dead, don't you? I don't pay no attention to her then, but bout ten minutes later I get to thinkin bout it and we rushes over there and it was true. He was deader'n a doornail."

"Why didn't Son tell me you were there at the time of the murder?"

P.M. shrugged. "Beats the hell outta me. That's between you and him."

"You didn't kill Tee, P.M.? You're not still working for Cunningham?"

P.M. looked like he was about to stub his toe on my nose. "Aw lissen, Campbell, I was runnin around like a brokehearted chicken with his head chopped off just trying to keep Tee Texas alive. And you know, he din't care. He'd just lost heart. The only thing I caint figger out is where Cunningham got up the emotion to go ahead and finish him off. Lord only knows where that kinda hatred comes from, I sure as hell don't." P.M. slowly got out of the car, brushing something off the knee of his pants. "All I can tell you, Campbell, if I was you, I'd watch my step. There's still plenty a that hatred still floatin around. You remember that, and that if you got one friend in this world, Campbell, it's ole P. M. Estep. I'll git back to you fore you can skin a cat." And P.M. was headed back down the hill.

I sat there a long time staring at my destroyed truck and the lost gun. I dropped the gun in my pocket and left the truck and went back down to the lodge.

P.M. was laughing hard and strained. He stood at the lower end of the patio, looking out toward the middle of the lake through a pair of binoculars. The others stood watching him, shaking their heads. Mabelline stood by his side, crying. When I approached, P.M. turned on me and in a cold fury shoved the binoculars into my hands, then walked back into the house, pushing those who had gathered around him out of his way. Mabelline turned her face away from me. "Don't look. It's got to be over by now." Through the binoculars I could see the boat far out on the lake, a figure at either end, one bent over so I could barely make it out, the other using an oar to strike at something floating in the water. Over and over the oar came down, slowly, silent, till the urn ruptured and sank.

For a while Son let the boat drift in the center of the lake; then he began rowing, very slowly, toward us. They had to help Adrienne out of the boat. She could barely walk up the stairs, clutching at Son for support. Her friends came behind, shuffling at the slow pace, their faces drawn, their heads lowered.

Adrienne and Son left immediately in the limousine. A few cars followed, but most of us hung back. Mabelline began cleaning the lodge, and I decided I had to get out of here. I caught a ride with the next group leaving. The woman next to me stared at the ruined, abandoned truck but said nothing.

About ten miles south of Estacado we came upon a group of people gathered at the side of the highway. Maury's gold Cadillac was parked on the left-hand side of the road, two other cars on the right. I had the driver let me out. Maury stood in the center of the group, his gestures weary and sad, like a preacher before his lost flock. With a green silk handkerchief he wiped tears away from his eyes. "There must a been two hundred cowboys lined up on Tule Ridge there this mornin. That's where the old man chose to bury his boy. There where the bone pile used to be. You boys know that story, where the last Comanches in these parts was beat. Ole MacKenzie had been up after Quannah Parker all summer and had finally run him to earth in October up behind Tule Canyon. The soldiers and the Injuns fought all day long, but toward evenin the Injuns was defeated and had begun to drift out onto the staked plains, to make their way back to Sill. My daddy said they was no longer yearnin for war. Ole MacKenzie let the Injuns go, but he had trapped all their ponies, fourteen hundred ponies, and he had them all rounded up in three big remudas; then he had his men encircle them. Some a them men rebelled at the orders and it took them most all the afternoon to shoot them Injun ponies down. Them was the three bone piles that had stacked up when I was a kid and they used to take us out there. It used to be that when the wind was comin right up the canyon that it blew through the bone piles so that you could hear the sound of ole Quannah Parker callin out for his ponies. But the bones is all gone now. Scattered to the four winds by the coyotes and them fuckin tourists.

"Anyway, there must a been two hunderd cowboys and their ponies lined up along Tule Ridge at dawn this mornin, silhouetted up there against the sky. The buryin was down by a little grove a elder trees and we all had to wait as the three Meskins dug out the hole. When that was finished, the old man started makin a speech. About the ranch like it was, or the compny, as he's always called it. But nobody could hear a word he was sayin and he couldn't finish. Miz Kitchens took the papers away from him and finished up the rest a the speech. He tole that tale about his granny livin out on Sour Tongue line camp and that last sack a white flour she traded away for that little pup. There was also a lot a good advice to the cowboys, what they should be doin with themselves now that the compny was breakin up.

"Then over the south ridge, from the direction a the old Tule line camp, comes the buckboard and a raw coffin. And followin along behind that, tethered to the tailgate, come ole Jinglebob, that old pinto a Tee's when he was a kid. They drawed the wagon up through the trees and six a us lowered the coffin into the hole and a preacher prayed over him and a boy from the high-school band played a trumpet over him. Then they led ole Jinglebob over to where the old man was settin and he took out his Bowie knife and he reached up and cut the cinch strap and the little Meskin saddle was laid in the hole and then alongside that they laid Tee's old .30-30. Then an ole Meskin man who had been at Toro longer than anybody, he took the pony off a little ways and then took the bridle off of him and quirted him on the rump and the old pony trotted on up the draw, farther on up Tule Canyon where it narrows. Then the old man raised up his hands and the Meskins took up their shovels and the cowboys up on the ridge, with the heavens behind them red as blood, they took their rifles outta their scabbards, and as the Meskins filled in the hole, the cowboys fired off their rifles and the sparrows that had been chirpin in the trees, they filled the sky so that it was near black, and then they turned in this great black cloud and flew off northwest where the sky was a vilet blue. And then when the grave was filled in and the last cowboy had emptied his rifle, there was this silence so awful that it was broke only by the sound a that boy's pore mama weepin."

We too were silent for a while; then a man spoke quietly, "Goddamn, two hunderd cowboys and all over a pine box full a rocks."

"Rocks, ashes," another man said, "what the hell difference does it make."

# 8

When I got back to Houston, Foose wasn't at home. June said he had been out investigating the murder in every beer joint in and around the Fairview district. There was something awfully damp about the place I found Foose in, crouched in a booth behind a jukebox whose songs hadn't been changed since January 1, 1953. "What the hell you been up to, Cammel?"

"What the hell have *you* been up to, Foose?"

"You see, it was"—Foose slipped in under Hank Snow's "Moving On"—"it was a philosophical decision. What we were after was not justice but retribution. One doesn't exist and the other's old-fashioned. Who is to say who is guilty? We are all murderers at heart, aren't we, Cammel? You know that. We are all guilty. No, wait. Maybe the murderer is the only one of us who is free. In the society of murder, the only free man is a murderer. You see the logic in that, don't you?"

"Let's go home and you can sleep it off, Foose."

"And the dead man is free too, but that's a different matter. That's a deeper question. Six *feet* deeper. We're all victims; I'm a victim, you're a victim, Cammel."

"I'm not a goddamn victim, Foose."

"But wait, that's carrying things too far. That's the law of the jungle. Dog eat dog. No, no, there are values in life. There are values."

"Like what?"

"Death is a value. Love is a value. Life is a value."

I said to hell with it. I needed a drink myself. "And what is a value?"

Several beers later: "A value is something that doesn't change. No matter how much we change, it's still there."

"And there are different ways to live and different ways to die and different things to die for."

"You've got me there, Cammel. A lot of the time the value of your death depends on the life you've led. So everything is relative, except for suicide, and that's a value."

"Why?"

"The murderer murders the murderer! Love is not a value, Cammel, love is a bunch a shit. You agree?"

"I agree."

"Do you realize how unscientific we are? Do you know how little we know? Do you realize how the twenty-second century will look down its long pointed nose at us? *They didn't even know what love was.*" Foose folded back in the booth, giggling. A tough old girl at the jukebox looked at us with sympathy. "Do you know what our century will be known as? The century that didn't know its ass from a hole in the ground!" Foose started to speak to the woman at the jukebox but she was gone. Foose became morose. "I've been wanting to tell you something, Cammel, you've been good for her."

"Good for who, Foose?"

Foose nodded reluctantly. "It's not just sympathy?" The little man shook his head, his eyes moist. "You really have fallen in love with her? No, don't speak, you love her. I know. I've seen you. One day I was up in the Rice library investigating the murder when I saw you and June walking across the campus and you were holding hands and you looked so happy. I tried not to watch, but I couldn't help it. I followed you around the library, peeking from window to window. You sat under that tree for the longest time. I knew what you were saying. Then I realized you were silent and content with one another. And then you kissed. And I was not jealous at all. Not much anyway."

I couldn't keep from smiling. "Foose, I haven't even been here. I've been in West Texas for four days."

"If it isn't love, it's better than love." He looked away. For some reason, probably just as foolish, I wanted to reach out and touch the face of this foolish man. "I've always fallen in love with the wrong woman and now I've done it again. I've fallen in love with June, Cammel, would you mind leaving her alone?" Foose got up and went to the rest room. When he returned, he had grown very tough. "I talked to Adrienne today. I appreciate your not trying to get in touch with her. But you know, she hasn't seen anyone. She won't even see me. She hasn't even seen Cunningham. Not since he brought her here." He paused. "You heard from him?"

"No, but I want to talk to him pretty soon."

"Adrienne thinks he's in Austin. Can you believe she actually *loves* that man? What are you going to do to him?"

"What do you mean, do to him?"

"You know."

"I don't know."

"She wants to know."

"Tell her I haven't made up my mind yet."

Foose nodded. "Have you heard what us big two-hearted liberals have been doing?"

"No, what have you been doing?"

"Kicking down the walls of conservatism and reaction. Their empire is tottering, diseased, their envoys are at their throats." Foose laughed. "I'm not as loony as you think. Dolly has talked to the feds. He's blown the whistle on the whole can of worms. He's squealing like a canary. Just made the papers today. You didn't hear about it? Cunningham didn't tell you about it?"

"No, I drove all last night. What's happening, Foose?"

Foose shook his whole body disagreeing with himself. "Francis Dolly has betrayed them all. He's going to betray Cunningham. Why don't you just let nature take its course?"

"What do you mean, he's betrayed them?"

"He's got immunity. Don't you think it's very weird for the top dog in a conspiracy to be given immunity just so they can nail the pups? They ought to be after bigger game."

"Like what?"

"You know that Son Cunningham is working for Adrienne's father now—with Tee's body still warm in the grave. He's Bob Zeeburg's assistant now. Zeeburg is

Gunther's Washington man. Son is in Austin right now lobbying before the Railroad Commission. You know that Gunther's deal with the Fath Foundation might fall through. He put down one million in cash to buy that newspaper and has only one month to raise the rest. It could be why he needs the insurance money. It's a funny thing, isn't it? Once again Cunningham is working for a man who desperately needs cash. Sugar"—he touched my arm like a conspirator—"why don't you let him go? Let this yellow slave break his back."

The bartender called out from the end of the bar: "Anybody around here named Foose? Moose? Wanted on the telephone." Foose's face had become still and white, as if he had suddenly grown old. But in a few minutes he returned, almost prancing, with the simplest, happiest look I have ever seen on anyone's face. He didn't sit down but raised his beer bottle in a toast. "It was June. Adrienne has just called. We're all forgiven. Everything is going to be just like it was. Drink up!" Foose was so ebullient that when we got back to the house he somehow managed to get the three of us—himself, June, and me—into one big warm hug. From there we carried him in and put him to bed.

# 9

"My arms have begun to heal," said June, smiling at the bandages on her wrists. "They look like sweatbands, don't they, like when you play tennis? Other than that I feel fine. My body feels fine. All those people, I try to pretend we've never met. Foose has helped me. We pretend that nothing has happened, that A. and Cunningham and Tee and Billy, that they were never born. Did Foose tell you he has fallen in love with me?"

"I think he did. Who did Adrienne want to talk to?"

"Adrienne? I think she wanted to talk to you. Has she fallen in love with you now?" The life in June's eyes was constantly dilating, shifting, the brightness at times sinking so tangibly that I felt by reaching out and touching her, I could bring it back. "Well, he has fallen in love with me. Hasn't he? Didn't he say he had?"

"He said he had, June."

"She left a number." She waved a hand toward something behind her. "You probably already know it."

"Where can I get an evening newspaper?"

"An evening newspaper? That's a funny thing to say. There's a drugstore four blocks down on Bissonnet. They might have one. They probably do."

"I'll be right back."

"Good."

I walked down to the drugstore on Bissonnet and bought the paper. The story was long and detailed. Francis Dolly had testified before a secret federal grand jury which, the article said, had handed down indictments against several former business associates of Dolly. Of the dozen or so names I recognized Marvin DeKalb and Mercury. There was no mention of Son. The defendants had been charged with juggling stock and cash among a welter of firms controlled by Dolly, his bank, and his insurance company. I drank a cup of black coffee and went back to Foose's house.

June was sitting in a chair in front of the TV, her consciousness so weak that when she said Son had called, it was as though she were talking in her sleep. On the kitchen table I found an envelope with two phone numbers scrawled on the back. One was an Austin number. I called Adrienne first, but there was no answer. I dialed the Austin number and a man told me Son would call me back in fifteen minutes. He knew where to find me. I waited in front of the TV set. The evening news was filled with what the announcers called the Dollywood scandal. Someone claimed it was all a Republican vendetta. Someone else said Dolly's only crime was living next door to the governor. After the news June switched off the TV. She sat on the floor by me and leaned her head against my leg. "If you go to Austin, will you do something for me? Will you tell Son that I am sick unto death? Will you tell him that what we've done is killing me? Tell him that he's got to help me now that Tee is gone. Sugar, have I ever told you I loved him? I must have. Tee told me I did. And he wouldn't lie, would he? Murder, steal, cheat, but he wouldn't lie. I would lie and lie and lie. Tee didn't like me. The only reason he took me in was so that he could waltz me in and say, 'Adrienne, dear A., isn't she perfect?' They were living in the Big House then, and she was sitting in the main dining room—it's so dark there and she's sitting at the far end of the longest table I have ever seen; she's playing solitaire and Tee says, 'Adrienne, look who I'm fucking now.' And she looked at me and, oh my God, I have never felt so pale, plain, so stupid. Her eyes, they're so black . . . she picked up a card and she tore it in half and then another and another and I knew I didn't have a chance . . ."

I waited till she had nothing else to say. "June, can you tell me what you've done? Can you tell me about those boys who died?" She was shaking her head. "Did Son have anything to do with them?"

"We were a den of vipers, all of us. Queers, murderers, liars. I can't talk about them, any of them. You'll have to ask your little questions of somebody else. Sure, ask Son Cunningham. Why not? Ask him, he knows it all by heart. I can't talk any more." Her head jerked to one side, as if it were trying to get away. "Talking can be a bad thing too. Talking is when I go crazy. You've got to tell me to shut up. My words start running away with my thoughts. Like little thieves . . . Sugar . . . say to me, Shut up, June, shut up, you crazy lady . . . say it," and she tried to smile, but she couldn't.

The telephone was ringing.

# 1 0

I hadn't slept in forty-eight hours. I don't remember how I got there, but three hours later I was parking in front of the Austin beer garden where I was supposed to meet Son. The capitol lay a few blocks to the south, the university about the same distance to the north. It was an easy sweet evening, the sound of the university carillon cushioned by the night heat. The beer garden occupied a weary yellow building, once the bund hall for the local German community; the floor sank beneath your feet, the light bulbs bobbed only a few inches above your head, old men slouched against the bar, abandoned there by the younger Germans. On the thick crumbling walls hung photographs of people from the old country stolidly suffering through your drinking so much watery beer. Out back was the beer garden proper cluttered with long, ramshackle, rambling tables, countless battered folding chairs, forests of pitchers, mugs, plastic trays, and baskets, slabs of pottery plates, dozens of shouting, singing drunks, all mixed together beneath great sorrowful trees that disappeared into the sky, their branches hung with lights and loudspeakers carrying jukebox polkas. I found Son Cunningham arguing with a puffy, seedy man who grinned as if a genie were trapped in his mouth. He was introduced as the editor of a liberal political weekly. I took a chair and the editor turned back to Son. "No, what I would really like to know, Cunningham, is what Bob Zeeburg is doing out here in the boonies."

"I told you, Rucker, he's showing the new boy around."

"What I want to know, Cunningham, is what a guy like you, one of Marvin DeKalb's asshole buddies, one of the Lubbock mafia, what one of Francis Dolly's errand boys is doing working for Dolph Gunther. Huh?"

"I told you, Rucker, I haven't worked for Dolly in ages."

"Is that why he let you off the hook, Cunningham? Do you expect me to believe that? You're as goddamned implicated in that stinking Dollywood mess as the rest of them."

Son kept smiling as he nodded at me. "This is one of the finest minds in Austin, Sugar. Glad you could make it."

The editor was looking at me but thinking about something else. "I just have to figure out why. Now I know that Gunther is hard up for cash, but I didn't think he'd ever get messed up with you. He's generally not that stupid."

"I think Dolph knows what he's doing, Rucker."

"You do?" The man's eyes glittered like soft jewels. "You know that Fath and the Foundation boys are going to fuck him over if they can."

"Rucker, you miss the point about that deal. Dolph would've taken half a dozen white elephants to get hold of that newspaper. Believe me, it was not essentially a commercial deal."

"What does Dolph want to be, Cunningham? Father of Houston?"

Son shrugged. "Why not?"

One of the men at the end of the table laughed abruptly,

the sound hacked off at both ends. "Well, he did get a fountain named after him. Even if he had to pay for it."

The editor smiled and ignored the man. "Who's going to make it around here now, Cunningham? You've killed them all off. There's nobody left. This town is a shambles. Some dark horse? Maybe a guy like you, Cunningham? Will you make it? The shadow behind the shadow."

The man who had put his foot in his mouth tried again. "I didn't think Gunther had that much interest in Austin, Son. Outside of the Railroad Commission, of course!" And everyone laughed.

Son said, "You know, I have been thinking a lot about the Railroad Commission lately." Not quite as much laughter this time.

Rucker swayed toward Son. "You know, Cunningham, you really are a strange choice for Gunther. Most of his men have been with him for years. Hell, Zeeburg came out of the oil fields. And there's your ties with DeKalb and Dolly. But what's really strange is your, let's say, involvement in Gunther's son-in-law's murder." He turned to the rest of us. "That young rancher who was thinking about running for lieutenant governor, if Rabine hadn't run for a second term."

Son's words moved slow but easy: "What involvement are you talking about, Rucker?"

"Well, Son, Baggy Bayer up in Tulia has written this article that makes it sound like you might've actually killed the guy. Did you? Ambitious courtier slays the crown prince, woos the princess, gains favor with the king, to ascend the throne at the king's demise. It's got the makings of a Greek tragedy. Tell us, Cunningham, tell us what happened that dark night of June whatever on that lonely isolated ranch in West Texas. Tell *me*, Cunningham. Every Oedipus needs his Sophocles . . . and vice versa."

"Nothing."

"What!"

"I don't know what happened, Rucker. Two spicks killed one of my best friends." Son's eyes were glazed by his smile. Something kept his hands lying limp on the table. The editor was about to go on, but the man with his foot in his mouth started barking. Everyone else at the table began barking too, till everyone in the garden was barking at a huge florid man standing on the steps of the beer hall. The man barked back; then he howled and waved his Stetson above his head and made his way through the crowd, shaking the paw of every barker.

The editor turned back. "Maybe we'll have Mad Dog for our next governor, Son. Or maybe some other mad dog."

Son was standing, smiling, his body moving uneasily from side to side. "I'd like to continue our little discussion sometime, Donnie, sometime soon. It's not often I get to philosophize these days, but right now I've got an appointment with Sugar here. I'm sure you understand."

Rucker was looking away. "Have a good time, Cunningham, while you can."

"Oh, we will. We're going out to the beer bust out at Delta's. Why don't you saddle up and come along, Rucker, and have a good time yourself?"

"Good night, Cunningham."

"Good night, Donnie." And Son and I made our way among the tables toward the street.

Son punched and grabbed the red Lincoln deep into the black ragged hills west of Lake Austin. Son didn't seem to be watching the road, only looking at it with detached curiosity; his feet and hands hammered at the car's controls. He abruptly twisted the Lincoln onto a narrow dirt road that wound through the cedar forest. Son had begun to laugh. There was something frightening, almost youthful in his eyes—it was his own fear that made him look so young. I looked away from him. I didn't want him to be afraid.

The Lincoln slid into a parking area that fronted on a wide grassy slope that ended a hundred yards below in the darkness of Lake Austin. When Son snapped off the engine, we could hear the water lapping against the shore and the boisterous laughter of a party rising from behind a fence that ran from the parking area down to the water. Except that most of the men were over fifty, it could have been a college fraternity beer bust. Son drew me aside. He spoke to everyone who came near, but his voice to me was cold and light: "Sugar, we've got to find a quiet place and have a little talk tonight."

"I want to talk to you too, Cunningham, and it's going to have to be soon. I can't remember the last time I've slept."

"I can't sleep either. Not at night. I've been trying to sleep in the daytime, but there's too goddamn much work to do. I wanted to get a hold of you after the funeral, Sugar, but I had to get A. away from there. The night after the funeral she insisted on spending the night in that goddamn house. I barely survived it myself. Have you seen the papers tonight?"

"Yeah, I have."

"Crazy, ain't it? Dolly's gone off his rocker. Mercury's the guy who's going to hang, not me. Mercury and that poor fucking Marvin. This whole goddamn town is coming apart. Nobody knows who's going to be next."

"Why didn't Dolly name you in his testimony?"

Son smiled. "Because I haven't done anything wrong. Don't laugh, it's true. I told you, I sold all my ABL stock before they started doing their funny little things. I didn't make a penny off that deal and Dolly knows it. He'd like to nail my ass tighter than anybody, but he hasn't got a goddamn thing on me. You don't think the timing of this was just a coincidence, do you?"

"I just don't know, Son."

"Naw, buddy, they're out to get my ass and you better believe it. I didn't make a penny off that deal and Dolly knows it better than his beddy-bye prayer."

A small, hairless, pear-shaped man who had been listening to our conversation moved in and planted his feet in front of Son. He was followed by several drunks. The pear-shaped man said, "You think you will survive, Son?"

"I haven't heard much about it."

"I imagine you will," said the pear-shaped man, "but in a manner you are accustomed to surviving in?" There was laughter from the drunks.

"They'll all make a pot off the deal," said one of the drunks, "but *I'll* end up in jail."

"I imagine you'll end up a state's witness like Dolly, won't you, Son? Your future father-in-law has some powerful friends that haven't been heard from yet. How does that immunity work, Son?"

"First you lean down, Dale, and then you spread your cheeks—"

"But why would they let a man like Dolly go—the man who conceived and contrived the whole affair—and then hammer down bottle washers like Mercury . . . but then of course there is Marvin DeKalb, and Lon—"

"And Watson and Lebarron—"

"And Baby Rabine."

"They'll never touch Baby."

"But they already have, Son. Business is a hardy plant— a weed—you can dance all over it and it'll spring back. But politics, politics is a fragile thing. One evil word and you're lost forever—"

"Are you trying to tell me you're an orchid, Dale?"

"Were you actually thinking about running for Railroad Commissioner, Son? To Railroad Commissioner in one bounce?"

"Why don't you fuck off, Dale."

"I'm sorry, Son, but everyone has to pay the devil his due. Even Baby Rabine. Of course there are tiers of guilt—or there will be tiers of punishment." The man smiled. "Lon will probably go directly to jail. Watson and Lebarron will be only politically damaged—though God only knows how Watson will earn an honest living. And then there's the tragedy of Baby Rabine—he'll never be governor, Son. You know, this whole thing has me terribly depressed. Brilliant young men like yourself and Rabine sullied if not destroyed, your great ambitions humbled, crippled, the state foundering without its young helmsmen—and all for a pot of filthy lucre. Was it worth it, was it worth it? What are we going to do now, Son, without our young heroes?"

"I imagine you'll figure something out, Dale."

"It's a terrible shame, Son. You would have been a great politician. I guess now you'll have to stick to business."

"I guess I will."

"You know, Son, at these wretched sorries I always long to see a Jay Gatsby strolling across the lawn . . . and this is what I get . . ." Almost everyone in the compound had turned to watch a smiling young man standing at the gate to the parking area. The young man's hair shone like gold, he was wide and athletic but still smaller than the three men who formed a fleshy wall around him. The young man smiled broadly and looked deep into all our eyes. In one hand he held a small cup and saucer; the other hand was lifted, but he did not wave. "Can you imagine, Son, that Baby Rabine thought that one day he would be President of the United States? Can you imagine that, can you imagine that now?"

"No," Son said, turning away, "I can't imagine that now."

# 1 1

From the middle of the lake they looked like dolls in a brightly lit store window. From this distance the dolls did not move, they only shrank till they disappeared into the cube of light cut into the dark hillside. Son took the outboard farther on up the serpentine lake, now as narrow as a river. To our right rose a cliff, to the left gently sloping hills. Son cut the motor and we drifted in a slow circle toward the cliff. "Goddamn, Sugar, am I ever stupid for hooking up with that old fool." He laughed to himself. "But I guess everybody got caught with their pants down in this market slump. I know Gunner lost his ass, some of the baby fat anyway. How's your investigating going these days?"

"I didn't even know you knew about it, Son."

"Oh, I know about a lot of things. How is it going?"

"It's going all right. We're doing pretty good for a couple of screwball amateurs."

Son took one of the oars from the bottom of the boat and dug it into the water so that we moved in a slow circle nearer the overhanging cliff. "You drawn any earth-shaking conclusions? Dug up anything the cops haven't already come up with?"

"No, we use what you would call the deductive method of detecting. We decide what the answer is—in this case, who killed Tee—and then we set out to prove it. It's nice and tidy."

"Don't keep me in suspense. Who did kill Tee?"

"You did."

Son laughed and gave the boat another turn. The cliff wall was so dark it could have been a cave. "You know, I almost did get my ass caught in a sling there with Dolly. It was close, very close."

"And you're out of it now?"

"Sure. You didn't really think I was as stupid as Marvin or that fucking Mercury, did you? Everything I did for Dolly was aboveboard. All the wheeling and dealing I did through third parties. I wasn't in that deep anyway, but when I played I played strictly for cash. No records, and dead men don't talk, right?" He laughed. "It is too bad ole Tee ain't around to see some of his adversaries biting the bullet, ain't it? Did I tell you what that goddamn Watson said today? He was having a press conference and somebody asked him how much money he had made while he was governor and Watson said he had made a little nest egg for himself and Winnie Wanda and the reporter said, 'Well, I've heard that you're worth a million dollars.' And ole Watson got red as a three ball and said, 'Worth a million? That's bullshit. If I had to liquidate in thirty days, I wouldn't be worth no more than a couple hundred million.' *'Million?'* 'A couple hundred thousand, I said!' Goddamn, this place is a joke. It's a three-ring circus. But then you're not laughing, son. Why is that, you take life too seriously?"

"I'll start laughing when murder gets funny, Cunningham."

"All right, Sugar, maybe murder is serious business. Maybe it's more serious than I ever thought anything would get." Son was silent for a moment. We had drifted against the cliff. I put my hand out and touched the cool soft rock. The boat had stopped moving. "I'm sorry I had to bring you all this way, Sugar, but I can't trust the telephone any more. I can't trust anything. I used to think

Dolly was crazy, with all his codes and secret rendezvous, but I don't think so any more. I had to talk to you and this was the only way. See, I was lying and I had to tell you." He stopped. "I had to tell someone the truth."

"All right."

"I know who the killers are. I know one of them. I recognized him."

"One of the Mexicans?"

"Yeah, they're real all right. They exist. They killed Tee. I guess they did. I'm no longer sure of anything. I lied to you, to everybody, to protect someone."

"Adrienne?"

"The funny thing is, Sugar, the funny thing is, I really was planning on killing him. It just didn't work out that way. I didn't even get close."

"How did it work out?"

"Like I told you, except . . . I left a few things out. O.K. When Tee came in, A. and I were talking in the Little Room—this was about midnight. Maybe a quarter hour later a car stops out front and in come P.M. and C.J. and Maury. Maury is mad as hell at Tee for dumping him in the goddamn lake. He says he's going to kill Tee and he takes a swing at him, but we pull him off. Tee is scared to death of the little bastard—I don't think I've ever seen a man in such bad shape. He's falling apart right before our eyes. Everybody sits down and we start hashing things out, so I go upstairs."

"Leaving who downstairs?"

"Just Tee and Maury and A. P.M. and C.J. went over to the Big House to report in, I figure."

"They were working for the old man?"

"Not for Malcolm directly. But they have the same interests. Or think they do. O.K., I go upstairs and I'm up there about ten minutes, no more. During that time I hear a car—arriving, leaving, I don't know, I don't pay that much attention. Then I hear the shot. At first I think it's just a backfire, but then I know it's not and I run downstairs. Tee is lying facedown in the middle of the room. This Mexican turns him over and starts pounding his face with his gun and I just stand there at the head of the stairs and I can't move. It seems like hours later I yell out at the Mexican and he raises the gun at me, but it won't fire. Somehow I'm down the stairs, the Mexican is still standing over the body, he can't move. I think I'm going to kill him, when someone called my name . . . *she* called my name, God, I swear, Sugar, it was *her* voice, I turned around and there was another Mexican standing in the shadows beneath the stairs. And he reached out toward me with his gun, and my arm exploded and then I guess the spick behind me hit me— The next thing I knew I was waking up, I guess it was a couple minutes later. I was in the room alone. I couldn't hear anything but the sound of her voice. I don't know if I thought maybe Tee was still alive— No, I wanted to make it look like I had killed him, so I took the branding iron and beat his face off his head. It's one of the reasons I have a hard time sleeping, Sugar."

"I guess that's when Tabor saw you."

He hesitated. "When was that?"

"Tabor woke up and saw you killing Tee. I guess he thought you were killing Tee."

"Tabor didn't tell you that."

"No, P.M. did. Tabor told him. They're big buddies now."

"You know, Sugar, if heads were legs and Estep was a horse, we'd have to shoot him. You know he's an insurance man."

"Hired to keep Tee alive?"

"They didn't give a shit whether he was dead or not. They just wanted to be sure that if he did die, that his dying was funny-looking enough that twelve of our peers wouldn't think it was natural. Nobody's ever going to get that money."

"So if Adrienne did kill him—or had him killed—it wouldn't have been for the insurance money."

"No, son, that wasn't it, it never would have been."

"Are you sure, Cunningham? I mean, six million bucks is a lot of money, even to a man like Dolph Gunther. Maybe especially to a man like Gunther, a man who's up to his eyeteeth in debt. A man whose empire is about to collapse."

"Sugar, you're overheating again. If you're talking about the deal with the Fath Foundation, you can forget it. This country's in business for Dolph Gunther to *make* money, not lose it. Anyway, it's good for the old man to have a taste of diversification, then he can get his ass back in oil where it belongs. And, Sugar, having your daughter kill her husband so that you can get his money—this ain't Italy."

"You recognized one of the Mexicans?"

"That's right. The frightening thing about it, Sugar, is that he used to work for me."

"And if they caught him, it might look like you hired him to kill Tee."

"It crossed my mind. He doesn't speak English and God knows what fucked-up story he'd come out with."

"What did this Mexican do for you?"

"It wasn't exactly illegal. Look, Sugar, tell you the truth, I am getting scared. She might've been there, she might've called out to me, she might've been standing in the shadows behind Raphael, but that doesn't mean she killed him or that she had anything to do with it. She could've just been there . . . They could have been hired by somebody else."

"Have you asked Adrienne about it?"

"That's just it, son, she can't remember a fucking thing.

Some things are coming back, but she can't piece together what's real and what's dream. What I want you to do for me, Sugar—for us both—is to find out what really happened. Why don't you talk to her first? Then go back to West Texas, do whatever you have to do, but find out the truth." He stopped. "Find out the truth, no matter what it is. Will you do it?"

"All right," I said and pushed the boat away from the cliff face, "but I'm going to need some money. A lot of money."

"I'll wire it to Foose in the morning and then I'll talk to Gunner about something more substantial and everlasting."

"If I'm going to find out what happened, Son, then I'm going to have to start with you. You've told me three different stories. They were all concocted to protect Adrienne, right?"

"That's right."

"So when I saw you right after the murder and you said you killed Tee, that was a lie?"

"It was a lie."

"You didn't kill Tee?"

"No, son, I didn't kill Tee."

"All right. And you don't really know who did?"

"The two Mexicans—"

"But you really didn't see them kill Tee, did you? You came downstairs when you heard the shot. Do you think Adrienne could have seen the murder? Is that what you're worried about?"

"That's right."

"Do you think she's in any danger?"

"She could be, but we've got a couple of Gunner's boys staying with her now."

"You're still lying."

"What do you mean?"

"There weren't any Mexicans. You killed Tee yourself and you didn't have anybody holding your hand while you did it."

He leaned forward and wrenched something out of himself. I barely understood the words. "I didn't, I swear I didn't."

"When Tabor said he saw you beating Tee, Tee was still alive, he wasn't dead. Tabor said Tee was screaming. You weren't beating a dead man, you were killing him."

Son rocked back in the boat, his hands clasped behind his head as if this were an idle excursion. "Look, we did have a fight, Sugar, that's what Tabor saw. When I heard Maury and A. leave, they went outside for something, I went back downstairs. Tee and I got into an argument and then we had a fight. I don't think Tabor saw a goddamn thing, but if he did, he saw me beating the hell out of Tee. But Tee wasn't dead, not then. He was dead the second time, and I didn't kill him."

"You beat the corpse, to make it look like—what? A crime of passion?"

"I guess it does."

"What if Tee killed himself?"

"I don't follow you."

"That would be a reason for you to do what you did. You don't follow me? So that Adrienne would get the insurance money, Son. Nobody collects on a suicide, right? I think it's a good idea, Son, I think you ought to keep it in mind. Maybe he killed himself with you two watching. That way you could be witnesses for each other. That would be a good tale. He walks in, his wife and her lover sitting on the couch holding hands, and he walks right up to you and pulls out a gun and blows his brains out. That would've destroyed you both. Right?"

"It would have. But he didn't kill himself."

"He shoots himself and then you panic. Let's say

Adrienne's not there. More than likely neither of you are. You hear the shot— Maybe Adrienne's already gone, that might be better. You hear the shot, you panic. Is the money worth the risk? But then you're not cozy with Gunther yet, are you? Maybe there's something else that *nobody* knows about. You can't stand the fact that he has killed himself. It drives you crazy. You beat his face off his head, you take the gun and shoot him again, and you shoot yourself and hide the gun, and now you've killed Tee Kitchens, what you've always wanted to do, you've finally done it."

"Now you're talking crazy, Sugar."

"Sure I am, but it's fun. You want them to know, to know you've killed him. But you don't want to die. So you come up with the story about the Mexicans and you have it all. Insurance and revenge and freedom. Like you say, it is crazy, but then maybe it's just crazy enough to be true. So why don't you tell me the final goddamn truth, Cunningham? No, we want to work up to it real nice and slow. We don't want to get there too fast— I mean, what do you have when you learn the truth? It's all over then. There's nothing left but the truth. Isn't that right, Cunningham?"

"All right, Campbell, you'll get your little piece of truth now and I hope you choke on it. I told you I watched Tee kill Billy O.; I watched him kill that boy, but that's not quite all of it, there was somebody else there with us. I'm not trying to kid you, I was all for Tee killing the kid; he was evil, the most thoroughly evil man—boy—I've ever seen. He was the one that killed Palmer, the cowboy, he dragged Tee into that. He killed him for fun, for sport, just to see what it's like to kill another man, except this was real, this was no goddamn book the kid was reading, something he never counted on. So they got Palmer all fucked up on something—that wasn't too hard to do, they had that cowboy mixing up chemicals in his belly like he was a test tube. And then the kid drove him out to this hole where him and Tee had been collecting snakes, they must've had a couple hundred of them by now, and they throw this stoned, miserable bastard down into this snake pit and then they drive away, so fucked up they didn't even know what they were doing. You know, they say he crawled three miles before he died. It was enough to drive a man crazy. The kid wasn't up to it. He started going crazy, he got sick with fear and guilt, I watched him crumble, he didn't have it. We had to do something about it, the kid was going to go to the sheriff and tell the whole story. It would all be over, for Tee, the ranch, everybody. She came to me, but I couldn't do it. Oh I wanted to, Sugar, but I couldn't. They tried to get somebody else to do it, but by then the kid knew what was going on. So Tee had to do it himself. He killed him. One day he comes up to A. and me and says he wants to take us for a little ride, he wants to show us something. We follow him out to a place beyond Soda Springs. There's an old line-camp dugout there. Tee tells us to wait outside. We hear voices, Tee and the kid screaming at each other, and we walk in the door and Tee's got the kid tied to a fucking bed, naked, and when we walk in the door, he smiles at Adrienne and he turns and blows the goddamn kid's brains out, right there in front of us. I'll have to give him credit, he did try to kill himself then, but the fucking gun jammed. Then he faints. There we are, we don't know what the hell to do, so we take Tee back and stuff him full of pills and come back that night and move the body to the shooting range. O.K., I did put the boots on him to make it look like the other murder. I was hoping Tee would hang for it. But then June sees us with the body and we're as implicated as Tee, but that doesn't make any difference, Tee starts telling everybody he killed the boy, and then he starts getting that same murderer's sickness, just like Billy, except with him

I know he's going to kill somebody else. Me, Adrienne, I don't know. And I go through all these plans of what to do—for some fucking reason I bring you in, P.M., the Mexicans, but nothing works. I know I'm going to have to kill him myself, before he kills her. So I lay my final plans and it works perfect, everything, down to the last detail. Tee goes down to Lake Snyder and acts crazy. You fall in, but Tee gets rid of you. He knows what role he has to play. The three of us are finally left there in the Little House, like it was a stage and we were actors; the curtain is about to fall, the audience, everybody knows it's time for the play to end, but the hero won't play his part. He won't kill the madman and save the lady. The hero tries, he beats him, but still he can't kill him. He goes upstairs and sits alone and he's shaking with fear. It's all over. It's all over and he's lost her. And he hears a cry; it was a terrible cry, Sugar, it was a plea for an ending. And then there's a gunshot and I go back down and I see this man, what used to be a man, crawling on the floor; he's not alive but then he's not dead, and I look into her eyes and they are black, burning, like they are on fire—" Then suddenly Son moved across the boat and grabbed my shoulders. It happened so quickly, these three things—I thought he was going to kill me, then that his action was sexual, then he ran his hands down my jacket to my empty pockets and smiled and leaned back in the boat. Like a magician at the end of his act, he held a gun in his hand as if he had taken it from me. "O.K., son, so I finished him off for her. We killed him together. What difference does it make? Too bad you didn't bring your little pistola along tonight. That's the only way you're going to get me and this is the last chance you'll ever have." He kicked the oars toward me. "Why don't you row back in, Sugar. I think we just ran out of gas."

# 1 2

I drove back to Houston that night and slept for twelve hours. Foose tried to talk to me but his mouth made slow barking sounds and then no sound at all. And then there were the same sounds but everything was dark. A fat man was sitting on my head. There was another one on my chest and four of his friends squatting on my feet and hands. I had to lie there and listen to Foose's whole story. "Well, do you believe him? Do you believe his pack of lies?"

"What are you talking about?"

"What am I talking about? I'm talking about Cunningham's wild accusations!" We settled down some. "See, he called me up while you were asleep. A lot of things have happened while you were asleep."

I rolled over and sat up. "Like what?"

"He told me the same story he told you."

My mind was mimicking rationality. "How do you know he told me the same story?"

"June has disappeared. She's left us." I lay back down. "Adrienne called. You. She wants to talk to you. They're having a party. They want us to come down to Galveston. I'm not sure I can go. I'm not sure I want to go."

"Where did June go?"

"I don't know. She left a note—she said she was sick of me." Foose covered his face. "I can understand why. All I've done is drink. I'm sick of myself." He tried to laugh. "I said, 'Our ships are passing in the night, June.' And she said, 'Your ship's about to sink, Foose.'"

"Which story did Cunningham tell you, Foose?"

"That Adrienne killed Tee."

"That's not exactly the same one he told me." I stood up. Foose watched me dress. I started toward the door and he stopped me.

"Where are you going? Don't go out there. It's miserable, it's an oven outside. Hundred degrees, maybe more. Let's talk in here. I go crazy out in that heat."

"Foose, what is there to talk about?"

Foose swung his head around so that I could see he was drunk. "You see, Campbell, I believe him."

"What else?"

"What *else?* You're not shocked . . . *dismayed?*"

"Yeah, maybe I'm dismayed."

"I'm not joking, Campbell. Listen to me. She's a murderess and he's protecting her. Look, I've been in love with her for years, so I ought to know her. What do you think? That maybe he killed Tee and she's protecting him?"

"I don't care who killed Kitchens. I don't even think."

"You don't care, you don't think," he sneered.

"Foose, it doesn't make any difference to me who killed Tee. I've decided who I'm going to get."

Foose started to speak, then yawned. But he wasn't bored. "Get? What do you mean by that?"

"Whatever you want it to mean."

"I get it. And you just haven't decided how?"

"Maybe."

"Cunningham?"

"What time is it, Foose?"

"But is Cunningham the one who killed Tee?"

"He's the one I'm going to get."

Foose slouched in the chair. "Then Adrienne could have killed her husband and you don't care. You don't care about *her* guilt!"

"That's right."

"But then maybe Cunningham put her up to it. Is that what you think?"

"Maybe. Did Adrienne say what she wanted to talk to me about?"

"She didn't say exactly, but I had the feeling . . . I had the feeling that Cunningham put her up to it. She called only thirty minutes after he had talked to me. It was fishy."

"You don't have any idea what she wanted to talk about?"

"Oh well, it was something about the murder, but then everything is. She said it was urgent."

"I want to talk to June before I see Adrienne."

"That's going to be impossible. She's disappeared. If you're worried she might do something . . . foolish, you can forget it. We talked about suicide and she's beyond it now." Foose took off his glasses and wearily stroked his eyes. "Oh my God, she couldn't've done it; but then how could he say she did? How could a man who loved her . . . I just don't understand them. Any of them."

"Foose, I want to find June and talk to her and I want to start right now."

"Are you in love with her too? No, but then you don't do anything for love, do you, Sugar? You're normal while the world is nuts! Did you know we pretended that we had just met. We pretended we were animals. That worked, but June couldn't keep quiet, she had to talk. I used to love words, but I hate them now—they were destroying us—the sound of her voice was like a caress. She was like a child and I knew that when she grew strong enough, she would leave me. Yesterday I came home and found her sitting at the dining-room table, sitting there with the telephone in her hands and it was making that horrible buzzing it makes when it's off the hook, and she was crying. It was so stupid, she said, so stupid to be crying when they were only having a party, they were only having a party and had invited her. Oh, that reminds me, a West Texas sheriff called. And then there was a man who wouldn't give his name. He jabbered a lot, he sounded hysterical."

"Which sheriff was it?"

"Which sheriff? Is there more than one? Ha ha ha."

"Do you know Maury Mueller?"

"His name was in the paper."

"He's the man who sold Tee his insurance policy. He talks fast."

"That's him then. He said they were after him. He said they were out to get him. He wants you to come up to Lubbock as soon as possible. He left a number. Somewhere. I'll find it. He wants you up there right away. But let's go down to Galveston first. We'll see Adrienne. We'll tell her what her treacherous lover is up to. She's innocent. She's got to be. Then we'll find June and bring her back here. Then you can go traipsing around West Texas to your heart's content."

"Did Maury say anything else?"

"Who?"

"The man who talked fast, did he say anything else, Foose?"

"It was a matter of life and death. What isn't?"

"What was the sheriff's name? Maxwell?"

"No."

"Tabor?"

"That's it. I think maybe he was the one who said it was a matter of life and death. Maybe they both did."

"You can't remember anything they said, Foose?"

"No, but I know what they meant. *He* was after them. *He* was going to get them."

I stood. "When's this party?"

"Right now!"

# 1 3

Galveston Island is the shape of a ragged knife, a thirty-mile-long strip of sand torn away from the peeling crust of the Texas Gulf coast. The city of Galveston sits at the eastern, the fat end of the island, Adrienne's beach house lay somewhere near the sharp tip, well beyond Fifteen Mile Road.

From the high bridge connecting the island and the mainland we saw the city of Galveston a few miles ahead, then to the right the slender body of the island stretching as far as the eye could see. We took a wide, palm-lined boulevard along the seawall which had been built after the 1906 hurricane had demolished the city. The seawall continued a mile or so beyond the western city limits, then ended abruptly, and the road dropped to the beach. From then on we followed the tracks the cars before us had worn in the sand, past a string of beach honky-tonks that sat on pilings back among the sand dunes, like giant gray crabs facing the sea. At first it seemed cooler here than in Houston, but as we drove farther down the island, the road through the sand became softer, less certain, the breeze dropped, and the heat seemed to take the form of light, so that when you closed your eyes to escape it, your mind burned like a coal.

The beach house stood alone and back from the beach, almost hidden among the sand dunes that on this end of the island had grown tall and wild like waves rising in a storm. We followed the ruts off the road and around a gate without a fence and parked behind the house, among the twenty or so cars already there.

We went inside, but Adrienne was not there. Someone said she had gone to a neighbor's house and would be back in a few minutes. We waited. The house was old and damp and cool; outside, the beach burned white as ashes. Overhead fans drew up silent spirals of air. Guests moved constantly around us, their bright witty talk trailed by their laughter. Foose went off to talk to a woman who wouldn't look at him. I walked out to the screened porch and was about to go outside when at the far end of the porch there was a crash that shook the house and then roared on for several seconds, like a baby grand piano that had been flipped on its back. Everyone had gathered around a huge red-faced man who lay on the floor, kicking and striking out at everyone who tried to give him a hand. A woman stood over the man, shaking a finger in his face. Nearby a bridge foursome braced themselves, tightly gripping their cards. The woman helped the man to his feet and they walked back and forth along the porch. The man wore an artificial leg and he lurched against the bridge table each time he passed and shouted at them: "Goddamn liberals beg you come to their goddamn parties and then they put goddamn snot on the doorknob! One two three four! Start up another fucking war!" Someone touched my arm and I turned around. Anna's face was gray and worried.

"Believe me, Campbell, I'm glad you came." She lit her cigarette. "They haven't come back yet. You haven't seen them, have you?"

"Seen who? Is Son here?"

She swung her head up, then down. "Yes, he's here and I don't like the looks of it. He's no good for our Adrienne, Campbell, they shouldn't be together. He's crazy; you know that, don't you? He's crazy as a loon. And so are all the others. What a madhouse this is."

"Where did they go, Anna? I've got to talk to her. Away from him."

"So you're afraid of him too." She shook her head. "She's moving into a bad period. I can feel it. I feel evil coming on like a barometer senses an approaching storm. In a couple of minutes I'm going out looking for them. You never can tell when there might be a new outbreak of violence. You know, that crazy bitch girl friend of Tee's has always thought Adrienne was plotting against him. Look, Campbell, I'm afraid—I don't know who to be afraid of—but I'm afraid for her life." Anna laid her face against the upturned palm of her hand; then she sat up and gave two distinct, piercing shrieks. I turned and saw a group of ten or twelve people coming in the front door. They were led by a large soft young man carrying a very long shotgun at port arms. He walked up to us, laid the shotgun on the bar, and stared wide-eyed at Anna.

"What in the hell is wrong with you?"

Anna gasped. "I thought you were going to shoot someone."

The young man's fleshy head swiveled left and right. His entourage had scattered into the crowd. No one had followed him to the bar. "Is Daddy here, Anna? If Daddy's here, I gotta get outta here."

A young woman appeared out of nowhere and started shoving the much larger man back against the bar. The way she flexed her fingers against the man's chest looked something like a pianist during the stormy part of a sonata. "Goerman, if you don't stay here and face down that pig chauvinist once and for all, I'm leaving you forever!"

The young man seemed willing to accept that, but a woman who was probably his mother came up on the other side and grabbed his arm so that he couldn't get away. "Goerman, you've got to get out of here. Your daddy is threatening to beat you up!"

The young woman sneered, "Why did you bring that gun here, Goerman?"

"Because I'm broke. I want somebody to buy it."

"All right, all right," said the mother. "Calm down. How much?"

"Twenty-five hundred."

"You idiot," the young woman said. "Did you pay twenty-five hundred dollars for a gun?"

The young man's eyes moved shiftily over the people standing near the bar. "Sure I did. I'm taking a beating on this gun. I paid five thousand bucks for it. It's a Forster—"

"God—"

"Oh, he stole it. You know that."

"Listen, Mommy—"

Anna drew me away. "Campbell, listen, I know I'm sounding melodramatic, but something bad has happened to our Adrienne and . . . and I think something bad is going to happen again."

"Has she said anything to you, Anna? Has she talked to you about Tee's death?"

Anna covered her face with her hands. "No, but I know she had something to do with it. Don't ask me what. Just find her, Campbell, just bring her back."

"It's all right, Anna. I'll find her. And she didn't have anything to do with Tee's death."

She looked up. "Are you sure?"

"I'm positive."

I didn't find Adrienne till dark. I had followed the directions of a man who had seen her and Son walking down to the beach, but I had gone the wrong way, and by the time I had doubled back, Son had gone. Gone to West Texas, Adrienne said, he had business there in the morning. She didn't know what. She was standing at the water's edge as if she had been there for hours, forgotten by her friends. She looked so different from the first time I had seen her. Her face tender and uncertain, she laughed tentatively when I told her about Anna's fears. "No, what a ridiculous idea," she said as we walked along the shore line, the Gulf almost perfectly still. "Anna's gone, let's say, slightly off-key since Tee died. You know how it is, sometimes you have to pretend to be a patient yourself to nurse someone back to health. No, we came out here to be by ourselves and talk. Son and I hadn't talked since . . . since that night. You know, Sugar, I was afraid that we would never be able to talk again, that Tee's death would have destroyed us. But it hasn't. We were able to talk and talk and talk."

"Sometimes too much talk can be bad."

"Sometimes." She smiled to herself. "Sugar, this afternoon Son and I saw this scene, it was out of *La Dolce Vita*. These fishermen had dragged in their fishnet and this couple from Chicago had gotten their Caddy caught in the sand. The man was dressed in one of those tacky suits with pegged legs, with the black shirt and white tie and sideburns that looked like a putting green dyed black, and she had on her hot pants with silver hip boots, except that the spike heels kept sinking into the sand, so that she was walking around hunched forward at the *knees*, and well, they were there yelling adenoidal epithets at the fishermen, waving twenty-dollar bills around like gay little flags at a parade, and all the while these fishermen were picking around in this pile of disgusting fish, yanking out these little sharks and hitting them over the head with a claw hammer; I mean, they were hammering hammerheads . . ." She tried to laugh. "I know I'm not being funny, I'm not even coming close, but I can't help it. I'm so goddamned tired. I still can't sleep. Not for very long. You know, I went crazy there for a while. We all must have. There had to be something terrible to end it, to break it. Do you know, the night of the funeral, the night after the funeral, I went back to the Little House. Son and I spent the night there. I wasn't there when they found him, but I know what he looked like. I know what he looked like when Son found him." She looked across the water as if searching for someone across a room, someone who had left the party early, before she had had a chance to talk to him. "I wandered through the house all night long. I must have looked like a ghost myself. The next morning Son took me away. He's helped us all so much, Sugar, you'll never know what he's done for me." Her eyes moved slowly over my face. "If you've come to see him, he's not here. He went back up to West Texas. He had some business, some last-minute business to take care of."

"You've already told me that, Adrienne."

"I have? So I have."

"Who was his business with?"

"Who was it with? I don't know who it was with."

"Was it with Mark Tabor?"

"No, not that I know of."

"And Maury Mueller?"

"I don't know. Is there any reason why it shouldn't be? He has business with Maury, all kinds of business all the time." She turned and walked along the beach. "I'm sick and tired of all this gossip. It's so boring, the people who indulge in it are so boring. Who killed Tee? Did you kill Tee? Did he kill Tee? Have you fucked him since Tee's death? Have you fucked anyone, are you going to fuck—"

"Adrienne, I didn't come here to talk about fucking."

She walked on a few yards, then came back. "I'm sorry, I really have been a terrible bitch. And you've been the kindest one of all. Let's walk, Sugar, I hate standing still." She touched my arm and we moved down the beach, which lay before us as dark as the water. "Did you know that June and I have talked? It was the first time June and I had ever really talked. She's very fond of you." We walked a short while in silence. "She says you and Foose are the only ones who've kept her sane. Son has been wonderful for me. So kind and gentle. He's the only thing that's kept me going. I used to pride myself on being so rational. Even during the worst times, I still thought the world was real. I no longer think so. It's the dreams I've been having, Sugar; it's not that they're terrible, it's that they go on and on . . . each night the dream starts in where it left off the night before. And in my dream I remember my waking moments and at times, like now, when I'm awake, I burst back into that other world . . . I break back into it *as if I were waking from a dream.* It's my life, not my dreams, that's the nightmare. Oh, how I long for sleep." She drew her lips back. "I'm sleepy now." We had stopped. In the distance we could see the lights of a beach community, a cluster of squat houses raised high on their spidery legs. Farther down we could see the lights of fishermen drawing their nets toward the beach. Then closer a flounderer moving along a sandbank fifty yards offshore. She covered her face with her hands. I tried to see her face, for the darkness made her voice so smooth and calm. "You don't hate yourself. I can tell, we can tell, we self-loathers. We feed on your love, why can't you ever see that? That's what destroyed Tee—" Her laugh cracked and she ran down the beach toward the fishermen's lights. But after a few yards she stopped and I caught her. I could now see her face in the darkness, I remembered her face. "Talk, can't you talk, Sugar? Tell me about you and June. Anything."

"No, I can't."

"Because it's not over."

"No."

"Is it over?"

"It never was, Adrienne. It never happened."

"I'm glad you don't love me. Son makes all the others

look pale. They disappear. I can't think of anyone but him. I can't think of anyone but him. I love him more than anything in the world."

"What would you do for him, Adrienne? Would you do anything in the world for him?"

"Why do you ask that? Yes, I would. I would do anything. Is that what you want me to say? *Is it?*"

"No, it's not."

"You bastards, you incredibly stupid bastards. You're one of them, aren't you? You're just like Foose and Malcolm Kitchens and all those creepy police, that mob of idiots. Do you want me to tell you who killed Tee, Sugar, *do you really want to know?*" We were silent for a long time; when she spoke her voice was flat: "He killed himself, help me, my poor friend has killed himself."

"No, he didn't kill himself, Adrienne."

"God, would you stop!"

"Do you remember what happened?"

"No! No, only these dreams . . . they can't be memories . . ."

"Son killed Tee, Adrienne."

"No, he didn't . . ."

"I'm going to stop him, Adrienne. I don't know how yet. I don't even know if he's sane or not. I'm afraid he might be."

She laughed. "Is sanity worse than madness these days, Sugar? I think you're the one who's insane, Sugar. You're looking strange these days."

"I'm going to need your help."

"I can't help you."

"I want you to write a letter to your father. I want you to say that I'm working for you."

"Is that all? Will you leave me alone then?"

"No. I want you to write down everything that happened—I don't care if you remember it as a dream or not.

I've got to drive back to West Texas tonight. I've got to find him before another accident happens. Then I'm going to see your father and we'll stop him."

"Sugar, don't do this. I know he's never killed anyone. He's told me so."

"He's lying."

"No, he's not lying."

"He told me you killed Tee, Adrienne. That's how desperate he is. He'll sacrifice anybody who gets in his way, including you."

She turned her back to me. "He didn't say that. Did he say he loved me?"

"He didn't mention it." I waited. "Will you write that letter now?"

She turned back to me. "All right, I'll write your fucking letter. And then I don't ever want to see you again. Ever." And she walked back down the beach without me.

When I got back to the beach house, Foose was waiting for me. There had been a phone call from West Texas. Mark Tabor was dead.


# 1 4


It was noon and I was driving north toward Toro. The earth looked like it had aged a hundred years in the last two months. The heat pushed down on Foose's old car, as if it were something crawling on the bottom of the sea. I parked across from the courthouse. The square was deserted. I didn't remember that most of the buildings' windows were broken or boarded up. Inside, the courthouse halls were coated with dust. The pretty secretary said that Sheriff Maxwell was out. Deputy Phelan was no longer with them. He had joined the Wichita Falls police force; he had been planning to quit for ages. The secretary told me I could find the sheriff in the café across the street.

Maxwell sat in the back booth of a large rusty diner on the south side of the square. A Greyhound bus was parked outside and the passengers lined up at the counter. After the bus pulled out, I went back and took a booth and stared at Maxwell. After a few minutes he spoke to the men he was with, then joined me, sliding across the deep bench, leaning against the wall. "Well, Campbell, I thought I told you never to show your face around here again." He smiled, but it didn't last long.

"I heard about Mark Tabor. I thought I might go to the funeral."

Maxwell wearily looked away. "What do you want, Campbell?"

"I want to know what happened the night of Tee's death."

The sheriff looked back at me, sitting on his hands like a bashful schoolboy. "Campbell, have a heart. You want *me* to tell *you* what happened that night?"

"I want to know what you think happened, Maxwell."

Maxwell stared at me for several seconds. "All right, you sonofabitch, I will. You and Cunningham and the widow set the whole goddamn thing up. You knew the ranch was going to be deserted. That was easy enough to arrange. Thanks to Cunningham, the goddamn place was falling apart. So you set up a little celebration down at Lake Snyder, to clear out what riffraff was still hanging around. Then you had the widow arrange a meeting between you and her and Kitchens and Cunningham for later that night. Nobody but the four of you. Oh, there was that poor fucking Tabor, but that was what we call an act of providence. Not even the servants were in that house. Most of the cowboys were gone. The only people around were the old folks over at the Big House. O.K., so P. M. Estep and his friends were there, but maybe they were part of it too. The meeting is easy to set up, isn't it? Kitchens is in love with his wife, he'd meet her in hell if that's what she wanted. So she calls him and says she wants to have a talk. She wants Cunningham there, maybe the three of them can get things straightened out. Maybe now that the ranch's problems are solved, maybe they can get back together, she tells him; she wants him there when they talk to Cunningham. He's a violent, crazy man. You're the only one who can handle him. That'll draw him back, won't it, Campbell? That'll draw him back every time. Now he's feeling confident. The ranch is saved, he thinks. His lady is coming back, he thinks. It's such a simple thing to take him away for a couple of hours and get him blind drunk, isn't it, Campbell? Your job is to get him drunk and lead him back to the trap. But that's only part of your role. You see, there has to be a third witness. There can't be just the three of them there—the murderer, the dead man, and his widow. No, there would be no one there to say it wasn't murder. No, Cunningham had to have a loyal stooge to hide his crime. He got cold-blooded bastards like you and P. M. Estep and Maury Mueller, and then he got a poor drunken fool like Mark Tabor. So you do your job perfectly, Campbell. You do it better than perfect, throwing Tabor in the back seat was a stroke of genius. I hope you got a bonus for that. After you get him there, I don't know what happens, not exactly. You're there, Estep is there, some place. The widow, Cunningham, I don't know exactly who pulled the trigger. For a while I was even giving some credence to the two-Mexicans theory. You have heard the latest development on that, haven't you?" Maxwell shook his head. "No, of course you haven't. You didn't even know that Tabor was going to die, did you? Well, the two Mexican killers have actually showed up.

Aw, don't look so surprised, Campbell. Shut your mouth, you'll catch a fly. The people you made up are dead, you don't have a thing to worry about." Maxwell took a cigar out of his pocket and took some time stripping off the cellophane. "Maybe you ought to stick around, Campbell. My job might be opening up pretty soon. You'd make a good sheriff in this rotten motherfucker. Honest Injun, I *try* to play it smart, but I just can't help myself, I just keep on nosing around in these closed cases." He paused. "So you really don't know what happened to your two Mexican killers."

"No."

"Well, O.K. It was just about all the Lubbock papers carried for the last couple of days. But then Houston papers don't much care what happens up here in West Texas, do they? They didn't even carry Kitchens's death, did they? Maybe a few lines. Well, all right. Do you know Ronnie Rice of the Lubbock P.D.?"

"It seems like I've heard the name."

Maxwell shrugged. "Ronnie was or is head of Lubbock's narcotic bureau. The name does ring a bell? Well, Rice is a zealous officer and he did a good job cleaning up Tamale Town in Lubbock. Cleaning up the small frijoles anyway. Well, one night a week or so ago one of Rice's snitches said he had a hundred pounds of cocaine tagged down near the Santa Fe yard. Rice set up a stakeout, and two days later twenty officers busted into this old garage apartment and blew the shit out of these two spicks. The trouble was, they got the wrong apartment and the wrong two spicks. No cocaine, no fifty thousand cash, no tommy guns, no nothing. Nothing but two dead Mexican laborers and their grief-crazed widows who can't even speak English, it's so terrible. Rice planted an ounce of grass on them and that was it. And you know what kind of car those two Mexican boys had? An old beat-up pink and white

Olds. O.K., so that's a coincidence. You know who one of Rice's biggest playmates is? The one who's going to pry him out of this wreck with nothing but a slapped wrist. Old Marvin DeKalb. You know another one of Rice's big buddies? Old Son Cunningham. O.K., that's a coincidence too." Maxwell leaned back and blew smoke and laughter across the table. "See, Campbell, maybe you didn't even know you weren't lying. Maybe there were two Mexican killers." He leaned toward me. "But they aren't killers any more, boy. If they ever were anything but patsies. Three down and how many to go? You and that fat insurance peddler, I guess. But maybe they can trust him. Maybe they're just after you. After you're gone that will leave the two of them." Maxwell stopped as if I had just walked in the door and kicked him; he grinned as if it didn't hurt. "You look so stupid, Campbell. You really aren't in on it, are you?"

"No, I'm not, Maxwell."

The sheriff held his cigar as if not to get fingerprints on it. "But you did deliver the body, at the right place and the right time. Is that just another coincidence?"

"No. I knew what was happening; it's just that I wasn't part of any plan. I wasn't part of their plan."

"What do you mean by that?"

"I was hoping that Tee would kill Cunningham—or that Cunningham would kill Tee. Something like that. I guess you could say I was planning it in some fucked-up way. I knew somebody was going to die that night, I just didn't know which one it was going to be. Hell, maybe I was even planning on killing Tee myself and setting Son up. But it didn't work out that way. I don't think I would have done it, but I don't know, I was a little crazy myself that night." I laughed. "Maybe I still am. I had this idea I would take Adrienne away from both of them and we would be very rich and happy."

"Tell me what happened."

"It's the same story I told before the grand jury. Without the true confessions."

"How about the Mexicans?"

"Maybe they were there before the murder. Maybe they beat Kitchens up. I don't know. Maybe Cunningham hired them, like you said, just to set them up."

"Maybe. All right, you and Kitchens drove out to Soda Springs and he dropped you off. Why did he do that?"

"Because he thought I was hired to kill him."

"But you weren't?"

"Hired is not the right word. Groomed. I was being groomed to kill him. But I guess that was just a setup too."

"I'm just a poor rustic, Campbell, you're going to have to explain that."

"I was being led—coaxed, enticed?—to a point in my life where I wanted him dead so bad that I would kill him."

"Enticed by Mrs. Kitchens?"

"She was the bait, I guess, but she didn't have anything to do with it."

"You were in love with her?"

"I was."

"And you're not now?"

"No— I don't know."

"All right. Kitchens gave you the slip and by the time you got back to the Little House he was dead."

"That's right."

"And Cunningham was standing over him with a smoking gun?"

"No, he was in the bathroom upstairs, washing his face and hands."

"Washing his face and hands?"

"Washing blood off his face and hands."

"Tee's blood?"

"I don't know. I thought it was Kitchens's, but it could've been his own."

The sheriff nodded. "Then Cunningham told you about the Mexicans?"

"Sometime that night. I don't remember when."

"And you didn't see any car leave the Little House when you were coming up from Soda Springs?"

"No. I saw one leave earlier, but I didn't recognize it. I didn't even see it very well. It could've been the Olds."

"But you believed Cunningham's story that night?"

"No, I've never believed him."

"You think Cunningham killed Kitchens."

"Who else is there, Maxwell?"

"Tee could've killed himself."

"Yeah, he shot himself between the eyes with a .45, pounded his face to a pulp with the butt, hid the gun where nobody would ever find it, then he laid down and died."

"Don't get cute, Campbell. Kitchens could have shot himself, then Cunningham could have done that to his face and hid the gun. He could've made it look like murder, to get the insurance money."

"I thought of that myself, but I don't think it works. From what I hear, they're not going to get any insurance money, not before they're two hundred years old anyway. And anyway, Adrienne doesn't need any more money. Six million bucks would just get lost."

"Six million bucks ain't ever going to get lost. I tell you, Campbell, if I were Cunningham, I'd have suicide as my ace in the hole. Now, it is a felony to mutilate a corpse and it's hell to pay to defraud an insurance company, but that's a lot better than murder." The sheriff thought a moment. "Of course, if he's willing to cop to that, it would mean he's in bad shape. Maybe she suspects he did it."

"I don't know."

"Maybe she knows. Maybe she was there."

"No, I don't think so, Maxwell. I saw her later that night. I was the one who told her he was dead. She might've known he was going to die, but believe me, she didn't know he was dead. She didn't kill him."

"You sound pretty sure of that."

"She didn't kill him, Maxwell."

"Murder one on Cunningham would leave you with the girl, wouldn't it?"

"No, it wouldn't, Maxwell, it would do just the opposite."

The sheriff shrugged. "The Mexicans weren't there. O.K., so Cunningham set them up, had them come in earlier. Adrienne Kitchens wasn't there. How about Estep and Mueller?"

"They didn't kill Tee, I don't even think they had anything to do with it. Maybe they saw it. Maybe Tabor did. He was asleep in a car parked in front of the Little House. Maybe he woke up and saw something he shouldn't have seen."

"And now he's dead." Maxwell drew on his cigar, then almost imperceptibly nodded his head. "Cracked up out on the Flavannah highway. Didn't make that one big ole curve coming off the cap. Funny thing, it happened the same night that Ronnie Rice blew out those poor fucking Mexicans. Almost the same exact time. Four-thirty a.m. in the morning. You feel like taking a little ride, we'll go out and have a look at the car. What's left of it."

We took Maxwell's car to a farmhouse three miles north of town. Behind the house sat a dilapidated barn where two old men toiled under a Hydra-Matic transmission. Maxwell took a key off a nail inside the door and we walked out to the pasture behind the barn. He unlocked a chain on a barbed-wire gate and we wandered through acres of derelict cars squatting like smashed insects in the jungle of tumbleweeds.

"I grew up in this goddamn place and I've never been able to get the stink of it out of my nose." Maxwell laughed absently. "That's my old man under that car back there. He's been under there for twenty years. It's funny but I can understand why Cunningham did it. But it's the people he thinks are protecting him who'll finally turn on him. You ought to tell him that, Campbell. If he doesn't already know." We stopped and Maxwell wiped his forehead with a white handkerchief. "This place has been crawling with insurance investigators. They talked to you yet?"

"No, they haven't found me yet. I've got a few more stops of my own before I see them."

Maxwell looked at me closely. "You're not planning anything extralegal, I hope."

"I sure as hell wouldn't tell you if I were, Maxwell."

"No? What if Cunningham turns on you, Campbell? What if he changes his song? What if he says he found you standing over the body with a smoking gun? He's already testified you came upstairs with a gun in your paw."

"It was a .38 that hadn't been fired. I wish he would turn on me, Maxwell."

The sheriff shrugged. "The law is a funny thing. It says you can tell me you're going to take the law into your own hands and that I can't do a damned thing about it till you do. But let me warn you, there's always the possibility that these accidents and coincidences aren't accidents or coincidences at all. He could be out to clear the rest of you folks off the board." We started walking again. "I don't really believe that, but Cunningham was registered in a Lubbock hotel the night Tabor died. And one of the state boys flagged him just last night, out on the Flavannah highway. Oh yes indeedy, if I were you I'd watch my step. Well, here we are."

We had stopped before a white Thunderbird whose front end was jammed back into the front seat. Maxwell knelt by the rear wheel and reached under the car. He felt around for a few seconds, then withdrew his hand, empty. "Funny thing, it really was an accident. Least it looks too good not to be. Rear brake line busted. Somehow got pushed up against the tail pipe and burned a hole right through it. Would've taken some time for that to happen, could've as easily gone out while he was driving five miles an hour down his driveway. Well, he wasn't much good at sheriffing anyway, was he?" The sheriff stood and looked out across the dry lake, the heat rising from it in a dusty shimmer. "Maybe I'm going crazy too—like my wife says —but I not only think Cunningham killed Kitchens, I think he was cool as a cucumber about it. I think he planned it from a long way back. I don't know about all these other folks—Tabor, the Mexicans, that kid, the cowboy—but I know he killed Kitchens. I know he's a murderer and I know he's going to get away with it and there's not one goddamn thing I can do about it. Ah hell, let's get out of here. They had to hack one of Tabor's feet off to get him out and the smell of it makes me sick to my stomach. Anyway, this case is closed."

"No, it's not closed, Maxwell, not yet."

"Oh yes, it is," the sheriff said, and we walked back to the car.

# 1 5

For two hours I sat in a booth at Tommy's Oil Well, listening to the ranchers talk, watching the cars pass on the highway. Tommy had a new waitress. I asked what was happening out at El Toro.

"Nothin. Nothin at all."

"But what's been happening since Tee Kitchens's death?"

"Look, buddy, not a goddamn thing far as I know."

For a long time I leaned against Foose's old Studebaker, looking at the melting strip of asphalt that led to Wadsworth. The snakes were gone. Tommy had put them back on the menu. The air was so hot and dry I could barely breathe. I drove aimlessly through Toro. The houses were all small and worn, the people poor and old. I finally came out on the Wadsworth highway south of town. I found myself turning off on the road that led to the ranch. A chain with a heavy padlock was draped across the stone arch. Signs posted on the arch said NO HUNTING, NO TRES- PASSING; someone's scrawl warned that if I passed this barrier I would be shot. I turned the old car around and drove to Flavannah.

I checked into the City Hotel and fifteen minutes later got a call from the Flavannah sheriff. He only wanted to know why I hadn't reported my pickup stolen. I told him I had forgotten about it while flying jets all over Texas. He said that the scrap metal would do for the towing and that if I felt like paying a fine I could drop by his office in the morning. Fifteen minutes after that, banker Dougherty called and told me that tomorrow morning was when he, Stigall, my aunt, and some other lawyers were meeting to decide who was going to get what from whom. I agreed to abide by their decision. I lay on the plywood mattress but I couldn't sleep.

Son's house looked the same as the first time I had seen it: abandoned. I had parked the old Studebaker down the block and had walked back. Merce's pickup was parked across the street, but it was shiny and new. A man was out behind the grade school driving golf balls. I thought I knew him but he never turned around. I could hear a bark- ing dog on the next block. Overhead a jet was passing, returning to Reese, shining like a star in the pale sky. I waited till its faint sound was gone, then walked up the front sidewalk. The door was locked, but my mind opened it and I walked in. I was so sure of what I was doing that I started laughing. I stood in that dark, musty room laughing, till the man in the back room could stand it no longer and came into the room after me. I hit him as hard as I could, but I felt nothing. He just gave up. He curled at my feet. He didn't care. He let me knock him down again. Finally he no longer got up. Like a child, he belonged to me. He gave me his gun without a struggle and I sat in a chair and watched him plead for mercy. Mercy, sure, I told him, but I had to kill him first. We laughed and laughed till our laughter woke me up.

I waited for dark in the hotel lobby. The old man and woman who ran the place shuffled in and out, keeping an eye on me. I guessed the problem was that the chair hadn't been sat in in years. There wasn't anything else in the lobby. Not even a newspaper. Maybe they hadn't rented a room in years. There was no one else but me in the hotel—they told me that twice. The old folks finally gave up on me and told me to lock the front door before I went to bed and then disappeared.

I studied Maury Mueller's number, his emergency number, the one Foose had taken down on a napkin. It took me a while to realize it was not a telephone number; the street had a number, not a name, and Maury's call had been confused. I noticed that a light shone over the hotel's front door. It was dark outside. I left ten bucks on the desk and drove to Lubbock.

The house that belonged to Maury's emergency address looked like it had been vacant for years. Railroad tracks ran down the middle of the street, and as I parked, the wandering eye of a switch engine flashed over me. Across the street thin brown children played in the dust. Over the roofs of the houses a huge neon sign slowly revolved. I followed a path beaten into the ground. The front steps were gone, so that I had to reach over my head to knock on the door. The door opened slowly and a hand reached down for me and I was pulled up into the dark house without having said a word.

Maury was panting. Even in the darkness I felt I could see him clearly, his words so faithfully recalled his visage. "I knew it was goin to be you, Campbell, so let's git it over with, I got to ast you right off. Are you with me or aginst me?"

"What?"

His flabby voice trembled. "Are you the one he sent to git me?"

"Nobody sent me here, Maury, you called me."

Maury pulled me back into the house, away from the front windows. "Yeah, but you never can be too careful." We were in the kitchen. The white appliances gleamed in the dark and something in the sink stank. Maury asked me if I had anything to eat. "I ain't been outta here in two days. Meskin kids been bringin me grub, but this morning they took off with the money. I lost my appetite anyway. I thank I got cancer. Mark Tabor is dead, did you know that? It wadn't no accident. See, Mark was tryin to put the bite on Cunningham. It was all my fault. See, I was the one who tole him I saw Cunningham murderin Tee. He didn't know nothin. He slept through the whole goddamn thing."

"You saw it?"

"I saw it. The tail end a it anyway. Right after it happened. How could I miss it with all that ravin and screamin going on. *She* was the one who saw all of it. Standin there like a statue. Didn't shed one goddamn tear. There was some shots, I was outside at the time, I heard em and run in and there was Son killin Tee with his bare hands."

"Cunningham claims he was only mutilating the corpse. To hide the fact that somebody else killed Tee."

"I don't like them fancy theories. There was the shots. If somebody else killed him it had to be her. She was the only one there. And if he was already dead, then who was doin that hollerin?"

"Maybe that was Cunningham."

"Aw, Campbell, that was a man bein killed, not the man doin the killin."

"You an expert on that, Maury?"

"Mebbe I am, mebbe I am."

"Sit down, Maury, and tell me what happened. There's nobody out after you."

"God, I wisht I could believe that was the truth."

"Tell me what happened, Maury."

Maury groaned and walked around the small room as if he were on a tether. "I wanted to kill him myself. You know that? It was terrible. All the way drivin back from the lake P.M. was eggin me on. No white man would take that shit. No white man would 'low his wife to do *that*. C.J. was already crackin up. Babblin like a bat. P.M. had this greasy look in his eye. I knew he was up to somethin. But I couldn't think, see, cause I was so upset at Tee for dunkin me in the lake. Anyways, when we got back to the ranch we was in a terrible state a agitation. P.M. was screamin bout doin you in, I was screamin bout Tee, and C.J. was goin on bout somethin nutty as a squirrel pie. We went chargin into the Little House yellin and cussin, but what we saw stopped us in our tracks. I thought I was seein things." Maury walked back and forth. "Why, it was him and her just standin there huggin. Naw, they just had their arms wrapped round one another like they was skeered little children and Tee Texas was a big bad wolf, hangin on to one another like they was the last ones on earth. I figgered that Son and A. had finally laid the law down to Tee, I figgered they had tole him they was runnin off with one another—Tee had this look on his face that I know from the inside. Whatever was goin on, we busted it up. P.M. went out lookin for yore ass. C.J. passed out. I started chewin Tee out, but my heart just wadn't in it. For the first time in my life he was skeered a me. I couldn't unnerstand it. Then it hit me. It wadn't me he was fraid of, no sir, it wadn't me or my words he was fraid of. He finally ast me to go over to the Big House, he wanted to talk to his daddy. He sounded just like a little boy. 'Go git my daddy for me,' he said. Somethin along them lines. Well, I went over to the Big House. On the way out I did look in the Pontiac and Tabor was passed out in the back seat. Well, over in the Big House everybody had done gone to bed and they wouldn't git up. I told Mr. Stanley that Tee really needed his daddy bad and Stanley shook his head and said he was sorry but the old man had wrote Tee off. He wadn't havin nothin to do with him no more. Then I walked back over to the Little House."

"When you went to the Big House, who was left in the Little House?"

"Son and A. and Tee. And C.J. passed out on the floor there. And when I got back, nobody was there."

"Nobody?"

"That's right. Nobody. There wadn't a soul in the Little Room. Not even C.J."

"Did you have any idea where they went?"

"Not at the time, no. I know where they said they was. P.M. had come back from lookin for you and had woke C.J. up and had took her out to walk her around and git her sobered up some. A. was somewheres in the Little House, I guess. Accordin to Son, she had gone upstairs, and then him and Tee had got into a fistfight and then Son had gone upstairs to look for A., cause Tee was threatenin to kill her. Tee hisself, I don't know where he was."

"What did you do then?"

"Well, I went back outside to try to gather up my thoughts. I was kinda walkin around nowhere in particular—that's when I heard the shots. Bout five minutes later. That's when I went runnin."

"As far as you know, Son and Adrienne and Tee were the only ones in the Little House at the time of the shots."

"To the best a my knowledge. Everybody else was out wanderin around or over to the Big House. And I had a purty good view a the front door, so there was nobody who coulda come or gone without me knowin it."

"How about coming in through the garage?"

"You woulda had to use the elevator and it was broke."

"Somebody else could have been in the house before you all showed up."

Maury shook his head at me. "Naw, there wadn't nobody else in that house but them three. And if yore thinkin I killed that boy, Campbell, you can forgit it. That's the last thing in the world I woulda done."

"When you heard the shots you went back inside?"

"Purty much like that. I was froze there for a couple a seconds, but them screams thawed me out."

"And when you came into the room, you saw Son beating Tee. And Adrienne was there."

"That's right. Then all of a sudden A. went dashin past me like a crazy horse. Son grabbed me up fore I knew what was goin on. I figgered he was goin to kill me too. I almost fainted on the spot. He had this wild look in his eye, but he was talking sense. He tole me things wadn't what they looked like and they had to git A. outta this. He tole me to go run after her and take her over to his place over in Lubbock. That's what I did. I was still in them goddamn bathin trunks, shakin like a granny, but I got her all settled down. Then I drove back to the ranch. By that time Tabor was in charge and everbody was runnin around like chickens with their heads chopped off."

"Did Adrienne say anything to you?"

"She did say one thing. She said she was sorry. Said it a coupla times, but it didn't make much sense." Maury drew a deep breath. "I guess she sounded a little crazy when you come right down to it."

"I don't think she knew Tee was dead. She can't remember it."

"Memry went blank, huh? Mebbe that's goin to work for her, Campbell, but if the likes a me and you tried it—" Then Maury leaped up in the air but didn't make a sound coming down. "Hey, wait a minute. Did you hear that?"

"I didn't hear anything."

"Yeah, you did. Lissen." Maury was creeping along the hall on his hands and knees. I walked along behind him. Maury crawled across the floor to the window, peered out, and then crawled back to me. He stayed on his hands and knees, as if that was going to be his means of locomotion from now on. "Oh my God," he said softly, "they're goin to git me sooner or later. Oh my God, it's all over now." Somewhere down the block a car door slammed and Maury flinched. I helped him to his feet and we moved to the rear of the house. "It's all over now. I got to think about Mabs now. She was goin to pick me up at midnight, we was shiftin south, but that's all over now. You gotta help me. You gotta head Mabs off. She caint come over here."

"I'll do whatever you want, Maury, but why don't you just come back to Houston with me—"

"You gotta cut that out, Campbell, they know all about you and Foose, they know everthing. It's just a matter a time now, just a matter a waitin. Don't feel bad about it, it don't make no difference. It was goin to happen no matter what I did. The minute I walked in the front door, my goose was cooked. But you gotta git Mabs outta here. You gotta git outta Lubbock, you gotta git outta West Texas. Go on down to Mexico, start a new life." He was crying now, he even cried fast. "You gotta pull outta this godforsaken state." He touched my arm and pulled me back into one of the empty rooms. "I got somethin here I wont you to keep. If anything happens to me, then the truth will be out. We wrote everthing down. If anything happens to me, you use it aginst him."

He handed me a roll of yellow paper. In my hands the papers curled open like a flower in sunlight. "Read it, read it now," and he moved me over to a window. The three pages were filled with large, neat handwriting. "It all began," it read, "when my husband, Maury Mueller, met Son Cunningham. Son Cunningham told him he could get rich. Before that Maury Mueller had never done one thing wrong . . ."

# 1 6

I drove to Maury's house in the southwest part of Lubbock, but Mabelline wasn't there; the house was empty and dark. I drove back to Maury's hideout, but now he was gone. It was as if I were still dreaming: I had never been here. I drove by Son's house in the hills above the country club, I drove back to Flavannah, by the house behind the grade school, past the City Hotel, past Hannah's. I drove to Toro, past Tommy's Oil Well and his empty snake pit. I drove south on the Wadsworth highway, and then about ten miles out I turned east and drove down to the Little House.

I parked in the side lot and walked around the huge, unadorned building. The doors were locked, the windows cloaked with heavy, colorless curtains. I stood on the front porch, where once they had danced, and recalled the sound of music drifting down from the roof.

It was past midnight but they dragged open the doors to the Big House as if they had been expecting me. I followed a Mexican servant deep into the house. On the second floor we stopped before a double door. The servant spoke quietly to me, pushed open the door, and went away. Inside the room I found Denton sitting in a leather armchair before a window overlooking the road I had just driven down. A book lay open on Denton's chest. He turned the reading lamp on me as if it were a spotlight. Someone lay curled beneath an Indian blanket on one of the couches. I walked over and looked at the face. Denton told me it was no one I knew. He was a man who looked like a boy, his sleeping face sullen and unformed, his mouth broken open by the force of his sleep. I walked around the room; there was nothing there but books. Denton followed me with the lamp, laughing quietly at his joke. I took a book off a shelf and sat across from him. He kept the light shining in my eyes, he kept laughing softly. "I didn't know you were a literary man, Campbell."

"I didn't even know you could read."

He switched off the lamp, but just as my eyes had quit throbbing, he switched it back on. "What are you doin nosin around here at this time a night, Campbell?" He switched the light off again. "Are you lookin for trouble?" And back on again.

"I want to talk to Malcolm Kitchens."

"You caint talk to him at this time a night, Campbell. The old man is dyin, he needs his sleep."

"Is he dying?"

"I said he was dyin. He's dyin."

"You think he might be interested in seeing his son's killer brought to justice before he dies?"

"No." And he turned the lamp off and left it off. My eyes felt like freed birds wandering out into the dark room. "If he wants anything, he wants him back alive. Back alive before things went bad."

"When did things go bad, Denton?"

"Things always been bad, Campbell, things always will—"

"Yeah, I've heard your back-to-Cain speech, Denton. I want to know when things started going bad here, at this ranch. And I want to know why."

"Things started goin bad when I showed up." He laughed to himself; his head turned toward the man on the couch. "That's when things started goin bad around here. At this so-called ranch."

"Did Tee kill Palmer?"

"Yes, Tee did kill Palmer."

"Did he kill Billy O.?"

"Yes, he did kill Billy O. I loved that boy, but he was a cocksucker."

"Who killed Tee?"

"I woulda killed him, but I was done with killin by then."

"I want to know who killed him, Denton."

He turned the lamp toward the couch and switched it on. The man groaned in his sleep, twisting his rubbery face against the armrest but unable to escape the glare even in his dreams. Denton turned the light off. "I don't know who did that, Campbell, but I know he needed to die. You know that happens sometimes. Men *need* to die."

"Why did Tee kill Billy O.?"

"Just to kill somebody."

"That's not true."

"You know, Campbell, I been thinkin about killin somebody. You know much about it?" He switched the lamp on and turned it into his own face. "Do you go to hell?"

"Can you tell me why he did it?"

Denton switched off the light. "He was tormented by his crime, his soul was twisted and ugly. He was afraid; he came to ask forgiveness, he came here to ask the father for forgiveness, but there was none. Not in this world. He came to confess his crime"—Denton laughed softly—"but everbody already knew. He was a killer in his heart"—he turned the light toward the couch, the squirming face— "and it drove him crazy."

"What do you think I ought to do, Denton?"

"About what?"

"About Tee's murder."

Again, like a harsh light, his laughter cut through the darkness. "Why don't you *kill him?*" He looked toward the couch. The man's eyes were open, gray, blank. "That's what you been wantin to do all along, ain't it?" The eyes closed. They had seen nothing. "I wisht I could help you, Campbell, but I caint. I wisht you could see to the bottom a my heart and then mebbe you could understand all this. But you caint."

"I can see to the bottom of my own."

"Then you can understand, caint you, what's growin there. There's flowers of evil growin there. A man's heart is a garden of evil, except"—he laughed silently—"except for that Cunningham, and his heart is a hothouse. We're goin to save that man a front-row seat in hell, Campbell . . ." and in the dark his laughter flashed against my face.

# 1 7

Foose wouldn't let me turn on the light. When I did, he hid his face, but I had seen enough. The sound of his voice was enough. I turned the light off and we sat in darkness. "I'm all right, believe me, I'm all right."

"Who did it?" He didn't answer. "Foose, did Cunningham do it?"

His voice shuddered beneath his words. "He broke me, he broke me down. But that's all right. I came through. I endured. In the end I was the victor and he the vanquished." I waited in the darkness, letting the silence draw him out. "It was Cunningham. He'd gone crazy. But I finally came through. In the end he was the one who broke down and cried."

"Before I go out and find him, tell me what happened."

"No, you can't. Promise me you won't retaliate. Promise me you won't even think about it!"

"I'm not promising anything. Tell me what happened."

"No. He had a reason. I know why—but we've got more important things to think about. We've got an emergency on our hands."

"What emergency?"

"It's June. She's been calling me up and . . . she's been telling me the Commies have taken over the radio stations. They've changed the commercials." His laughter scratched like something trying to get out of a box. "They do sound like they have taken them over." He laughed again.

"All right, Foose, start from the beginning. What's been happening since I've been gone?"

"He's afraid he's losing Adrienne. That's why he's been lying like he has. That's why he's doing what he's done. He loves her so much."

"Did he tell you that?"

"No. Not in words. Who needs words? Only the stupid and the dull. He's afraid he's losing her and it's driving him crazy. It's not that she's fallen in love with someone else. Nobody that he can touch." He paused. "See, that's my theory. I think she's fallen in love with Tee, now that he is dead. I called him up and told him that. That's why he beat me up."

"Foose . . . go on."

"He knows we have been investigating the murder. He threatened to kill us if we didn't stop. See, I called him up and told him I finally agreed with him. I think Adrienne did kill her husband. That's why he beat me up."

"You told him that?"

"I talked to her."

"Did she tell you she killed Tee?"

"Not in so many words—"

I walked around the room for a minute, slamming the walls. "*All right*. What did she say?"

"She said—"

"I want the story just like she told it to you. None of your bullshit."

"I'm not sure if I can. I'm not too linear tonight—I'll do the best I can. Cunningham picked her up at the airport that night. They drove back to the ranch and they were sitting in the Little Room talking. They were going to tell Tee that she was leaving him. She was going to marry Cunningham. When Kitchens came in, he was very calm, very composed. They told him their plans and he said all right, but that he wanted to talk to his wife alone. He asked Cunningham to leave them alone for a while and Cunningham did so, going upstairs." Foose took a harsh breath. "They talked for a while and then . . . then he said he was going to kill her and he hit her. Then she blacked out. She can't remember what happened. She found herself out in an open space. It was dark and she was running, running, and voices were pursuing her. You have killed him! they were saying. And then she woke up and you were standing over her; she was in a strange house, and you were saying, You killed him, *you killed him* . . . But then it came back to her. Her dream, parts of her dream began to come back to her. He hit her and there was the sound of it and she lost consciousness and then she was running down the south road, away from the ranch

. . . and then she stopped and saw she held a gun in her hand. She turned around and went back. Tee was dead. Son was alone with him in the Little Room. He was kneeling beside the body, as if he was waiting for it to come alive. He told her he had killed him, but she knew he was lying. She knew he was lying, not to protect her from punishment, but to protect her from the truth. Now she can face that truth—you helped her face that truth, she said—but she had to face it alone. That's why Cunningham came here and did what he did. What he has done. You see, someone has saved your life, but your debt to the savior is too strong for love—"

"Foose—"

"He sent her away with somebody. He took her gun and put her in a car and sent her to his place in Lubbock. He went back inside and took another gun—a larger-caliber gun—and he fired a shot through the same wound. And then he beat the face . . . and then he shot himself in the arm and hid the guns. You came in, but he got rid of you. Then the dead sheriff and P.M. helped him carry out the rest of the plan. He didn't tell them the truth, of course—he let it look like he had killed Tee and was trying to hide the truth. Don't you see, it has three layers. It wasn't the story of the two Mexicans that was to cover his crime—it was the idea of his guilt that was to hide her crime!"

"Shut up! *Shut up!* Don't you know that's a goddamn pack of lies! Don't you know that he's willing to convince Adrienne that she killed Tee just to save his own skin! Don't you know he's capable of killing her if she stands in his way!"

"No! *No!* I've finally learned the truth and I won't let it go!" He went down the hall to the bathroom. In a few minutes he came back, breathing heavily. The room was still dark. "He was going crazy, that's all I know. So was I.

I think I might've hit him first. Still, he didn't want to hurt me, I know that. He just wanted me to be quiet. He just wants to save Adrienne. I know that." He was silent. "He was looking for you, he said. I think he wanted to tell you something. Maybe he wanted to tell you they're getting married, did you know that . . ."

"When?"

"I don't know when. Who cares when. They're the ones who have everything their way. And we have nothing. Nothing . . ."

"How much of what you told me is true?"

"It's all true."

"What about June?"

"I haven't been able to reach her in three days. I'm worried sick about her, Campbell."

"Do you know where June lives?"

"Yes. I was out there—the other night."

"All right, Foose, let's go find June. And then I'll take care of Cunningham."

"That's right, Campbell, we're going to learn the truth. Even if it kills us." And he crashed against the wall.

An hour of cold showers and hot coffee later we were headed north on the freeway over the top of Houston, the city's skyscrapers huddled together like headstones. Foose was silent now. Occasionally he would rock forward and grasp his head. The freeway ended north of the bayou which crept through the heart of Houston, and soon we were following a narrow, winding road through what not that long ago had been fields of grass and rice. We seemed to drive forever.

Foose finally spoke and I turned off Main onto Little York and then shortly onto a narrow, ditched road. We couldn't find the house and had to turn around and drive back. Finally Foose told me to stop. We looked at a line of small frame houses—they were all alike and Foose couldn't remember a number. We walked the block but June's car wasn't there. It was still dark and across the road I could hear the sound of cattle moving toward pasture. A semi-tractor roared by, and in its high beams I saw fear in Foose's eyes. "This is the one," he said and I followed him up the sidewalk to the narrow, pinched house. His voice shaking, he told me he would go in first.

But the door was locked; the key, still on a ring with several other keys, jammed in the lock. Foose stood jerking at the knob while I went around the side of the house. A dog in the next back yard began to bark and an angry voice called out in Spanish. A light in the rear of the house illuminated a strip of the back yard; an old abandoned Pontiac sat in the light, grinning like a skull. The back door was unlocked. I took a slow breath and pushed open the door.

The kitchen was littered with weeks of eating. Cartons, boxes, packages torn open and left to rot and mildew; meat, milk, bread, cheese, everything covered with a gray, furry slime. Pans, dishes were arranged in wild towers. A bag of flour had fallen onto the floor and broken open. Cockroaches as big as mice scrambled out of the darkness when I switched off the light.

I walked through to the front room. Foose was still on the porch, shaking the door, calling out June's name. I let him in and went into the small back bedroom. Foose followed me to the door. There was a sleeping bag on the bed, no blankets or sheets. A long table occupied most of the far wall; on it piled books, papers, and magazines. Beneath them I found a pistol and a box of ammunition; in the closet a cheap pump shotgun. I found no shells for the shotgun. "She bought it because she thought they were going to come and take her away. Here, you can see where she was going to saw it off." Foose's finger jerked across a thin line scratched around the barrel.

"When was the last time you talked to her?"

"Friday. Friday night. Where do you think she is? What do you think she's done?"

"How was she acting?"

"I told you. She was going crazy again. She thought Tee was still alive. She was talking about meeting him some place." He buried his face in his arms. "She even called me by his name."

"Look, it's all right."

"*Is it?* Did you know I had been sleeping with her? Did you know I'd been *drilling* her, Campbell . . ."

I waited. "Maybe we ought to go by Moser's."

"Moser?"

"He might know where she is, Foose."

"No, he won't. They hate each other's guts."

"Is there any other place you can think of?"

"No place. There's a beer joint on Little York, but she wouldn't be there now. It's too early." He began to laugh. "I think she's probably all right. I think we're being alarmist. I mean, she's perfectly normal except she thinks Tee is alive and well in West Texas." And he walked over and picked up June's pistol and aimed it at the light and pulled the trigger. The empty gun snapped. He pulled the trigger again and then again; he tossed it on the desk. "I'm sorry, Sugar, I've got to get control of myself. She's not at Moser's . . . he's gone." He shook his head. "I guess they could've gone off together—but that doesn't seem likely after Friday night." He gestured to keep from speaking; his hand fluttered like a handkerchief. "I wasn't going to tell you about Friday night, but I guess I'd better. I'm responsible for everything." Foose's voice was now steady and quiet: it was as if I were listening to a different man.

"I've been so foolish trying to solve this ridiculous murder, haven't I? When I should have been trying to keep her alive."

"I imagine she's still alive, Foose. What happened Friday night?"

"Friday night I humiliated Moser in front of all his friends. I beat him up. June was there too. This was later. And Adrienne. That's why Cunningham attacked me. I wasn't going to tell you that. Moser was having one of his going-away parties. He was leaving for San Francisco again. We had invited all our friends and almost everyone came. But Moser was brutal, you know how frank he can be. It's only honesty, I kept saying, don't go! But by midnight we were practically alone. June was there, but she was asleep again. Payne had gone to pack her bags and had locked the door. Moser was beside himself. He pounded on the door and begged her to stay. There were still a few people leering from their shadowy corners. Laughing at his misery, grinning in their cups. Then he began to call up his wife. She's gone, Sugar, God knows where. Kansas, remarried, living some place in Kansas, he couldn't even remember her new name. Now even the people in the corners had begun to leave. And then Adrienne came in. Oh God, why did I ever ask her . . . my poor tangled web . . . Can you believe I was planning a confrontation of all the suspects? Adrienne had been to a party and was with a girl friend, and their dresses were long and silky and they were so beautiful, so incredibly beautiful. She walked in as Moser was groveling in front of Payne. They had a Mexican chauffeur with them. Moser started yakking about his seesters. They had to make the man wait in the car. Payne left. Then Moser got mean. He attacked June. He began to tell about their love life. It's never happened. I know that if I know anything. He made her kiss his feet. Like a coward I sat there and watched her crawl across the floor. He kept moving away—tiny little baby steps—she kept crawling after him. Adrienne broke into tears. He forgot June. We were going to play a game, he said, we were going to perform a play called *Kitchens's Death,* he said, and he was going to play the role of Kitchens and I . . . I was going to play the murderer . . . and I hit him. I had never hit a man in my life. I hit him till he fell down and I kept hitting him. There was blood on my hands and he kept crying out! Adrienne caught my arms and I looked into her eyes . . . and I stopped. It had felt so good to hit him, Sugar. Then they drove away. I followed them. God, I was so drunk. I started walking, running. I ended up in this bar; the people were staring at me, talking about me. Sometime that night I found myself in this apartment building; they had me pinned against the floor, kicking me. I was screaming and cursing. I thought they were dragging me in for murder." Foose had been pacing back and forth, but now he fell into a chair. He made himself laugh. "I don't remember how but I had a bag of dirty laundry with me and they thought I was burglarizing the place. I told the winos in the tank I was a murderer. They wanted to kill me when the cops let me go the next day. I had become their hero. Have you ever wanted to be a murderer?" He turned his old face to me. "Well, *have you?*"

"Go on, Foose."

"It was Cunningham who came and got me out and beat me up. And I deserved every blow."

We didn't speak for a while. "You just need some sleep, Foose. I think we both do. Just a couple hours and then we'll see what we can do."

Foose tried to lift his head but couldn't. "A couple of hours of anything will be a matter of life and death. Like your dead sheriff told me on the phone, a matter of life and death."

And then the phone in the hall began ringing. Neither of us could move for a second; then Foose rose and said he would get it. When he came back there were tears in his eyes. "She's crazy, all right," he said, "but she's still alive. And that's what counts, isn't it?"

# 1 8

They had found June wandering along the freeway that runs through Austin. The cops had taken her to the city jail for the night, but this afternoon were transferring her to the state mental health center. Foose and I spent most of the morning working with a lawyer, then drove to Austin that afternoon. The center, on the fringe of the city's Mexican barrio, occupied a long one-story building on the corner of a block dominated by a used-car lot. Pennants, bunting, catchy slogans were slapped on the windshield of each car. Across the street sat a high-backed ambulance; painted gold and silver, it shone in the bright afternoon sun. We found June inside the center. I barely recognized her.

She sat in a chair beside the receptionist's desk, her head resting on her arms. She raised her head when I spoke her name. It was as if her face were being erased. Her hair was stringy, dark, it fell across her eyes. She was dressed in white, like the first time I had seen her, and held a pair of shoes in her lap. The shoes of an old woman. She tried to smile, but it was too hard. She tried to smile at the receptionist too and laid her head back on the desk, her arms falling limp at her sides. The receptionist worked on something busy and kept up a stream of talk. She was telling June her friends had come to get her. June raised her head and smiled at the ambulance drivers, who were dressed like cops, in crash helmets and heavy boots. "They have been nice to me," she said to them.

Foose would not get close to her. He went off to find the psychiatrist, someone in charge. June leaned against me, her head hanging back so that she stared up into my face. She didn't take her eyes off mine till a man who said he was a doctor came in. He was so smooth he could have been on wheels. He smiled at June and she smiled at him. He looked like a bitchy old wino they had cleaned up because he almost fit the previous doctor's yellow and green sport coat. His face was wrinkled with hundreds of feathery purple veins; his hair glistened and rippled like a hot tin roof; his breath smelled sweet, like Sen-sen and Southern Comfort. He ushered us into a stark, windowless room that had only a desk and three straight-back chairs. The walls were blank, an oily green that you felt would come off on your hands. The doctor gave us the chairs and leaned against the desk. He talked to Foose about June, legal talk. Foose said all the right things. I could not take my eyes off June. She had grown alert; she no longer smiled, or looked dreamy. She would not look at me. She watched the doctor as he talked about her. Everything had been agreed upon. The doctor turned to June and spoke through his smile, but she no longer saw smiles or heard our pleasant lies.

"I want this door open," she said. "I don't like what's going on in here."

"Now, Jane." The doctor smiled. "The door is closed for a very good—"

"No, I want this door open!"

The doctor adopted a sterner attitude. "Now, Jane, if I say the door stays closed—"

"No! This door is open!" She went over and opened the door and walked out of the room. She was out the front door before we could catch her. The doctor, Foose, and I stood outside watching her walk down the sidewalk. She suddenly ran across to the other side of the street, heading toward Congress Avenue.

"You'll have to catch her and bring her back," the doctor said petulantly and disappeared inside the center.

I told Foose I would bring her back, and he nodded and said he would like to take care of the paper work.

By the time I got to the first corner, June was disappearing around a second. When I caught her she refused to look at me or listen to what I said. I grabbed her by the arms and made her stop. "No, I won't go back there. I know who they are. I know what they're going to do." She wouldn't look at me; her eyes kept running over the people who passed us by.

"Look, June, we want to take you back home with us. We're going to take you back to Houston."

She began struggling to get free. "I don't want to go back to Houston. I want to go to Toro. I want to see Tee. *You're one of the ones who's doing this to us!*" I told her I had changed my mind. I didn't want to take her back, I just wanted to walk with her. She thought it over. "You can walk with me. But you have to walk behind me. Ten feet behind me." She walked off very quickly, singing a children's song.

We walked away from downtown, on a street of leaning, faded houses. Occasionally June would glance at me with exaggerated suspicion. I tried to get her to go back in the other direction. We had gone a dozen blocks, more. She began running again. She ran up to a man getting into his car and began slapping the windows, yelling for help, pointing at me and yelling. The man sat in his car, windows rolled up, doors locked, his hands at his sides, his head thrown back, staring straight ahead, till June grew bored and we went away.

For a while June forgot I was with her. She stopped and looked around with puzzlement. "I know where I am. I know someone who lives here. I left my car here last night." She walked up the sidewalk to an old two-story house and rang the bell. A frightened young woman answered the door. "I was wondering if you know who owns that car," June said, peering past the woman into the house. "For a minute I thought it was mine."

"What car are you talkin about?" The woman's hand moved up toward the screen latch, then moved back to her side. There was a small child behind her whom she kept kicking back out of sight. "Which car are you talkin about?"

"That one," said June, waving her arm behind her. "I wonder if I could have a glass of water." The woman shook her head and closed the door.

We stood on the sidewalk in front of the house, June worriedly looking up and down the street. "Let's go back this way, June," I said and touched her arm. She smiled knowingly at me.

"Why do you want to go *that* way?"

"Because I'm tired, June, I want to go home."

"I'm tired too." She ran out into the street in front of an oncoming car, waving her arms. We began walking, and for a while she followed me, but she turned abruptly toward downtown. "I'm not going back home." She stopped. We stood in a parking lot filled with shining new cars. "Why are you following me?"

"I'm not following you. I can walk along with you, can't I?"

"You can walk with me. Let's run!" But she grew tired and again we were walking. We crossed Congress, about two blocks north of the center, and turned into an alley off East Seventh. June said she was thirsty and we went into a Mexican bar. We sat at the bar. June told the woman she wanted to read the paper; then put her head on the counter and closed her eyes. Mariachis blared on the jukebox. I tried to talk to the woman in Spanish. Her husband came down the bar. "Ella está loco . . . hay un teléfono?"

The husband shook his head suspiciously. "No, aquí no. En la esquina . . ."

A withered old man sat to my right. On the other side of June stood a thick, well-dressed Mexican—his teeth, skin, sunglasses, hair, suit, everything glittered. He spoke English and told the barman the problem, but the barman shook his head and said something to his wife, who rolled out a jumble of soft Spanish. "Esick?" said the bartender and touched his temple with his finger.

"Yes, she's sick." I touched my temple with the tip of my finger. "I need a telephone, to call my friend, my friend who has a car . . ." I turned back to the glittering Mexican. "Can you ask him to look after her till I get back. I've got to call my friend on the telephone . . ."

"O.K. O.K. O.K., vaya, vaya," said the bartender, sweeping me out the door with his hands.

"¡Vaya con Díos!" said the glittering Mexican, and the withered old man folded over with laughter. As I looked back through the front window I saw that the wife had taken a dry bar towel and put it under June's head.

I found a phone in the pinball parlor on the corner. I called the number of the center, but Foose wasn't there, the woman said, he had left to look for me. I persuaded her to put the doctor on the phone. "Oh yes," he purred, "Mr. Foose has gone to look for you. He said he would be back."

"Look, I've found her—she's sleeping, I don't know where, somewhere on East Sixth. Can you send somebody over to pick us up?"

"I'm sorry, we don't have facilities here for that. I wish I could. Mr. Foose said he would call back. Do you want to leave a message? Well, whatever you do, remember we close at five-thirty. There'll be no one here after that." And he hung up.

I saw June on the other side of Congress, standing in front of a newspaper box. She was trying to break through the box's thick plastic shield, trying to borrow a dime from a passerby. "I've got to find out what's happened today. I've got to find out if it's happened today."

"All right, June, I'll buy you a paper if you'll promise to come back with me, if you'll come home with me. I'll buy you a paper and we'll see what happened today." She looked at me as if I were the last person on earth she could trust. "We'll see what Tee is doing today," I said finally, and she reached out her hand and I took it and we went back to the center.

Foose had returned and we signed the papers and took June home with us.

# 1 9

Gunther Oil had its headquarters just beyond downtown Houston, in a large red tin building that looked like a barn that had made good. On top of the building, like a weathervane, perched a brightly painted globe belted by the company's revolving name. Two wide picture windows flanked the front door; they were curtained on one side and draped with chain-link mesh on the other. Behind the headquarters stood a giant crane. I had been watching the entrance of the building for ten minutes and no one had come in or out. It was seven o'clock and the evening traffic was thin.

I rolled up the newspaper I had been pretending to read and walked across the street. On the front page of the paper was a picture of Maury Mueller coming out of the federal courthouse in Dallas. The building grew larger and larger as I drew near. The grass had never been stepped on, the sidewalk looked as pure as cake. I deposited the newspaper in the first wastebasket I saw and asked to see Dolph Gunther on a matter concerning the health and safety of his daughter.

"Would you repeat that, please," said the receptionist. "Would you wait here, please," she said when I did and "Would you follow me, please," when in a few minutes she came back. We walked down a long hall, turning several times. There weren't many doors in the walls and all of them were shut. We stopped in front of a door that was taller, broader than the rest. "Would you go in, please." She didn't move till the door was closed behind me.

In the corner of the leather-padded office sat young Gunner as motionless and well preserved as the game trophies which surrounded him. Dressed casually in white, as if he had been playing tennis, he sat with his legs crossed, staring at the wall only a few feet from him. He asked me to sit down without moving his eyes from the wall. "I was handling contract negotiations when I was fifteen years old. My freshman year in college I crossed the Atlantic eighteen times. I carried the title searches to the Plaquemines Parish when I was fifteen years old. My old man hasn't made a deal that I haven't sat in on since I was eighteen years old. Then they write this crap about a poor little rich boy who's going to lose his tuxedo in the racing game." He snorted. The pronghorn antelope above him didn't move. "I know they got spies working in my shop. One mechanic is on the GM payroll. It doesn't bother us. You remove the human element and we'll still win. What do you want?" He finally stared at my right shoulder.

I walked across the carpet, trying not to stumble on the braid. Gunner drew back in his chair, grasping the arms as if it were about to drop out from under him. I stopped and he relaxed. "I'm representing your sister." I held out Adrienne's letter.

"On the desk." He watched me walk. "What's wrong with you? You been in an accident?"

"I'm all right. I haven't been sleeping well lately."

"Sit down before you fall down." I moved to a chair away from the desk, and Gunner reached across and with his fingers speared the letter. On either side of my chair ivory tusks grew out of the floor, leaning on me like talons. "Yeah," Gunner said, reading the letter, "we met before, didn't we? Up at Toro."

"At the ranch."

"That's right." He folded the letter and put it in his pocket. "What do you want?"

"I wanted to warn you, and your father, that Adrienne is being framed for murder."

"You don't say."

"Son Cunningham killed Tee and he's setting it up to look like Adrienne did it. Just in case something goes wrong. Just in case."

"They're getting married in the fall, buddy."

"He's marrying her for her money."

Gunner laughed. "More likely she's marrying him for his." He waved his hand. "People hate you for what you've got. I've got eighteen cars. When some snooty bastard pulls up in his Triumph, I tell him I've got a Maserati, a Scarabe, four Lotuses, and you ought to see the look in his eye. Pure spite."

"I don't think you understand what I'm trying to tell you."

He was looking at the wall again, as if he were surreptitiously studying my reflection there. "What are you going to tell me that I don't already know?" He snorted again. Maybe the antelope's nose did quiver. "I already knew that Cunningham pulled the string on Kitchens. I figured it."

"Did you figure he's trying to set up your sister for murder?"

"I don't know that. What we don't know is who you are." I almost laughed. Who *was* I? "Well?" he said.

"I started out as a friend of Cunningham's and then I worked for him a while, but I don't work for him any more and now I want to stop him. He killed Adrienne's husband and now he's trying to blame her for it. I've got to stop him."

"Maybe she did kill him."

"No, she couldn't have. She couldn't have."

"Too sweet?"

"No—"

"What kind of work did you do for Cunningham?"

"I think at first he wanted me to kill Tee, but I couldn't."

"Why couldn't you kill the little bastard? Too sweet too?"

"No, I just couldn't kill him, I don't know why. Maybe I'm a coward. I hated his fucking guts."

Gunner nodded. "What else?"

"What?"

"What else did you do for Cunningham?"

"I investigated Tee's murder for him."

Gunner laughed at the wall. "He paid you to prove that he killed Kitchens?"

"I think he wants me to know. He wants somebody to know."

Gunner hadn't stopped laughing. "Is he so racked with guilt that he wants to get caught?"

"No. He just wants me to know. It will drive him crazy if somebody else doesn't know. He wants Adrienne to know but he can't tell her. He's got to make her think she did it or he'll lose her." For the first time I found Gunner looking at me. "He's going mad. He loves her, but he's destroying her."

Gunner slid into a chair behind his desk, moving as if his legs were paralyzed. "Well, I think you're crazy myself, but I guess it bears looking into." He pressed a button on an intercom. He licked his lips before he spoke. "Marianne, would you have Bob Zeeburg step into my office for a moment, please. You don't have to know if it's important or not, just have him step in here." He leaned back in his chair. Now he couldn't take his eyes off me. "I'll have to ask Cunningham what it's like."

"What?"

"Killing a man." It was a youthful gesture: he opened his arms above his head. "I've killed about everything else. I haven't killed a rhino either." He pitched his body forward. "I read a story once, about a hunter growing bored with death. It's an interesting idea. I'm beginning to like it." He moved in his seat. "Had he ever killed a man?"

"Cunningham? I don't know."

"Tee and I used to talk about this. About killing a man for sport. Actually he was the one who told me that story, about the man who grows bored with killing animals and decides to kill a man. I forget how it goes exactly, but they're on an island and one man is a prisoner and the other his jailer and the jailer gives the prisoner his chance for freedom. He is going to turn him loose and hunt him. I forget how it ends." He shrugged and thought a moment. "Do you know if Tee killed that kid that was fucking A.?"

"I think he did."

"I've always thought so, too. He used to tell me as much. That he hunted him down like an animal. But then Tee was always so full of shit. I don't suppose you know for sure, do you?"

"No, but you can ask Cunningham. I think he knows."

"But then perhaps after killing a man—'The Most Dangerous Animal,' that's what the story was called—after that maybe he even grew bored with that. Maybe the only excitement left in life was to become the hunted. Do you think that could've happened? Maybe he wanted to be hunted."

"I think Cunningham would like us to think so. He would like for us to think he was mad, he was driven to it; he would like for us to think he killed Tee in a rage, to protect Adrienne, in self-defense, anything, *anything* to keep us from knowing the truth. The truth is that he killed Kitchens slowly, gradually; he killed him over many months of planning and waiting . . ."

Gunner let his words drift. "He hunted him."

"If you want to call it that. That's why I've got to talk to your father. If we can convince him, then we might be able to stop Cunningham . . . before it's too late."

"The old man won't care if he killed Kitchens. He might like the idea."

"What about his daughter?"

"Maybe," said Gunner and pressed the button on the intercom. "Would you get my sister on the phone, please. Pronto. And where's Bob? He's on his way," he said as if I hadn't heard. "Don't say anything about that story—the men hunting each other. Anything else you want to tell me before Bob gets here?"

"I'm worried that he might actually kill her."

"You are?" Then a small man stepped through a door hidden in the wall. "Come in, Zee," Gunner said. "This man here says that Son Cunningham killed Tee Kitchens."

Small, about fifty, dressed in a Western suit with a vest, the man went so quickly to a chair on the other side of the desk that I thought he was intent on taking it with him. He sat down and looked at me—one eye was glass. He propped a notebook on his knee. "What's your name?" I told him and he wrote it down. "Telephone number." He wrote it down. "Address." Like the phone number, I gave him Foose's. Gunner watched his writing out of the corner of his eye. Zeeburg studied my answers, checking each one. "What proof do you have that Son Cunningham killed Tee Kitchens?"

"He told me he did."

"Anybody else hear his confession?"

"No. We were alone."

"Where?"

"Austin."

"Where in Austin?"

"On Lake Austin. We were in a boat on Lake Austin."

"When?"

"A week ago, less than a week ago. I can't remember the day—"

"Less than a week ago and you can't remember the day?"

"Wednesday. Last Wednesday night."

Zeeburg tapped his pencil against the pad. Gunner watched the pencil bounce. "What in the hell were you and Cunningham doing in a boat in the middle of Lake Austin at night?"

"I think he wanted to kill me. But he couldn't."

Zeeburg closed his notebook. "Is this what you brought me in here for?"

Gunner's voice was hollow and strained. "I think you ought to hear him out, Bob. It might come in handy later on."

Zeeburg pried open his notebook. "Were there any witnesses to the murder?"

"Adrienne was there, I think, but she doesn't remember anything."

Zeeburg pulled the intercom around to him. "Marianne, would you get Adrienne on the phone, please."

"I've already done that, Bob."

"Anybody else?"

"Mark Tabor was there and Maury Mueller, but I don't think—"

"Marianne, would you get Maury Mueller on the telephone, please."

"They weren't eyewitnesses, Bob."

"Repeat the other name."

"Mark Tabor, but he's dead."

"Dead?"

"He was killed in a car wreck. I think Cunningham was responsible for it."

"How?"

"Someone burned through the brake lines . . . The Toro sheriff thought he could have done it . . ."

Zeeburg's eyes focused beyond his notebook. "The sheriff was the one who was killed."

"No, that's Wadsworth County. Mark Tabor was sheriff of Wadsworth County, the county to the south of El Toro. Maxwell is the sheriff of Toro County. He's still alive."

"This Sheriff Maxwell of Toro County thinks the other sheriff could have been murdered?"

"Why don't we call him up on the telephone, Bob?"

Zeeburg nodded. "Marianne, would you see if you could get a Sheriff Maxwell of Toro County on the phone. Toro County, that's right. No, just hold all other calls. To both of us. That's right." Zeeburg leaned back in his chair, his notebook closed. "So the official version of Tee's death is a lie."

"That's right."

"I never believed it either. All right, let's have your side of it. From the beginning."

I didn't tell them all of it, just what they wanted to hear. I told them that Son Cunningham had brought me to Texas to help him kill Tee, but then things changed, or maybe all along I was just to be blamed for the death. Maybe I was to die for Tee, maybe I was just there to watch. I told them about the two men who had died before, and who had killed them. I told them about the insurance and the search for money. I told them about Francis Dolly and Son Cunningham's treachery and ambition. I told them about June and her strange love for Tee. I told them about the trip to Mexico and about Foose and P.M. and the dead man in the hotel room. I told them about Tee's death, about his wanting to die. I told them about the night of his death and the following days. I told them how the lake looked that afternoon, gray, like steel. I told them about the ring of winos who thought I was going to kill Tee. I told them about the ruined pickup, I told them about the smell of burned meat and alcohol, I told them about the ghost that Tee had hit on the road. I told them about the piss flooding from the telephone booth, about the white straight line down the center of the highway. I told them about the couples dancing, about the man with the dirty face and the hard hat whose finger struck my chest like a knife, about how Tee's face leaped away from his head when the man hit him, how he screamed and beat the car till he was quiet and said he knew what he had to do. How he looked as we drove to the place where he had killed a man. I told them about the sound of the gunshot in that black pit of trees, about the sound of my own voice calling out his name, about the car turning, the light honk of the horn, and the long slow walk back to the ranch. I told them where I stood when I knew for sure that Tee was dead. I told them how he looked dead, how his body had seemed to fall apart inside his clothes, that only his life had held it together. I told them that his face was missing. I told them about Malcolm Kitchens handing the reins of his horse to a younger man and how the reins had slipped from his hands. I told them about the sound of water running above me and someone laughing or crying. I told them how I climbed the stairs and how the gun in my hand pushed open the door. And I told them how I saw Son Cunningham with blood on his hands and his face, how the blood clung to his face like a mask and to his hands like gloves, and he could not take them off. I told them how Son had admitted his crime. But I did not tell them how the gun in my hand rose and leaped at him over and over again. I did not tell them how I had killed him long after he was dead. I didn't tell them that I had wanted to kill him, but that I hadn't. That I couldn't. I didn't tell them that.

We waited in silence, but I didn't say anything else. Then Zeeburg said, "Well, what do you think of that?" He had a telephone cradled against his ear. He was reading over his notes. "Yeah. All right." He looked up at me. "I don't know. No, no, we don't operate like that. O.K. Tuesday, then. Fine." He held the phone away from his face and pressed a button on the receiver's base. "O.K., Son, you're on the box now."

Son's voice filled the room. "We're on the squawk box?"

"That's right, Son. On this end there's myself and Gunner and this man Campbell."

"Hello, Son," said Gunner.

"Hello, Gunner," the voice said, "how're things going down Houston way?"

"Pretty good, Son. D.G. ought to be back in town end of the week, let's get together."

"You just give me a ring and I'll fly back. The conversations with the poet are coming along real good, Gunner." The voice laughed. "Real good."

"That's good, Son," Zeeburg cut in, "but we'll get into that when Dolph gets back. What did you think about your friend's tale and what do you think we ought to do about it?"

"I think with friends like that I don't need any enemies,

Zee." There was a silence; then the voice spoke thought-fully: "Sugar, are you there?"

"I'm here."

"Sugar, where do you think up all these crazy stories?"

"That's no crazy story, Son, that's the truth."

"If it's the truth, Campbell, why didn't you tell it to the authorities when you had the chance? Why, I just got through talking to Maxwell the other day—Sheriff Maxwell, Zee, up in Toro County. He's the law officer in charge of investigating the murder and he told me that you had confessed to lying at the coroner's jury. He said you had broken down and admitted to perjury. The district attorney could be drawing up indictments against you right now, Sugar, if you keep on with these fool tales. And another bone I've got to pick with you is these stories you've been scaring poor ole Maury Mueller with. Now ole Maury's in poor enough shape as it is, Sugar, without you scaring the wits out of him with these crazy stories about P. M. Estep murdering poor ole Mark Tabor and all this crap about me out to kill Maury because he supposedly saw me killing Tee Texas. Now, sometimes crazy stories are funny and sometimes they're sad and sometimes they're just downright criminal. Did you know that you've just about driven poor Mabelline Mueller to the verge of a nervous breakdown with all your crazy stories? Now, I don't know what we're going to do about all this, Sugar, but we sure as hell are going to have to stop it, aren't we? Do you know what I just did to a man who'd been spreading wild and malicious and crazy stories about people? A man who had been spreading the filthy lie that our Adrienne had killed her husband. Son, I beat him to an inch of his life and I told him that if I ever heard one more peep out of him as long as he lived that I was coming back and would finish up the job. Now, are we going to have to do something like that to you, Sugar, to get you to stop spreading these vicious lies? Are we? Well, are we? Or are we going to have to take more drastic steps? Are we going to have to do something like A. suggested? Are we going to have to put you away for a while so your mind can get a little rest? Are we going to have to put you behind lock and key and have somebody wash all these goddamn lies out of your head, Sugar? *Well, are we?*"

"No," I finally said. "No, that won't be necessary. It's all over now."

"That's right, son, that's all she wrote, there ain't no more."

The receptionist came and led me back outside.

# 2 0

I got a room at a hotel down on 75th because it looked like a good place to kill somebody. I forget the hotel's real name but Heartbreak was what the manager called it. So many people splitting the blanket, running away from somebody or something, coming down here to suffer a few weeks before moving on. Across the street was a slave-labor hall, and I sat by the window and listened to the sounds of the drifters who had lost their jobs, were looking for other jobs, finding them, losing them, drifting away again. I sat with my back to the window and listened. I waited till dark, till most of the men had come in, collected their eight bucks, and left, and then I walked across the street and sat in the phone booth in the corner of the hall. Nobody paid any attention to me. I fit right in.

I called Son's River Oaks apartment and got the answering service. The girl was so glad they had found me. She had practically been out looking for me herself. She didn't know where Son was, though. "No, no," she said as carefully as if she were reading a message, "but Mr. Cunningham wants to see you very badly."

"I want to see him too."

"He would like for you to stay in his apartment while he's gone. No, he's not out of town. He's in Houston elsewhere, though we don't have that number. But he would like for you to stay in his apartment till tomorrow when he can get free to talk to you."

"I can't do that. I'm leaving town first thing in the morning. I've got to see him tonight. Tomorrow morning I'm going back up to see Maxwell in Toro. Write that down. Maxwell in Toro. I'm going back up to Toro, and if I don't see him tonight, I'm going to give Maxwell something that will put Cunningham in jail for the rest of his life. You can write that down too."

"I don't know anything about any of this."

"Tell him to meet me at eleven o'clock at the turning basin at the ship channel. Eleven o'clock at the observation point overlooking the turning basin. Have you got it? That's eleven o'clock tonight."

"Where are you staying now?"

"Have you got my message?"

"Mr. Cunningham would like to know where you are staying now."

I thought a moment, then told her the address of the hotel and hung up. The dispatcher in his glass cage was watching me. He was a tall skinny man; his face had been caught by something, he looked weary and frightened. Another wino came stumbling in from the dark and the dispatcher turned his attention toward him. His voice was angry and unyielding. More workers came into the hall, collecting their pay; they were all drunk. One of the stragglers was given the job of sweeping the hall. I watched how slowly, gently he collected the dirt. He made ridges, then mounds, then larger ridges. He finally reached the back of the hall. For no reason he turned his face to me; his mouth made a sound.

"What?"

"You gotta leave now. We're goin to clean the phone booth." He was tired of life, I could tell. "This ain't no hotel," he said. "They ketch you sleepin in here and they thow you out."

"My watch has stopped. What time is it?"

"Time fer you to go."

"What goddamn time is it?"

"O.K. O.K." Like drawing water from a well, the old wino pulled a fat watch out of his pocket. "Niner clock."

"I've got two hours to kill. Two hours before I kill a man."

The old man peered into the booth. "You in trouble with the law?"

"You don't get in trouble with the law for killing a man. Didn't you know that? Not down here in Texas you don't."

"Beats me," said the old man.

"Do you really have to sweep out this fucking phone booth? Why don't you tell the boss to shove that broom up his ass."

"Shit," said the old man and wiped his brow, "why don't you nuts leave me alone."

I'm not a nut, I said to myself as I walked along 75th Street, I'm no nut. Another wino stopped me for a match, sucking on his cigarette hard enough to break a rib. His hand drifted against my sleeve as soft as a breeze; then he looked into my eyes and hurried on. I'm not a nut, I went on, I just look like a nut. I went back to the Heartbreak and took a shower and shaved and changed into clean clothes. I polished my boots till it was too dark to see them shine. I don't remember how long I sat in the dark before I went across to the dresser and opened a drawer and took out the Llama automatic, the little gun I had lost in Mexico. I sat on the edge of the bed and polished the gun with a cloth. I removed the bullets and polished them too and then reloaded the gun and put it in my pocket and then walked down 75th Street toward the ship channel.

For an hour they had been unloading the ship below me, but now they were through. Deck hands were tying things off for the night; a group of longshoremen moved easily along the dock toward the parking lot which lay to the left and below the observation tower where I stood. The empty ship was moored at the very end of the ship channel, the widened basin where all ships had to be turned before they could make their way back out the narrow channel to the Gulf. From my vantage point I had a good view of the Canal Street gate to the docks. I watched an orange Mustang stop at the dock gate, then drive along the road to the parking lot below me, park, the lights flash off, and a huge fat man slide from under the wheel. He pawed at the ground like a buffalo before he headed up the observation platform stairs.

Pork Man was still dressed like a Sunset Strip plantation owner. The fat man stood at the far end of the platform, pretending to check out the ship channel through the observation telescope. I walked down closer. "What are you doing here, P.M.?"

P.M. had turned the telescope, peering at me through it. He gave the telescope a whirl and leaned back against the railing. "I want to give you a piece a good advice. Come on back to California with me. I'll give you a ride outta here right now tonight. Git outta this fucked-up state while the gittin's good." He thought a second. "I lifted Maury's credit cards, so's you don't even have to worry bout gas." For some reason that pissed him off. "You cheap fuckin bastard."

"I'm not going back to California. Not right now, anyway. I've got some business to take care of."

P.M. snorted. "You ain't got no business around here,

Campbell. Yore belly-up in this goddamn state, buddy."

"What are you doing here? Your boss send you to take care of me?"

P.M. scowled. "Nobody sent me nowheres. I come here on my own." He studied me out of the corner of his eye. "I come here as yore buddy, asshole."

"Then how come you got that gun in your pocket?"

"How come *you* got that gun in *yore* pocket?"

"Because I'm going to use it to kill Cunningham."

P.M. scowled some more. "What bushit, Campbell, you ain't killin nobody and you know it. Yore just tryin to look good for the girls. You fuckin hot dog."

"I asked you a question. If you just came down here to give me some friendly advice, how come you're carrying a goddamn gun?"

P.M. grinned. "Why, I figgered I'd kill two dodos with one rock. I'm goin to unload this sonofabitch right now." And with a sudden, smooth motion P.M. took the .45 out of his belt and, like a discus thrower, flung the gun far out into the darkness. A long time passed; then there was a splash off the bow of the ship. P.M. was still grinning. "Now I talk some sense into yore head and git a gold star." He went back to fiddling with the telescope. "I bet this sonofabitch don't work. I bet it gobbles up dimes like a candy-bar machine."

"Why don't you give me your advice and get it over with."

That meant it might take hours before Pork Man talked, so I said something nice and he nodded, looking down into the water. "You know what that was, don'tcha?"

"What? It was a gun."

"That's right. You know what gun that was, don'tcha?"

"No. I don't."

"That was the murder weapon, killer. The one yore buddy got Tee Texas with." P.M. turned his face so that I could have a full view of his smirk. "Actually, that ain't the fact. It's just the one everbody *thanks* Tee Texas got it with."

"What are you talking about?"

"It ain't the real murder weapon. The gun that killed Tee Texas is in yore pocket right now." My hand clenched the weapon and Pork Man laughed. "Gives you the shudders, don't it? Be the best thang to give it the heave-ho right now, buddy."

I took the Llama out of my pocket and pointed it at P.M. "How do you know this is the gun that killed Tee?"

"Cause I seen it with my baby-blue eyes, Campbell."

"So you did see it . . . Tell me what happened, P.M."

"You are one a the nosiest bastards I have ever seen— All right, don't git yore bowels in a uproar. Put that sonofabitch away and I'll tell you what happened till yore blue in the face. That a deal?"

"Does Son know you saw it?"

"He's got just enough suspicion to keep him on his toes, and not quite enough so's he'd ever decide to raise his hand against his ole buddy, P. M. Estep."

"All right. I already know that you and C.J. and Maury came back to the ranch and found Tee and Adrienne and Son in the Little Room. Right?"

"That's right. We came in boilin mad. I was goin to git you, Maury was after Tee, he hits him—I knew that was the end a Tee right there, letting that little cocksucker slap him around."

"I've heard that part."

"O.K. Then Maury goes off over to the Big House; I drags C.J. out to the car and pours her in the back seat. She has passed out on us."

"All right, that leaves Tee, Son, and Adrienne inside. Wait—you told me at the funeral that you and C.J. were over at the Big House around the time of Tee's death."

"Lissen, I had to perteck myself. Shore, C.J. was conked out durin the whole shootin match, but she don't know that. She'll tell em anything I want her to." Pork Man spat out over the railing almost as far as he had thrown the gun. "All right, so's Maury's out wonderin around some place hootin and hollerin, 'Ah hit mah best butty, ah hit mah best butty,' some kinda snivelin shit. Anyways, I git C.J. laid out in the car and I go back inside and nobody is there in the Little Room. And that is funny, since I had only been gone two, three minutes. I poke around downstairs and there ain't nobody there that I can find. I try the elevator and it's busted. So I walk up the stairs to the roof but there ain't nobody there. I check it out. Nobody. I look off the roof there, but there ain't nothin movin around the headquarters neither. They gotta still be some place inside the Little House."

"Did you know that Son was going to kill Tee?"

Pork Man thought a moment. "Yeah. Up until that night I was workin for Cunningham—I was takin his money— but I wadn't in on it. Not that night. By that time he had gone off on his own. I figger he had decided to git it done, he was goin to have to do it hisself." He paused. "But I knew that was the night. I reckon everbody did. O.K., so's I go down and check out the third floor and there ain't nobody there, and I check out the second floor and there ain't nobody there. Well, I was headin back downstairs, not knowing what the hell is goin on, when I heard voices. Now you know how them stairs kinda curl around behind that big chimley; well, I was blocked outta sight but I could hear everthin that was goin on. Campbell, it was like the three a them was talkin tongues, babblin all at onct. I creeps down a little bit and I can see A. and she's standin there with her hands clapped over her ears, and then I go on down one more step, stayin in the shadders, and I see Cunningham and Tee. Tee was holdin this

brandin iron, but it ain't like he's goin to use it—it's like
he was wavin it around to skeer Cunningham off with it.
And then all of a sudden there, Cunningham raises up
yore little popper there and shoots that boy right between
the middle a the eyes. It was like he didn't even aim it—
there's a pop and there's a little red hole right smack in the
middle a Tee Texas's forehead. Then Tee and his lady
both go down like a shot—it was like she was shot herself,
she falls down in a dead faint. Then like some kinda goddamn movie star, I whip out my gun and rush down into
the middle of it, instead a tiptoein right back up them
stairs. But it's like I ain't there, Cunningham don't pay a
goddamn bit of attention to me. He's standin there over
Tee's body, lookin down at him like he's hopin he'll wake
up." Pork Man stopped. "He starts askin me if I think he's
still alive and we look at him, but just cause somebody is
twitchin don't mean they are alive. Then Son reaches out
and takes my .45 from me and says we gotta make sure and
he puts the .45 over the first hole and well, ole buddy, I
got a strong tummy, but Lord, it was a mess. Ole Cunningham was gaggin hisself."

"Why in the world did he do that?"

"Mebbe he thought he wadn't dead. Mebbe he did it to
save yore ass." The fat man grinned. "But that don't make
sense, does it, killer?"

"I just don't understand it. I don't understand it."

"It ain't that hard, Campbell. After I found yore little
.380 in my buddy's cab down in ole Mexico, I decided to
keep it, just in case I ever wanted to hang yore ass. I ran
down the pawn shop you bought it at, and five hunderd
bucks said the old boy wouldn't have problems remem-
berin you buyin it. I had that sonofabitch draggin after
yore ass like a tail."

"Five hundred bucks?"

"Shore. Cunningham paid me five thousand bucks for

the gun, if I could set you up with it. Come on, Campbell, who the hell did you think you was messin around with anyway? Yore buddy Cunningham is one cold sonofabitch. That's why I don't figger why he did what he did. He pays five thousand for that gun, shoots Tee with it, he's got you out wonderin around with no alibi, A. passes out and don't remember nothin, and for fifty thousand I woulda took the witness stand and swore you pulled that trigger— I just don't figger it. Mebbe I do. It was that goddamn broad, she didn't want you set up. That's one time in yore life, Campbell, that bein a lover boy didn't git yore ass in a crack. I never could figger out you boys chasin after that ole gal. You and Tee and Cunningham, you coulda had the run a things, but you was always fuckin up over her."

"You miss the point, P.M. She's got the treasure. She *is* the treasure."

"Oh yeah? Anyways, me and Cunningham is both staggerin around swallerin puke when we looks over and see that A. has woke up. She starts in yellin Murder and all that shit, and then I looks over and see Maury standin in the doorway, his eyes bulgin so big it looks like he's wearin goggles. He's lookin right through me, he don't even see me, and then I hear this fuckin noise, sounds like somebody taking a dull ax to a rotten stump, and I turn around and see that Cunningham has gone berserk. I thought he was flippin his fuckin lid. I was beginnin to wisht I hadn't give my gun up, but it turns out he was cool as a cucumber bout it. He'd already figgered out the two Meskins and he was just puttin the finishin touches on it." P.M. hesitated. "Then A. starts screamin and she runs out. Son grabs Maury and sends him after her. Then he comes over to me and says he figgers he better be found here alone and I says that suits me just fine. Then he picks up my .45 and I say to myself, P.M., you slow turd, it's all over now, but then he shoots hisself with it. Then he hands me the gun, both the guns, and he tells me to lose em. I go out and do some hard thinkin. I get in the car and drive around and decide that I'm goin to keep these guns, just in case I ever need em agin. To perteck myself, if you foller me. So I burry em and come back and park in the trees down by the bunkhouse and wait awhile and then you come along and go inside, and well, you know the rest of it. After you git Tabor up and take off, I wake C.J. up and we go back inside." We were both silent for a while. "So that's it, buddy. Come on, deep-six that gun and come on to California with me. Where they sleep out ever night."

"Not yet."

P.M. shook his head. "Campbell, he can kill you any time he wants to and git away with it, but you ain't ever goin to clip a hair on his head and end up a free man."

"Maybe not. Who killed all those other people, P.M.?"

"What other people?"

"Mark Tabor. Did you kill Mark Tabor, you sonofabitch?"

"Shit, Campbell, I ain't killed nobody since that spick in Mexico and that was *his* fault. I'm gittin too old for that shit." After a while P.M. spoke in a different voice; it sounded like he might have almost grown fond of me. "Look, Campbell, I'm as wary a Cunningham as the next man, but he ain't responsible for everbody who's been dyin around here. Now he did Tee in and mebbe he'd been plannin it, but that's all I know of and that's the truth. What I don't understand, Campbell, is why yore holdin this grudge aginst him. Hell, you didn't give a shit bout Tee Texas, how come you give a shit if somebody kills him? Tell you the truth, I always thought you wanted to do him in yoreself." P.M. drew himself up and buttoned his jacket. "My advice is to git shed a that gun, then we can abduct some teenyboppers and drive to California."

"Not yet, P.M. Maybe I'll see you out there later."

P.M. nodded. "Whatever you say. I think I might drive over to Shrevesport and see if I can shake C.J. loose from that nuthouse. She'd fit right in out there in the Golden West. Both a you would. See you in the funny papers, Campbell. And one more thing. Anybody ever tell you you look like a idiot in a cowboy hat?" And the big man ambled back to the orange Mustang, weighted down one side of it, and drove back out the dock gate.

# 2 1

The road that became 75th Street climbed steeply from the docks; the first few blocks were a wilderness of destroyed, vacant buildings. The old Wobbly hall sat empty; the glass from its shattered windows sparkled on the sidewalk. Across the street two black men leaned their chairs back against the Kitty Kat Klub. Farther up the street an old gas station sat abandoned as if cars had become extinct, the pillars of its overhang as thick as houses. I walked past the Seamen's Mission, a Mexican grocery, a pastelería, then onto Harrisburg Avenue; all the bright new cars sliding from downtown to Pasadena and back again. Beyond that, like pulling a sheet over your face, lay the quiet, numb streets of Houston.

I walked back to the Heartbreak. A long shiny Cadillac was parked just off the side street. A white convertible with tags from a dealer in River Oaks. The car was locked. On the front seat lay a pair of women's leather gloves— white too—and on the back seat a book with a painting of the bright, hazy face of a clown on the cover. The hood was warm and the tires were rimmed with damp mud.

I went upstairs. The room was filled with the dusty smell of Adrienne's cigarette. She lay on the bed, a dark twisted form against the white sheets. She could have been asleep. I took the chair with my back to the window. Adrienne said, "We got your message, Sugar." She stopped. "How have you been?"

"I've been all right. I'm all right now. But then I guess you didn't know that, did you?"

She shook her head. "He's so sorry, Sugar, he's so sorry for those things he said."

"Adrienne—"

"Even Gunner was appalled. It must've been Bob Zeeburg. He's so cold—he makes other people as cold as he is. Son wants to talk to you, to try to explain some of the things we've been through these last few weeks. Sugar, you have no idea what he has been through. Really." And like the first time I met her, her hand reached out toward me but did not touch me. "Will you talk to him, Sugar? For his sake."

I laughed. "He didn't have to send you here—"

"My God, Sugar, don't you realize that I know he killed Tee and that I don't care!"

I couldn't get away from her. I closed my eyes and it was all still there, everything, the picture of Son killing Tee—she couldn't have seen it any clearer. "Adrienne, sometime I would like you to tell me what he's like, what he's really like. I really would like to understand a man cold enough to murder a man for his woman and her money, and I would like to understand a woman who would marry a man who's killed her husband. If you ever feel like explaining something to me, you can explain that."

She sat up slowly. Her voice was cold and fast. "Explain it to you? You bastard. Don't you realize the hell we've been through, you bastard, you sanctimonious bastard!

Who gives a goddamn about you and your little games, vicious gossiping and prying. Explain it to you, my God, you are a despicable man—now I know why he despises you so much, you pretend to be so pure, so righteous, so *above* everybody—and really you just wallow in our cheating and lying, the murder, always the murder. But you're such a goddamn coward, you can't get down in the dirt and grovel with the rest of us. No, you're a coward, a voyeur. What we have to do, you keep locked up in your head—oh sure, you suffer, you think you do, but really it's a luxury. What destroys us, *almost* destroys us—for you it feeds and feeds and feeds your crippled pointless fucking existence. Did you really ever think I could love you? You must be out of your head. You're nothing compared to him, you're nothing. You want me to explain what we're like? Do you *really* want to know what we're like? Did you know it was *my* idea to kill my husband, it was my idea all along? Do you want that explained? I was the one who came to him and said, You've got to destroy him before he destroys us. Would you like me to tell you about the look on Son's face when I told him I wanted to destroy that demented bastard? Would you like to *see* that, Sugar? That's your reality, *that's* the truth you think you're looking for, but then that's not what you're interested in, is it, Sugar? You're not interested in the real world, you're just interested in your daydreams, the big dragons and sweet princesses in your head. No, no, Adrienne is a dear sweet tender innocent woman—no, no, no, it would take another man to kill a man. Well, I'll tell you, it was the sweet innocent girl who pushed him and pushed him and pushed, and still he wouldn't do it; he still wouldn't take another man's life, no matter how vile that life was. He couldn't kill him, Sugar, but I made him. It's almost driven me crazy, but now I've done it and we're living through it. We're going to live through it. We're going to be so fucking happy." Her voice had grown quiet and now it drifted into silence. "It's not pretty, is it?" she finally said. "But then that's the way the world is. And now, Sugar, will you give me the gun and leave us alone?"

I laughed. "So that's why he sent you here. He's really that afraid of me."

"He's not afraid of you, Sugar, I am. Could you give me the gun now? Please."

I tossed the gun on the bed and she quickly picked it up and put it in her purse, snapping the catch. "Thank you." With the same precise movements she went to the door and turned toward me. "By the way, Sugar, we're having a little function to celebrate our engagement and we'd like you to attend, before you return to California. If this is your address while you're in Houston, I'll mail the invitation here. What's the name of this dump anyway?"

"The name? I don't know if it has a name. They call it the Heartbreak Hotel."

"The Heartbreak Hotel," she said. "Well, that fits you just perfectly, doesn't it?" And she walked out the door.

# 22

"It was so good of me to have invited you," said Anna with her cracked smile and took my hand and led me down into the garden where Son Cunningham and Adrienne Gunther Kitchens were informally celebrating the announcement of their wedding engagement. Dolph Gunther's French château rose behind us like a fortress. The garden—a lawn of African Bermuda grass dotted with a rich mixture of rose shrubs and every conceivable variety of fruit tree—sloped down a hundred yards or more to the wilderness of Buffalo

Bayou. Like candy figures the guests had been carefully placed among the roses, the trees, the white skeletal lawn furniture. Dolph Gunther himself was one of the few not able to attend—he had not been able to delay oil negotiations in Libya. But Adrienne's mother had flown back from Hong Kong and her brother had even taken off a few days from interfering with his racing team's time trials. Almost everyone I had ever known or ever would need to know, Anna told me, was here. "Everyone but the West Texas crowd, of course." Of course.

So Anna was my guide as we stepped off the château's broad polished stairs into the spongy Bermuda grass. "Now, I don't mean it's *the* event of the decade—the fiancé simply comes from *too* egalitarian a background." She touched my arm and gave a musical laugh her best. "Of course, if you're aware you *have* a background, you're not real society. Have you heard the latest trash? About the boy friend who beat up the husband at the graveside of the wife? The grief of the living, I would call it." Anna started making little leaps to see over the heads of the people who seemed to be overrunning us, though we were the ones who were moving among them. "I suppose you're going to want to see Adrienne."

"I've already talked to her."

Anna stopped leaping, and suddenly I could hear the conversation of those around us. Someone was speaking a foreign language. It took all I had to understand Anna. "Cunningham wants to talk to you. Later on."

"It's the reason I came, Anna."

"He's upstairs now. On business." She suddenly looked around her as if the people had all turned to stones—smooth, polished, identical—and we had gone too far and were lost among them. "I've finally gotten over Adrienne. Have you? You look so tired, Sugar, what have you been up to?"

"Sleeping. Not sleeping."

"I've fallen in love again. My God, I thought it was all over, that I was too big for that. She's so beautiful, so . . . well, beautiful." And as if she too were beautiful, she turned her face to me. "Sugar, she's so sorry for what you had to go through. I was wrong, so wrong . . . she looks so right now. What do you think of our job of rehabilitation? I can no longer tell." She covered her face with her hands.

"I think she looks fine, Anna. I think she's going to be happy."

"Happy? None of us is innocent, Campbell. I feel the burden of guilt, just like you. We all killed him, we all wanted him dead. You're not the only one. I loved her too. We're all like Audie Murphy, aren't we? We've been to hell and back. He was in love with her too, Campbell. All his life he loved only one woman. *That* is what is terrible—to love only one person. Only one way out of that prison of love," and she smiled. "Maybe his death was an act of love."

"An act of economics," said a voice from one of the groups drifting nearby, a crusading liberal journalist, Anna whispered to me, from Austin. The journalist looked so young, dressed neatly in a suit with wide lapels and flared pants, and he smoked a pipe and always seemed to be losing interest in what was being said, even when he was the speaker. Beside him stood a young woman with slim, athletic legs. The only woman in the group, she stood in attitudes she knew only a body such as hers could sustain. On the far side of the circle I saw Foose; he held a drink in his hand and stared at the ground. Anna spoke to the group: "I wonder why Dolph isn't here."

"Old Dolph may not have got the word yet," said an earnest young man in horn-rim glasses. "Maybe they don't sell the *Examiner* in Tripoli."

"If Rosemary has given her blessings, that's all the cover Son needs."

"*That's* a true fact." Several people laughed. The

woman with the beautiful legs was watching another
woman with beautiful legs. The soft young journalist was
studying a distant airplane as if he were hoping it would
drop. The earnest young man in horn-rim glasses was saying, "Actually, I hear that Dolph is quite fond of Son.
Treats him like a son."

One person laughed.

"I hear Cunningham's closest friends call him Herbie,"
said the journalist.

"I don't believe that."

"His real friends call him a dirty dog!" said Foose and
gave me a wink and a grin he couldn't quite manage: it
kept leaping up at me at all the wrong times. They tried to
crowd him out but he lowered his head and would not be
moved. "I need to *siddown*."

"After Kitchens, I suppose anything's an improvement."

No one laughed at that.

"Do you think his murder was really an act of economics, Wiley?"

"Why not? Everything else seems to be." Suddenly the
journalist stood on tiptoe. "Is that goddamn Rucker here?
That goddamn sonofabitch, honey, I don't want to see him
now." He grasped the elbow of the woman with the beautiful legs. It made her smile.

"Have you told them what Rucker said about the murder, dear?"

"Yeah, tell us what Rucker said, dear," said Foose.
"Then *siddown*."

The journalist matched the woman's smile. "Some of his
usual bullshit about murder and capitalism—"

"Ontogeny recapitulates phylogeny." The woman
smiled.

"Sure. Come on, honey, let's get outta here."

The circle began to break up. Wiley, Anna, the woman
with the beautiful legs moved away. "Aw, you're an incur-

able romantic, Wiley!" Foose called out, but they were already gone. "That's what they tell *me*. Let's *siddown* under one of these fucking trees. It's good for you to get drunk every once in a while; let's *siddown* under one of these cute little trees. Boy, I never feel more liberal than when I come to one of these fucking garden parties. How come you haven't come by and see us, Sugar? Did you have a hissy and storm off in a huff? Are you in a snit? You noticed I was really keeping up the end of the stick there with Wiley. You can't let them get away with a thing. Come on, Sugar, let's *siddown*. I'll *siddown* if you'll *siddown*." And I sat and Foose lay facedown under an apple tree. There was a number pinned on its trunk and while Foose and I were talking, groups of guests with clipboards would come by, study our tree, then move on to the next tree. Below us, toward the dark thicket of the bayou, a group of guests had stripped a tree of its balloons and were gently tapping them to one another, trying to keep them from striking the ground. The late-summer twilight had begun to fade; a touch of cool night was in the air and the grass was cold. The Japanese lanterns had begun to glow, and the sound of the guests' voices had grown musical, like a breeze disturbing a crystal chandelier. "I miss my ole buddy Moser. I knew I would miss him. He won't write. He never will. Maybe you can look him up when you get back to California."

"Maybe."

"Maybe . . ."

"How is June?"

"June . . . June is fine." Foose turned on his side, facing me. "She really is. I've got her working in my garden. She likes it. She's very good. Except *she won't kill bugs*."

"Tell her I said hello."

"O.K. Come by and say goodbye before you go."

"I'll try."

"Maybe you will and maybe you won't. But probably not. I'm sorry it didn't work out for you, Sugar. You're not a nice man, but you're a pretty good old boy. Pretty good. Old boy. Cunningham is a dirty dog, but he only did what he had to do. Is that why you showed your face around here, Sugar, to see if he only did what he had to do?"

"I didn't come here to kiss him goodbye."

"I was hoping that you were going to kill him. There was a time when you would've killed him. Wasn't there?"

"No."

"No?" He shrugged and turned back on his face. "I guess you want to see Adrienne, but she won't see you. Oh, she'll talk to you, but she won't see you. You know, Sugar, I'm forty-seven years old and I haven't done one thing with my life that I wanted to and I no longer give a shit. I used to think I was so special, I used to think I was the Great Foose. Do you see me standing out there, Sugar, reaching out for those distant green lights? You know, Cunningham is our hero, our real hero. He was poor and went to an orphanage and was saved by a rich old man, and he loved this girl so much, this beautiful rich girl. He fought, cheated, lied, schemed, betrayed his friends, and finally he killed a man—all because he loved this beautiful rich girl. That's right, isn't it?"

"I don't think so."

"Neither do I." Foose turned his face away from me. "I know I'm ridiculous, Campbell. I know I'm a fool and a drunk and that they all laugh at me behind my back. I know she doesn't really love me, I know I'm not the Great Foose, but by goddamn, I'm the Little Foose." And after a while he said, almost as if he were talking in his sleep, "Would you *siddown*, Campbell . . ."

I said so long to the little man sleeping it off under the apple tree.

# 2 3

Once night got started it came on fast. I stood alone on the steps of the château, probably looking as small as I felt. The guests who remained had gathered at the bottom of the garden. Searchlights were piercing the wilds of the bayou cypress and occasionally laughter would rise from the party.

The servants operated like polite but efficient guards. They let me in the house and ushered me upstairs without a word. Son was standing at the far end of a spacious room, looking out across the garden toward the bayou. No lights were on in the room, only the twilight from the wall of windows glazing everything a hazy ivory. Over the cypress I could see a stream of silent headlights disappearing into a freeway. In the garden beneath us the paper lanterns bobbed on the evening breeze like small boats moored in a bay. The room was covered with maps. Maps hung in layers on the walls, which were papered with maps. Down the center of the room ran a long table covered with maps, stacks of maps. Cabinets of maps, rolls of maps, globes, atlases, even the rug was a huge map of Texas. Son remained at the window, looking out at the party, which had descended into the bayou, the laughter and the lights gone. The garden had grown dark and silent. "This is where I hide out when the old man's not around," he said. "When I was a kid I was crazy about maps. I used to send off to Havana, Acapulco, and they would send me maps. I'm up to here in maps now, but we don't keep them here. Men are killed over the maps I play with now." Son was silent for a moment. "I'm glad you came, Sugar. I didn't really think you would."

"There was no reason not to. I've got a lot of time on my hands these days."

Son made an abrupt gesture. "Did you see Adrienne? She was looking for you."

"We had a nice talk the other night."

Son nodded. "So I heard. Do you know who I was thinking about today, Sugar? Carver Stansell. Do you remember him, Sugar?"

"I remember he's dead."

Son was silent for a while. "I think you were already gone, so you probably don't remember. He came back home after a couple of years in New York—he was a stock specialist or something—he came back home and rented a half section out near Mize and started farming. I still remember how funny he looked coming into town on Saturdays—khakis starched like bread, tweed coat, little leather cap—he always looked like a business executive out working in his garden. Spent more time playing golf than on a tractor. One night he was over in a poker game in Lubbock and he didn't make that curve out by Sand Hill. Going a hundred and twenty. My old man used to tell me that for a place with no oceans to walk into or bridges to jump off of, it wasn't a bad way to go. I guess that's the way Mark Tabor died."

"I guess it was."

"Didn't make that big sweeping curve coming off the cap. Did you ever meet Stansell's wife? She was French, of all goddamn things, a lovely lady. After Carver died she moved over to Lubbock—God only knows why she didn't go back home. Anyway, the last I heard she had married an old boy over in Littlefield and was having a family. Married a farmer. A real one this time. Well, son, I slipped this one in on you. You thought I was just reminiscing about the good old days, when I was setting you up for a little philosophy. How does the old saying go? You can fool all the people some of the time and some of the people all the time, but you never can fool yourself. I've been thinking about Carver Stansell a lot lately and about people fooling themselves about who they are." He came over and sat at the long table. "You know, I used to be some philosopher when I was a kid. Used to write little essays like Montaigne. 'On Stupidity.' 'On Greed.' 'On the Fear of Death and the Eternity of Hell.' I used to read a lot of Nietzsche when I got to college. I was an arrow of longing for the other shore. But it was ole Plato, he was the one who pushed me out of my shell and into the real world. For a while there the *Republic* was my Bible. You ever read any Plato?"

"Some."

"There's a part in the *Republic* about the golden son. You ever read that? Ole Socrates and one of his buddies are having one of their little chats, and they start talking about this royal lie they're going to tell the people to keep them under control. The lie goes something like everybody in the country inhabits his station because of a certain quality given to him by the gods. The rulers are men of gold, merchants and bureaucrats are made of silver, and workers and farmers and the like are made of brass and iron. But this quality is not transmitted from father to son. Each child receives his talent from the gods, so that a man of gold may have a son of brass and a man of iron may have a golden son. Now the royal lie comes in, Socrates says, in that the state must be eternally vigilant so that the golden sons become the new rulers no matter where they come from and that the sons of the old rulers, if they're made of brass, must become workers and toil in the fields. For if the state is ever ruled by men of brass, then it will be destroyed. And then old Socrates' buddy says, Do you think the people are going to believe this lie? Socrates says, Long enough for us to get em into this war, Jack." Son laughed. "Oh man, I used to laugh my ass off reading ole Plato. Folks thought I was crazy. I used to tell Tee, Tee, ole buddy, I'm a son of gold, a golden son, and you're a son of brass, a sonofabitch. We would laugh our asses off. Tee always thought I was crazier than he was. That's why we got along, both of us crazy as cats. But I don't guess you came here to talk about Tee, did you?"

"No, I didn't."

Son reached out and touched a globe sitting on the desk. He spun the ball and we watched it till it ran down. "Life plays strange tricks on us, Sugar, awfully strange little tricks. We're going to get that oil concession over in Libya because I used to write poetry. Yeah, ole Fahiz is a poet and we sit around examining our pentameters. As a hobby he's also the Libyan oil minister. I'm flying out to Paris tomorrow morning and we'll walk the banks of the Seine and despair over short lines and free verse and it'll make ole Gunther millions of dollars. I might even make a few myself."

"You going to make enough to keep you out of jail?"

"I'm not going to jail, son. Not for the Dolly business, if that's what you mean. You got to remember I'm in the back room now. The concession we're getting in Libya is so big they're dividing it in two, and there's still more oil in the little one than in this whole fucking state. Adrienne's coming over in about a month. Like little morons we're going to drive across the Sahara. Speaking of morons, did I ever tell you what Dolly and I—ah, I guess I'd better start being a bit more modest—did I ever tell you what ole Francis Dolly was up to? It was incredible, it was all paper, son, a goddamn pyramid of paper. The market started slipping a little bit and all this pyramid of paper started to collapse, and pretty soon there's nothing but this swirl of paper, it looks like a goddamn white tornado. And to build up this little paper empire ole Dolly had to drag in all sorts of bankers and politicians and insurance men . . . Well, I don't know if they're going to have to redraw the maps, but a good number of these paper millionaires are going to be repairing rocks. Now, there's some of these good ole boys that a speck of jail might straighten out, but there's some of them, like Maury and poor ole Marvin DeKalb, that I kinda hate to see go. Pore ole Marvin, he's probably the saddest one of all, he really believed that bear grease and a grin were going to carry him all the way to the White House. I guess you heard about Maury's testimony."

"I read about it."

"It's tough for a man of his age having to go to jail. I think he's got some kind of stomach trouble on top of that. When your troubles start, it seems like they pile in from every direction. But if he keeps his mouth shut, maybe he can get out in a couple of years. Ah, but then sometimes life seems too soft and long anyway. What's on your feeble mind, Sugar? You didn't come here with money on the brain. Or did you? No, what's your weakness, son? Crime and punishment?"

"Crime and reward looks more like it."

Son looked around the darkened room and laughed. "Crime and reward—ole Feodor would have shit a brick. All right, let's assume this is the reward—what's the crime? Not all these banking shenanigans, is it? What is your crime, Sugar? Is it still murder? Are you still interested in Tee Kitchens's murder, son? For a while there, you and that Foose had that boy's murder on the brain, but I hoped you'd forgotten all about that. I thought A. told me you had decided to put childish things aside." I didn't say anything, just watched him. When he finally spoke, his voice was so changed that for an instant I thought he was pretending to be someone else. "Did I ever tell you that we had to do it, that we didn't have a choice?" He was silent again. "Do you know when it was that I first got the idea to ask you to come back home? It was back when things were looking pretty good for me and A. Back before they had found Palmer. A. and I were out riding one day and we ended up down at the swimming hole at Roaring Springs. You remember the place from high school. A god-damn ratty swimming pool and a jukebox and a concrete slab to shuffle around on, it hasn't changed a bit, still the most exciting place on the face of this earth. Anyway, A. and I were cooling our heels in the springs and there was a high-school class on their senior trip there, swimming, more like doing their damnedest to drown one another, dancing, strolling hand in hand out into the bushes to stir up the chiggers— Well, I got to telling A. that that could've been us twenty years before and she started asking questions what it was like, growing up in a little West Texas town. And I told her about it. I told her who those kids were. I said that one's me and he's still a virgin and he's in love with that dark-haired girl over there, and I said that one's Kenny and that one's Idalou, and I told her about them, and then I said that one was you; I said, That's my best friend there; I sometimes think I wouldn't have made it through high school without that crazy ole boy being around. I said it always seemed like he's already been through every bad problem there is in life and he always knows how to help you make it through yourself. Some-thing like that. Then later on, after they'd found Palmer and we had buried Billy O., A. and I were having one of our crying, talking jags, trying to figure out what in the world we were going to do, when A. said, Why don't we ask your friend to help us? Why don't we have him help us straighten things out? Well, I don't know what I had in mind when I wrote you—maybe in a strange nostalgic way

I did think you could help out. That you just being around would change things."

"But I didn't change things, did I, Son?"

He shook his head. "Things had already changed by the time you got here. We had already decided to kill him. You know, he knew what was going on. I think he wanted to die, up to the very end, and then he changed his mind. That's what was so bad, Sugar. We all wanted to stop, but we couldn't." Son had moved over against the wall so that I couldn't see him. "That last twenty-four hours I couldn't think about anything else—but I guess I've already told you about that." Son moved back to his chair, his head bowed wearily. "Speaking of *Crime and Punishment*, the novel, have you read it?"

"No."

"I haven't in a long time. I read it in college, I hated the book then, or I hated the hero. I can't remember much about it except how shocked I was when the kid murdered the old woman so soon, so near the beginning of the book. I thought, What the hell, this book is about murder and it's over with in seventy pages, but then it wasn't, was it? Murders don't happen and end. They go on for a long time. I wonder just how long." He pressed his fingers against his eyes. "I remember how real the murder was, how much I believed it and how bored I was with the rest. When I was planning on killing Tee, when I was thinking about how I would do it and how he would look and how it would feel, I'd find myself thinking about that goddamn book, and I began to see how unreal the murder was, how easy it was for him to kill the old woman, when really it should've been so fucking hard. And I saw how real the guilt was, how real the punishment was." Son made a sound, not like laughter. "But now I'm boring you, aren't I, son? With all my cracker-barrel philosophy. You'll have to excuse us country boys, we get a bright idea and we just get all carried away. We figure that nobody in the whole wide world has ever had *that* idea before." Son paused. "I'm not trying to run you off, Sugar, but I've got a couple of phone calls to make. Won't take more than thirty minutes, and we can have a drink downstairs."

"No, that's all right. I've got to be going."

"Which way are you headed, Sugar?"

"I'm going to drive back up to Flavannah tonight. And then I'll decide which way I'm going. Maybe back to California."

Son swiveled his chair toward the window. "Radio said there was a bad storm up somewhere around Dallas. Maybe you ought to pack it in tonight and head out tomorrow morning."

"No, I want to see how far I can get tonight."

Son turned his chair around. Except for the windows behind him, the room was now totally dark. Music came from somewhere in the house, so faint I could not distinguish the instruments. "Sugar, I hope you won't hit me for saying it, but I'm glad you came back. I was glad you showed up. I don't know . . . I guess that's it."

"I'd never hit you, Son, because I know if I ever started, I'd never stop."

We were both standing. Son reached into the desk drawer in front of him and drew out a small silver object; it shone in the dark. It's hard to describe how I felt—a thrill maybe; it had nothing to do with fear. Son looked at the small gun, then put it on the desk and slid it toward me. "It's your property, son. A. got her wires crossed the other night, it was another gun of mine that was missing." I picked up the gun. "It's loaded, Sugar, so I wouldn't be pointing it at anybody . . . unless of course you want to shoot them. But then you don't want to shoot anybody, do you? You never have. I thought you'd want to take something back to California with you, to remind you of your little homecoming."

"A souvenir? Why not, you never can tell, I might be needing it someday."

"I hope not, Sugar. As far as I'm concerned, those days are over."

"Maybe. I do have one question before I go, Son. When I found you in the bathroom upstairs, right after you killed Tee, why did you tell me you killed him? Why didn't you come out with your two-Mexicans story then? According to P.M., you already had it planned."

Son had walked over to the window; he was staring down into the garden. "That's easy, Sugar. If I hadn't confessed then, you would have killed me. I knew that look on your face. It's the only thing that saved my life." He turned around. "See, I've got one weakness now that I've got everything I want. I don't want to die. I know it sounds strange, but Tee beat me in the end. He didn't care any more, and I did. He wins."

"That's bullshit, Son. You win and everybody knows it. You beat Tee, Adrienne, me, Dolly, everybody. You losing is bullshit, just like your cornball philosophy and your stories about our youth and your crime-and-punishment bullshit—it's all bullshit to cover up the fact that you know exactly what you're doing, you've known all along, every step. It came out just like you had planned, didn't it, Son? Down to the last sorry fucking detail. You didn't bring me back here because of some weird nostalgia. You had a reason, just like you've got a reason for everything you do. But I finally have figured it out, figured out why you dragged me back—you had to have a straw man, didn't you? You had to have a fool to act out and then tell the truth. Since everybody knew that you were going to kill Tee and that you did kill Tee, you had to have fools like

Foose and me out there acting out this fucking farce so everybody could see how foolish the truth was. That's why you told me you killed Tee. That's why you got Foose and me together. In the end your only real problem was Adrienne, wasn't it? But you did another fine job there. You got her to believe that she plotted and planned the whole thing, you got her to believe that she actually was the murderer, that you might have pulled the trigger but that she was the real murderer. You were the tormented killer, driven to a point where you had to kill Tee, there was no other way out. What bullshit, Cunningham. You felt no pain, no remorse, no pleasure, and no guilt—for you it was like changing a dollar bill. It was something you had to do yourself, to get it done right, and you did it. I told Adrienne that I wanted to know how you felt killing a man for his wife and her fortune, but now I know. You didn't feel a goddamn thing. And you knew all along I wouldn't kill you. You set that up too. It's like P.M. says, I'm not the type. Am I? That's my weakness, I'm afraid to kill a man. See how afraid I am." We were both so calm, watching the gun in my hand, watching it stretch out toward Son as if I were trying to touch him. "You know, the only thing I hadn't figured out, Son, was why I came back here and why I stayed. But now I've even figured that out. But this gun isn't loaded, is it, Cunningham? There're no bullets in it. I can't kill you with it, can I?"

"There's one way to find out, Campbell."

"You're right. There is only one way to find out." I pulled the trigger and the snap the hammer made against the firing pin was dry, like something breaking. I pulled the trigger again and the gun snapped again. I found myself laughing. "See, I was right. There weren't any bullets in it. I couldn't kill you with it."

Son was pressing a button on the desk, and somewhere

in another part of the house I could hear a buzzer and then footsteps coming up the stairs.

"Well, son, I hope you've got that out of your system now. But just to be sure, I'm going to have a couple of my new friends see you out. And, son"—he smiled when I got to the door of the room—"I've known all along why you came back and why you stayed. You were just homesick, now ain't that right?"

"Homesick." I was still laughing. "Maybe I was."

Son's new friends were waiting outside the door. "Sugar—" He paused as the door opened, then smiled and nodded. "So long, son."